The first romance stories Stephanie Laurens read were set against the backdrop of Regency England, and these continue to exert a special attraction for her. As an escape from the dry world of professional science, Stephanie started writing Regency romances, and she is now a *New York Times*, *USA Today* and *Publishers Weekly* bestselling author.

Stephanie lives in a leafy suburb of Melbourne, Australia, with her husband and two daughters, along with two cats, Shakespeare and Marlowe.

Learn more about Stephanie's books from her website at www.stephanielaurens.com

Also by Stephanie Laurens

Captain Jack's Woman

A Bastion Club Novel

Stephanie
LAURENS

piatkus

PIATKUS

First published in the US in 1997 by Avon Books,
an imprint of HarperCollins Publishers, New York
First published in Great Britain as a paperback original in 2009 by Piatkus
by arrangement with Avon

5 7 9 10 8 6

A CIP catalogue record for this book
is available from the British Library.

ISBN 978-0-7499-4018-8

Typeset in Baskerville by M Rules
Printed and bound by CPI Group (UK) Ltd, Croydon CR0 4YY

Papers used by Piatkus are from well-managed forests
and other responsible sources

Piatkus
An imprint of
Little, Brown Book Group
Carmelite House
50 Victoria Embankment
London EC4Y 0DZ

An Hachette UK Company
www.hachette.co.uk

www.littlebrown.co.uk

Prologue

April 1811
The Old Barn near Brancaster
Norfolk, England

Three horsemen pulled out of the trees before the Old Barn. Harness jingled, faint on the night breeze, as they turned their horses' heads to the west. Clouds shifted, drifted; moonlight shone through, bathing the scene.

The Old Barn stood silent, watchful, guarding its secrets. Earlier, within its walls, the Hunstanton Gang had gathered to elect a new leader. Afterward, the smugglers had left, slipping into the night, mere shadows in the dark. They would return, nights from now, meeting under the light of a storm lantern to hear of the next cargo their new leader had arranged.

"Captain Jack!" As he swung his horse onto the road, George Smeaton frowned at the man beside him. "Do we really need to resurrect him?"

"Who else?" Mounted on his tall grey, Jonathon Hendon, better known as Jack, gestured expansively. "That was, after all, my *nom de guerre.*"

"Years ago. When you were dangerous to know. I've lived the last years in the comfortable belief that Captain Jack had died."

"No." Jack grinned. "He's merely been in temporary retirement." Captain Jack had been active in more devil-may-care days, when, between army engagements in the Peninsula, the Admirality had recruited Jack to captain one of his own ships, harassing French shipping up and down the Channel. "You have to admit Captain Jack's perfect for this job – a fitting leader for the Hunstanton Gang."

George's snort was eloquent. "Poor blighters – they've no idea what they've let themselves in for."

Jack chuckled. "Stop carping – our mission's proceeding better than I'd hoped, and all in only a few weeks of coming home. Whitehall will be impressed. We've been accepted by the smugglers – I'm now their leader. We're in a perfect position to ensure no information gets to the French by this route." His brows rose; his expression turned considering. "Who knows?" he mused. "We might even be able to use the traffic for our own ends."

George raised his eyes heavenward. "Captain Jack's only been with us half an hour, and already you're getting ideas. Just what wild scheme are you hatching?"

"Not hatching." Jack threw him a glance. "It's called seizing opportunity. It occurs to me that while our principal aim is to ensure no spies go out through the Norfolk surf, and perhaps follow any arrivals back to their traitorous source, we might now have the opportunity to do a little information passing of our own – to Boney's confusion, needless to say."

George stared. "I thought that once we'd investigated any recent human cargoes, you'd shut the Hunstanton Gang down."

"Perhaps." Jack's gaze grew distant. "And perhaps not." He blinked and straightaned. "I'll see what Whitehall thinks. We'll need Anthony, too."

"Oh, my God!" George shook his head. "Just how long do you imagine the Gang will swallow your tale that we're landless mercenaries, dishonorably discharged no less, particularly once you take full command? You've been a major for years, landed gentry all your life. It shows!"

Jack shrugged dismissively. "They won't think too hard. They've been looking for months for someone to replace Jed Brannagan. They won't rock the boat – at least not soon. We'll have time enough for our needs." He twisted, glancing back at the third rider, a length behind to his left. Like himself and George, a native of these parts, Matthew, his longtime batman, now general servant, had merged easily into the smuggling band. "We'll continue to use the old fishing cottage as our private rendezvous – it's secluded and we can guard against being followed."

Matthew nodded. "Aye. Easy enough to check our trail."

Jack settled in his saddle. "Given the smugglers are all from outlying farms or fishing villages, there's no reason they should stumble on our real identities."

Checking his horse, Jack turned left, into the narrow mouth of a winding track. George followed; Matthew brought up the rear. As they climbed a rise, Jack glanced back. "All things considered, I can't see why you're worrying. Captain Jack's command of the Hunstanton Gang should be plain sailing."

"Plain sailing with Captain Jack?" George snorted. "When pigs fly."

Chapter 1

May 1811
West Norfolk

Kit Cramner sat with her nose to the carriage window, feasting on the landmarks of memory. The spire atop the Customs House at King's Lynn and the old fortress of Castle Rising had fallen behind them. Ahead lay the turning to Wolferton; Cranmer was close at last. Streamers of twilight red and gold colored the sky in welcome; the sense of coming home grew stronger with every mile. With a triumphant sigh, Kit sat back against the squabs and gave thanks yet again for her freedom. She'd remained "cabin'd, cribb'd and confin'd" in London for far too long.

Ten minutes later, the entrance to the park loomed ahead in the gathering dusk, the Cranmer arms blazoned on each gatepost. The gates were open wide; the coach trundled through. Kit straightened and shook old Elmina awake, then sat back, suddenly tense.

Gravel scrunched beneath the wheels; the carriage rocked to a halt. The door was pulled open.

Her grandfather stood before her, his proud head erect, his leonine mane thrown into relief by the flares flanking the large doors. For one suspended moment, they stared at each other, love, hope, and remembered pain reflected over and over between them.

"Kit?"

And the years rolled back. With a choked "Gran'pa!" Kit launched herself into Spencer Cranmer's arms.

"Kit. Oh, *Kit!*" Lord Cranmer of Cranmer Hall, his beloved granddaughter locked against his chest, could find no other words. For six years he'd waited for her to come back; he could barely believe she was real.

Elmina and the housekeeper, Mrs. Fogg, fussed and prodded the emotion-locked pair inside, leaving them on the *chaise* in the drawing room, before the blazing fire.

Eventually, Spencer straightened and mopped his eyes with a large handkerchief. "Kit, darling girl – I'm *so* glad to see you."

Kit looked up, tears unashamedly suspended on her long brown lashes. She hadn't yet recovered her voice, so she smiled her response.

Spencer returned the smile. "I know it's selfish of me to wish you here – your aunts pointed that out years ago when you decided to go to London. I'd given up hope you'd ever return. I was sure you'd marry some fashionable sprig and forget all about Cranmer and your old grandfather."

Kit's smile faded. Frowning slightly, she wriggled to sit straighter. "What do you mean, Gran'pa? I never wanted to go to London – my aunts told me I had to. They told me you wanted me to contract a fine alliance – that as the only girl in the family, it was my duty to be a credit to the Cranmer name and further my uncles' standing." The last was said with contempt.

Spencer's pale gaze sharpened. His bushy white brows met in a thunderous frown. "*What?*"

Kit winced. "Don't bellow." She'd forgotten his temper. According to Dr. Thrushborne, his health depended on his not losing it too often.

Rising, she went to the fireplace and tugged the bellpull. "Let me think." Her gaze on the flames, she frowned, long-ago events replaying in her mind. "When Gran'ma died, you locked yourself up, and I didn't see you again. Aunt Isobel and Aunt Margery came and talked to you. Then they came and told me I had to go with them – that my uncles were to be my guardians and they'd groom me and present me and so on." She looked directly at Spencer. "That was all I knew."

The angry sparkle in the old eyes holding hers so intently was all the proof Kit needed of her aunts' duplicity.

"Those conniving bitches! Those witches dressed up in silks and furs. Those hell-born harpies! The pair of them are nothing but –"

Spencer's animadversions were interrupted by a knock on the door, followed by Jenkins, the butler.

Kit caught Jenkins's eye. "Your master's cordial, please Jenkins."

Jenkins bowed. "At once, miss."

As the door closed, Kit turned to Spencer. "Why didn't you write?"

The pale old eyes met hers unflinchingly. "I didn't think you'd want to hear from an old man. They told me you wanted to go. That you were bored, buried here in the country, living with old people."

Kit's violet eyes clouded. Her aunts were truly the bitches he called them. Until now, she'd never appreciated just how low they'd stooped to gain control of her so they could manipulate her to suit their husbands' ambitious ends. "Oh, Gran'pa." Sinking onto the *chaise*, her elegant gown sushing softly, she hugged Spencer for all she was worth. "You were all I had left, and I thought you didn't want me." Kit buried her face in his cravat and felt Spencer's cheek against her curls. After a moment, his hand rose to pat her shoulder. She tightened her arms fiercely, then drew back, eyes flaming with a light Spencer remembered all too well. She rose and fell to pacing, skirts swishing, her vigorous strides well beyond society's dictates. "Ooooh! How I wish my aunts were here now."

"Not half as much as I," Spencer growled. "Those *mesdames* will get a lambasting from me when next they dare show their faces."

Jenkins noiselessly entered; coming forward, he offered his master a small glass of dark liquid. With barely a glance, Spencer took it; absentmindedly, he quaffed the dose, then waved Jenkins away.

Kit paused, slender and elegant, before the mantelpiece. Spencer's loving gaze roamed her fair skin, creamy rather than white, unmarred by any blemish despite her predilection for outdoor pursuits. The burnished curls were the same shade he remembered, the same shade he'd once possessed. The long tresses, confined in plaits at sixteen, had given way to cropped curls, large and lustrous. The fashion suited her, highlighting the delicate features of her small heart-shaped face.

From age six, Kit had lived at Cranmer, after her parents, Spencer's son Christopher and his French emigrée wife, had died in a carriage accident. Spencer's gaze dwelled on the long lines of Kit's figure, outlined by her green traveling dress. She carried herself gracefully even now as she resumed her angry pacing. He stirred. "God, Kit. Do you realize we've lost six years?"

Kit's smile was dazzling, resurrecting memories of the tomboy, the hoyden, the devil in her blood. "I'm back now, Gran'pa, and I mean to stay."

Spencer leaned back, well pleased with her declaration. He waved at her. "Well, miss – let me see how you've turned out."

With a chuckle, Kit curtsied. "Not too deep, for after all, you are just a baron." The twinkle in her eye suggested he was the prince of her heart. Spencer snorted. Kit rose and dutifully pirouetted, arms gracefully extended as if she were dancing.

Spencer slapped his knee. "Not bad, even if I say so myself."

Kit laughed and returned to the *chaise*. "You're prejudiced, Gran'pa. Now, tell me what's happened here."

To her relief, Spencer obliged. While he rattled on about fields and tenants, Kit listened with half an ear. Inside, she was still reeling. Six years of purgatory she'd spent in London, for no reason at all. The months of misery she'd endured, during which she'd had to come to grips with the loss of not only a beloved grandmother, but effectively of her grandfather as well, were burned into her soul. Why, oh why had she never swallowed her pride and written to Spencer, pleaded with him to allow her to come home? She'd almost done it on countless occasions but, deeply wounded by his apparent rejection of her, she'd always allowed her stubborn pride to intervene. Inherently truthful, she'd never dreamed her aunts had been so deceitful. Never again would she trust those who professed to have her welfare at heart. Henceforth, she silently vowed, she'd run her own life.

Gazing at her grandfather's white mane, Kit nodded as he told her of their neighbors. The six years had wrought their inevitable changes in him, yet Spencer was still an impressive figure. Even now, with his shoulders slightly stooped, his height and strength made a definite impact. His patrician features, his hooked nose and piercing pale violet eyes shaded by overhanging brows, commanded attention; from his rambling discourse, she gathered he was still deeply involved with county matters, as influential as ever.

Inwardly, Kit sighed. She loved Spencer as she did no other on earth. And he loved her. Yet even he was demonstrably fallible, no real protection against the wolves of this world. No. If she was to come to grief, she'd rather it was self-inflicted. From now on, she'd make her own decisions, her own mistakes.

Later that night, finally alone in the bedroom that had been hers for as long as she could remember, Kit stood at the open window and gazed at the pale circle of the moon, suspended in night's blackness over the deep. She'd never felt so alone. She'd never felt so free.

Kit was astonished at how easily she slipped back into her Cranmer routine. Rising early, she rode her mare, Delia, then breakfasted with Spencer before turning to whatever task she'd set herself for the day. The afternoon saw her riding again, before evening brought her back to her grandfather's side. Over dinner, she'd listen to his account of his day, giving her opinions when asked, shrewdly interpolating comments when she wasn't. Between them, the six years of separation were as though they'd never been.

From that, Kit took her direction. It was useless to wail and gnash her teeth over her aunts' perfidy. She was free of them – free to forget them. Her grandfather was in good health and, she'd learned, would remain her legal guardian until she was twenty-five; there was no chance of her aunts interfering again. She would waste no more time on the past. Her life was hers – she would live it to the full.

Her daily tasks varied from helping Mrs. Fogg about the house, in the stillroom or the kitchen, to visiting her grandfather's tenants, who were all delighted to welcome her home.

Home.

Her heart soared as she rode the far-flung acres, the sky wide and clear above her, the wind tugging at her curls. Delia, a purebred black Arab, had been a gift from Spencer on Kit's eighteenth birthday. Since he'd taught her to ride and had always taken enormous pride in her horsemanship she hadn't placed any undue emphasis on the gift. Now, she saw it as a call from a lonely and aching heart, a call she had not, in her innocence, recognized. It only made her love Delia more. Together, they thundered over the sands, Delia's hooves glistening with wave foam. The sharp cries of gulls came keening on the currents high above; the boom of the surf rumbled in the salt-laden air.

Word of her return spread quickly. She dutifully sustained visits from the rector's wife and from Lady Dersingham, the wife of a neighboring landowner. Kit's *ton*nish grace impressed both ladies. Her manner was assured, her deportment perfection. In the faraway capital she might hold herself insultingly aloof, but at Cranmer, she was Spencer's granddaughter.

Chapter 2

On the afternoon of her third day of freedom, Kit donned her green-velvet riding habit and asked for a sidesaddle to be put on Delia. When with Spencer or alone, she'd taken to riding astride, scandalously dressed in breeches and coat. The clothes had been made for her years before; Elmina had let down the hems and remade the breeches to fit. The coat was an old one of her cousin Geoffrey's, recut to her slighter frame but still loose enough to disguise her figure should the need arise. Now that her hair was cropped, leaving the flame-colored curls rioting about her head, she hardly needed the protection of the old tricorne that completed her highly irregular outfit. When garbed in her male attire, a hat shading her features, her sex was moot.

Today she was bound for Gresham Manor. Her closest friend, whom she hadn't seen in years, lived quietly there with her parents. Amy had never had to go to London. She'd contracted a suitable alliance with a local gentleman of acceptable birth and reasonable fortune; that much, Kit knew from her letters. Amy's gentleman was with Wellington's forces in the Peninsula; their wedding would take place once he returned.

Kit rode up the long drive of Gresham Manor and directly around to the stables.

"Miss Cranmer!" The groom came running to take her horse's bridle. "Didn't recognize you for a minute there, miss. Back from London town, are ye?"

"That's right, Jeffries." Kit smiled and slid from Delia's back. "Is Miss Amy in?"

"*Kit?* It *is* you!"

Turning, Kit barely had time to verify that the figure descending on her was indeed Amy, golden hair in fashionable ringlets, peaches-and-cream complexion still perfect, before she was enveloped in a warm embrace.

"I saw you ride past the library windows and wondered if Mr. Woodley's sermons had sent me to sleep, and I was dreaming."

Kit laughed. "Goose! I've been back only a few days and couldn't wait to see you and hear all your news. Is your fiancé back yet?"

"Yes! It's the most wonderful thing!" Amy gripped Kit's fingers, her eyes shining. "First him – now you. Clearly the gods have decided to be especially kind."

Amy drew back, holding Kit at arm's length to study her elegant attire, the short velvet coat, clasped with gold frogs, and the gracefully sweeping velvet skirts. Amy's brown gaze returned to Kit bobbed curls, and she grimaced. "Drat! You make me feel positively dowdy. I don't know whether I'll introduce you to George after all."

Kit laughed and drew Amy's arm through hers. "Fear not. I've no designs on your fiancé – very likely he'll be either terrified or disapproving of my wild ways." They started for the house.

"George," Amy declared, "is utterly sensible. I'm sure you'll approve of each other. But I'm dying of curiosity.

Why are you back? And why didn't you write and warn me?"

Kit smiled. "It's a long story. Perhaps I should meet your mother first, then maybe we can find a nice quiet nook?"

Amy nodded; arm in arm, they entered the house. Lady Gresham, a motherly woman who ruled her household with a firm but benevolent hand, had always had a soft spot for Kit. She insisted the girls take tea with her but, beyond extracting the information that Kit was still unbetrothed, made no effort to learn more of her recent past.

Eventually released, Amy and Kit took refuge in Amy's bedchamber. Settled in the billows of the bed, Kit smiled. She and Amy had been closer than sisters since the age of six; six years' separation, bridged by letters, hadn't dinted their easy familiarity.

At Amy's prompting, Kit recounted the tale of her aunts' machinations and how they'd contrived to hold her for six long years. "If it hadn't been for my cousins, I'm sure their persuasions to marry would have been a great deal more drastic. Once, they locked me in my room for two days, until Geoffrey appeared on the doorstep and insisted on seeing me." Kit grimaced. "After that, they were reduced to nagging. But when they wheeled in the earl of Roberts, I decided enough was enough. The man was old enough to be my father!" Kit frowned. "And he was altogether . . . not nice," she ended lamely. "After that, my aunts finally conceded defeat and declared me unmarriageable. So I was allowed to come home – I knew Gran'pa would at least give me houseroom."

Amy sent her a stern look. "He was heartbroken when you left. I did tell you."

Kit's eyes clouded, viola hazed with grey. "I know, but my aunts were very clever." A short silence fell; Kit broke it with a sigh. "So now I'm finished with London *and* with men. I can live very happily without either."

Amy frowned. "Is it wise to go that far? After all, who knows what delicious gentleman might be lurking around the next bend in your road?"

"Just as long as he stays *out* of my road, I'll be satisfied."

"Oh, *Kit*. Not all men are old dodderers or fops. Some are quite personable. Like George."

With a "Humph," Kit turned on her stomach and propped her chin in her hands. "Enough of my affairs. Tell me about this George of yours."

George, it transpired, was the only son of the Smeatons of Smeaton Hall, located some way beyond Gresham Manor. He was twelve years Kit's senior; she could not recall meeting either him or his parents before.

"It's reassuring knowing I'll not be too far away," Amy concluded. "We must have you and your grandfather over for dinner and introduce you to George and his parents."

Noting the happiness shining in Amy's face, Kit agreed with what enthusiasm she could. It was obvious to the meanest intelligence that Amy was head over heels in love with George, and that soon Kit would lose her best friend to matrimony. Amy chattered on; eventually, a frown tugging at her brows, Kit broke into her narrative. "Amy, why do you want to marry?"

"Why?" The question stopped Amy in her tracks. Then realizing Kit meant the question literally, she marshaled her thoughts. "Because I love George and want to be with him for the rest of my life." She looked hopefully at Kit, willing her to understand.

Kit stared back, violet eyes intent. "You want to marry him because you love him?" When Amy nodded, she asked: "What's love feel like?"

15

Brow furrowed, Amy considered. "Well," she began, "you know all about the . . . the act, don't you?"

"Of *course* I know about that." They were both country bred – such matters were inescapable facts of country life. "But what's that got to do with love?"

"*Well,*" Amy continued, "when you love a man you want to . . . do that with him."

Kit frowned. "Do you really want to do that with your George?"

Blushing furiously, Amy nodded.

Kit's brows rose, then she shrugged. "It seems such a peculiar undertaking – so undignified, if you know what I mean."

Amy choked.

"But how do you know you want to do that with George?" Kit focused on Amy's face. "You haven't, have you?"

"Of course I haven't!" Amy stiffened.

"How then?"

Drawing a deep breath, Amy fixed Kit with a long-suffering look. "You can tell because of what you feel when a man kisses you."

Kit frowned.

"You've been kissed by a gentleman, haven't you? I mean, not one of your relatives. What about your London gentle-men – didn't they?"

It was Kit's turn to blush. "Some of them," she admitted.

"Well? What did it feel like?"

Kit grimaced. "One was like kissing a dead fish, and the others were sort of hot wriggling things. They tried to put their tongues in my mouth." She shuddered expressively. "It was awful!"

Amy bit her lips, then drew an unsteady breath. "Yes, all

16

right. That's probably just as well – that means you don't want to go to bed with any of them."

"Oh." Kit's face cleared. "What should it feel like if I do want to . . ." She gestured. "You know."

"Sleep with a man?"

Kit glared. "Yes, damn it! What does it feel like to want a man to make love to you?" She turned onto her back and, dropping her head into the pillows, stared upward. "Take pity on me, Amy, and tell. If you don't, I'll probably die ignorant."

Amy chuckled. "Oh no, you won't. You're just in the doldrums, what with your aunts' machinations and all. You'll come about and meet your man."

"But I might not, so just tell me. Please?"

Amy smiled and settled beside Kit. "All right. But you must remember I haven't had much experience of this either."

"You've had more than me, and it's only fair to share."

"And you've got to promise you won't be shocked."

Kit came up on one elbow and looked into Amy's face. "You said you didn't . . ."

Amy blushed. "I – we haven't. It's just that there are . . . well, preliminaries, that might be a bit more than you expect."

Kit frowned, then dropped back onto the bed. "Try me."

"Well – when he kisses you, you should like it for a start. If you're revolted, then he's not the man for you."

"All right. He's kissed me, and I like it. What then?"

"You should want him to go on kissing you, and you should like it when he puts his tongue in your mouth."

Kit bent a skeptical look on her friend.

Amy frowned. "It's true. And you should feel all hot and flushed – like having a fever only nicer. Your knees tend to

17

go weak, but that doesn't matter because he'll be holding you. And for some reason, you can't hear very well when you're kissing – I don't know why. It's just as well to remember that."

"Sounds like a disease," Kit muttered.

Amy ignored her. "Sometimes it's a bit hard to breathe, but somehow you manage."

"Wonderful – suffocation as well."

"He might kiss your eyes and cheeks and ears, too, and then move on to your neck. That's always nice."

A distinct purr was slowly infusing itself into Amy's soft voice; Kit blinked.

"And then," Amy went on, "depending on how things are going, he might touch your breasts, just gently, sort of squeezing and stroking. It always feels as if my laces are too tight by that stage."

Kit stared, openmouthed, but Amy was well launched on her subject.

"Soon, my nubbins go all hard and crinkly, which is a rather odd feeling. And then comes the hot flushes."

"Hot flushes?"

"Mmm. They start in your breasts and move down."

"Down? Down where?"

"To between your legs. And then – and this is the important bit." Amy wagged a finger. "If you feel all hot and wet down there, then he's the man for you. But you'll know that anyway because all you'll be thinking about by then is how nice it would feel if only he'd come into you."

Aghast, Kit stared. "It sounds positively dreadful."

"Oh, *Kit.*" Amy threw her a commiserating glance. "It's not awful at all."

"I'll take your word for it. Thank you for warning me."

Kit lay silent, staring at the ceiling. Her one brush with

love hadn't been anything like that. From Amy's description, it was clear that she, Kit, had never been touched by love. Feeling as if she'd succeeded in understanding some particularly difficult point that had eluded her for years, Kit shook her head. "I can't see myself getting hot and wet for any man. But then, I'm obviously not destined for love at all."

"You can't say that."

Kit lifted a haughty brow, but Amy was not to be gainsaid.

'You can't just *decide* you're not susceptible. With the right man, you won't be able to help yourself. It's just because you're . . . innocent of love that you say so."

Kit's eyes widened. "Innocent? Did I tell you I lost my innocence one fine summer evening on my Uncle Frederick's terrace?"

Amy gaped.

Kit shook her head. "Not physically. But I found out what most men think of love that night. I grant your George may be different – there are exceptions to every rule. But I've learned that it's women who fall in love and men who take advantage of our weakness. I've no intention of succumbing."

"What happened on your uncle's terrace?"

Kit grimaced. "I was eighteen. Can you remember what eighteen felt like? I suppose I'd started to get over leaving Cramner. My uncles and aunts had already been urging me to marry. Then, miraculously, I found myself in love. Or so I thought." Kit paused, eyes fixed on the ceiling, then she drew a deep breath. "He was beautiful – a captain of guards, tall and handsome. Lord George Belville, the second son of a duke. He said he loved me. I was so happy, Amy. I don't think I can explain what it felt like, to have someone who really cared about me again. I was . . . oh – as you are

19

now. Over the moon with joy. My aunts gave a ball, and Belville said he'd use the opportunity to ask my uncle for my hand. They disappeared into the library mid-way through the evening. I was so excited, I couldn't bear not knowing what was being said. So I slipped out on the small terrace and listened outside the library windows. What I heard –" Her voice broke. She drew another breath and forged on. "All I heard was them laughing at me."

Amy's hand found hers amid the bedcovers; Kit barely noticed. "It was all deliberate. They'd presented me with four suitors up till then, all much older men, none particularly attractive. My aunts had decided I was too much of a romantic – tainted with the wildness of my father's and mother's blood was the way they put it – to accept such eminently suitable alliances. So they'd searched out Belville. He was as ambitious as they were. He was destined for some position in military affairs, something high, organized through his connections. Through our marriage, he'd get the backing of my uncles in furthering his career. They'd get his support in furthering theirs. I was the token to cement their alliance. It was all made perfectly clear while I listened. Belville spoke of how easy it had been to ensnare me."

Kit stretched her arms out, forcing her long fingers to straighten from the claws they'd curled into. She uttered a hollow laugh. "They were so sure of themselves. When I refused Belville the next day, they couldn't believe it."

Abruptly, she sat up, swinging about to face Amy. "After that, I always listened to my so-called suitors' meetings with my guardians. Most instructive. So, you see, Amy dear, while I may envy you your experience, I know how rare it is. I don't expect love as you know it to find me. It's had six years to do so and failed. I'll soon be well and truly on the shelf."

Kit saw sympathy in Amy's brown eyes and, smiling rue-fully, shook her head. "There's no earthly point feeling sorry for me, for I don't feel the least sorry for myself. What man do you know would allow me the freedom I presently enjoy – to go about as I please, to be myself?"

"But you don't do anything scandalous."

"I see no point in inviting the attentions of the gabble-mongers, and I would never bring scandal to my grandfather's name. But I recognize no restrictions beyond those. A husband would expect his wife to behave in accord with certain strictures, to be at home when he was, not riding the sands. He'd expect me to follow his dictates, have my world revolve about him, when I'd be wanting to do something quite different."

Amy frowned. "I can understand your disillusionment, but we vowed we'd marry for love, remember?"

Kit smiled. "We'd marry for love – or not at all."

Amy flushed, but, before she could speak, Kit went on, her tone one of acceptance: "*You're* marrying for love; *I'm* not marrying at all."

"*Kit!*"

Kit laughed. "Don't fuss so, my dearest goose. I'm enjoy-ing myself hugely. I promise you – I don't *need* love."

Amy held her tongue but, to her mind, love was the very thing Kit did need to make her whole.

Chapter 3

Kit spent the following two days paying visits to various tenants' wives, hearing about their families their troubles, renewing the women's direct contact with Cranmer Hall, which had lapsed since her grandmother's death. Yet between the chatter-filled visits, she brooded, surprised at herself yet unable to shake free.

Discussing love with Amy had been a mistake. Ever since, she'd been restless. Until then, Cranmer had seemed the perfect haven. Now, something was missing. She didn't appreciate the feeling.

Luckily, the next day was too busy for brooding, filled instead with preparations for the dinner Spencer had organized to reintroduce her formally to their neighbors. Kit managed to squeeze in a ride in the afternoon but returned in good time to change.

The guests arrived punctually at eight. Waiting to greet them at the drawing room door, Kit stood beside Spencer, impressive in a silk coat and white knee breeches, his white mane wreathing his proud head. His expression was one of paternal pride, for which Kit knew she was directly responsible.

She'd chosen her gown carefully, rejecting fine muslins and low-cut satins in favor of a delicate creation in aquamarine silk. The free-flowing material did justice to her slender length; the neckline was scooped and scalloped as befitted her age but remained high enough for propriety. The color heightened the glow of her burnished curls and drew attention to the creaminess of her skin.

Her eyes sparkled as she curtsied to the Lord Lieutenant, Lord Marchmont, and his wife, drawing an appreciative look from his lordship.

"Kathryn, my dear, it's a pleasure to see you back in the fold."

Kit smiled easily. "Indeed, my lord, it's a pleasure to be back and meeting old friends."

Lord Marchmont laughed and tapped her cheek. "Very prettily said, my dear."

He and his wife moved into the room to make way for the next guests. Kit knew them all. She couldn't help comparing the real joy she felt in such a simple affair with the boredom she'd found in the elaborate entertainments of the *ton*.

The Greshams were the last to arrive. After exchanging compliments with Sir Harvey and Lady Gresham, Kit linked her arm in Amy's. "Where's your George?" At her suggestion, the Greshams' invitation had included Amy's betrothed. "I'm dying to meet this paragon whose kisses get you hot and wet."

"Sssh! For heaven's sake, Kit, keep your voice down." Amy's eyes were fixed on her mother's back. Perceiving no sign that her ladyship had heard, she switched her gaze to Kit's teasing face. And sighed. "George had to cry off. It seems he's still on duty – assigned to some special mission." Amy grimaced. "He does steal time to drop by now and then, but it's hardly what I'd hoped – I haven't seen much of him in the last few weeks."

"Oh," was all Kit could find to say.

"But," added Amy, drawing herself up, "it will only be for another few months. And at least he's safe in England, not facing the French guns." Smiling, she squeezed Kit's arm. "Incidentally, he said he was most desirous of making your acquaintance."

Kit looked her disbelief. "Did he really say that or are you just being loyal?"

Amy laughed. "You're right. What with his apologies for not being able to accompany us, I'm afraid we never got around to discussing you."

Kit nodded sagely. "I see. Too feverish for sense."

Amy grinned but refused confirmation. Together, they strolled among the guests, chatting easily. The conversation in the drawing room revolved around farming and the local markets, but once they were all seated about the long dining table, the talk shifted to other spheres.

"Hendon's not here, I see." Lord Marchmont sent a glance around the table, as if the recently returned Lord Hendon might have slipped in unnoticed. "Thought he would be."

"We sent a card, but his lordship had a prior engagement." Spencer nodded to Jenkins; the first course was promptly served, footmen ferrying dishes from the kitchen.

Pondering a dish of crab in oyster sauce, Kit realized it was rather odd of Lord Hendon to have a prior engagement. With whom, when all the surrounding families were here?

"Pity," Spencer continued. "Haven't met the fellow yet."

"I have," replied Lord Marchmont, helping himself to the turbot.

"Oh?" said Spencer. All paused to hear his lordship's response.

Lord Marchmont nodded. "Seems a solid sort. Jake's boy, after all."

Jake Hendon had been the previous lord of Castle Hendon. Kit's memory supplied a hazy figure, broad, powerful, and extremely tall with a pair of twinkling grey eyes. He'd taken her for a ride on his stallion when she'd been eight years old. She couldn't recall having met his son.

"What's this I hear about Hendon's appointment as High Commissioner?" Sir Harvey glanced at his lordship. 'Another attempt to stamp out the traffic?"

"So it appears." Lord Marchmont looked up. "But he's Jake's boy – he'll know how to pace his success."

All the men nodded, comfortable with that assessment. Smuggling was in the Norfolk blood; control was one thing, suppression unthinkable. Where else would they get their brandy?

Lady Gresham looked pointedly at Lady Marchmont. "Amelia, have you met this paragon?"

Lady Marchmont nodded. "Indeed. A most pleasant gentleman."

"Good. What's he like?"

Amy and Kit exchanged glances, then rapidly looked down at their plates. While the men ignored the very feminine question, the ladies fastened their attention on Lady Marchmont.

"He's tall, just like his father. And he's got the same odd hair – you remember, Martha. I believe he's been in both the army and the navy, but that might not be right. It doesn't sound normal, does it?"

Lady Gresham frowned. "Amelia, stop beating about the bush. *How much* like his father is he?"

Lady Marchmont chuckled. "Oh, that!" She waved dismissively. "He's as handsome as sin, but then, all the Hendons are."

"Too true," agreed Mrs. Cartwright. "And they can charm the birds from the trees."

"That, too." Her ladyship nodded. "A silver-tongued devil, he is."

Lady Dersingham sighed. "So pleasant, to know there's a personable gentleman about one has yet to meet. Heightens the anticipation."

There were nods of agreement all around.

"He's not married, is he?" asked Lady Lechfield.

Lady Marchmont shook her head. "Oh, no. You may be sure I asked. He's only recently returned from active service abroad. He still carries a wound – a limp in his left leg. He said he expected to be very much caught up in executing his commission as well as taking up Jake's reins."

"Hmm." Lady Gresham's gaze rested on Kit, seated at the end of the table. "Thinks he'll be too busy to find a wife, does he?"

Lady Dersingham's gaze had followed her ladyship's. "Perhaps we could help?" she mused.

Kit, busy conveying her compliments to their chef via Jenkins, did not catch their assessing glances. She turned back to see the ladies Gresham and Dersingham exchanging satisfied nods with Lady Marchmont.

As the ladies' attention returned to their plates, Kit caught a quizzical glance from Amy. Briefly Kit grimaced then looked down, eyes gleaming cynically. A silver-tongued devil as handsome as sin sounded far too much like one of her London suitors. Just because the man was tall, wellborn, and not positively ugly, he was immediately considered a desirable *parti*! Stifling an unladylike snort Kit attacked her portion of crab.

Chapter 4

Shortly after eleven, the coaches rumbled down the drive, well lit by a full moon. Beside Spencer on the steps, Kit waved them away, then impulsively hugged her grandfather.

"Thank you, Gran'pa. That was a lovely evening."

Spencer beamed. "A rare pleasure, my dear." Arm in arm, they entered the hall. "Perhaps in a few months we might consider a dance, eh?"

Kit smiled. "Perhaps. Who knows – we might even entice this mysterious Lord Hendon with the promise of music."

Spencer laughed. "Not if he's Jake's lad. Never could stand any fussing and primping, not Jake."

"Ah, but this one's a new generation – who knows what he'll be like."

Spencer shook his head. "As you get older, my dear, one thing becomes clear. People don't really change, generation to generation. The same strengths, the same weaknesses."

Kit laughed and kissed his cheek. "Good night, Gran'pa."

Spencer patted her hand and left her.

But once in her room, Kit couldn't settle down. She let Elmina help her from her gown, then dismissed her;

enveloped in a wrapper, she prowled the room. The single candle wavered and she snuffed it. Moonlight streamed in, shedding more than enough light. Thinking of Spencer's dance, Kit bowed and swayed through the steps of a cotillion. At its end, she sank onto the window seat and stared out over the fields. In the distance, she could hear the swoosh of the waves, two miles away.

The odd emptiness remained, that peculiar feeling of lack that had settled deep inside her. In an effort to ignore it she fixed her senses on the ebb and surge of the tide, letting the sounds lull her and lead her toward slumber. She'd almost succumbed when she saw the light.

A flash of brilliance, it flared in the dark. Then, just as she'd convinced herself she'd imagined it, it came again. There was a ship offshore, signaling to – to whom? On the thought, the muted reflection of an answering flash from beneath the cliffs gleamed on the dark water.

Kit searched the blackness, separating the darker mass of the cliffs from the background of the Wash. Smugglers were running a cargo on the beach directly west of Cranmer Hall.

Within minutes, she'd pulled on her breeches and bound her breasts in the cloths she used for support when riding. She pulled a linen shirt over her head and shrugged on her coat without stopping to tie the shirt laces. Stockings and boots followed. She jammed on her hat, remembering to wrap a woollen scarf about her throat to hide the white of her linen. She headed for the door but paused at the last. On impulse, she turned back and crossed to where, above a dresser against the wall, a rapier with an Italianate guard lay in brackets, crossed over its belted scabbard. It was the work of a minute to free both. Seconds later, Kit slipped out of the house and headed for the stables.

Delia whinnied in welcome, then stood quietly as Kit threw a saddle onto the black back, expertly cinching the girth before leading the mare, not into the yard where the clop of iron-shod hooves would rouse the stablelads, but into the small paddock behind the stables. Swinging into the saddle, she leaned forward, murmuring encouragement to the mare, then set her directly at the fence. Delia cleared it easily.

The black hooves effortlessly ate the miles. Fifteen minutes later, Kit reined in under cover of the last trees before the cliff's edge.

Fitful clouds had found the moon. Her senses straining into the sudden darkness, Kit heard the soft splash of oars, followed by an unmistakable "scrunch." A boat had beached. In the same instant, a jingle fiom her left drew her eyes. The moon sailed free, and Kit saw what the smugglers on the beach beneath the cliffs couldn't see. The Revenue.

A small troop was picking its way across the grassy headland. For a full minute, Kit watched. The soldiers were armed.

What crazy impulse prompted her she never knew. Perhaps a vision of fishermen' s children playing under nets on the beach? She'd seen such a sight just that afternoon, while riding past a fishing hamlet. Whatever, she pulled her scarf high, covering nose and chin, and yanked her hat down. Drawing Delia around, she set the mare on a silent course parallel to the shore. There was no pathway where the Revenue were headed. Kit knew every inch of this stretch of coast, the section she most frequently visited on her rides. She left the Revenue behind but didn't turn Delia to the shore until she was out of their sight. The clouds were unreliable; she couldn't afford to be seen.

Once on the beach, she turned the mare's head for the

smugglers, a dark blotch on the shore. Praying they'd realize a single rider was no threat, she galloped directly toward them. The dull drubbing of Delia's hooves was swallowed by the crash of the surf; she was nearly upon them before they realized. Kit had a momentary vision of stunned faces, then she saw moonlight flash on a pistol's mounts. Struggling to turn Delia, she all but snarled in fright: "Don't be a fool! The Revenue are on the cliff. They're some way from a path, but they're there. Get out!"

Wheeling Delia, Kit glanced back. The smugglers stood frozen in a knot about their boat. "Go!" she urged. "*Move* — or they'll nail your hides to the Custom House in Lynn."

Afterward, she realized it was her use of the shortened name for the town, a habit with locals, that prompted them to turn to her. The largest took a tentative step toward her, warily eyeing Delia and her iron-tipped hooves. "We've a cargo here that's got nowhere to go. All our blunt's sunk in't. If we don't get it out, our families'll starve."

Kit recognized him. She'd seen him that afternoon at the hamlet, busily mending nets. Fleetingly, she closed her eyes. Trust her to stumble onto the most helpless crew of smugglers on the English coast.

She opened her eyes, and the men were still there, mutely begging for help. "Where are your ponies?" she asked.

"Didn't think we'd need 'em, not for this lot."

"But . . ." Kit had always thought smugglers had ponies. "What were you going to do with it then?"

"We normally put stuff like this in a cave up beside the knoll yonder." The big man nodded southward.

Kit knew the cave. She and her cousins had played in it often. But the Revenue troop was between the smugglers and the cave. Moving the goods in the boat was impossible; with the moon out they'd be seen.

On the other hand, a boat could be a perfect distraction. "Two of you. Take the boat out to sea. You've got nets in it, haven't you?" To her relief, they nodded. "Get the cargo out. Put it close to the cliffs." She glanced at the cliffs, then up at the moon – a large cloud swept up and engulfed it. Thanking her guardian angel, Kit nodded. "Now! Move!"

They worked fast. Soon, the boat was empty. "You two!" Kit called to the pair elected to remain with the boat. The surf was pounding in; she had to yell to be heard. "You're out fishing, understand? You pulled in here for a break, nothing more. You don't know anything about anything except fish. Take the boat out and act as if you really are fishing. Go!"

A minute later, the oars dipped and the small boat struggled out through the surf. Kit wheeled Delia and made for the cliff.

The large man was waiting for her there. "What now?"

"The Snettisham quarries." Kit kept her voice low. "And no talking. They must be close above us. Head north and keep in the lee of the cliff. They'll be expecting you to go south."

"But our homes are south."

In the blackness, Kit couldn't tell who'd said that. "Which would you rather – being late home or ending in the cells beneath the Custom House?"

There was no further argument. Huffing and puffing, they followed her. Once they were clear of where she'd seen the Revenue, Kit found a path to the cliff top. "I'm going to find out where they are. There's no sense in walking into an ambush with your arms full."

Without waiting for their opinion, she set Delia upward. She followed the cliff edge back toward the soldiers, keeping under cover. She was in a stand of oak waiting for the next spate of moonlight to study the area ahead when she heard them coming. They were grumbling, loud and long, having belatedly realized they were nowhere near a path downward. The moonlight strengthened, and she could see them gathering in a knot in the middle of the grassy expanse directly in front of her.

A shout came from the cliff's edge. "There's a path here, Sergeant! What are we to do? The boat's gone, and there's nought to be seen on the sands."

A burly man nudged his horse to the cliff and looked down. He swore. "Never mind that now. We saw that boat. Half of you – down onto the sand and go south. The rest keep to the cliffs. We're bound to come up with them, one way or t'other."

"But south's Sergeant Osborne's region, Sergeant."

The burly man cuffed the speaker. "I know that, fool boy! But Osborne's out to Sheringham way, so's it's up to us to police this 'ere stretch. On you go, and let's see what we can find."

To Kit's delight, she saw them split, then both groups head south. Satisfied, she returned to the small band trudging doggedly northward, still on the sands.

"You're safe. They've gone south."

The men downed their burdens and sat on the sands. "Thanks be we only had one boatload." The speaker glanced toward Kit and explained: "Normally we have a lot more."

The large man, who seemed to be their spokesman, looked up at her. "This quarry you spoke of, lad. Where be it?"

Kit stared. It had never occurred to her that they wouldn't know Snettisham quarries. She and her cousins had spent hours playing there. It was a perfect hiding place for anything. But what if she took them there?

Delia pranced sideways; Kit gentled her. "I'll give you directions. You won't want me to know exactly where you've stowed your goods." Using the mare's nervousness as an excuse, Kit backed her up. At least one man had a pistol.

"Hang about, lad." The large man stepped forward. Delia took exception and danced back. He stopped. "You've got nothing to fear from us, matey. You saved us back there, no mistake. Smugglers' honor says we offer you a cut of the booty."

Kit blinked. Smugglers' honor? She laughed lightly and drew Delia around. "Consider it a free service. I don't want any booty." She set her heels to the sleek black sides and Delia surged forward.

"Wait!" The panicky note in the man's voice made Kit rein in and turn. He stumbled through the sand toward her, stopping when he was close enough to talk. For a moment, he stared at her, then looked to his companions. In the dim light, Kit saw their emphatic nods. The spokesman turned back to her.

"It's like this, lad. We don' have a leader. We got into the business thinking we could manage well enough, but you saw how 'tis." His head jerked southward. "You thought fast, back there. I don' suppose you'd like to take us on? We got good contacts an' all. But we're not good on the organization, like."

Disbelief and consternation warred in Kit's brain. Take them on? "You mean . . . you want me to act as your leader?"

"For a slice o' the profits, o'course."

Delia shifted. Kit glanced up and saw the others hoist their burdens and draw nearer. She didn't need to fear a pistol while they were so laden. "I'm sure you'll manage well enough on your own. The Revenue just got lucky."

But the big man was shaking his head. "Lad, just look at us. None of us knows where these quarries of yours be. We don' even know what's the best road home. Like as not, as soon as we're back on the cliffs, we'll run slap bang into the Revenue. And then it'll all be for nought."

The moon sailed free and Kit saw their faces, turned up to her in childlike trust. She sighed. What had she got herself into now? "What do you run?"

They perked up at this sign of interest. "Show 'im, Joe." The big man waved the smallest one forward. The man shuffled over the sand, one wary eye on Delia. He smiled up at Kit as he drew near – an all but toothless grin – then stopped beside the mare and peeled back the oilskin enclosing the packet he bore, a rectangle about three feet long and flatish. Grubby hands brushed back layers of coarse cloth.

Moonlight glimmered on what was revealed. Kit's eyes grew round. Lace! They were smuggling Brussels lace. No wonder the packages were so small. One boatload, carried to London and sold through the trade, would surely feed these men and their families for months. Kit rapidly revised her assessment of their business acumen. Organizationally hopeless they might be, but they knew their cargoes.

"We sometimes get brandy, too, depending." The big man had drawn closer.

Kit's eyes narrowed. "Nothing else?" She'd heard there were things other than goods brought ashore in the boats.

Her tone was sharp, but the man's face was open when he answered: "We ain't done no other cargoes – this's been enough t'present."

She could sense their entreaty. Her Norfolk blood stirred. A leader of smugglers? One part of her laughed at the idea. A small part. Most of her unconventional soul was intrigued. Her father had led a band for a short time – for a lark, he'd said. Why couldn't she? Kit crossed her hands over her pommel and considered the possibilities. "If I became your leader, you'd have to agree to doing only the cargoes I think are right."

They glanced at each other, then the big man looked up. "What cut?"

"No cut." They murmured at that; behind her muffler, Kit smiled. "I don't need your goods or the money they'll bring. If I agree to take you on, it'll be for the sheer hell of it. Nothing more."

A quick conference ensued, then the spokesman approached. "If we agree, will you show us these quarries?"

"If we agree, I'll take over right now. If not, say so, and I'll be off." Delia pranced.

The man sent a glance around his companions, then turned back to her. "Deal. What moniker do ye go by?"

"Kit."

"Right then, young Kit. Lead on."

It took them an hour to reach the quarries and find a suitable deserted tunnel to use as a base. By then, Kit had learned a great deal more of the small band. They contracted for cargoes through the inns in King's Lynn. Whatever they brought ashore, they hid in the cave for a few nights before transferring it by pack pony to the ruined abbey at Creake.

"S'been a clearinghouse for years, hereabouts. We show the goods to the old crone who lives in the cottage close by, and she's always got our cut ready an' waiting."

"The old woman has the money?"

"Oh, aye. She be a witch, so the money's safe with her."

"How very convenient." Someone, somewhere, had put considerable effort into organizing the Norfolk smugglers. An unwelcome thought surfaced. "Are there any other gangs operating about here?"

The large man went by the unenviable name of Noah. "Not on the west here, no. But there's a gang east of Hunstanton. Big gang, that is. We've never come across 'em, though."

And I hope you never will, Kit thought. These poor souls were a remarkably simple lot, not given to unnecessary violence, fisherman driven to smuggling in order to feed their families. But somewhere out there lurked real smugglers, the sort who committed the atrocities proclaimed in the handbills. She'd no desire whatever to meet them. Keeping clear of this Hunstanton Gang seemed a good idea.

Once the lace was stored, she gave orders, crisply and clearly, about how they were to pass the cargo on. She also insisted they operate from the quarries henceforth. "The Revenue men will be suspicious of that stretch of beach, and the cave's too close. From now on, we'll work from here." Kit threw out a hand to indicate their surroundings. They were standing before the dark mouth of the abandoned tunnel in which they'd stashed their goods. "We'll be safer here. There are places aplenty to hide, and even in broad daylight it's not easy to follow people through here." She paused, then paced before them, frowning in concentration. "If you have to go out in your boats to bring in the cargo, then the boats should just land the goods and go directly back to your village. If the rest of you bring ponies, then we can load the goods and transfer them here. When it's safe, they can go on to Creake."

They agreed readily. "This be a dandy place for hiding, right enough."

As they stood to leave, Noah noticed the rapier at Kit's side. "That's a right pretty toy. Know how to use it?"

A heartbeat later, he was blinking at the soft shimmer of moonlight on steel, the rapier point at his throat.

Swallowing convulsively, his gaze traveled the length of the wicked blade, until, over the top of the ornate guard, he met Kit's narrowed eyes. She smiled tightly. "Yes."

"Oh." The big man remained perfectly still.

Kit relaxed and expertly turned the blade and slid it back into the scabbard. "A little conceit of mine."

She turned and walked to where Delia waited, ears pricked. Behind her, she sensed the exchanged glances and hid a smug smile. She swung up to the saddle, then looked back at her little band.

"You know the road home?"

They nodded. "And we'll keep a watch for the Revenue, like you said."

"Good. We'll meet here Thursday after moonrise." Kit wheeled and set her heels to Delia's sides. "And then we'll see what comes next."

Chapter 5

"Damn!" George flung his cards down on the rough deal table and glared at Jack. "Nothing's changed in well-nigh twenty years! You still win."

Jack's white teeth showed in a laughing smile. "Console yourself it's not the title to your paternal acres that lie under my hand." He lifted his palm, revealing a pile of woodchips.

Pushing back his chair, George snorted disgustedly. "As if I'd risk anything of worth against such a dyed-in-the-wool gamester."

Jack collected the cards and reshaped the pack, then, elbows on the table, shuffled them back and forth, left hand to right.

Outside, the east wind howled, whipping leaves and twigs against the shutters. Inside, the lamplight played on Jack's bent head, exposing the hidden streaks of gold, bright against the duller brown. Aside from the table, the single-room cottage was sparsely furnished, the principal items being a large bed against the opposite wall and an equally large wardrobe beside it. Yet no farmworker would have dreamed of setting foot in the place. The bed was old but of polished oak, as was the wardrobe. The sheets were of linen and the goosefeather quilt simply too luxurious to permit the fiction of this being a humble dwelling. True, the deal table was just that, but smoothed and cleaned and in remarkably good condition. The four chairs scattered about the room were of assorted styles but none bore any relation to the crude seating normally found in fishermen's abodes.

Jack slapped the pack on the table and, pushing his chair back, stretched his arms above his head.

Hoofbeats, muffled by the wildness outside, sounded like a ghostly echo. Dragging his gaze from the flames flickering in the stone hearth, George turned to listen, then sent an expectant look Jack's way.

Jack's brows rose fleetingly before his gaze swung to the door. Seconds later, it burst open to reveal a large figure wrapped in heavy frieze, a hat pulled low over his eyes. The figure whirled, slamming the heavy door against the tempest outside.

The tension in Jack's long frame eased. He leaned forward, arms on the table. "Welcome back. What did you learn?"

Matthew's lined face emerged as the hat hit the table. He shrugged off his coat and set it on a peg beside the door. "Like you thought, there's another gang."

"They're active?" George drew his chair closer.

At Jack's nod, Matthew pulled another chair to the table. "They're in business, all right. Ran a cargo of brandy last night, somewhere between Hunstanton and Heacham, cool as you please. I heard talk they did that consignment of lace we refused – the run that clashed with that load of spirits we took out Brancaster way."

Jack swore. "Damn! I'd hoped that night was all a piece of Tonkin's delusions." He turned to George. "When I went into Hunstanton yesterday, Tonkin was full of this gang he'd surprised running some cargo south of Snettisham. Preening that he'd found another gang operating on Osborne's turf that Osborne hadn't known about. I spoke to some of Tonkin's men later. It sounded like they'd seen a fishing boat pull in for a break and Tonkin invented the rest." Jack grimaced. "Now, it seems otherwise."

"Does it matter? If they're a small operation . . ." George broke off at Jack's emphatic nod.

"It matters. We need this coast tied up. If there's another gang operating, no matter how small, who's to tell what cargoes they'll run?"

The wind whistled down the narrow chimney and played with the flames licking the logs in the hearth. Abruptly, Jack pushed away from the table. "We'll have to find out who this lot is." He looked at Matthew. "Did you get any hints from your contacts?"

Matthew shook his head. "Not a whiff of a scent."

George frowned. "What about Osborne? Why not just get him to clamp down along that stretch?"

"Because I've sent him to clamp down on the beaches between Blakeney and Cromer." Exasperation colored Jack's tone. "There's a small outfit operating around there, but for most of that coast, the silts are so unpredictable no master in his right mind will bring his ship in close. The few reasonable landings are easy to patrol. But I sent Osborne to ensure the job was done. Aside from anything else, it seemed preferable to make certain he wouldn't get wind of our activities and seek to curtail them. Tonkin, bless his hopeless heart, is so bumblingly inept we stand in no danger from him. Unfortunately, neither does this other gang."

"So," George mused, "Tonkin's now effectively responsible for the coast from Lynn to Blakeney?"

Jack nodded.

"Whoever this other lot are," said Matthew, "seems like they know the area well. There's no whispers of pack trains or any such, but they must be moving the goods, same as us."

"Who knows?" Jack said. "They might actually be better set up than us. We're only novices, after all."

George turned a jaundiced eye on Jack. "I don't believe any man in his right mind would call Captain Jack a novice – not at this sort of devilry."

A broad grin dispelled Jack's seriousness. "You flatter me, my friend. Now, how are we to meet this mystery gang?"

"Must we meet them?"

"How else, oh knowledgeable one, are we to dissuade them from their illegal pursuits?"

"Dissuade them?"

Jack's face hardened. "That – or do Tonkin's job for him."

George looked glum. "I knew I wasn't going to like this mission."

Jack's chair grated on the floor as he rose. "They're smugglers, for Christ's sake."

George sighed, dropping his eyes from Jack's stern grey gaze. "So are we, Jack. So are we."

But Jack had stopped listening. Turning to Matthew, he asked, "What cargoes do they usually take?"

Chapter 6

A week later, from the cliff top screened by a belt of trees, Kit watched her band beach their boats at much the same spot as on the night she'd first rescued them. This time, there was no Revenue troop about; she'd reconnoitered the cliffs in both directions.

Still she was nervous, twitchy. Since she'd taken over, her band had run five cargoes, all successfully. Her band. At first, the responsibility had scared her. Now, each time they came off safely, she felt a thrill of achievement. But tonight was a special cargo. An agent, Nolan, had met them in Lynn last night. For the first time, she'd joined Noah for the negotiations. Just as well. She'd intervened and driven their price up – because Nolan was in a fix. He had a schooner with twenty bales of lace and no one to bring it in. They were his last resort. She'd already heard of the Revenue raids about Sheringham and, for some reason, the Hunstanton Gang had refused the run. Why, she didn't know – which was the root cause of her nervousness.

Everything, however, was going smoothly. The night was dark, the sky deepest purple. Beneath her, Delia peacefully cropped, undisturbed by an owl hooting in the trees behind them.

Watching the orderly way the men swiftly unloaded the boats, Kit smiled. They were not unintelligent, just unimaginative. Once she showed them a better way of doing things, they caught on quickly.

Suddenly, Delia's head came up, ears pricked, muscles tensing. Kit strained her senses to catch what had disturbed the mare. Nothing. Then, far to the left, another owl hooted. Delia sidled. Kit stared at the great black head. *Not an owl?* She didn't wait for confirmation. Pulling Delia around, she set the mare onto the path down to the sands.

In the trees on the cliff top, two riders met a third.

"Spotted them," Matthew murmured, as Jack and George came up, walking their horses over the thinly grassed ground. He pointed to where ten ponies were being loaded with the consignment of lace they'd refused. As they looked, a mounted figure all in black broke from the shadow of the cliff and raced across the sands. "Cripes," muttered Matthew. "What's that?"

"A lookout we've alerted," came George's laconic answer.

"But where did a smuggler get a horse like that?" Jack watched as horse and rider flew toward the boats, a single entity in effortless motion. "This gang has signed up a little unexpected talent."

George nodded. "Do we go down now that they know we're here?"

Jack grimaced. "Let's wait. They might think we're the Revenue."

It appeared he was right. The rider reached the group on the sands. Immediately, their pace increased. Within minutes, the boats pulled out to sea. The rider backed from the ponies as the men tugged straps and girths tight. The black horse danced; the rider scanned the cliffs. He did not look directly their way.

Squinting, George whispered: "The horse – is it all black?"

Jack nodded. "Looks like it." He took up his reins. "They're heading in. Let's follow. I've a desire to see where they're stashing their goods."

Kit couldn't get rid of the feeling of being watched. Like Delia, her nerves were at full stretch. She hadn't explained to Noah why she came bolting out of the dark, urging him on. She'd just issued a warning: "There's someone out there. I didn't wait to find out who. Let's get going."

Five minutes later, she and Delia gained the cliff top. She waited until Noah, walking beside the lead pony, crested the cliff, then leaned down to say: "Go east by Cramner woods, then cut back to the quarries. I'll scout around to make sure we're not followed."

She wheeled Delia and made off into the surrounding trees. For the next hour, she tracked her own men, sweeping in arcs across their trail. Time and again, Delia skittered. And every time, Kit felt the hair on her nape lift.

In the end, she realized it was she, the rider, the unknowns were tracking. Abruptly, Kit drew rein. Her followers were mounted, else they wouldn't have kept up thus far. They weren't trying to catch them but were following them to their hideout. But they were on Cranmer land and none knew that better than she. Her men would soon be turning north toward the quarries. She, with her unwelcome escort, would continue east.

Kit patted Delia's glossy black neck. "We'll have a run soon, my lady. But first let's do a little deceiving."

They were nearing the village of Great Bircham when Jack realized they'd lost the pack train. He reined in on a crest overlooking a moonlit valley. Somewhere ahead, the rider still ranged. "Damn! He's moving too fast to be following ponies. We've been had."

George stopped beside him. "Maybe the ponies were faster through the woods. The rider went slow there."

Jack shook his head emphatically. Then, as if to confirm his deduction in the most mocking way, the rider appeared, crossing the fields below at full gallop, a streak of black against the silvered green.

"Christ!" breathed George. "Will you look at that."

"I'd rather not look at that," Jack replied. After three seconds of silence, in which the rider gathered the fluid black into a soaring leap over a pair of hedges, he continued grudgingly: "Well, whoever he is, he can ride."

"What now?" asked Matthew.

"We go home and try to figure out another way of contacting this accursed gang." With that dampening answer, Jack shook his reins and set his grey stallion, Champion, down the ridge.

Kit raced with the wind, the scenery a blur about her. She took her usual route to Gresham Manor, circling it, then pulling up on a hill overlooking the house to let Delia rest.

What would Amy say if she went down and threw gravel at her window? Kit grinned. Amy had a streak of conservatism that was quite wide, despite her predeliction for becoming hot and wet for her George.

Sighing, Kit folded her hands across her pommel, staring at the dreaming countryside. She hadn't thought of Amy's disturbing revelations for weeks, not since she'd taken up smuggling. Had excitement filled in that odd gap in her innermost self? After a moment's consideration, she admitted it had not. Rather, the demands of smuggling had left no time for dwelling on ill-defined regrets. Which was just as well. Shaking the cramps from her shoulders, Kit picked up the reins. It was time for the quarries.

The trio of riders cantered north in no great hurry. Jack drew rein as they topped a hill and turned to George, who pulled up beside him. Champion's head came around, but not to look at George, or George's gelding. The grey stallion shifted, craning his long neck to stare past George. The movement caught Jack's attention; he followed the horse's gaze.

"Hold very still," he commanded, his voice a bare murmur. Carefully, he turned in the saddle and looked back. The flash of black that had caught Champion's attention appeared in the fields behind them, this time heading west. Then horse and rider crossed the road, still flying. Jack watched until they disappeared into the trees bordering the next field.

Only then did he relax his rein and let Champion turn. The horse came about and stared in the direction the unknown rider had taken.

A grin of diabolical delight spread over Jack's features. "So that's it."

"What?" asked George. "Was that the rider again? Why aren't we giving chase?"

"We are." Jack set Champion back down the road, waiting until George and Matthew caught up before shifting to a canter. "But we mustn't get too close and warn him. I've been wondering what gave us away. I'd wager that black is a mare. Not having been introduced to Champion here, like any other well-bred female, she gets skittish whenever he gets close."

"Can Champion lead us to them?"

"I've no idea." Iack patted the silky grey neck. "But we can't risk getting too close until the rider dismounts."

Kit reached the quarries as the last pony was unloaded. Noah and the others greeted her with relief.

"Thought as how somethin' might have come upon you, lad."

Feeling thoroughly alive, her blood stirred by her long gallop, Kit swung her leg over Delia's neck and slid to the ground. "I'm sure we were followed, but I didn't catch sight of anyone. I went a very long way around, just in case." She looped Delia's reins to a wooden strut at the edge of the clearing, well away from the men, who had an almost superstitious fear of the black horse. "What's the stuff like?" She headed for the tunnel entrance.

Noah waved to a packet opened on a rock. "First-class stuff, it looks."

Kit bent over the lace, resting both palms on the rock to protect against the impulse to draw off her gloves and finger the delicate tracery, a far too feminine gesture. "This is better than that other stuff you ran. What's the price?"

The other men sat in the cave entrance, chewing baccy and talking quietly, while she and Noah reviewed their plans.

What warned her, she never knew. The hairs on her nape lifted. The next instant, she whirled, her rapier singing from its sheath, sweeping in an arc before the three men silently approaching.

What happened next made her blink. The foremost man – tall, well built, and hatless was her first impression – took one step back and her rapier clashed against solid steel. Kit's eyes grew round. She swallowed a knot of cold fear at the sight of her elegant blade countered by a longer, infinitely more

47

wicked-looking sword. The two men following the first drew back, leaving a wide area to the fighters.

Heavens! She was involved in a sword fight!

Resolutely, Kit quelled the impulse to drop her rapier and flee. Drawing a deep breath, she forced her mind to function. If this man was a smuggler, he'd have no knowledge of the finer points of swordsmanship. She, on the other hand, had been trained by an Italian master, a close friend of Spencer's. She hadn't practiced for years but, as her opponent drifted left, she instinctively drifted right, the blades hissing softly.

He made the first move, a tentative prod Kit easily pushed aside. She followed immediately with a classic counter, and was dismayed to meet the prescribed defense, perfectly executed. Two more similar exchanges sent her heart to her boots. The man could fight and fight well. The strength she sensed behind the long sword was frightening.

In growing panic, she glanced at her opponent's face. The moon shone over her shoulder, leaving her own face in shadow. Even in the weak light, she saw the frown on the handsome face watching her. A second later, the effect of that face hit her. Kit blinked and dragged her mind and her gaze back to her blade, poised against that other. But her disobedient eyes flicked upward again, drawn by that face. She sucked in a painful breath. *God, he is beautiful.* Sculpted features, aquiline planes below high cheekbones, lips long and firm above a stubbornly square chin. His hair was fairish, streaked silver in the moonlight. Despite her every effort, Kit's senses refused to bend to her will, irresponsibly continuing their dangerous detachment, roaming over the outline of the large body facing hers.

An odd sensation bloomed in Kit's midsection, a warm weakness that sapped what little strength she had. She wondered whether it was fear of impending death. At the thought, from deep inside, she heard a laugh, a warm, rich, seductive laugh. *What are you waiting for? You've been fantasizing about meeting a man who could do to you what George does to Amy – here he is. All you have to do is put down your rapier and step forward.*

Kit's guard wavered – she came to herself with a sickening start. In that instant, her opponent launched an attack. Her blade had nowhere near enough strength to counter the sword effectively. By dint of sheer luck and fancy footwork, she survived the first rush, her heart pounding horribly, a metallic taste in her mouth. She knew she'd never survive the second.

So much for my dream come true, she sneered at her inner self. The man's about to skewer me, no thanks to you.

But the clash she feared never came. Her opponent took a decisive step back, just one, but it was enough to get him out of her reach. His sword was slowly lowered until it pointed at the ground.

Glancing up at that distracting face, Kit saw his frown deepen.

Jack's mind was reeling, overloaded by conflicting and confusing information. Champion had led them unerringly in the wake of the black mare. As soon as they saw the jumble of jagged rocks on the horizon, they'd recognized their destination. Respect for the smaller gang grew – the quarries were a perfect hideaway, made to order. They'd left their horses at the edge of the quarries, to ensure that Champion's presence did not give them away.

They'd come into the clearing openly but quietly. He'd immediately seen the slim figure in black poring over something on the opposite side. His feet had taken him in that direction. That was when his problems started.

Even before the lad whirled to face him, sword in hand,

he'd been conscious of a quickening of his pulse, an increase in his heartbeat, a tightening of expectation which had nothing to do with the dangers of the night. Being presented with a rapier, wrong end first, only compounded the confusion. His reaction had been instinctive. It was not common practice for men to wear swords, but neither he nor George had yet adjusted to walking abroad without theirs on their hips. His hand had grasped his hilt the instant he'd heard the hiss of steel leaving a scabbard.

The poor light put him at a disadvantage from the first. The young lad was an outline, nothing more. Straining into the gloom, he'd moved cautiously, testing his opponent, despite the likelihood he could walk over the lad without difficulty. His opening move had been tentative. The lad's response had been another revelation – who'd have expected Italian ripostes from a smuggler? But the following moves left him wondering what was wrong with the lad. The arm wielding the rapier had no strength in it.

He'd peered hard at the boy then, and the impulse to shake his head grew. Something was damnably wrong somewhere. Despite not being able to see the lad's eyes, he could feel the boy's gaze and knew he was staring. At him. It was the effect of that stare that totally threw him. Never before had his body reacted so definitely, certainly never in response to a stare from a male.

The lad's point had wavered, and he'd pressed forward, without any real aim, more a matter of keeping up pretenses while he decided what to do. The lack of response made his mind up for him. He didn't know enough about the gang, and about this strange boy, to make forcing a submission wise. The lad was no fool; he'd know a fight between them could have only one end; they both knew that now. He stepped back and lowered his sword.

The boy's head came up.

A moment passed, pregnant with expectation. Then the rapier lowered. Inwardly, Jack sighed with relief.

"Who are you?" Fear had tightened Kit's throat; her voice came out gravelly and, if anything, even deeper than usual. Her eyes remained fixed on the man before her. His head turned slightly, as if to catch some half-heard sound, yet she'd spoken clearly. His unnerving frown didn't waver.

Jack heard the question but couldn't quite believe what he'd heard. His senses registered not the fear, but the underlying quality in the husky voice. He'd heard voices like that before; they didn't belong to striplings. Yet what his senses kept telling him, his rational mind knew to be impossible. It had to be some peculiar effect of the moonlight. "I'm Captain Jack, leader of the Hunstanton Gang. We want to talk, nothing more."

The lad stood perfectly still, shrouded in shadow, his face invisible. "We're listening."

Moving slowly, deliberately, Jack sheathed his sword. The tension eased, but he noted that the stripling kept his rapier in his hand. His lips quirked. The lad had his wits about him – if their situations had been reversed, he'd have done the same.

Kit felt much safer when the long sword settled back into its scabbard and felt no compulsion whatever to sheathe hers. The man was more than dangerous, particularly when his features eased, as they'd just done. The slight smile, if it was even that, drew her eyes to his lips. What would they feel like against hers? Would they make her feel . . . Kit dragged her errant thoughts from the brink of certain confusion. Then another thought struck, out of the blue. What would she feel if he smiled?

But he was talking. Kit struggled to concentrate on his

51

words, rather than letting her mind slide aimlessly into the rich, velvety-deep tones.

"We'd like you to consider a merger." Jack waited for some response; none came. His cohorts shifted, but the lad made no sign. "Equal footing, equal share in the proceeds." Still nothing. "With our gangs working together, we'd tie up the coast from Lynn to Wells and farther. We could set our conditions, so we get a decent share of the profits, given the risks we take."

That idea caused a stir. Jack was pleased with the result given that only half his mind was concentrating on his arguments. The better half was centered on the lad. Now, with his mates looking pointedly to him, the boy shifted slightly. "What exactly's in this for us?"

It was a sensible question, but Jack could have sworn the lad paid scant attention to his answer.

While ostensibly listening to Captain Jack extoll the obvious virtues of operating as part of a larger whole, Kit wondered what on earth she was to do. The merger would be in the best interests of her small band. Captain Jack had already demonstrated an uncommon degree of ability. And good sense. And he didn't seem overly bloodthirsty. Noah and company would be as safe as they could be under his guidance. But for herself, every sense was screaming the fact that remaining anywhere near Captain Jack was tantamount to lunacy. He'd eat her for breakfast, or worse. Even in bad light, she wasn't sure of her ability to fool him – he seemed suspicious already.

He'd come to the end of his straightforward explanation and was waiting for her reply. "What's in a merger for you?" she asked.

Jack's feelings for the stripling became even more confused as grudging respect and exasperation were added to the list. He hadn't entered the clearing with any real plan; the idea of a merger had leapt ready-formed to his mind, more in response to a need to accommodate the lad than anything else. His explanation of the benefits to them had been easy enough, but what possible benefits were there to him? Other than the truth?

Jack looked directly at the slim figure, still wreathed in shadows before him. "While you're operating independently, the agents can use you as competition to force us to accept whatever price they offer. Without competition, we'd be better off." He stopped there, leaving the other way of reducing competition unvoiced. He was sure the lad would get the message.

Kit did, but she was not convinced she understood the full ramifications of a merger, nor that she ever would, not while Captain Jack stood before her. "I'll need time to consider your offer."

Jack smiled at the formal phrasing. He nodded. "Naturally. Shall we say twenty-four hours?"

His smile was every bit as unnerving as his frown. In fact, Kit decided, she preferred his frown. She only just managed to stop her bewildered nod. "Three days," she countered. "I'll need three days." Kit glanced around at the faces of her men. "If the rest of you want to join them now . . ."

Noah shook his head. "No, lad. You rescued us, you took us on. Decision's yours, I'm thinking." A murmur of agreement came from the rest of the group.

Jack's look of surprise was fleeting, wiped from his face by the lad's next words.

Kit spoke to Noah. "I'll be in touch." Inside, she was feeling most peculiar. Decidedly fluttery and weak at the knees. She had to get out of this, and soon, before she did something too feminine to overlook. Steeling herself, she faced

Captain Jack and inclined her head regally. "I'll meet you here, seventy-two hours from now, and give you our answer."

With that, Kit walked off toward Delia, praying their unexpected and unnerving guests would accept their dismissal.

Her unconscious arrogance left Jack reeling again. He recovered his equilibrium in time to see the slim figure swing up to the saddle of the black. The horse was pure Arab, not a doubt about it, and a mare as he'd supposed. Jack's eyes narrowed. Surely there'd been too much swing in the lad's swagger? When on a horse, it was difficult to judge, yet the boy's legs seemed uncommonly long for his height and more tapered than they ought to be.

With no more than a nod for his men, the lad headed the mare out of the clearing. Jack stared at the black-garbed figure until it merged into the night, leaving him with a headache and, infinitely worse, no proof of the conviction of his senses.

Chapter 7

By the time they reached the cottage that night, Jack didn't know what he thought of Young Kit. They'd learned the lad's name from the smugglers, but it was clear the men knew little else of their leader. They were sensible, solid fishermen, forced into the trade. It seemed unlikely such men, many fathers themselves, rigidly conservative as only the ignorant could be, would give loyalty and unquestioning obedience to Young Kit if he was other than he pretended to be.

Leaving Matthew to see to the horses, Jack strode into the cottage. George followed. Halting by the table, Jack unbuckled his sword belt and scabbard. Turning, he went to the wardrobe, opened it, and thrust the scabbard to the very back, then shut the door firmly. "That's the end of that little conceit." Flinging himself into a chair, Jack rested both elbows on the table and ran his hands over his face. "God! I might have killed the whelp."

"Or he might have killed you." George slumped into another chair. "He seemed to know what he was about."

Jack waved dismissively. "He's been taught well enough, but he'd no strength to him."

George chuckled. "We can't all be six-foot-two and strong enough to run up cathedral belltowers with a wench under each arm."

Jack snorted at the reminder of one of his more outrageous exploits.

When he remained silent, George ventured, "What made you think of a merger? I thought we were just there to spy out the opposition."

"The opposition proved devilishly well organized. If it hadn't been for Champion, we wouldn't have found them. There didn't seem much point in walking away again. And I've no taste for killing wet-behind-the-ear whelps."

A short silence descended. Jack's gaze remained fixed in space. "Who do you think he is?"

"Young Kit?" George blinked sleepily. "One of our neighbors' sons, I should think. Where else the horse?"

Jack nodded. "Correct me if I'm wrong, but I don't know of any such whelp hereabouts. Morgan's sons are too old – they'd be nearer thirty, surely? And Henry Fairclough's boys are too young. Kit must be about sixteen."

George frowned. "I can't recall anyone that fits, either. But perhaps he's a nephew come to spend time on the family acres? Who knows?" He shrugged. "Could be anyone."

"*Can't* be just anyone. Young Kit knows this district like the back of his hand. Think of the chase he led us, the way he rode across those fields. He blew every fence, every tree. And according to Noah, Kit was the one who knew about the quarries."

George yawned. "Well, we knew about the quarries, too. We just hadn't thought of using them."

Jack looked disgusted. "Lack of sleep has addled your wits. That's precisely what I mean. We know the area because we grew up here. Kit's grown up here, too. Which means he should be easy enough to track down."

"And then what?" mumbled George, around another yawn.

"And then," Jack replied, getting to his feet and hauling George to his, "we'll have to decide what to do with the whelp. Because if he is someone's son, the chances are he'll recognize me, if not both of us." Propelling George to the door, he added: "And we can't trust Young Kit with that information."

What with seeing the somnolent George on his way before riding home with Matthew and stabling Champion, it was close to dawn before Jack finally lay between cool sheets and stared at the shadow patterns on his ceiling.

Neither George nor Matthew had found anything especially odd about Young Kit. Questioned on the way home, Matthew's estimation had mirrored George's. Kit was the son of a neighboring landowner, sire unknown. There was, of course, the possibility that Kit was an illegitimate sprig of some local lordly tree. The horse might have been a gift, in light of the boy's equestrian abilities, or alternatively, might be "borrowed" from his sire's stables. Whatever, the horse provided the best clue to Young Kit's identity.

Jack sighed deeply and closed his eyes. Kit's identity was only one of his problems and certainly the easier to solve. His odd reaction to the boy was a worry. Why had it happened? It had been decades since any sight had affected him so dramatically. But, for whatever incomprehensible reason, the slim, black-garbed figure of Young Kit had acted as a powerful aphrodisiac, sending his body into a state of immediate readiness. He'd been as horny as Champion on the trail of the black mare!

With a snort, Jack turned and burrowed his stubbled

cheek into the pillow. He tried to blot the entire business from his mind. When that didn't work, he searched for some explanation, however insubstantial, for the episode. If he could find a reason, hopefully that would be the end of it. There was a strong possibility that it might prove necessary to include Young Kit in the Gang. The idea of having the young whelp continuously about, wreaking havoc with his manly reactions, was simply too hideous to contemplate.

Could it have been some similarity to one of his long-discarded mistresses, popping up to waylay him when he least expected it? Perhaps it was simply the effect of unusual abstinence?

Maybe it was just wishful thinking on his part? Jack grinned. He couldn't deny that a nice, wild woman, the sort who might lead a smuggling gang, would make a welcome addition to his current lifestyle. Elsewise, the only sport to be had in the vicinity consisted of virtuous maids, whom he avoided on principle, and dowagers old enough to be his mother. Ever fertile, his brain developed his fantasy. The tension in his shoulders slowly eased.

Insidiously, sleep crawled from his feet to his calves to his knees to his hips, ever upward to claim him. Just before he succumbed, Jack hit on his cure. He'd unmask Young Kit – that was it. The sensation would disappear once Kit was revealed as the male he had to be. George was sure of it, Matthew was sure of it. Most importantly, the smugglers who followed Kit were sure of it, and surely they must know?

The problem was, *he* was far from sure of it.

Kit spent the following day in a distracted daze. Even the simplest task was beyond her; her attention constantly drifted, lured in fascinated horror to contemplation of her dreadful dilemma.

After incorrectly mixing a potion for the parlor maid's sore throat, twice, she gave up in disgust and headed for the gazebo at the end of the rose garden. The morning had cleared to a fine afternoon; she hoped the brisk breeze would blow away her mental cobwebs.

The little gazebo, with its view of the rose beds, was a favorite retreat. With a weary sigh, Kit sank onto the wooden bench. She was caught, trapped, squarely between the devil and the deep blue sea. On the one hand, prudence urged that she accept Captain Jack's proposal for her crew and decline it for herself, slipping cautiously into the mists, letting Young Kit disappear. Unfortunately, neither her men nor Captain Jack would be satisfied with that. She knew them – knew them far better than they knew her. She didn't, in truth, know Captain Jack, and if she was intent on following prudence's dictates, she never would.

Coward! sneered her other self.

"Did you see him?" Kit asked, annoyed when her heart-beat accelerated at the memory.

Oh, yes! came the thoroughly smitten answer.

Kit snorted. "Even in moonlight he looked like he could give the London rakes lessons."

Indubitably. And just think what lessons he could give you.

Kit blushed. "I'm *not* interested."

Like hell you're not. You, my girl, turned a delicate shade of green when Amy was describing her experiences. Now fate hands you a gilded first-ever opportunity to do a little experiencing of your own and what do you do? Run away before that gorgeous specimen gets a chance to raise your temperature. What's happened to your wild Cranmer blood?

Kit grimaced. "I've still got you to remind me I haven't lost it."

Putting a lid on her wilder self, Kit brooded on her folly in getting involved with smugglers. That didn't last long.

She'd enjoyed the past weeks too much to dissemble, even to herself. The excitement, the thrills, the highs and lows of tension and relief had become a staple in her diet, an addictive ingredient she was loath to forego. How else would she fill in her time?

The alternative to disappearing grew increasingly attractive.

Resolutely, she shook her head. "I can't risk it. He's suspicious already. Men can't be trusted – and men like Captain Jack are even less trustworthy than the rest."

Who said anything about trust? If he realizes Young Kit's not all he seems, well and good. You might even learn what you're dying to know – what price a little experience against the years of lonely spinsterhood ahead? You know you'll never marry, so what good is your closely guarded virtue? And who's to know? You can always disappear, once your men have settled in with his.

"And what happens if I get caught, if things don't go as planned?" Kit waited, but her wild self remained prudently silent. She sighed, then frowned as she saw a maid looking this way and that amongst the rosebushes. With a rustle of starched petticoats, Kit rose. "Dorcas? What's amiss?"

"Oh! There you be, miss. Jenkins said as you might be out 'ere."

"Yes. Here I am." Kit stepped down from her retreat. "Am I wanted?"

"Oh, yes, if you please, miss. The Lord Lieutenant and his lady be here. In the drawing room.'

Hiding a grimace, Kit headed indoors. She found Lady Marchmont ensconced on the *chaise*, listening with barely concealed boredom to the conversation between her husband and Spencer. At the sight of Kit, she perked up. "Kathryn, my dear!" Her ladyship surged up in a froth of soft lace.

After exchanging the usual pleasantries, Kit sat on the *chaise*. Lady Marchmont barely paused to draw breath. "We've just come from Castle Hendon, my dear. *Such* an impressive place but sadly in need of a woman's touch these days. I do believe Jake hadn't had the curtains shaken since Mary died." Lady Marchmont patted Kit's hand. "But I don't suppose you remember the last Lady Hendon. She died when the new Lord Hendon was just a boy. Jake raised him." Her ladyship paused; Kit waited politely.

"I thought I should pass the word on directly." Lord Marchmont's voice, lowered conspiratorially, came to Kit's ears. She glanced to where Spencer and the Lord Lieutenant sat on chairs drawn together, the two grey heads close.

"Mind you, such being the case, it's a wonder he's not positively wild. Heaven knows, Jake was the devil himself in disguise, or so many of us thought." Lady Marchmont made this startling revelation, a dreamy smile on her lips.

Kit nodded, her eyes on her ladyship's face, her attention elsewhere.

"Hendon's made it clear he's not particularly interested in the commercial traffic, as he put it. He's here after bigger game. Seems there's word about that this area's a target for those running cargo of a different sort." Lord Marchmont paused meaningfully.

Spencer snorted. Kit caught the sharpness in his comment, "What's that supposed to mean?"

"But I dare say one shouldn't judge a book by its binding." Lady Marchmont raised her brows. "Perhaps, in this case, he really is a sheep in wolf's clothing."

Kit smiled, but she hadn't heard a word. She was far too concerned with learning what sort of cargo interested the new High Commissioner.

"Human cargo," Lord Marchmont pronounced with heavy relish.

"But what it's better the other way around." Lady Marchmont brightened.

"Seems they've blocked the routes out of Sussex and Kent, but they didn't catch all the spies." Lord Marchmont leaned closer to Spencer. "They think those left will try this coast next."

"But just fancy, my dear. He keeps city hours down here. Doesn't rise until noon." An unladylike humph escaped Lady Marchmont. "He'll have to change, of course. Needs someone to help him adjust. Must be hard to pick up country ways after so many years."

A frown nagged at Kit's brows. As Lady Marchmont's bemused stare penetrated her daze, she wiped her expression clean and nodded seriously. "I dare say you're right, ma'am."

Her ladyship blinked. Kit realized she'd slipped somewhere and tried to focus on her ladyship's words, rather than her lord's.

Lady Marchmont's face cleared. "Oh – are you imagining he's a fop? Not a bit of it!" She waved one plump hand, and Kit's mind slid away.

"Hendon suggested I quietly let the message get about. Just to the right people, y'know." Lord Marchmont set down his teacup.

"His dress is very precise – the military influence, I dare say. But you'd know more about that than I, being so newly returned from the capital." Lady Marchmont chewed one fat finger. "Elegant," she pronounced. "You'd have to call him elegant."

Kit's eyes glazed. Her head was spinning.

"Did he now?" Spencer eyed Lord Marchmont shrewdly.

Lady Marchmont leaned forward and whispered: "Lucy Cartwright's got her eye on him for her eldest, Jane. But nothing'll come of that."

"Seemed to think he might need a bit of support if it came to a dustup," Lord Marchmont said. "The Revenue are stretched thin these days."

"He doesn't strike me as being the sort of man who'd appreciate having a young girl to wife. He's a serious man, thirty-five if he's a day. A more mature woman would be much more useful to him. Being the Lady of Castle Hendon is a full-time occupation, not the place for a giddy girl."

Spencer's barking laugh echoed through the room. "That's certainly true. Have you heard of the raids out Sheringham way?"

Her grandfather and his guest settled to review the latest exercises of the Revenue Office. Kit took the opportunity to catch up with her ladyship.

"Of course, there's the limp, though it's not seriously incapacitating. And he's at least got the Hendon looks to compensate."

Kit attempted to infuse some degree of mild interest into her features.

Lady Marchmont looked positively thrilled. "Well, Kathryn dear, we really must see what we can organize, don't you think?"

The predatory gleam in her ladyship's eyes set alarm bells ringing; Kit's interest fled. *Good God – she's trying to marry me off to Lord Hendon!*

To Kit's immense relief, Jenkins chose that precise instant to enter with the tea tray. If not for the timely interruption, she'd never have stilled the heated denial that had risen, involuntarily, to her lips.

Conversation became general over the teacups. With the

ease born of considerable practice in company far more demanding than the present, Kit contributed her share.

Suddenly, Spencer slapped his thigh. "Forgot!" He looked at Kit. "There's a letter for you, m'dear. On the table there." His nod indicated a small table by the window.

"For me?" Kit rose and went to fetch it.

Spencer nodded. "It's from Julian. I got one, too."

"Julian?" Kit returned to the *chaise*, examining the packet addressed in her youngest cousin's unmistakable scrawl.

"Go on, read it. Lord and Lady Marchmont'll excuse you, I'm sure."

Lord Marchmont nodded benignly, his wife much more avidly. Kit broke the Cranmer seal and quickly scanned the lines, crossed and recrossed, with two blots for good measure. "He's done it," she breathed, as Julian's meaning became clear. "He's enlisted!"

Her face alight, Kit looked at Spencer and saw her happiness for Julian mirrored in his eyes. Spencer nodded. "Aye. About time he went his own road. It'll be the making of him, I don't doubt."

Blinking, Kit nodded. Julian had wanted to join the army forever but, as the youngest of the Cranmer brood, he'd been protected and cosseted and steadfastly refused permission to break free. He'd reached his majority a fortnight ago and had signed up immediately. A passage toward the end of his letter sent a stab of sheer, painful pride through her.

You broke free, Kit. You made up your mind and went your own way. I decided to do the same. Wish me luck?

Her grandfather and Lord Marchmont were discussing the latest news from Europe; Lady Marchmont was eating a queen cake. With a happy sigh, Kit refolded the letter and laid it aside.

Jenkins returned, and the Marchmonts rose to take their leave, Lady Marchmont evolving plans for a ball to introduce the new Lord Hendon to his neighbors. "We haven't given a ball in years. We'll make it a large one – something special. A masquerade, perhaps? I'll want your advice, my dear, so think about it." With a wag of her chubby finger, Lady Marchmont sat back in her carriage.

On the steps, Kit smiled and waved. Beside her, Spencer clapped the Lord Lieutenant on the shoulder. "About that other matter. Tell Hendon he can count on support from Cranmer if he needs it. The Cranmers have always stood shoulder to shoulder with the Hendons through the years – we'll continue to do so. Particularly now we've one of our own at risk. Can't let any spies endanger young Julian." Spencer smiled. "Just as long as Hendon remembers he's Norfolk born and bred, that is. I've no mind to give up my brandy."

The twinkle in Spencer's eye was pronounced. An answering gleam lit Lord Marchmont's gaze. "No, b'God. Very true. But he keeps a fine cellar, just like Jake, so I doubt we'll need to explain that to him."

With a nod to Kit, Lord Marchmont climbed in beside his wife. The door shut, the coachman clicked the reins; the heavy coach lurched off.

Kit watched it disappear, then dropped a kiss on Spencer's weathered cheek and hugged him hard before descending the steps. With a last wave to Spencer, she headed for the gardens for a last stroll before dinner.

The shrubbery welcomed her with cool green walls, leading to a secluded grove with a fountain in the middle. Kit sat on the stone surround of the pool, trailing her fingers in the water. Her pleasure at Julian's news gradually faded, giving way to consideration of Lady Marchmont's fixation.

It was inevitable that the local ladies would busy themselves over finding her a husband; they'd known her from birth and, naturally, not one approved of her present state. With the appearance of Lord Hendon, an apparently eligible bachelor, on the scene, they had the ingredients of exactly the sort of plot they collectively delighted in hatching.

Grimacing, Kit shook the water from her fingers. They could hatch and plot to their hearts' content – she was past the age of innocent gullibility. Doubtless, despite his eligibility, Lord Hendon would prove to be another earl of Roberts. No – he couldn't be that old, not if Jake had been his father. Fortyish, a dessicated old stick but not quite old enough to be her father.

With a sigh, Kit stood and shook out her skirts. Unfortunately for Lady Marchmont, she hadn't escaped London – and her aunts' coils – to fall victim to the schemes of the local *grandes dames*.

The sun dipped beneath the horizon. Kit turned back toward the house. As she passed through the hedged walks, she shivered. Were spies run through the Norfolk surf? On that subject, her opinions matched Spencer's. The trade was tolerable, as long as it was just trade. But spying was treason. Did the Hunstanton Gang run "human cargo"?

Kit frowned; her temples throbbed. The day had gone and she was no nearer to solving her dilemma. Worse, she now had potential treason to avoid.

Or avert.

Chapter 8

A quiet dinner with Spencer did not advance Kit's thoughts on Captain Jack's offer. She retired early, intending to spend a few clear hours pondering the pros and cons. But once in her bedroom, the fidgets caught her. In desperation, she threw on her masculine clothes and slipped down the back stairs.

She'd become adept at bridling and saddling Delia in the dark. Soon, she was galloping over fields intermittently lit by a setting moon, half-hidden by low, scudding clouds. On horseback, with the breeze whistling about her ears, she relaxed. Now, she could think.

Try as she might, she couldn't see a way off the carousel. If Young Kit simply disappeared, then riding alone dressed as a youth, by day or by night, became dangerous in the extreme. Young Kit would have to die in truth. Of course, Miss Kathryn Cranmer could still ride sedately about the countryside. Miss Kathryn Cranmer snorted derisively. She'd be dammed if she'd give up her freedom so tamely. That left the option of joining Captain Jack.

Perhaps she could retire? Individual members often

withdrew from the gangs. As long as the fraternity knew who their ex-brothers were, no one minded. "I'll need to develop an identity," Kit mused. "There must be some place on Cranmer I could call home – some family with whom the smugglers have no contact." An old mother hysterical over the wildness of her youngest son, the last of three left to her . . . Grimly, Kit nodded. She would need to concoct a convincing reason for Young Kit's early retirement.

Which brought her to the last, nagging worry, a hovering ghost in the shadows of her mind. Were the Hunstanton Gang aiding and abetting spies?

If they are running spies, shouldn't you find out? If you join them for a few runs and see nothing, well and good. But if they do make arrangements to run "human cargo," you can inform Lord Hendon.

Kit humphed. Lord Hendon – wonderful! She supposed she'd have to meet the man sometime.

She turned Delia northeast, toward Scolt Head, a dense blur on the dark water. The sound of the surf grew louder as she approached the beaches east of Brancaster. She'd ridden north from Cranmer, passing in the lee of Castle Hendon, an imposing edifice built of local Carr stone on a hill sufficiently high to give it sweeping views in all directions.

Delia snuffed at the sea breeze. Kit allowed her to lengthen her stride.

Surely it was her duty to join the Hunstanton Gang and discover their involvement, if any, with spying? Particularly now that Julian had joined the army.

The ground ahead disappeared into blackness. At the edge of the cliff, Kit reined in and looked down. It was dim and dark on the sands. The surf boomed; the crash of waves and the slurping suck of the tide filled her ears.

A muffled shout reached her, followed by a second.

The moon escaped the clouds and Kit understood. The Hunstanton Gang was running a cargo on Brancaster beach.

Blanketing arms recaptured the moon, but she'd seen enough to be sure. The figure of Captain Jack had been clearly visible at the head of one boat. The two men who'd been with him the other night were there, too.

Kit drew Delia back from the cliff edge into the protection of a stand of stunted trees. The gang was nearly through unloading the boat; soon, they'd be heading . . . where? In an instant, Kit's mind was made up. She turned Delia, scouting for a better vantage point, one from which she could see without being seen. She eventually took refuge on a small tussocky hill in the scraggy remnants of an old coppice. Once safely concealed, she settled to wait, straining eyes trained on the cliff's edge.

Minutes later, they came up, single file, and passed directly beneath her little hill. She waited for Captain Jack and his two cohorts, bringing up the rear, to clear her, then counted to twenty slowly before taking to the narrow path in their wake. She followed them in a wide arc around the little town of Brancaster. In the fields west of the town, the cavalcade went to ground in an old barn. Kit watched from a distance, too wary to get closer. Soon, the men started leaving, some on foot, some riding, guiding ponies on leading reins.

At the last, three horsemen drew away from the barn. The moon smiled; Kit caught the gleam of Captain Jack's hair. The trio divided, one heading east. Captain Jack and the third man went west. Kit followed them.

She kept Delia on the verge, the drum of hooves of her quarries' horses making it easy to follow them. Luckily, they weren't riding fast, else she'd have had difficulty keeping up without taking to the telltale road herself.

They traveled the road for no more than a mile before turning south along a narrow track. Kit paused at the turn. The sound of heavy hooves at a walk reassured her. She pressed on, careful to hold Delia back.

Jack and Matthew set their mounts up the steep curve that took the track over the lip of the meadowland. At the highest point, just before the track curved into the trees edging the first Hendon field, Jack glanced down onto the stretch of track below. It was a habit instituted long since to ensure none of the Hunstanton Gang followed them to their lair.

The track was a pool of even, uninteresting shadow. Jack was turning away when a slight movement, caught from the corner of one eye, brought every faculty alert. He froze, gaze used to the night trained on the track below. A shadow darker than the rest detached itself from the cover of the trees and crept along the verge.

Matthew, warned by the sudden silence, had reined in too, and stared downward. He leaned closer to whisper in Jack's ear. "Young Kit?"

Jack nodded. A slow, positively devilish smile twisted his long lips. "Go on to the cottage," he whispered. "I'm going to invite our young friend for a drink."

Matthew nodded, urging his horse to a walk, heading south along the narrow track.

Jack nudged Champion off the path and into the deeper shadows by a coppice. Young Kit's excess of curiosity was perfectly timed; he hadn't been looking forward to another night like the last, tossing and turning while grappling with his ridiculous obsession with the stripling. What better way to cure his senses of their idiotic misconception than to invite the lad in for a brandy? Once revealed in full light for the youth he was, Young Kit would doubtless get out from under his skin.

Approaching the upward sweep of the trail, Kit heard the steady clop of hooves above cease. She reined in, listening intently, then cautiously edged forward. When she saw where the track led, she stopped and held her breath. Then the hoofbeats restarted, heading onward. With a sigh of relief, she counted to twenty again before sending Delia up the track.

She crested the rise to find the track, innocent and empty, leading on across the meadowland. Ahead, a coppice bordered the trail, darker shadows pooling on the track like giant ink puddles. She paused, listening, but the hoofbeats continued on, the riders invisible through the trees ahead.

All was well. Kit put her heels to Delia's sleek sides. The mare sidled. Kit frowned and urged the mare forward. Delia balked.

The sensation of being watched enveloped Kit. Her stomach tightened; her eyes flared wide. She glanced to the left. Fields opened out, one adjoining the next, a clear escape. Without further thought, she set Delia at the hedge. As eager as she to get away, the mare cleared the hedge and went straight to a gallop.

In the trees bordering the track, Jack swore volubly. Be damned if he'd let the lad lose him again! He set his heels to Champion's sides; the grey surged in pursuit.

Champion answered the call with alacrity, only too ready to give chase. Jack held him back, content to keep the bobbing black bottom of Young Kit in clear view, waiting until the Arab started to tire before allowing the grey stallion's strength to show.

The thud of hooves behind her told Kit her observer had come into the open. She glanced behind and her worst fears

71

were confirmed. Damn the man! She hadn't seen anything worthwhile, and he must know he couldn't catch her.

By the time the end of the fields hove in sight, Kit had revised her opinion of Captain Jack's equestrian judgment. The grey he had under him seemed tireless and Delia, already ridden far that night, was wilting. In desperation, Kit swung Delia's head for the shore. Riding through sand would hopefully slow the heavier grey more than the mare.

She hadn't counted on the descent. Delia checked at the cliff's edge and took the steep path in a nervous prance. The grey, ridden aggressively, came over the top in a leap and half slithered through the soft soil to land on the flat in a flurry of sand, mere seconds behind her.

Kit clapped her heels to Delia's sleek flanks; the mare shot forward, half-panicked by the advent of the stallion so close.

To Kit's dismay, the tide was in and just turning, leaving only a narrow strip of dry sand skirting the base of the cliffs. She couldn't risk getting too close to the rocks and boulders strewn at the cliff foot. There was nowhere else to ride but on the hard sand, dampened and compacted by the retreating waves. And on such solid ground, the grey gained steadily.

Crouched low over Delia's neck, the black mane whipping her cheeks, Kit prayed for a miracle. But the sound of the grey's heavy hooves drew inexorably nearer. She started considering her excuses. What reason could she give for having followed him that would account for her bolting?

There was no viable answer to that one. Kit wished she'd had the nerve to stand her ground rather than fly when confronted with her nemesis. She glanced forward, contemplating hauling on the reins and capitulating, when, wonder of wonders, a spit of land loomed ahead. A tongue of the cliff, it cleaved the sands, running out into the surf, its sides decaying into the sea. If she could gain the rough-grassed dunes, she'd have a chance. Even tired as she was, climbing, Delia would be much faster than the heavy grey. As if to light her way, the moon sailed free of its cloudy veils and beamed down.

A length behind, Jack saw the spit. It was time to wind up the chase. The lad rode better than any trooper he'd ever seen. Once in the dunes, he'd be impossible to catch. Jack dropped his reins. Champion, sensing victory, lengthened his stride, obedient to the direction that sent him inland of the black mare, cutting off any sudden change of tack.

Kit was breathless. The wind dragged at her lungs. The dunes and safety were heartbeats away when, warned by some sixth sense, she glanced to her left. And saw a huge grey head almost level with her knee.

She only had time to gasp before two hundred odd pounds of highly trained male muscle knocked her from the saddle.

The instant he connected with Young Kit, Jack realized his error. He tried to twist in midair to cushion her fall but was only partially successful. Both he and his captive landed flat on their backs on the damp sand.

The breath was knocked out of him but he recovered immediately, sitting up and swinging around to lean over his prize, one leg automatically trapping hers to still her struggles. Only she didn't struggle.

Jack frowned and waited for the eyes, just visible beneath the brim of her old tricorne, to open. They remained shut. The body stretched beside and half under his was preternaturally still.

Cursing, Jack pulled at the tricorne. It took two tugs to free it. The wealth of glossy curls framing the smooth, wide brow sent his imagination, already sensitized by her near-ness, into overload.

Slowly, almost as if she might dissolve beneath his touch, Jack lifted a finger to the smooth skin covering one high cheekbone, tracing the upward curve. The satin texture sent a thrill from the tip of his finger to regions far distant. When she gave no sign of returning consciousness, he slid his fingers into the mass of silky hair, ignoring the burgeoning sensations skittering through him, to feel the back of her skull. A lump the size of a duck egg was growing through the curls. In the sand beneath her head, he located the rock responsible, thankfully buried deep enough to make it unlikely it had caused any irreparable hurt.

Retrieving his hands, Jack eased back to stare at his captive.

Young Kit was out cold.

Grimacing, he eyed the heavy muffler wound over her nose and chin, concealing most of her face. The conversion of Young Kit into female form was certain to wreak havoc with his plans, but he may as well leave consideration of such matters until later. Right now, he doubted he could raise a cogent thought, much less make a wise decision. Which was simply proof of how much of a problem she was destined to become.

He should get that muffler off – she'd recover faster if she could breathe unrestricted. Yet he felt reluctant to bare any more of her face – or any other part of her for that matter. What he'd already seen – the perfect expanse of forehead, gracefully arched brows over large eyes set on a slight slant and delicately framed by a feathering of brown, the rioting curls, glossy even in moonlight – all attested to the certainty that the rest of Young Kit would prove equally fatal to his equanimity.

Jack swore under his breath. Why the hell did he have to

get a case of the hots just now? And for a smugglers' moll, no less!

Metaphorically, and in every other way he knew, he girded his loins and reached for the muffler. She'd wound it tight, and it was some moments and a good few curses later before he drew the woollen folds from her face.

Just why she wore a muffler was instantly apparent. Grimly, Jack considered the sculpted features, rendered in flawless cream skin, the straight little nose, the pert, pointed chin and the full sensuous lips, pale now but just begging to be kissed to blush red. Young Kit's face was an essential statement of all that was feminine.

Intrigued, Jack let his gaze slide over the figure lying inert beside him. The padding in one shoulder of her coat was pressed to his arm, explaining that point. He stared at her chest, slowly rising and falling. The fullness of her shirt made it difficult to judge, but experience suggested her anatomy was unlikely to be quite so uneventful. Jack decided he wasn't up to investigating how she accomplished that feat of suppressing nature and turned instead to an expert inspection of her legs, still entwined with his. They were, in his experienced opinion, remarkably remarkable, unusually long and slender but firm with well-toned muscle.

Jack's lips curved appreciatively. She obviously rode a lot. How did she perform when the roles were reversed? He allowed his imagination, rampant by now, a whole three minutes to run riot, before reluctantly calling his mind to order. With a sigh, he gazed once more at Young Kit's pale face. Female skulls were weaker than male. She might take a few hours to come to.

Jack looked along the sands to where Champion stood in the lee of the dunes, reins dangling. Beside him stood the black mare, uncertain and skittish. Disengaging his legs from Kit's, Jack stood, brushing sand from his clothes. He whistled, and Champion ambled over. The mare hesitated, then followed.

Catching Champion's reins, Jack murmured soothing nothings to the great beast while watching the mare. The Arab approached slowly, then veered to come up on Kit's other side. The black head went down. The mare softly huffed into the bright curls. Kit didn't stir.

"What a precious beauty you are,' Jack breathed, edging closer. The black head came up; one large black eye looked straight at him. Slowly, Jack reached for the mare's bridle. To his relief, she accepted his touch. He lengthened the reins, then looped the ends through a ring on his own saddle. Then he stood back to see how Champion would take to the arrangement. The big stallion did not normally tolerate other horses too close, yet a single minute served to convince Jack he didn't need to worry about the Arab. Champion clearly possessed equine manners when he chose to employ them, and he was all out to make a good impression on the mare.

Grinning, Jack turned to consider the female he had in charge. He bent and lifted Kit from the sands, then sat her in his saddle and held her draped over the pommel while he mounted behind her. Swinging her once more into his arms, he settled in the saddle, balancing Kit across his thighs, her head cradled against his chest.

Jack turned Champion toward the dunes, touched his heels to the grey's flanks, and set course for the cottage.

Chapter 9

By the time he reached the cottage, Jack's jaw was clenched with the effort of ignoring the thoroughly female body in his arms. With every stride, Champion's gait pressed the warm swell of Kit's bound breasts against Jack's chest, alternating with the even more unnerving rub of her firm bottom against his thigh. The ride was torture – a fact he was sure Kit, whoever she was, would delight in, if he was ever fool enough to tell her. He suspected she'd wake with a headache. On the sands, he'd felt a touch guilty about that. Now, he considered it only her due – he was sure he'd have a splitting head by dawn. And no chance of sleep, either.

Champion's hooves thudded on the packed earth before the cottage. The door opened, and Matthew came out. "What happened?"

Jack drew rein some paces from the door. "The lad didn't take kindly to my invitation. In fact, he didn't even wait to hear it. I had to exert my powers of persuasion."

"So I see." Matthew advanced, clearly intent on taking Jack's burden from him.

Jack brought his leg over the pommel and slid to the

ground, Kit's inanimate form clasped to his chest. He brushed past Matthew and headed for the door. "Stable Champion and the mare. I doubt she'll give you much trouble." Jack paused in the doorway and looked back. "Then you may as well go home. He's apt to be out for a while." He smiled. "I think Young Kit would probably feel more comfortable if he thought no one but me had seen him *in extremis.*"

Wise in the ways of lads and young soldiers, Matthew nodded. "Aye. You'll be right enough there, no doubt. I'll be off then." So saying, he caught Champion's reins and headed for the small stable beside the cottage.

Jack entered the cottage and kicked the door shut, leaning back on the rough panels to juggle the latch with his elbow. Then he straightened and looked down at his burden. Thank God he'd put Kit's hat back on. The wide brim had shaded her face enough for him to get her past Matthew. Quite why he was keeping her little secret from his unquestionably loyal henchman he wasn't entirely certain. Perhaps because he hadn't yet had time to consider just what Kit's secret meant and how he was going to deal with it, and, from long experience, he knew Matthew would unhesitatingly avail himself of the license accorded long-time servitors to disapprove, vociferously, should his master elect to follow some less than straightforward course.

But before he could think of anything, he had to get rid of the distracting body in his arms.

Jack strode to the bed and dropped Kit onto the coverlet as if she was a lump of hot iron. In truth, she'd set him alight, and he couldn't see any prospect of dousing the flames. Making love to unconscious women had never appealed to him. He stared down at the slender and still silent form. The muffler had shaken loose and lay about her throat. Her hat had fallen off, exposing her curls and telltale face to the lamplight.

Abruptly, Jack took a step back.

Now that she was out of his arms, he could think clearly. And it didn't take much thought to conclude that making love to Kit at any time was likely to prove dangerous, if not specifically to himself, then certainly to his mission. He'd already dropped the appellation "Young" – having carried her for half an hour, he knew she wasn't that young. Certainly not too young.

With a growl of frustration, Jack swung around and crossed to the sideboard. He poured himself a generous brandy, wryly wondering if Kit actually drank the stuff. What would she have done if he'd invited her back to share a bottle?

Jack grinned; the grin faded when he glanced toward the bed. What the hell was he to do with her?

He prowled the room, intermittently shooting glances at the figure on the bed. The brandy didn't help. He drained the glass and set it aside. Kit hadn't stirred. With a long sigh, Jack approached the bed and stood beside it, staring down at her.

She was too pale. Tentatively, he touched her cheek. It was reassuringly warm. Leaning over her, he pulled off her leather gauntlets and chafed the small hands, fine-boned and delicate. It didn't help. Jack grimaced. Her breathing was shallow, her chest constricted by the tight bands she wore to conceal her breasts. He'd felt them when he'd carried her.

His arms felt leaden; his feet wouldn't move. His body definitely didn't like what his brain was telling it. But there was no help for it. And the sooner he got it over with, the better.

Jack forced his limbs to function. He turned Kit over, making sure she didn't suffocate in the soft folds of the coverlet. He bundled her out of her coat, then pulled her shirttails free of her breeches, trying to ignore the most unmasculine curve of her buttocks. Pushing the back of the shirt up to her shoulders, he located the flat knot securing the linen bands, craftily tucked under one arm. The knot was well and truly tight. Jack swore as he tugged and fumbled, fingers brushing skin that felt like cool silk and burned like a brand. By the time the knot finally gave, he'd exhausted his repertoire of curses, something he'd hitherto believed impossible.

He sat on the edge of the bed, garnering strength for the next move, willing his mind not to see the beauty revealed to his senses, the slim back, delicate shoulder blades sheathed in ivory silk. With slow deliberation, he loosened the bindings and shifted them until they gave. Quickly, he pulled the shirt back down, wisely refraining from tucking it in and, rising, turned Kit onto her back once more.

Almost immediately, her breathing deepened. Within a minute, her color improved, but still she didn't stir. Resigned to more waiting, Jack drifted to the table and pulled out a chair. Leaning back, he gazed broodingly at his unconscious visitor. He reached for the brandy bottle.

Consciousness trickled into Kit's mind in dribs and drabs, a flash of memory, a tingle in her fingertips. Then her eyelids fluttered, and she was awake. And confused. She kept her eyes shut and tried to think. The memory of the wild chase on the beach, and Captain Jack riding her down – it must have been his body that had hit her – crystallized in her brain. That was all she could recall. Warily, she let her senses search out her surroundings, stiffening with apprehension at the incoming information. She was lying on a bed.

From under her lashes. Kit surveyed what she could see of the room – rough walls and an old oak wardrobe. Beyond confirming the fact she was in someone's bedroom, in someone's bed, they told her little.

But you can guess who that someone is, can't you? And now you're in his bed.

Don't be silly, Kit lectured her wilder self. *I'm still dressed, aren't I?* On the thought, the looseness of her bands registered. Kit sat up with a gasp.

The bands immediately slipped lower, freeing her breasts. Her head swam. With a weak, "Oh," Kit fell back on her elbows, closing her eyes against the pain in the back of her head. When she opened them, she saw Captain Jack watching her from across the room. He was lounging in a chair on the other side of a table, a look of aggravation on his handsome face.

For the life of him, Jack couldn't tear his gaze from the proof of Kit's womanhood, thrust provocatively against the fine cotton of her shirt. The front was pulled taut by her reclining position, revealing the rich swells beneath tipped by the tight buds of her nipples. When she just lay there and stared at him, Jack felt his temper stir. Hell and the devil! Was she doing it on purpose?

Kit raised a hand to her head, stifling a groan. "What happened?"

The shirt eased, and Jack could breathe again. 'You hit your head on a rock buried in the sand."

Kit sat up and gingerly felt her skull. She'd forgotten how velvety deep his voice was. Her fingers found a sizable lump on the back of her head. She winced and shot a frowning glance at her nemesis. "You could have killed me with that foolish stunt."

The accusation brought Jack upright, the legs of his chair

crashing onto the floor. "Foolish stunt?" he echoed in disbelief. "What the hell do you call a woman masquerading as a boy and leading a gang of smugglers? Sensible?" Real anger at the risks she'd courted rose up. "What the hell do you think would have happened after your first slip? Do you swim well with rocks tied to your feet?"

Kit winced. "Don't bellow." She dropped her head into her hands. She didn't feel all that well. Coping with Captain Jack at any time would have proved problematical, but right now, feeling as woozy as she did, this was shaping up to be a disastrous encounter. And he was already annoyed though what he had to be annoyed about she couldn't imagine. She was the one with the lump on her head. "Where are we?"

"Where we won't be interrupted. I want some answers to one or two questions – understandable in the circumstances, don't you think? We can start with the obvious – what's your name?"

"Kit." Kit grinned into her hands. Let him make what he liked of that.

"Catherine, Christine, or what?"

Kit frowned. "You don't need to know."

"True. Where do you live?"

Kit reserved her answer to that one. Her head ached. A quick reconnoiter yielded the information that they were in a small cottage, alone. The fact that the door led directly outside was reassuring.

Frowning, Jack stared at the glossy curls crowning Kit's bent head. In the lamplight, they glowed a rich coppery red. In sunlight, he suspected they'd be redder and brighter still. The color tugged at his memory, an elusive recognition that refused to materialize. When she pulled her knees up, the better to support her hands which in turn were supporting her head, Jack grimaced. He supposed he should give her some brandy, but he didn't really want to get closer. The table was a protective barricade and he was loath to leave its shelter. At least he was wearing his "poor country squire" togs; the loosely fitting breeches gave him some protection. In his military togs, or, heaven forbid, his town rig, she'd know immediately just how much she was affecting him. It was bad enough that he knew.

Her head was still down. With an exasperated sigh, Jack reached for the bottle. Rising, he fetched a clean glass and half filled it with the best French brandy to be found in England. Glass in hand, he approached the bed.

She'd glanced up at the sound of his chair on the boards. Now, she raised her head, to look first at the glass, then into his face.

Memory returned with a thump. Jack stopped and blinked. Then he looked again and suspicion was confirmed. "Kit," he repeated. "Kit Cramner?" He allowed one brow to rise in mocking question. Her eyes staring up at him, liquid amethyst, were all the answer he needed.

Kit swallowed, barely aware of his words. Heavens – it was worse than she'd thought! He was perfectly gorgeous – mind-numbingly, toe-curlingly gorgeous – with his wild mane of hair, wind-tousled brown streaked with gold. His brow was wide, his nose patrician and autocratic, his chin decidedly square. But it was his eyes that held her; set deep under slanted brows, they gleamed silver-grey in the lamplight. And his lips – long and rather thin, firm and mobile. How would they feel . . .

Kit clamped off the thought. Parched, she reached for the proffered glass. Her fingers brushed his. Ignoring the peculiar thrill that twisted through her, and suppressing the panic that swam in its wake, Kit sipped the brandy, very aware of the man beside her. He'd stopped by the side of the bed, towering over her. Entranced by his face, she'd spared no more than a glance for the rest of him. How did he measure up? She leaned back on her elbows the better to bring him into view.

Her shirt drew taut.

Beside the bed, Jack stiffened. Kit shifted to stare up at him. She saw his jaw clench, saw the planes of his face harden. Then she noticed his gaze was not on her face. She followed its direction, and saw what was holding him transfixed. Smoothly, she sat up, taking another sip of brandy, telling herself it was just the same as when London rakes had sized her up. There was no need to blush or act like a missish schoolgirl. Another sip of brandy steadied her. She hadn't answered his question. Perhaps it would be wise to do so. Trying to hide her paternity was hopeless; the Cranmer coloring was known the length and breadth of Norfolk.

"Now you know who I am, who are you?" she said.

Jack shook his head to clear his befogged senses. Christ! It'd been too long. His mission was in grave danger. With some vague idea of safety, he walked to where a chair stood against the wall and, swinging it about, sat astride, resting his arms on its back, facing her. He ignored her question; at least she hadn't recognized him.

"I doubt that you're Spencer's." He watched her closely but could detect no reaction. Not the current Lord Cranmer's child, then. "He had three sons, but if memory serves, the elder two don't have the family coloring. Only the youngest had that. Christopher Cranmer, the wildest of the bunch." Jack's memory lurched again. His lips twisted wryly. "Also known as Kit Cranmer, as I recall." A lifting of the corners of Kit's lips suggested he'd hit the target. "So you're Christopher Cranmer's daughter."

Kit allowed her brows to rise. Then she shrugged and

nodded. Who was he, to have such detailed recollections of her family? At the very least, he was a local, yet she'd never seen him before yesterday. From under her lashes, she glanced at the broad shoulders and wide biceps, bulging as he leaned forward on his forearms. There was no padding in the simple jacket – those bulges were all perfectly real. Powerful thighs stretched his plain breeches. Seated as he was, she couldn't see much beyond that, but anyone who rode as he did had to be strong. The lamplight didn't illuminate his face, but she supposed him in his thirties. There was no chance she would have forgotten such a specimen.

"Who was your mother?"

The question, uttered in an amiable but commanding tone, jerked Kit's mind back from whence it had wandered. For a full minute, she stared uncomprehendingly. Then the implication of Jack's question struck her. Her eyes kindled; she drew breath to wither him. Belatedly, her wilder self tumbled out of its daze and scrambled to clamp the lid on her temper.

Hang on a minute – stop, cease, desist, stow it, you fool! You need an identity, remember? He's just handed you one. So what if he thinks you're illegitimate? Better that than the truth – which he wouldn't believe anyway.

Kit's eyes glazed. She blushed and looked down.

The odd expressions that passed over Kit's face in rapid succession left Jack bewildered. But the blush he understood immediately. "Sorry," he said. "An unnecessarily prying question."

Kit looked up, amazed. He was apologizing?

"Where do you live?" Jack remembered her mare. The stubborn pride of the present Lord Cranmer was as well-known as his family's coloring. Jack hazarded a guess. "With your grandfather?"

Slowly, Kit nodded. Her mind was racing. If she was her father's illegimate daughter, nothing would be more likely. Her father had been Spencer's favorite. Her grandfather would naturally assume responsiblity for any bastards his son had left behind. But she had to tread warily – Captain Jack knew far too much about the local families to allow her to invent freely. Luckily, he obviously didn't know Spencer's legitimate granddaughter had returned from London.

"I live at the Hall." One of her cousin Geoffrey's maxims on lying replayed in her head. *Stick to the truth as far as possible.* "I grew up there, but when my grandmother died they sent me away." If Jack was a local, he'd wonder why he'd never seen her about.

"Away?" Jack look interested.

Kit took another sip of brandy, grateful for the warmth unfurling in her belly. It seemed to be easing her head. "I was sent to London to live with the curate from Holme when he moved to Chiswick." Kit grabbed at the memory of the young curate – the image fitted perfectly. "I didn't really like the capital. When the curate was promoted, I came back." Kit prayed Jack didn't know the curate from Holme personally; she'd no idea if he'd been promoted or not.

Neither did Jack. Kit's tale made sense, even accounting for her cultured speech and sophisticated gestures. If she'd been brought up at Cranmer under her grandmother's eye, then spent time in London, even with a boring curate, she'd be every bit as confident and at ease with him as she was proving to be. No simple country miss, this one. Her story was believable. Her attitude suggested she knew as much. Jack's eyes narrowed. "So you live at the Hall and Spencer openly acknowledges you?"

Now that, my fine gentlernan, is a trick question. Kit waved airily.

86

"Oh, I've always lived quietly. I was trained to look after the house, so that's what I do." She smiled at her inquisitor, knowing she'd passed the test. Not even Spencer would raise a bastard granddaughter on a par with the trueborn.

Grimly, Jack acknowledged that smile. She was certainly quick, but he could do without her smiles. They infused her face with a radiance painters had wasted lifetimes trying to capture. Whoever her mother had been, she must have been uncommonly beautiful to give rise to a daughter to rival Aphrodite.

"So by day, Spencer's housekeeper; by night, Young Kit, leader of a smuggling gang. How long have you been in the trade?"

"Only a few weeks." Kit wished he'd stop scowling at her. He'd smiled at her once at the quarries. She'd a mind to witness the phenomenon in the stronger lamplight, but Jack didn't seem at all likely to oblige. She smiled at him. He scowled back.

"How the devil have you survived? You cover your face, there's padding in your coat – but what happens if one of the men touches you?"

"They don't – they haven't." Kit hoped her blush didn't show. "They just think I'm a well-born stripling, not built on their scale."

Jack snorted, his gaze never leaving her face. Then his eyes narrowed. "Where did you learn to swagger – and all the rest of it? It's not that easy to pass as a male. You've not trod the boards, have you?"

Kit met his gaze – and chose her words with care. She could hardly lay claim to her cousins, much less their influence. "I've had opportunity aplenty to study men and how they move." She smiled condescendingly. "I'm more than passing familiar with the male of the species."

Jack's brows rose; after a moment, he asked: "How long did you intend playing the smuggler?"

Kit shrugged. "Who knows? And now that you've found me out, we'll never learn, will we?" Her smile turned brittle. Young Kit's short career was at an end – the excitement and thrills were no longer to be hers.

Jack's brows rose higher. "You plan to retire?"

Kit stared at him. "Aren't you . . ." She blinked. "Do you mean you won't give me away?"

Jack's scowl returned. "Not won't – can't." He'd never thought of himself as conservative – Jonathon was his conservative side and at the moment he was definitely Jack – but the thought of Kit trooping about in breeches before a horde of seamen, laying herself open to discovery and God only knew what consequences, awoke in him feelings of sheer protectiveness. Outwardly, he frowned. Inwardly, he seethed and swore. He'd known she'd be trouble; now, he knew what sort.

He stifled a groan. Kit was looking at him, uncertainty plainly writ in her fine features. He drew a deep breath. "Until your men are safely accepted as part of the Hunstanton Gang, Young Kit will have to continue a smuggler."

Kit heard but was barely listening. She knew she wasn't an antidote; if she'd wanted it, she could have had men at her feet the entire time she'd been in London. Yet Captain Jack, whoever he was, wasn't responding to her in the customary way. He was still scowling. Deliberately, she lay back on her elbows and surveyed him boldly. "Why?"

The sudden stiffness that suffused his large frame was unnerving to say the least. Deliciously unnerving. Kit moved her shoulders slightly, settling her elbows more firmly, and felt her shirt shift over her nipples. She looked up to see how Jack was taking the display, ready to smile condescendingly at his confusion. Instead, she froze, transfixed by an overwhelming sense of danger.

His eyes were silver, not grey, clear and sparkling, like polished steel. And they weren't looking at her face. As she watched, a muscle flickered along his jaw. Suddenly, Kit understood. He wasn't responding because he didn't wish to, not because she wasn't affecting him. Only his control stood between her and what he would do – would like to do. Abruptly, Kit rolled to the side, on one hip, ostensibly to take a sip of brandy.

Shaken, Jack drew a deep breath, grimly wondering if the silly minx knew how close she'd come to being rolled in the bed she was lolling so provocatively upon. Another second, and he'd have given in to the urge to stand up, set the chair aside, and fall on her like the sex-starved hellion he was.

Luckily, she'd drawn back. Later, he fully intended to pursue a more intimate relationship with her, but at the moment, business came first. What had she asked? He remembered. "I want to make one gang out of two. If I expose you, your men will be a laughingstock, which won't help me in my aims. If you suddenly disappear, your men will think I've done away with you – scared you off at the very least. They'll probably decide not to join us so there will still be two gangs operating along this coast."

Kit frowned and looked down into the amber fluid swirling in her glass. He was suggesting she remain a boy – her true sex known only to him and herself – for an indefinite time. She wasn't sure she could keep up the pretense for a day. It was all very well to prance about in breeches when everyone watching thought you were male; she suspected it would be quite a different matter when one watcher, this particular watcher, knew the truth. Besides, she didn't really want to play the boy with Jack. Determinedly, Kit shook her head. "If I explain it to them –"

"They'll think I've scared you off."

Kit glared and sat up. "Not if I tell them –"

"Regardless of what you tell them."

The finality in his deep tones was not encouraging. But his scheme was the epitome of madness. "You said yourself it was a foolish thing to do. What if they, and the rest of your gang, discover the truth?"

"They won't. Not while I'm there to make sure of it."

His conviction sounded unshakable. How illogical, Kit thought, to be arguing for an outcome she didn't really desire. Yet the more she considered his scheme, the more dangerous it seemed. Luckily, she had herself well in hand. He was offering just the sort of excitement that appealed to her wilder self. She narrowed her eyes and chose her words carefully. "How do I know you won't give me away?"

Jack's eyes glittered. She was getting very close to the bone. What did she think he was – an overreactive schoolboy? Coolly, deliberately, he let his gaze wander, lingering on her breasts – not visible anymore, but he knew they were there – before drifting downward for a leisurely perusal of her long legs.

Kit blushed. And pounced the instant before he did. "Like that!" It hadn't been what she'd meant, but it would prove her point.

Jack blinked, then flushed with annoyance. He scowled ferociously. "I won't! What would I have to gain from giving you away?" His eyes narrowed as he studied her. "I can assure you I'll behave exactly as if you were the lad they all think you are." He didn't consider it wise to tell her what it was more likely the men would think if they realized he was overly interested in Young Kit. "I can't, of course, answer for your reactions."

Kit's temper ignited. Of all the insufferable, conceited louts she'd ever faced, Jack took the cake. Presumably he knew he was gorgeous. Doubtless scores of women had told him so. Hell would freeze before he heard those words from her! Kit tilted her nose in the air. "What reactions?"

Jack hooted with laughter. Abruptly, he stood and flung the chair aside. All thought of his mission, of sense and safety, fled at her challenge. No reactions to him? He advanced on the bed.

Kit's eyes felt as if they'd pop from her head. Horrified, she tried to shuffle back in the bed but her elbows tangled in the covers and she sprawled full-length instead. Then he was towering over her, his shadow engulfing her. Hands on hips, he looked down at her from the foot of the bed. He held out one hand. "Come here."

He was mad. She had no intention of going anywhere near him. He was smiling now, devilishly. She decided she preferred his scowl – it was infinitely less threatening. She tried a scowl of her own.

Jack's smile gained intensity; his eyes grew brighter. He had every intention of putting the vixen in her place once and for all. She was giving him more trouble than a troop of drunken cavalry. First she played the tease, curling on the bed so much like a cat he was quite sure that if he'd stroked her she'd have purred. Now, because he'd forced her into a blush, she was playing the threatened virgin.

But he wasn't so far gone in lunacy as to get on the bed with her. When she continued to scowl, her amethyst eyes spitting purple chips, he made a grab for her hand.

Unfortunately, Kit chose the same moment to sit up, the better to deliver a verbal broadside. She saw his movement; he saw hers. Both tried to compensate. Jack's fingers curled about her hand as he tried to straighten to avoid a collision of heads. Kit half rose, then fell back, wrenching her hand in an effort to free it. The result was the reverse of both their intentions. Jack's leg hit the bed end and he stumbled, then was pulled off-balance by the unexpected violence of Kit's tug. He landed on the bed beside her.

Kit smothered a shriek and tried to roll off the bed. A large hand grabbed her hip and rolled her back. A curse she didn't comprehend fell on her ears. Memories of tussles with her cousins awoke in her brain. Instead of fighting the pull, she turned with it.

It was purely reflex action that saved Jack's manly parts from Kit's rising knee. Giving up any attempt at gentlemanly behavior, he grabbed both her hands and swung over her, straddling her hips, pinning her beneath him.

To his amazement, she continued to struggle, her hips writhing between his thighs.

"Be still, you witless wanton, or I won't answer for the consequences!"

That stopped her. Wide eyes stared up at him. The front of her shirt rose and fell rapidly. Jack couldn't see through it, but the memory of what lay beneath it acted powerfully on his brain. The temptation to let go of her hands and cup the sweet mounds grew stronger by the second. His palms tingled in anticipation.

Jack forced his gaze upward. He met her eyes and saw the panic there. Panic? Jack closed his eyes against the plea in the violet depths and drew a deep breath. What the hell was going on? Now, she even looked like a threatened virgin. As sanity slowly seeped back into his brain, the rigidity of the slim form between his thighs registered.

Could she be a virgin? Jack's worldly brain rejected that idea out of hand. A woman of her background, of her age, with her attributes – one who declared herself "more than passing familiar" with men – could not be a virgin. Besides, she'd made moves enough that smacked of experience. No. The truth was, she didn't, for whatever reason, want him. Because he wanted her? Some women were like that. Jack prided himself on his knowledge of the female sex. He'd spent fifteen and more years in an extensive study of the fascinating creatures. In between fighting a few wars. If she really had taken an aversion to him, he could use it to his advantage in the short term. And when the need for Young Kit had passed, he could look forward to spending countless interesting hours changing her mind.

Jack opened his eyes and studied Kit's face. She was scowling again. He smiled crookedly. He was aching with need, but she wasn't about to welcome him aboard. Not yet.

He changed his hold on her hands, so that his thumbs rested in her palms. Slowly, deliberately, he moved his thumbs in a circular motion, caressing her sensitive skin. He watched as her eyes grew larger, rounder.

Kit was speechless. Worse, she was close to mindless. Neither her own experiences nor Amy's had prepared her for the effect Jack was having on her. Despite the fact that he hadn't even kissed her, she couldn't think straight. His touch on her palms was driving little shivers down every nerve, focusing her mind on her hands, as if to distract her from the heat seeping insidiously through every vein, radiating from the junction of her thighs. There was a complementary heat above, where he straddled her. Dimly, she sensed a growing urge to lift her hips and press heat to heat. She resisted it, struggling to break free of his spell. "Let me go, Jack." Her words were soft, feminine, not the decisive demand she intended at all.

Jack grinned, inordinately pleased to hear his name on her lips. "I'll let you go if you promise to do as I ask."

Kit frowned. Was he threatening her? It was an effort to put her thoughts into words. Particularly when he looked as if he'd like to eat her. Slowly. "What do you mean?" She asked.

"Be Young Kit for two months. After that, we'll arrange your retirement." *And you can start your next assignment – as my mistress.* Jack smiled into her beautiful eyes. He was sure they'd turn deepest violet when she climaxed. He was looking forward to conducting that experiment.

Kit couldn't steady her breathing. She shook her head. "It'll never work."

"It'll work. We'll make it work."

The idea was tempting, very tempting. Kit struggled to get a grip on the situation. "What if I won't?"

Jack's brows rose but he was smiling – that devilish smile again. Then he sighed dramatically and stopped stroking her palms. Kit relaxed, relief surging through her. Only to be overridden by panic when he raised her hand to his lips and kissed one fingertip. Her lips formed an O of sheer shock.

Watching her, Jack nearly laughed. No reaction to him? If she was any more responsive she'd be climbing the walls. "If you won't join me in a business venture, we'll just have to consider what other type of . . . partnership we can enjoy."

Kit stared at him in undisguised horror.

Jack turned her hand over to press a kiss to her palm. He felt her entire body tense. "The first thing we'll have to investigate is whether this aversion of yours is any more than skin deep." Involuntarily, his gaze dropped to her shirt and his mind shifted to a contemplation of the delights it concealed. Just a single thickness of material was all that protected her breasts from his hungry gaze. And his ardent attentions. Almost, he wished she'd hold firm to her resolve

94

not to be Young Kit. At least long enough to make a little persuasion necessary.

Kit's mind was sluggish. Aversion? Her aversion? Here she was, in a flat panic lest he realize just how very attracted she was, and he thought she held him in aversion? She almost laughed hysterically. If she hadn't been so frightened by her response to him, she would have. Having him so close drained her willpower; every little attention he bestowed only made matters worse. Another few moves and he'd have her egging him on. The idea of what would happen if he kissed her brought her to a rapid decision. "All right."

Jack hauled his gaze back to her face and his mind back to her words. "All right?"

Kit heard the disappointment in his voice. He'd have carried out his threat with enthusiasm. "Yes, all right, damn you!" She pushed hard at his hands. "If the others agree, I'll be Young Kit, but only for a month. Until my men settle in with your gang."

Jack's sigh was heartfelt. Reluctantly, he released her. Before moving off her, he smiled winningly, directly into the large eyes lit by violet sparks. "Sure you won't change your mind?"

The look he got set him chuckling. He rolled to her side and lay back on the pillows, content for the moment. Her capitulation wasn't exactly complimentary, but he'd a month to work on that.

Beside him, Kit lay still, struck by the revelation that, although he was still close, now that he wasn't touching her, her mind was functioning again. Recalling her uncertainties about the Hunstanton Gang's cargoes, she remembered what had led her to such questions. "I take it you've heard about Lord Hendon, the new High Commissioner, and his interest in the trade?"

Jack managed to suppress the start her words gave him. What had she heard? He settled his hands behind his head and spoke to the ceiling. "It's well known the Revenue are working out an excess of zeal about Sheringham."

Kit frowned. "That's not what I meant. I heard that Lord Hendon has been appointed specifically to take a greater interest in the traffic."

From under his lashes, Jack watched her profile. "Who told you that?"

"I overheard someone tell my grandfather about it."

"Who?"

"The Lord Lieutenant."

Jack pursed his lips. It wasn't exactly the message Lord Marchmont had been sent to deliver, but it was close enough. He was sure the Lord Lieutenant would have communicated his message accurately but if Kit had been flapping her ears at a distance, she might not have caught the whole of it. He couldn't imagine the two peers openly discussing such business in front of Spencer's housekeeper. "If that's the case, we'll have to keep a close eye on his lordship's activities."

Kit snorted derisively and sat up. "If he ever actually stirs himself to anything that can be so described. I'm beginning to think he's gone to ground in that castle of his and just issues orders to the Revenue from his daybed."

Jack looked at her in amazement. "What makes you think that?"

"He's never seen about, that's why. He's been here for a few months, yet most people haven't sighted him. I know because Spencer gave a dinner party. Lord Hendon was invited but had a prior engagement."

The disgust in her voice made Jack blink. "What's wrong with that?"

Kit's lip curled. "A prior engagement with whom – when all the surrounding families were at Cranmer that night?"

Jack looked much struck, a fact Kit missed. She found the glass of brandy, now empty, amid the covers and, with the trailing ends of her muffler, ineffectually dabbed at the small stain where the dregs had spilt in their tumble. Suddenly, she giggled.

"What's funny?"

"I was just wondering if I should pity the poor man, when he finally condescends to make a public appearance. The ladies of the neighborhood are all so *anxious* to meet him. Mrs. Cartwright has designs on him as a husband for her Jane, and Lady Marchmont –" Kit broke off, horrified by what she'd nearly said.

"Who's Lady Marchmont got in mind for the poor devil?" The laughter bubbling beneath the smooth surface of Jack's voice was encouraging.

"Someone else," Kit replied repressively. "And I don't envy the chit one bit."

"Oh?" Jack turned a fascinated eye on her. "Why's that?"

Kit was enjoying the unexpected sensation of sitting beside Jack, feeling oddly at ease and totally unthreatened, despite the panic of only minutes ago. For some inexplicable reason, she was quite sure he intended her no harm. His conviction that he could make her welcome his advances was frightening purely because she knew it was the truth. But when he wasn't engaging in that sort of play, she felt completely at one with him, perfectly ready to share her opinion of the new High Commissioner. She pulled an expressive face. "From all I've heard, Hendon sounds a dry old stick, positively fusty." She studied the glass in her hand. "He must be fifty and he limps. Lady Marchmont said he was 'Hendonish' but I've no idea what that means – probably stuffy."

Jack's brows had risen to considerable heights. He could have informed Kit precisely what "Hendonish" meant – she'd just been treated to a sample, albeit restricted – but he didn't. He was too taken up with grappling with a sense of outrage. "You've met the man, I take it."

"No." Kit shook her head. "Hardly anyone has, so he can hardly take exception to our visions of him if they're unfairly unflattering, can he?"

And that, thought Jack, was a deucedly difficult argument to counter.

A sudden shriek of wind brought their situation forcibly to Kit's mind. Heavens! Here she sat in Captain Jack's bed, with him beside her, chatting the night away. She must have rocks in her head! She wriggled toward the edge of the bed. "I must go."

Long fingers encircled her wrist. Jack didn't exert any great pressure, yet Kit didn't fool herself into thinking she could break free. "I take it we're agreed, then. Your men and mine to join from now on."

Kit frowned. "If the others agree. I'll have to ask them. I'll meet you at the quarries as we planned and tell you what we've decided."

She glanced at Jack. His face was blank, his expression unreadable. But she sensed he didn't like her conditions. Unconsciously, she tilted her chin.

Jack pondered her defiant expression and considered the advisability of pulling her to him and kissing her into agreement. Her lips were temptation incarnate, soft and full and devastatingly feminine. Particularly in their present half pout. Abruptly, he dragged his mind from its preoccupation. What she'd suggested was fair enough, but he didn't trust her in the quarries. He'd a shrewd suspicion she knew them better than he did. "I'll agree to wait two nights for your answer on the condition that you, personally, bring it to me here – not at the quarries."

Kit forced herself not to look down at the hand trapping hers or at the long body stretched at ease on the covers. She needed no demonstration to understand her vulnerability. She looked into Jack's eyes and read cool determination in their depths. Did it really matter if she came here again?

How deliciously dangerous, her wilder self purred.

"Very well." The hand about her wrist was withdrawn. Kit stood. Then immediately sank back on the bed, blushing furiously. Her bands were still undone. She couldn't ride back to Cranmer with them about her waist; and she didn't fancy the idea of stopping along the way to get undressed and do them up.

It took Jack a moment to work out the reason for her blush. Then he laughed, a low chuckle that set Kit's nerves skittering. He sat up. "Turn around and let me do them up for you." When Kit sent him a scandalized look, he grinned wickedly. "I undid them, after all."

At his teasing tone, Kit blushed again and reluctantly turned about, wriggling to work the bands into position. What else could she do? He'd already seen her naked back – and her seminaked front, too. She felt his weight shift on the bed, then he rolled up the back of her shirt.

"Hold them where you want them tied."

Kit slipped her hands beneath her shirt to settle the bands over her breasts. "Tighter," she said, as she felt him cinch the ends only just tight enough to stay up.

An unintelligible mutter came from behind her, but he tightened the knot.

"More."

"Christ, woman! There ought to be a law against what you're doing."

Kit took a moment to work that out, then giggled. "There won't be any permanent damage."

The knot was tied, just tight enough, and her shirt pulled down. Kit stood and tucked the shirt into her waistband, then shrugged on her coat before winding the muffler tight about her nose and chin.

Lounging on the bed, Jack watched the transformation critically. Even knowing she was a woman, he had to admit her disguise was good. "Your mare's in the stable out back, keeping company with my stallion. Don't get too close to him; he bites."

Kit nodded. She found her tricorne in the corner by the bed and crammed it over her curls. "You didn't say where we are."

"About two miles north of Castle Hendon."

Beneath her muffler, Kit's lips twisted wryly. Jack seemed a man very much after her own heart. "You do like to live dangerously, don't you?"

Jack smiled brilliantly. "It keeps boredom at bay."

With a regal inclination of her head, Kit sauntered to the door.

Jack grinned. With her husky voice and the mannish airs she assumed with such ease, he was confident they'd manage her charade for the requisite month.

At the door, Kit paused. "Until the night after tomorrow, then."

Jack nodded, his expression leaching into impassivity. "Don't try to disappear, will you? Your men might do something rash. And I know where to find you."

For the first time that night, Kit confronted the side of Captain Jack that had, presumably, made him the leader of the Hunstanton Gang. She decided she wasn't going to give him the joy of knowing how unnerving she found it. With a flourish, she swept him a bow before unlatching the door and pausing on the threshold to say, "I'll be here."

Then she left.

In the cottage, Jack dropped back onto the pillows and fell to a contemplation of the first woman to have ever left his bed untried. A temporary aberration but a novel one. He was deep in dreams when the quick clop of hooves told him Kit was on her way. With a sigh, he closed his eyes, wishing that Young Kit's month of service was already past.

Chapter 10

Next morning, Lord Hendon, the new High Commissioner for North Norfolk, visited his Revenue Office in King's Lynn, accompanied by his longtime friend and fellow ex-officer, George Smeaton.

His long limbs elegantly disposed in the best chair the Office possessed, his shoulder-length hair confined by a black riband at his nape, Jack knew he looked every inch the well-to-do gentleman lately retired from active service. His left leg was extended, kept straight by the discreet splint he wore under his close-fitting breeches. He'd carried such an injury for months after the hell of Corunna; the splint jogged his memory into a limp, increasing the overt difference between Lord Hendon and one Captain Jack.

One long-fingered hand languidly turned a page in the Office's logbook, the sapphire in his signet ring catching the light, splintering it through prisms of blue. His ears were filled with the drone of Sergeant Tonkin's explanations for his continuing lack of success in apprehending the smuggling gang operating between Lynn and Hunstanton. George sat by the window, a silent witness to Tonkin's performance.

"A devilish wise lot, they are, m'lord. Led by one of the more experienced men, I'd say."

Jack suppressed a smile at the thought of what Kit would say to that. He made a mental note to tell her when she returned to the cottage. Listening with apparent interest to Tonkin's summation, he was very aware that just the thought of that problematical female had been enough to instantly transform his body from listless lassitude to a state of semiarousal. Deliberately, he focused on Tonkin's words.

A burly, barrel-chested individual, Tonkin's coarse, blunt features were balanced by cauliflower ears. Since Tonkin's reputation was murky, bordering on the vicious, Jack had sent the efficient Osborne out of the area of their operations, leaving Tonkin to bear any odium as a result of the continuing high level of traffic. "If we could just lay hands on one of this 'ere lot, m'lord, I'd wring the truth from 'im." Tonkin's beady eyes gleamed. "And then we'd string a few up on our gibbets – that'd teach 'em not to play games with the Revenue."

"Indeed, Sergeant. We all agree this gang's got to be stopped." Jack leaned forward; his gaze transfixed Tonkin. "I suggest, as Osborne is engaged around Sheringham, you concentrate on the stretch of coast from Hunstanton to Lynn. I believe you said this particular gang operates only in that area?"

"Yes sir. We ain't never got a whiff of 'em elsewheres." Trapped beneath Jack's penetrating stare, Tonkin shifted uneasily. "But if you'll pardon the question, m'lord, if I'm to send my men down this way, who's tb watch the Brancaster beaches? I swear there's a big gang operating thereabouts."

Jack's face expressed supercilious condescension. "One thing at a time, Tonkin. Lay the gang operating between Hunstanton and Lynn by the heels, then you may go haring off after your 'big gang.'"

His insultingly cynical tones struck Tonkin like a slap. He came to attention and saluted. "Yes, m'lord. Is there anything else, m'lord?"

With Tonkin dismissed, Jack and George quitted the Custom House. Crossing the sunny cobbled square, George adjusted his stride to Jack's limp.

Artistically wielding his cane, Jack struggled to ignore the stirrings of guilt. He hadn't told George about Kit. Like Matthew, George would disapprove, insisting Kit be retired forthwith, somehow or other. Basically, Jack agreed with the sentiment – he just didn't see what the "somehow or other" could be, and he was too experienced an officer to put the safety of a single woman before his mission.

The other matter troubling his conscience was a sinking feeling he should have behaved better with Kit, that he shouldn't have stooped to sexual coercion. Henceforth, he'd ensure that his attitude toward her remained professional. At least until she retired from the gang. After that, she'd no longer be tangled in his mission, and he could deal with her as personally as she'd allow.

Fantasizing about dealing with her personally had kept him awake for much of last night.

"Lord Hendon, ain't it?"

The barked greeting, coming from no more than a yard away, startled Jack from his reverie. He glanced up; a large man of advanced years was planted plumb in front of him. As his gaze took in the corona of curling white hair and the sharp eyes, washed out but still detectably violet-hued, Jack realized he was facing Spencer, Lord Cranmer, Kit's grandfather.

Jack smiled and held out his hand. "Lord Cranmer?"

His hand was enveloped in a huge palm and crushed.

"Aye." Spencer was pleased to have been recognized. "I

knew your father well, m'boy. Marchmont spoke to me t'other day. If you need any help, you need only ask."

Smoothly, Jack thanked him and introduced George, adding: "We were in the army together."

Spencer wrung George's hand. "Engaged to Amy Gresham, ain't you? Think we missed your company, some nights back."

"Er – yes." George rolled an anguished eye at Jack.

Jack came to the rescue with consummate charm. "We were sorry to miss your dinner, but friends from London dropped by with news of our regiment."

Spencer chuckled. "It's not me you should be making your excuses to. It's the ladies get their noses out of joint when eligible men don't join the crowd." His eyes twinkled. "A word of warning, seeing you're Jake's boy. You'd do well to weather the storm before it works itself into a frenzy. Fighting shy of the *beldames* won't scare them off – they'll just try harder. Best to let them have their try at you. Once they're convinced you're past praying for they'll start off on someone else."

"Great heavens! It sounds like a hunt." Jack looked taken aback.

"It is a hunt, you may be sure." Spencer grinned "You're in Norfolk now, not London. Here they play the game in earnest."

"I'll bear your warning in mind, m'lord." Jack grinned back, a rogue unrepentant.

Spencer chuckled. "You do that, m'boy. Wouldn't want to see you leg-shackled to some drab female who's the dearest cousin of one of their ladyships, would we?" With that dire prediction, Spencer went on his way, chuckling to himself.

"The devil!" Jack heaved a sigh. "I've a nasty suspicion he's right." The memory of Kit's words, uttered while she'd been sitting on his bed last night, echoed in his brain. "Fighting shy of society seemed a wise idea, but it looks like we'll have to attend a few balls and dinners."

"*We'll?*" George turned, eyes wide. "Might I remind you I've had the good sense to get betrothed and so am no longer at risk? I don't have to attend any such affairs."

Jack's eyes narrowed. "You'd leave me to face the guns alone?"

"Dammit, Jack! You survived Corunna. Surely you can fight this engagement unsupported?"

"Ah, but we haven't sighted the enemy yet, have we?" When George looked puzzled, Jack explained: "Lady Whatsit's drab cousin. Just think how you'll feel if I get caught in parson's mousetrap, all because I didn't have you to watch my back."

George pulled back to eye the elegant figure of Lord Hendon, at thirty-five, a man of vast and, in George's opinion, unparalleled experience of the fairer sex, consistent victor in the amphitheaters of *ton*nish ballrooms and bedrooms, a bona fide, fully certified rake of the first order. "Jack, in my humble opinion, the ladies of the district haven't a hope in hell."

There was no moon to light the clearing before the cottage door. Kit stopped Delia under the tree opposite and studied the scene. A chink of lamplight showed beneath one shutter. It was midnight. All was still. Kit slackened her reins and headed Delia toward the stable.

In the shadow of the stable entrance, she dismounted, drawing the reins over Delia's head. The mare tossed her head sharply.

"Here. Let me."

Kit jumped back, a curse on her lips. A large hand closed

about hers, deftly removing the reins. Jack was no more than a dense shadow at her shoulder. Unnerved, her wits frazzled by his touch, Kit waited in silence while he stabled Delia in the dark.

Were there others about? She peered into the gloom.

"There's no one else here." Jack returned to her side. "Come inside."

Kit had to hurry to keep up with Jack's long strides. He reached the door and entered before her, heading straight for the table to take the chair on the far side. Irritated by such cavalier treatment, Kit bit her tongue. She closed the door carefully, then turned to survey him, pausing to take stock before sauntering across the floor to the chair facing his.

He was scowling again, but she wasn't about to try for one of his smiles tonight. Pulling off her hat, she unwound her muffler, then sat.

"What's your decision?" Jack asked the question as soon as her bottom made contact with the chair seat. He'd been steeling himself for this meeting for more than twenty-four hours; it was galling to find the time had been wasted. The instant she'd appeared on his horizon, the only thing he could think of was getting her back onto his bed. And what he'd do next. He wanted this meeting concluded, and her safely on her way, with all possible haste.

From her expression, he knew his frown didn't meet with her approval. Right now, she didn't meet with his. She was the cause of all his present afflictions. Aside from the physical ramifications of her presence, he was having to cope with untold guilt over his deliberate support of her hoax. He hadn't told Matthew or George. And now he was uncomfortably aware of Spencer, previously a shadowy figure he'd had no difficulty ignoring, transformed by their meeting into a flesh-and-blood man, presumably with real affection for his wayward granddaughter, even if she was illegitimate. Impossible to tell him, of course. What could he say? "A word in your ear, old man – your bastard granddaughter is masquerading as a smuggler"?

Dragging his gaze from Kit's lamplight-sheened curls, Jack stared into her violet eyes, alike yet quite different from Spencer's.

Kit's response to Jack's abrupt question had been to pull off her riding gloves, with infinite slowness, before glancing up to meet his gaze. "My men have agreed." She'd met her little band earlier that evening. "We'll join you as of now, provided you let us know what the cargoes are beforehand." It was her condition; the fishermen had been only too glad to accept Jack's offer.

Impassivity overtook Jack's scowl. Why the hell did she want to know that? His mind ranged over the possibilities but could find none that fit. "No." He kept the answer short and waited for her reaction.

"No?" she echoed. Then she shrugged. "All right. But I thought you wanted us to join you." She started to draw her gloves back on.

Jack abandoned impassivity. "What you ask is impossible. How can I run a gang if I have to check with you before I accept a cargo? There can be only one leader, and in case you've forgotten, I'm it."

Kit leaned one elbow on the table and cupped her chin in that hand, keeping her eyes on his face. It was a very strong face, with its powerful brow line and high cheekbones. "You should be able to understand that I feel responsible for my little band. How can I tell if you're doing right by them if I don't know what cargoes you're accepting or declining?"

Jack's exasperation grew. She'd hit on the one argument

he couldn't, in all honesty, counter. If she'd been a man. he'd have applauded such a reason – it was the right attitude for a leader, of however small a troop. But Kit wasn't a man, a fact he was in no danger of forgetting.

Artfully, Kit continued. "I can see it might prove difficult to keep an agent waiting for confirmation. But if I was with you when you arranged the cargoes, there'd be no time lost."

Jack shook his head. "No. It's too dangerous. It's one thing to fool semicivilized fishermen; our contacts are not of that ilk. They're too likely to penetrate your disguise – God only knows what they'll make of it."

Kit received the assessment coolly, drawing her gloves through her fingers. "But you deal mostly with Nolan, don't you?"

Jack nodded. Nolan was his primary source of cargoes although there were three other agents in the area.

"I've already met Nolan without mishap, so I doubt there's any real danger there. He'll accept me as Young Kit. Seeing me with you will confirm we've joined forces, so he won't go trying to contact my men behind your back. That's what you wanted, wasn't it – a monopoly on this coast?"

Jack made no comment. There wasn't any he could make; she was dead on target with her reasoning, damn her.

Kit smiled. "So. Where and when do you make contact?"

Jack's expression turned grim. He'd been maneuvered into a corner and he didn't like it one bit. Their meeting place had been expressly chosen to be as unilluminated as possible, to ensure Nolan and his brethren had little chance of recognizing him, or George or Matthew. He was most at risk – he'd learned long ago that effectively disguising the streaks in his hair was impossible – so they'd found a venue where the light was always bad and keeping their hats on

109

raised no eyebrows. But taking Kit to a hedge tavern frequented by local cutthroats and thieves was inconceivable.

"It's out of the question." Jack sat up and leaned both elbows on the table, the better to impress Kit with the madness of her suggestion.

"Why?" Kit fixed him with a determined stare.

"Because it would be the height of lunacy to take a woman, however well disguised, into a den of thieves." Jack's growl was barely restrained.

"Quite," Kit affirmed. "So no one will imagine Young Kit to be anything other than a lad."

"Christ!" Jack ran long fingers through his hair. "I wouldn't give a *sou* for Young Kit's safety in that place – male or female."

For a minute, Kit stared at him, incomprehension stamped on her fine features. Then she blushed delicately. Determined not to lower her head, she let her gaze slide to a consideration of the brandy bottle. "But you'll be there. There's no reason why any of them should . . ."

"Proposition you?" Jack kept his voice hard and matter-of-fact. If there was any possibility of scaring her off, he'd take it. "Allow me to inform you, my dear, that even I don't frequent such places alone. George and Matthew always accompany me."

Kit perked up. "So much the better. If there's four of us, and the three of you are large, then the danger will be minimal." She cocked an eyebrow at Jack, waiting for his next argument.

Her attitude, of patiently awaiting his next quibble in the calm certainty that she'd top it, brought a wry and entirely spontaneous grin to Jack's lips. Damn it – she was so cocksure she could pull the thing off, he'd half a mind to let her try. She wouldn't find the Blackbird at all to her liking;

maybe, after her first trip there, she'd be content to let him manage their contacts on his own.

His thoughts reached Kit. She smiled, only to be treated immediately to a scowl.

Hell and the devil! He was going mad. Jack fought the impulse to groan and bury his head in his hands. The effort of ignoring his besotted senses, and the pressure in his loins, was sapping his will. If only she was angry or frightened or flustered, he could cope. Instead, she was calm and in control, perfectly prepared to sit smiling at him, trading logic until he capitulated. He could render her witless easily enough, but only by unleashing something he was no longer sure he could reharness.

"All right." His jaw set uncompromisingly. "You can come with us next Wednesday night provided you do exactly as I say. Only I know your little secret. I suggest we keep it that way."

Content with having gained her immediate goal, Kit nodded. She was perfectly prepared to do as Jack said, as long as she could learn, firsthand, of the cargoes on offer. If there was any "human cargo," she'd have time to sound the alarm without risking her little troop, and, if possible, without endangering Captain Jack or his men, either.

Pleased, she reached for her hat. "Where do we meet?"

Engaged in an inventory of all the dangers attendant on taking Kit to the Blackbird, Jack shot her a decidedly malevolent glare. "Here. At eleven."

Kit grinned, then hid her face with her muffler. Her mood was buoyant; she wished she dared tease him from his grouchy attitude, but her instinct for self-preservation hadn't completely deserted her.

Jack slouched in his chair. This wasn't how this meeting was supposed to have gone, but at least she was leaving. He watched her assume her disguise and decided against going to the stable to help her with her horse. She could saddle her own damned mare if she was so keen on playing the lad. He acknowledged her flippant bow with something close to a snarl, which didn't affect her in the least. She seemed impervious to his bad temper – thrilled, no doubt, to have got her way. The door shut behind her, and he was alone.

Jack stretched but didn't relax until the sound of the mare's hooves died. He wasn't looking forward to Wednesday – the potential horrors were mind-numbing. To cap it all, he'd have to watch over her without letting on it was a *her* he was watching. Freed of Kit's inhibiting presence, Jack groaned.

Chapter 11

Kit's initiation into the dim world of the Blackbird Tavern was every bit as harrowing as Jack had anticipated. Sidelong, he studied the top of her hat, all he could see of her head as she sat at the rough trestle beside him, her nose buried in a tankard of ale. He hoped she wasn't drinking the stuff; it was home brewed and potent. He had no idea if she was wise to the danger. The fact that he wasn't sure of her past experience only further complicated his role as her protector. And Young Kit certainly needed a protector, even if the blasted woman didn't know it.

She'd seemed oblivious of the stir her appearance at his elbow had caused. Garbed in severe black, her slim form drew considering glances. Luckily, the Blackbird's patrons were not given to overt gestures. He and George had made straight for their usual table, taking Kit with them. He'd wedged her between the wall and his own solid bulk. The curiosity of the motley crew who'd taken shelter within the Blackbird's dingy walls on this drizzily June night washed over them, Young Kit its focus.

"Where the hell's Nolan?" George growled. Sitting

opposite Kit, he nervously eyed the section of the room within his orbit.

Jack grimaced. "He'll be here soon enough." He'd warned both George and Matthew of Kit's heritage but continued to keep her sex a secret. Her coloring was so obvious it was impossible not to comment; to them, she was Christopher Cranmer's bastard son who lived at the Hall under Spencer's wing. Over "the stripling's" wish to join them in negotiations over cargoes, George's tendency to watch over youngsters had been of unexpected help.

He'd agreed Kit should accompany them. "If the place serves to put the lad off smuggling, so much the better," he'd said. "At least in our company he'll see a bit more of life in greater safety than might otherwise be afforded him."

It was a view that had not occurred to Jack – he wasn't sure he agreed with it. Certainly, George had not foreseen the interest Young Kit would provoke. Like him, both George and Matthew were edgy, nerves at full stretch. The only one of their company apparently unaffected by the tension in the room was its cause.

His gaze slid to her once more. She'd lifted her head from the tankard, but her gaze remained on the mug, cradled in both hands. To any observer, she gave every appearance of unconcerned innocence, idly toying with her drink, completely ignorant of the charged atmosphere. Then he noticed how tightly her gloved fingers were curled about the handle of the tankard.

Jack smiled into his beer. Not so ignorant. With any luck, she'd be scared witless.

Kit was certainly not unaware of the cloying interest of the other men in the room. The reason for it she found distasteful in the extreme, but she could hardly claim she hadn't been forewarned. For all she knew, Jack was relying on her disgust to make her balk at similar excursions in the future. But as long as the men in the room stared and did nothing, she couldn't see any real reason for fear. She'd been stared at aplenty, and far more overtly, during her Seasons in London. And Jack was only an inch or so away, on the crude bench beside her, an overwhelmingly large body that radiated warmth and security, reassuring with its aura of commanding strength governed by steely reflexes.

A stir by the door heralded an arrival. Jack looked over Matthew's shoulders. "It's Nolan."

The agent went to the bar and ordered a tankard, then, after scanning the room, made his way without haste to their table. He drew up a rough stool and perched at Jack's left, his eyes going to Kit. She'd raised her head at his approach and returned his stare unblinkingly.

Nolan's eyes narrowed. "You two in league?" He asked the question of Jack.

"A merger. To our mutual benefit."

Jack smiled, and Kit was very glad he didn't smile at her like that. The thought brought a shiver, which she sternly repressed.

"What does that mean?" Nolan didn't sound pleased.

"What it means, my friend, is that if you want to run a cargo into North Norfolk, you deal with me and me alone." Jack's deep voice was steady and completely devoid of emotion. In the hush, it held a menacing quality.

Nolan stared, then switched his gaze to Kit. "This true?"

"Yes." Kit kept it at that.

Nolan snorted and turned to Jack. "Well, leastways that means I won't have to deal with young upstarts who skim a man's profit to the bone." He turned to receive his tankard from a well-endowed serving wench, and so missed the inquiring glance Jack threw at Kit. She ignored it, letting her gaze slide from his, only to fall victim to the serving wench's fervent stare. Abruptly, she transferred her attention to her tankard and kept it there.

Once Jack and Nolan were well launched on their dealings, Kit looked up. The serving girl had retreated to the bar but her gaze was still fixed, in a drooling fashion, on her. Under her breath, Kit swore.

"Twenty kegs of the best brandy and ten more of port if you can handle it." Nolan paused to swill from his tankard. Kit wondered how he could; the stuff tasted vile.

"We can handle it. The usual conditions?"

"Aye." Nolan eyed Jack warily, as if unable to believe he wasn't going to push the Gang's cut higher. "When do you want it?"

Jack considered, then said: "Tomorrow. The moon'll be new – not too much light but enough to see by. The delivery conditions the same?"

Nolan nodded. "Cash on delivery. The ship's the *Mollie Ann*. She'll stand off Brancaster Head after dark tomorrow."

"Right." Pushing his tankard aside, Jack stood. "It's time we left."

Nolan merely nodded and retreated into his beer.

Hurriedly standing, Kit found herself bundled in front of Jack. Matthew led the way and George brought up the rear. Their exit was so rapid that none of the other customers had time to blink. Outside, she, Jack, and George waited in the road while Matthew fetched their horses. Even in the gloom, Kit sensed the meaningful look Jack and George exchanged over her head. Then they were mounted and off, across the fields to the cottage.

There, they all sat around the table. Jack poured brandy, raising a brow in Kit's direction. She shook her head. The few sips of ale she'd taken had been more than enough. Jack

116

delivered his plans in crisp tones that left Kit wondering what he'd been before. A soldier, certainly, but his attitude of authority suggested he hadn't been a trooper. The idea made her grin.

"How many boats can your men muster?"

Jack's question shook her into life. "Manned by two?" she asked. When he nodded, she replied: "Four. Do you want them all?"

"Four would double our number," put in George.

"And double the speed we could bring the barrels in." Jack looked at Kit. "We'll have all four. Get them to pull inshore just west of the Head – there's a little bay they'll likely know, perfect for the purpose." Turning to Matthew and George, he discussed the deposition of the rest of the men. Kit listened with half an ear, glancing up only briefly when George left.

Matthew followed. "G'night, lad."

Kit returned the words with a nod and a smile, hidden by her muffler. As soon as the door shut behind him, she tugged the folds free. "Phew! I hope the nights don't get too warm."

Replacing the brandy bottle on the sideboard, Jack turned to stare at her. In a month, long before the balmy nights of August, she wouldn't have need of her muffler. In a month, she wouldn't be masquerading as a smuggler. In a month, she'd be masquerading as his mistress. The thought brought a frown to his face. He'd still be masquerading, too, for he couldn't tell her who he was until his mission was complete. With an inward sigh, Jack focused on the present. "I take it you were edified by the company at the Blackbird?"

Kit lounged in her chair. "The company I could do without," she admitted. "But everything passed off smoothly.

117

Next time, they'll recognize me, and I'll be less of an attraction."

Jack's exasperated look spoke volumes. "Next time," he repeated, drawing a chair to the other side of the table and straddling it. "I assume you're aware that the only reason you came off safely was because George and Matthew and I were there, rather too large to overlook?"

Kit opened her eyes wide. "I hadn't anticipated going there alone."

"Christ, *no!*" Jack ran his fingers through his hair, the golden strands catching and reflecting the lamplight. "This idea of yours is madness. I should never have agreed to it. But let me educate you on one point at least. If you'd made the slightest slip back there, unwittingly led one of the men to believe . . ." Jack struggled to find the right words for his purpose. One glance at Kit's open face, her eyes clearly visible now that she'd removed her hat and muffler, made it clear she wasn't entirely *au fait* with the way things were in dens of iniquity. "Led them to believe it'd be worthwhile to make a push for you," he continued, determined to bring her to a sense of her danger, "then we'd have had a riot on our hands. What would you have done then?"

Kit frowned. "Hid behind a table," she eventually conceded. "I'm no good with my fists."

The answer overturned Jack's deliberate seriousness. The idea of her delicate hands bunched into fists was silly enough; the notion of them doing any damage was laughable. His lips twisted in a reluctant grin.

Kit smiled sweetly. Immediately, all traces of mirth fled Jack's face, replaced by the scowl she was starting to believe was habitual. Dammit – he could smile, she knew he could. Charmingly.

Go on! Make him smile.

Shut up, Kit told her inner devil. *I can't afford a tussle with him – if he touches me, I can't think and then where will I be?*

Flat on your back, with any luck, came the unrepentant answer.

All I want is a smile, Kit told herself, repressing the inclination to scowl back. "You worry too much," she said. "Things will work out; it's only for a month."

Jack watched as she wound her muffler loosely into place and jammed her hat over her curls. He knew he should put his foot down and end her little charade, or at least restrict it to those areas he believed inevitable. He knew it, but couldn't work out how to do it. He argued and she returned a glib answer, then smiled, scattering his wits completely, leaving only an urgent longing in their place. He'd never worked with a woman before; socially, they were a pushover but professionally – he obviously didn't have the knack.

The scrape of her chair as she stood brought Jack's gaze back to Kit's face. "Until tomorrow, then." She smiled and felt a distinct pang of irritation when Jack glared back. Deliberately, she sauntered to the door, allowing her hips full license in their sway. She paused at the last to raise a hand in salute; his scowl was now definitely black. Her teeth gleamed. "Good night, Jack."

As she closed the door behind her, Kit wondered if the low growl she heard was from the distant surf or a somewhat closer source.

The run was her first taste of Jack's planning in action. All went smoothly. She was the main lookout, stationed on the cliff above and to the east of the bay into which they ran the goods. In answer to her protest that surely any danger would come from the west, Jack had pulled rank and all but ordered her to the headland. She had a fine view of the beach. Her men were there. They dropped the cargo, then, together with the others in boats, pulled out into the Roads and headed straight home. The land-bound smugglers transferred the barrels to pack ponies, and the cavalcade headed inland. This time, Jack chose to hide the cargo in the ruins of an old church.

Overgrown with ivy, the ruins were all but impossible to discover unless you knew they were there. The old crypt, dark and dry, provided a perfect spot for their cache.

"Who owns this land?" Kit turned to Jack, sitting on his stallion beside her. They'd pulled back into the trees to keep watch over the gang as they worked, unloading the barrels and carting them down the steps to the crypt.

"It used to belong to the Smeatons."

Jack's tone suggested it no longer did. "And now?" Kit asked.

She knew the answer before he said, "Lord Hendon."

"Do you have a fetish of sorts, to constantly operate under the new High Commissioner's very nostrils?" Delia sidled to avoid the grey's head. Kit swore, and reined the mare in. "I wish you'd make your horse behave."

Jack obediently leaned forward and pulled Champion's ears. "Hear that, old fellow?" he whispered *sotto voce*. "Your advances are falling short of the mark. But don't worry. Females are contrary creatures at the best of times. Believe me – I know."

Kit ignored the invitation to take exception to his state-ment, quite sure there'd be a trap concealed amongst his words. In their few exchanges since the previous night she'd detected a definite edge to Jack's remarks; she assumed it sprang from a corresponding sharpening of his temper. "You were about to tell me why you use Lord Hendon's lands."

Jack's lips twisted in a smile Kit couldn't see. He hadn't been about to do any such thing but hers was a persistent curiosity, one he should perhaps allay. She was also a persistent distraction, a persistent itch he couldn't yet scratch. But soon, he vowed, soon he'd attend to her as she deserved. The vision of her bottom, swaying in deliberate provocation as she'd walked to the door of the cottage wasn't a sight he was likely to forget. "Sometimes, the safest place to hide is as close to your pursuer as possible."

Kit thought about that. "So he overlooks you while searching farther afield?"

Jack nodded. The men came out of the crypt; the last barrels had been stowed. Jack urged Champion farward.

Within minutes, the gang was scattering, ponies led off, other men disappearing on foot. Soon, the only souls left were Kit, Jack, Matthew, and George. They waited a few minutes, to make sure all the men were safely away. Then George nodded to Jack. "I'll see you tomorrow."

George rode into the trees. At Jack's signal, Matthew drew away, to wait for him just beyond the clearing.

Kit looked up; it was time for her to depart. She smiled, not knowing how weary she looked. "My men and I'll come up for the meeting on Monday. That's right, isn't it?"

Jack nodded, wishing he could escort her home. He hadn't thought of her riding alone through the dark before; he'd never watched her leave the cottage. To let her head into the night, tired and solitary, seemed an act of outright callousness. He considered insisting on escorting her, but rejected the idea. She'd refuse and argue, and he'd probably lose. And he didn't wish to remind her of his very real interest in her just at present. Ignoring her while she believed he was uninterested was hard enough. Ignoring her once she knew he was hooked would be impossible if her actions of last night were any guide. Like any other woman, she'd be incapable of leaving him alone, teasing him for attentions he was too wise to bestow – at least, not yet.

Half-asleep and dreaming, Kit found she was staring at the pale oval of Jack's face. She shook herself awake. "I'll be going then. Good night."

Jack bit his tongue. Rigid, he watched her leave the clearing, heading south on a ride of close to six miles through the dark.

Stifling a curse, he turned Champion to the east and found Matthew. Wordlessly, they set off, Champion leading Matthew's black over fields and meadows, somnolent under dark skies. They'd covered nearly a mile when Jack abruptly drew rein, startling Matthew who'd been asleep in his saddle.

"Dammit! You go on ahead. I'll be in later." Jack wheeled Champion and set his heels to the grey's sleek sides, leaving a bemused Matthew in his wake. When he reached the ruined church, Jack turned the grey's head south and loosened the reins. He was sure Champion would follow his Arab mare no matter which way Kit had gone.

Chapter 12

After that first run, Kit had been sure she'd face no real problem in being Young Kit for the requisite month. Unfortunately, affairs did not run so smoothly. Her pride was her problem: it rose to the fore on two different counts, both stemming directly from Jack's irritating behavior.

In the third week of their association, she sought solitude in the gazebo to thrash out how to counteract Jack's stubborn refusal to deal reasonably with her. She was always the lookout – that she could understand – but for all his apparent experience, Jack persisted in placing her to the east of the run area, away from Hunstanton. Yet if the Revenue were to mount a sortie, surely they'd be coming *from* Hunstanton?

Plonking herself down on the gazebo's wooden seat, Kit stared at the roses. Any attempt to question Jack's peculiar orders met with a highly discouraging scowl, topped by a growl if she pushed him. A snarl would no doubt be next, but she'd never had the nerve to test him. She had the distinct impression she was being bundled aside, out of harm's way. Kit narrowed her eyes. It was almost as if Jack knew there'd be no interference from the Revenue but sent her in the opposite direction just in case.

Damn it! It had been at *his* insistence she'd continued her charade; being given token tasks was not what she'd expected. Enough! She'd have it out with him this evening. There was to be another run, on the promontory between Holme and Brancaster. Since they'd joined forces, the traffic had been constant – two runs a week, always on different beaches, mostly for Nolan, once for another agent. Spirits and lace had been the staple fare, high-quality merchandise that brought good returns to the smugglers.

With a rustle of skirts, Kit stood. Descending from the gazebo, she wended her way between the rose beds, indifferent to the perfect blooms nodding on every side. Lack of meaningful participation in the gang's affairs was one of her points of contention. Her personal interaction with Jack, or rather, lack of personal interaction with Jack, was the other.

His behavior during her first visit to the cottage she'd understood. What had her confused was all that had, or hadn't, come since. He'd blown hot for her initially, but ever since that night he'd appeared uninterested, as if he'd found her unattractive on second glance. For one who'd had the rakes of London at her feet, Jack's failure to succumb was galling.

Kit dropped the petals she'd pulled from a fading white rose and headed for the house. All the other personable males who'd hovered on her horizon had done so without her exerting any effort to attract their notice. Jack's notice, short-lived though it had been, had stirred her interest in a way none of the others had. She wanted more. But Jack damn his silver eyes, seemed distinctly disinclined to supply it. He now acted as if she was a lad in truth – as if he couldn't be bothered responding to her as a woman.

Climbing the steps to the terrace, Kit realized her teeth were clenched. Forcibly relaxing her jaw, she made a vow. Before she quit the Hunstanton Gang, she'd have Captain Jack at her feet. A rash resolution, perhaps, but the thought sent a thrill of delicious daring through her.

Her lips quirked upward. This was what she craved – what she needed. A challenge. If Jack insisted on removing all chance of other thrills, surely it was only right he provide her with suitable compensation?

Entering the morning room, Kit sank onto the *chaise* and considered the possibilities. She'd need to be on guard to ensure Jack didn't take things farther than mere dalliance. His behavior on that first night in his cottage had been ample proof that he could and would take matters far farther than she would countenance. He was not of common stock. No fisherman had such an air – of command, of authority, and, frequently, of sheer arrogance. His diction, his knowledge of swordplay, his stallion – all bore witness that his origins were considerably higher than the village. And, of course, he was gorgeous beyond belief. Nevertheless, a liaison, however brief, between Lord Cramner's granddaughter and Captain Jack, leader of the Hunstanton Gang, did not fall within the bounds of the possible.

But he thinks you're illegitimate, remember?

"But I'm not illegitimate, am I?" Kit pointed out to her wilder self. "I couldn't possibly forget what I owe the family name."

Why? The family was ready enough to sacrifice you for their own ends.

"Only my uncles and aunts – not Spencer or my cousins."

Sure it's not just an old-fashioned dose of maidenly nerves? How will you learn if Amy's right if you don't give it a try? And if you're ever going to take the plunge – he's the one. Why not admit you go weak

125

at the knees at the thought of all that lovely male muscle and those silver devil's eyes?

"Oh, shut up!" Kit reached for her embroidery. Prying her needle free, she poked it through the design. Drawing the thread through, she set her lips. She was bored. Excitement was what she needed. Tonight, she'd make sure she got some.

The roar of the surf as it pounded the sand filled Kit's ears. She stood in the lee of the cliff, holding Delia's reins, watching the Hunstanton Gang gather. The men huddled in small groups, their gruff voices barely audible above the surf. None approached her. They all viewed Young Kit as a delicate youth, a young nob, best left to Captain Jack to deal with.

Kit looked up and saw Jack approaching, mounted on his grey stallion and flanked by George and Matthew. Her confidence in Jack's ability to organize and command was complete. She'd heard tale, some decidedly grisly, of the Hunstanton Gang's activities before Jack had taken over. In the past three weeks, she'd seen no evidence of such excesses. Jack didn't even exert himself to impress his will — the men obeyed him instinctively, as if recognizing a born leader.

Kit peered out at the waves, black tipped with pearl in the weak moonlight. She could see no sign of the boats.

Jack drew rein some yards away and the men gathered about to receive their orders. Then they were off down the beach to wait, huddled on the sand like rocks just above the waterline. Dismounting, Jack set Matthew and George to watch for the signal from the ship that would tell them the boats were on their way in, then trudged through the sand toward Kit.

He stopped in front of her. "Up there should give you a good view."

To Kit's surprise, he indicated the cliff above the western end of the beach. Then she remembered they were out on the headland – if the Revenue came from anywhere it would have to be from the east; beyond the western point was sea. Her time had come. "No!" She had to shout over the din of the waves.

It took Jack a moment to realize what she was saying. He scowled. "What do you mean, 'No'?"

"I mean there's no sense in my keeping a lookout from that position. I may as well stay on the beach and watch the boats come in."

Jack stared at her. The idea of her scurrying around among the boats, being shoved aside by the first fisherman into whose path she stumbled, was one he refused to contemplate. A shout told him the signal had come. Soon, the boats would be beaching. He eyed the slight figure before him and shook his head. "I haven't time to argue about it now. I've got to see to the boats."

"Fine. I'll come, too." Kit looped Delia's reins about a straggling bush clinging to the cliff and turned to follow Jack.

"Get up to that cliff top immediately!"

The blast almost lifted her from her feet. Kit stepped back, eyes widening in alarm. Jack towered over her, one arm lifted, one finger jabbing at the western cliff. Transfixed, she stared at him. And saw him set his teeth.

"For Christ's sake, get moving!"

Shaken to her boots, furious to the point of incoherence, Kit wrenched Delia's reins from the bush and swung up to the saddle. She glared down at Jack, still standing before her, fists on hips, barring the way to the beach, then hauled on the reins and sent Delia up the cliff path.

On the western cliff top, Kit dismounted. She left Delia to graze the coarse grasses a few yards back from the edge. Seething, she threw herself down on a large flat boulder and, picking up a small rock, hurled it down onto the sands. She wished she could hit Jack with it. He was clearly visible, down by the beaching boats. A slingshot might just make it.

With a disgusted snort, Kit sank her elbows into her thighs and dumped her chin in her hands. God – could he shout. Spencer bellowed when in a rage, but the noise had never affected her. She'd always considered it a sure sign her grandfather had all but lost the thread of his argument and would soon succumb to hers. But when Jack had bellowed his orders, he'd expected to be obeyed. Instantly. Every vestige of defiant courage she possessed had curled up its toes and died. The idea of her doing anything to overcome such an invincible force had seemed patently ridiculous.

Thoroughly disgusted with her craven retreat, Kit glumly watched the gang unload the boats.

When the last barrel was clear of the surf and the pack ponies were all but fully laden, Kit stood and dusted down her breeches. Whatever happened, however much Jack bellowed, this was the last, the *very last time* she'd keep watch from the wrong position for the Hunstanton Gang.

"Well? What is it?" Jack dumped the keg he'd brought back from the run on the table and swung to face Kit. George had ridden straight home from the beach and, after one glance at Kit's rigid figure, Jack had sent Matthew directly on to the Castle. On the beach, he'd hoped that her knuckling under to his orders meant she'd forget her grievance over being a redundant lookout. He should have known better.

Kit ignored his abrupt demand and closed the door. With

128

cool deliberation, she walked forward into the glow of the lamp Jack set alight. Pulling her hat from her curls, she dropped it on the table, then, in perfect silence, unwound her muffler.

Straightening from lighting the lamp, Jack pressed his hands to the table and remained standing. He felt much more capable of intimidating Kit when upright. Assuming, of course, that she, too, was upright. If she didn't hurry up and get to her point, he wouldn't give much for her chances of remaining so. Jack set his teeth and waited.

When her muffler had joined her hat, Kit turned to face Jack. "I suggest that in future you rethink your lookout policy. If you order me to a position in what is obviously the wrong direction, I'll move to a more sensible place."

Jack's jaw hardened. "You'll do as you're told."

Kit lifted a condescending brow.

Jack lost a little of his calm. "Dammit – if you're on lookout and the Revenue appear, how the hell can I be certain you won't do something stupid?"

Kit's eyes blazed. "I wouldn't just run away."

"I know that! If I thought you *would* run away, I'd have no qualms about putting you on the Hunstanton side."

"You admit you've been deliberately putting me on the wrong side?"

"Christ!" Jack raked a hand through his hair. "Look – you can't unload the boats, so you may as well be our lookout. As it happens –"

"At the moment you don't actually need a lookout." Kit's tone dripped with emphasis. "Because, as you well know, the Hunstanton Revenue men have been ordered to patrol the beaches south of Hunstanton."

Jack's eyes narrowed. "How did you know that?"

Kit lifted one shoulder. "Everyone knows that."

"Who told you?"

Kit eyed Jack warily. "Spencer. He had it from the owner of the Rose and Anchor in Lynn."

The muscles in Jack's shoulders eased. She didn't have any contact within the Revenue Office. He'd been away so long, he'd forgotten how things got about in the country. "I see."

"I take it that means I won't have to stay stuck on a cliff twiddling my thumbs next time?" Kit's look dared him to disagree.

He ignored it. "What the hell else can you do?"

"I can help unload the lace," Kit stated, chin high.

"Fine," said Jack. "And what happens the first time someone hands you a keg instead? Here, take this to the sideboard." Without warning, he lifted the keg he'd brought in and handed it to her.

Automatically, Kit put out her hands to take it. Jack let go.

Jack could carry the keg under one arm. He didn't have any idea how much Kit could carry, but he didn't expect her to sink under the weight.

Kit's knees buckled. Her arms slipped about the keg as she struggled to balance the weight against her own and failed. She went down, bottom first, and the keg rolled back to flatten her. The instant before it did serious damage, Jack lifted it from her.

In awful silence, Kit lay flat on the floor and glared at Jack. Then she got her breath back. Her bound breasts, swelling in righteous indignation, fought against the constraining bands; her eyes spat purple flame. "You bastard! What kind of a stupid thing was that to do?"

Carefully, Jack set the keg back on the table. He glanced once at Kit, sprawled at his feet, then rapidly away, biting his lips against the laughter that threatened. She looked fit to kill. "Here, let me . . ." Reaching down, he grasped both her hands. Gently, he hauled her to her feet. He didn't dare meet her gaze; it was sharp enough to slice strips off him. Doubtless, her tongue soon would.

Back on her feet, Kit was agonizingly aware that a certain portion of her anatomy was very bruised. "Dammit – that hurt!"

The accusation was softened by the way her lips trembled. She frowned, and Jack felt a patent fool. He'd been trying to protect her and instead, he'd nearly squashed her to death.

"Sorry." He was halfway into an apologetic smile, designed to charm her from her anger, when he remembered what would happen if he did. She'd smile back. He could just imagine it – a small, hurt little smile. He'd be felled. "But I'm afraid that's precisely what will happen if you play the lady smuggler with me." Realizing how close to danger he stood, Jack stalked back around the table.

Kit's spine stiffened. Her fingers curled in fury. Her wilder self came to life. *Remember your alternative to smuggling thrills?*

Kit smiled at Jack and noted his defensive blink. Her smile deepened. She put her hands behind her waist and turned slightly, grimacing artistically. "How right you are," she purred. "I don't suppose you have anything here for bruises?" She let her hands press down and over the ripe curves of her bottom.

Despite years of training in the art of dissembling, Jack couldn't tear his eyes from her hands. His body made the switch from semiarousal, his usual state in Kit's presence, to aching hardness before her hands reached the tops of her thighs. His brain registered the implication in her husky tone and scrambled what few wits he had remaining. Only his instinct for self-preservation kept him rooted to the floor with the table, a last bastion, between them.

It was the silence that finally penetrated Jack's daze. He glanced up and caught a gleam suspiciously like satisfaction in the violet eyes watching him.

"Er . . . no. Nothing for bruises." He had to get her out of here.

"But you must have something," Kit said, her lids veiling her eyes. Her glance fell on the keg. Her smile grew. "As I recall, there's a rub made with brandy." She looked up to see Jack's face drain of expression.

A brandy rub? Jack's mind went into a spin. The image her words conjured up, of him applying a brandy rub to her bruised flesh, his hand stroking the warm contours he'd just watched her trace, left him rigid with the effort to remain where he was. Only the thought that she was deliberately baiting him kept him still. Slowly, he shook his head. "Wouldn't help."

Kit pouted. "Are you sure?" Her hands gently kneaded her bottom; "I'm really rather sore."

Forcibly, Jack clamped an iron hold over every muscle in his body. His fists bunched; he felt as if he had lockjaw as he forced out the words: "In that case, you'd better get on your way before you stiffen up."

Kit's eyes narrowed, then she shrugged and half turned to pick up her muffler and hat. "So I can help with the boats from now on?" She started winding the muffler about her face.

Further argument was beyond Jack, but he'd be damned if he'd let her best him like this. "We'll talk about it tomorrow." His voice sounded strained.

Kit pulled on her hat and swung about to discuss the

matter further, only to find Jack moving past her on his way to the door.

"We'll see what cargo Nolan has lined up for us. After all, you've only got a week more to go." Jack paused with his hand on the door latch and looked back, praying she'd leave.

Kit moved toward him, a considering light in her eyes, a knowing smile on her lips. "I thought you wanted two months?"

She was getting far too close. Jack drew a ragged breath and pulled open the door. "You agreed to one month, and that'll serve our purpose. No need for more." No need for further torture.

Kit paused beside him, tilting her head to look up at him from beneath the brim of her hat. "You're sure one month will be long enough?"

"Quite sure." Jack's voice had gained in strength. Encouraged, he grasped her elbow and helped her over the threshold, risking the contact in the interests of greater safety. "We'll meet here at eleven as usual. Good night."

Kit's eyes widened at his helping hand but she accepted her departure with good grace, pausing in the patch of light thrown through the open door to smile at him. "Until tomorrow, then," she purred.

Jack shut the door.

When the sound of the mare's hooves reached him, he heaved a huge sigh and slumped back against the door. He glanced at his hands, still fisted, and slowly straightened his long fingers.

A week to go. Christ – he'd be a nervous wreck by the end of it!

Pushing away from the door, he headed for the brandy keg. Before he reached it, the image of his torment, riding alone through the night, surfaced. Jack dropped his head back to stare at the ceiling and vented his displeasure in a frustrated groan. Then he went out to saddle Champion.

Chapter 13

"Well, Kathryn dear, you're our local expert. If it's to be a real masquerade, with no one knowing who anyone is, how shall we manage it?"

Lady Marchmont sipped her tea and looked inquiringly at Kit.

Acquainted with her ladyship of old, Kit hadn't imagined she'd forget her notion of a ball. It was patently clear to all in Lady Marchmont's drawing room – Lady Dersingham as well as Lady Gresham with Amy in tow – that the ball was to serve a dual purpose, winkling the elusive Lord Hendon from his castle, and introducing Kit to him. Having expected as much, Kit had given the matter due thought. A masquerade provided a number of advantages.

"For a start, we'll have to make it plain the ball is a real masquerade – not just dominos over ball gowns." Kit frowned over her teacup. "Do you think there's enough time for people to get costumes together?"

"Time aplenty." Lady Dersinghan waved one white hand dismissively. "There aren't that many of us, when all's said and done. Shouldn't be any problem. What do you think, Aurelia?"

Lady Gresham nodded. "If the invitations go out this afternoon, everyone will have a week to arrange their disguises." She smiled. "I must say, I'm looking forward to seeing what our friends come as. So revealing, to see what people fancy themselves as."

Sitting quietly on the *chaise* beside Kit, Amy shot her a glance.

Lady Marchmont reached for another scone. "We haven't had such promising entertainment in years. Such a good idea, Kathryn."

Kit smiled and sipped her tea.

"If you can't recognize anyone, how are you going to be sure none but the guests you've invited attend?" asked Lady Dersingham. "Remember the trouble the Colvilles had, when Bertrand's university chums came along uninvited? Dulcie was in tears, poor dear. They quite ruined the whole evening with their rowdiness and, of course, it took ages to discover who they were and evict them."

Neither Lady Marchmont nor Lady Gresham had any idea. The company looked to Kit.

She had her answer ready. "The invitations should have instructions about some sign the guests must present, so you can be certain only those you invited come but no guest identifies themselves beyond giving the right sign."

"What sort of sign?" asked Lady Marchmont.

"What about a sprig of laurel, in a buttonhole or in a lady's corsage?"

Lady Marchmont nodded. "Simple enough but not something anyone would guess. That should do it."

All agreed. Kit smiled. Amy raised a suspicious brow. Kit ignored it.

The ladies spent the next hour compiling the guest list and dictating the invitations to Kit and Amy, who dutifully acted as scribes. With the bundle of sealed missives handed into the butler's hands, the ladies took their leave.

Lady Dersingham had taken Kit up in her carriage; Amy and her mother had come in theirs. While they waited on the steps for the carriages to be brought around, Amy glanced again at Kit. "What are you up to?"

Her mother and Lady Marchmont were gossiping; Lady Dersingham had moved down the steps to examine a rose-bush in an urn. Kit turned to Amy. "Why do you suppose I'm up to anything?"

Her wide violet eyes failed to convince Amy of her innocence. "You're planning some devilment," Amy declared. "What?"

Kit grinned mischievously. "I've a fancy to look Lord Hendon over, without giving him the same opportunity. Be damned if I let them present me to him, like a pigeon on a platter, a succulent morsel for his delectation."

Amy considered defending their ladyships, then decided to save her breath. "What do you plan to do?"

Kit's grin turned devilish. "Let's just say that my costume will be one no one will anticipate." She eyed Amy affectionately. "I wonder if you'll recognize me?"

"I'd recognize you anywhere, regardless of what you were wearing."

Kit chuckled. "We'll find out how good your powers of observation are next Wednesday."

Amy got no chance to press Kit for details of her disguise. The carriages rounded the corner of Marchmont Hall, and she was forced to bid Kit farewell. "Come and visit tomorrow. I want to hear more of this plan of yours."

Kit nodded and waved, but her laughing eyes left Amy with the distinct impression that she did not intend to reveal more of her plans.

*

Jack stood, feet planted well apart, resisting the tug of the surf surging about his knees. He glanced at Kit, slender beside him, and prayed she didn't overbalance. Even in the shadowy night, soaked to the skin, her anatomy was sure to show its deficiencies.

The yacht they'd been waiting to board came over the next wave and slewed as the helmsman threw the rudder over. Matthew, some way to their right, steadied the prow. Kit grasped the side of the boat with both gauntleted hands and hauled herself aboard. Or tried to.

Anticipating her helplessness, Jack planted a large palm beneath her bottom and hefted her over the side. He heard her gasp as she landed on the deck in a sprawl of arms and legs. Then he remembered her bruised posterior. He grimaced and followed her. Serve her right if she felt a twitch or two. He was in constant agony with a pain she delighted in compounding.

Kit scurried to get out of Jack's way as he clambered into the yacht, glaring through the night at him once he'd arrived on her level. She'd love to give him a piece of her mind, but didn't dare open her mouth. Just being where she was had stretched the tension between them to the breaking point; she was too wise to add fuel to the fire just at present.

As far as she was concerned, tonight was a once-in-a-life-time chance, and she'd no intention of letting Jack spoil it. She'd gone with them to the Blackbird as usual on Wednesday, two nights ago. An agent had approached them with an unusual cargo – bales of Flemish cloth too unwieldy to be loaded into rowboats. To her surprise, Jack had accepted. The money on offer was certainly an incentive, but she couldn't imagine where he'd get large enough boats to do the job.

But he had – she knew better than to ask how.

She'd come to the beach tonight prepared to do battle if he dared suggest she be lookout. Although he'd eyed her with misgiving, Jack had included her in the group to go in the boats. The relief she'd felt when she'd learned she was to accompany Jack and the taciturn Matthew on board the yacht, rather than going on one of the other boats with the other men, was something she'd never admit. Its dampening effect was counteracted by her excitement over the yacht being the fastest boat in the small fleet. She'd always dreamed about sailing, but Spencer had never allowed her to indulge that particular whim.

Kit stood by the railings as the yacht cleaved through the swell. The ship they were to meet was a pinprick of light, gleaming occasionally well out in the Roads.

Jack kept his distance. He'd brought Kit along, unwilling to risk leaving her beyond his reach. Forcing his gaze from the slim figure with the old tricorne jammed over her curls he focused on their destination, a black shape on the horizon, growing larger with every crest they passed. Via Matthew, he'd already started rumors of Young Kit's difficulties in continuing as part of the Gang. The stories revolved about Kit's grandfather, unidentified, kicking up a fuss at his grandson's frequent nocturnal absences.

Young Kit's retirement could not come soon enough. Jack gritted his teeth as memories of their last evening at the Blackbird replayed in his mind. Kit had sat beside him in her usual place. But instead of keeping her distance as she'd done in the past, she'd shuffled closer, far closer than had been detectable from the other side of the table. The insistent pressure of her thigh against his had been bad enough. He'd nearly choked when he'd felt her hand on his thigh, tapered fingers stroking down the long muscle.

Luckily, she'd stopped when the agent appeared, else he'd

never have had the wits to negotiate. In fact, he doubted he'd have had the strength to resist paying her back in her own coin which, given the predilection of females for forgetting where they were and what they were doing at such times, would probably have landed them in an unholy and potentially fatal mess.

After that, he'd kept Matthew with him, a fact that had his henchman puzzled. But he'd rather face a puzzled Matthew than a female determined to bring him low in typical female fashion. She might call him a coward – as she had last night when Matthew had dutifully followed them into the cottage after the meeting at the barn – but she didn't know what type of explosive she was playing with. She'd find out soon enough. Salacious imaginings of exactly how he'd exact his retribution filled his sleepless nights.

The yacht overtook three slower, square-rigged luggers, the rest of the Hunstanton Gang's fleet, then slewed sharply to come alongside the hull of the Dutch brigantine. Matthew stood in the prow, a coiled rope in his hands. The other two crewmen brought down the sails. As the waves drifted the hulls closer, Matthew threw the rope to waiting hands. Within minutes, they were secured against the Dutchman's side.

Jack turned to the helmsman. "Lash the wheel and let the boy watch it." The man obeyed; Jack turned to see Kit already on her way midships. He grinned. Bales of cloth were not packets of lace.

They unloaded the cargo smoothly, lowering the bales on sets of ropes over the brig's side, directly into the hold of the yacht.

Her hands on the fixed wheel, Kit watched, her heart leaping when one bale swung crazily toward her, threatening to slip free of its lashings. Jack jumped onto the cabin roof directly between the wheel and the hold and steadied the large roll, reaching high with both hands and leaning his entire weight into it to counter its swing. Relief swept Kit when the bale settled; it was lowered without further drama.

The Dutch ship had been carrying a full load; at the end, each of the four smugglers' boats was fully laden, even carrying bales on deck, lashed to the railings. The entire process was accomplished in total silence. Sound traveled too well on water.

The men worked steadily, stowing the bales. Kit's mind drifted to the comment Jack had made the night before, when she'd been late for the meeting in the barn. She'd slipped unobtrusively around the door, but Jack had seen her instantly. He'd smiled and asked if she'd had trouble with her grandfather. She'd had no idea what he'd meant but had scowled and nodded, and then been astounded by the laughing understanding that had colored many of the men's faces. Later, she'd learned enough to guess that Jack had started paving her way out of the Gang. Clearly, he'd meant what he'd said about one month being more than long enough.

She'd gone on being Young Kit under duress; now, she was reluctant to part with her alias, her passport to excitement.

And you haven't had him at your feet yet, have you?

Kit eyed Jack's broad shoulders, presently directly in front of her, and fantasized about the muscles beneath his rough shirt. Before she broke with him, she was determined to convert at least some of her fantasies to reality. Thus far, the only response her tricks had brought was a general stiffening of his muscles, a clenching of his jaw. She was determined to get more than that.

A low whistle signaled that they were done. Ropes were

141

released; the smaller boats poled off from the brig's hull, drifting until they were out of the larger ship's wind shadow before hoisting their sails.

Relieved of her watch by the wheel, which had been every bit as useless as her lookout duty but infinitely more exciting, Kit strolled down the deck, heading for the bow. She'd cleared the cabin housing when the yacht passed the brig's prow and the wind caught its sails. The yacht leapt forward.

Kit screamed and just managed to stifle the sound. She was flung against the bale lashed to the railing. Her desperately groping fingers tangled in the lashings. Drawing a deep breath, she hauled herself upright.

Immediately she'd regained her feet, she heard an almighty crack, like a tree branch snapping.

"*Kit! Duck!*"

She reacted more to Jack's tone than his words, but duck she did. The boom went sailing past, level with where her head had been split seconds before. Kit stared at the long pole swinging outward over the waves, a rope dangling behind it. She grabbed the rope.

Instantly, she realized her mistake. The sudden tug on her arms was horrendous, and then she was being hauled in the wake of the boom, the wind filling the sail and causing the heavily laden yacht to list to starboard.

Kit's eyes widened in fright. She looked over the railings at the black waves and remembered she couldn't swim.

Her belly hit the bale. The next gust of wind would lift her from her feet, half over the rail. She was no expert seaman, but if she let go of the rope, the yacht looked set to capsize.

Hard hands locked about hers on the rope and hauled back. Kit added her weight to Jack's and the boom swung back. But the wind retaliated, filling the sail once more. The jerk on the rope pulled Kit hard against the bale, her arms outstretched over the railing. Jack slammed into her back.

Kit forgot the boom, the wind, the sail; forgot the waves and the fact that she couldn't swim; forgot everything but the awesome sensation of a very hard male body pressed forcibly against hers. She was jammed between the bale and Jack. She could feel the muscles in his chest shift against her as he struggled to haul in the boom. She could feel the muscles of his stomach brace into hard ridges as he used his weight to maintain their balance. She could feel the solid weight of his thighs pressed hard against her bruised bottom. On either side of her slender legs, she could feel the long columns of his legs like steel supports anchoring them to the deck, defying the wind's shrieking fury. She could also feel the hard shaft of desire that nudged into the small of her back. The discovery held her riveted.

Uninterested, was he? Found her unattractive, did he? What sort of game was he playing?

"For God's sake, woman! Lean back!"

Jack's furious whisper recalled Kit to the urgency of the situation. She dutifully added her weight to his as he drew in the boom.

Behind her, Jack was facing a conundrum unlike any he'd ever experienced. Having Kit trapped against him was pure hell. He'd give anything to be able to push her aside but didn't dare; he needed her additional weight to balance the wind in the sail. And he couldn't relax the tension on the rope long enough to wrap it about the rail.

The yacht raced before the wind, tearing through the waves. The helmsman tacked so they were driven by the wind-filled sail and were no longer in danger of capsizing.

Matthew appeared at Jack's shoulder, and shouted over the wind: "If you can hold it like that, we'll be all right."

143

Jack nodded and turned his head, intending to have Matthew replace Kit on the rope, but Matthew had already deserted him. He glared in disbelief at his henchman's retreating back.

Quite where the idea sprang from, Kit wasn't sure, but it suddenly occurred to her that Jack was every bit as trapped as she was. And, that being so, this was a perfect opportunity to further her aims in reasonable safety. She was screened from the other men by Jack's bulk. He had his hands full of rope, and he could hardly do much when the beach was only five minutes away. With a view to determining the possibilities, Kit pressed back against him.

A sharply indrawn breath just above her left ear was the result.

Her action had given her a little more room to maneuver. She wriggled her bottom, slowly, and felt a ripple of tension pass through the muscles in his thighs. The shaft rising between them was like iron, a solid but living force. Moving slowly, keeping her weight braced against the rope, Kit rubbed her body, from shoulders to hips and beyond, side to side against the man behind her.

Jack bit back an oath. He clamped his teeth over his lower lip to stifle a groan of frustration. Damn the woman! What devil possessed her wild senses to make her choose this precise moment to give him a demonstration of her potential? He could feel every undulation of her slender form, every purring stroke. She moved like a cat, sinuously against him.

The wind tugged again, and they were jammed together once more. Jack closed his eyes and forced his mind to concentrate on keeping his grip on the rope. His grip on his mind was dissolving.

Slamming into the bale knocked the breath out of Kit.

She waited, but Jack made no move to pull back. His breath wafted the curls above her left ear.

Jack was content to remain where they were. He'd no intention of giving her the leeway to continue her little game. He considered whispering a few carefully worded threats but couldn't think of anything appropriate. He'd a nasty suspicion his voice would betray him if he tried to speak at all. He set his jaw and endured, cataloging every little move she made into his ledger of account against the time, almost a week distant, when payment would fall due. He'd every intention of making sure she paid. In full. With interest.

The sight of the beach was more welcome than the cliffs of Dover had ever been. Jack saw the helmsman wave. "Let go of the rope. Slowly."

Kit did as she was told, wary of the wind-whipped sail. Jack held on until he was sure her hands were free, then he let go as well. The boom swung away, but the wheel was also swung; the yacht slewed and slowed as the wind emptied from the sail. The boom swung inboard.

Jack was watching it. He ducked, taking Kit to the deck with him. She sprawled full-length beside him.

A quick glance showed Jack that the helmsman was concentrating on his yacht while the other men, including Matthew, were busy securing the boom. The moment was too tempting to pass up.

Kit had seen the boom returning but had not been expecting Jack's hands to close so abruptly on her shoulders. The deck was hard and uncomfortable, but it was doubtless better than a broken head. She saw the men struggling to tie the wretched boom back into position and placed her hands palm down on the deck. She braced herself to rise. Instead, she froze as a large hand splayed across her bottom.

Kit stopped breathing. The hand pressed gently, moving in a slow, circular motion, then its orientation shifted. Damp heat spread over her rear. Two long fingers slipped between her thighs.

With an audible gasp, Kit shot to her knees, but that only pressed her bottom more fully into that caressing hand, leaving her more open to those intimately probing fingers.

Too shocked to think, she leaned back on her haunches. The long fingers pressed deep. Kit leapt to her feet, her face flaming.

From behind came a mocking, very male laugh. "Later, sweetheart."

Two hard hands set her aside, and Jack moved past to check the boom.

Kit escaped Jack's dangerous presence as soon as she possibly could. Furious, nervous, and shaken, she bided her time until the difficult unloading operation began. Then she sought out Matthew. "I'll go up on the cliff and keep watch."

Matthew nodded. Unaided, Kit slipped over the side of the yacht, gently bobbing on the shallow swell, and waded to shore.

On board the yacht, Jack saw her in the surf. He swore and stepped to the rails, hands on hips. "Where the hell's he going?"

Matthew was passing. "Young Kit?" When Jack nodded, he replied: "Lookout."

Matthew moved on and so missed the devilish grin that broke across Jack's face.

Was he supposed to understand she'd rather do lookout duty than stay in his vicinity? Jack felt laughter bubble up. Like hell! He'd felt her heat, even in those few minutes on the deck. She was as hot for him as he was for her, his little kitten. And soon, very soon, he was going to have her purring and arching like she'd never done before.

With an effort, Jack forced his mind back to the mundane but difficult task of unloading bales.

Kit waited only until she saw the first men leave. Then she pressed her heels to Delia's sleek sides and headed home, her face still several shades too pink. She couldn't stop dwelling on those few minutes on the deck. And on the promise in Jack's final words.

Gone was any idea that he wasn't attracted to her. Instead, her most pressing concern should doubtless be whether it wouldn't be wise never to see him again.

To Kit's consternation, her mind flatly refused to consider such an option.

At least now you know a little of what Amy meant.

Oh, God, Kit thought, *that's all I need. I can't possibly be in love with Jack. He's a smuggler.*

Memories of how she'd felt on the deck crowded her mind. Even now, the skin on her bottom felt feverish as she recalled the play of his hand. Her bruises throbbed. Her memory rolled relentlessly on, to the delicious thrill she'd experienced when his fingers had probed the soft flesh between her thighs. Kit blushed. As her memory replayed his words, her heart accelerated. What if he really meant it?

She considered the implications and swallowed.

What did he actually mean? Was he really intending to . . .?

Kit's thighs tightened, and Delia's stride lengthened alarmingly.

A mile behind Kit, Jack swung up into Champion's saddle. The last of the men had left, the cargo cleared. He turned to Matthew. "I'm going for a ride. I'll be in later."

With that, he set Champion up the cliff track, onto Delia's trail. Jack was very tired of his nocturnal rides, but he couldn't have slept, even uneasily as he did, without knowing Kit was safely home. At least he only had less than a week to go before Young Kit left the Hunstanton Gang. When they met at night after that, if she left him at all, it would be at a safer hour – one much closer to dawn.

Afternoon sunlight turned the streaks in Jack's hair to brightest gold as he sat, lounging elegantly, in the carved chair behind his desk. Huge and heavy, the desk was located before the library windows, its classic lines complementing the uncluttered bookshelves lining the walls.

Bright blue fractured light fell from Jack's signet ring onto the pristine blotter as his long fingers toyed idly with an ivory letter opener. His attire proclaimed him the gentleman but as always held a hint of the military. No one, seeing him, would find it difficult to credit that this was Lord Hendon, of Castle Hendon, the High Commissioner for North Norfolk.

A distant frown inhabited the High Commissioner's expressive eyes; his grey gaze was abstracted.

Before the desk, George wandered the room, glancing at the numerous sporting and military publications left lying on the side tables before stopping before the marble mantelpiece. A large gilt-framed mirror reflected the comforting image of a country squire's son, soberly dressed, with rather less of the striking elegance that characterized Jack, a more easygoing nature discernable in George's frank brown eyes and gentle smile.

George tweaked a gilt-edged note from the mirror frame. "I see you've got an invitation to the Marchmonts' masquerade. Are you going?"

Jack lifted his head and took a moment to grasp the question. Then he grimaced. "Pretty damned difficult to refuse. I suppose I'll have to put in an appearance." His tone accurately reflected his lack of enthusiasm. He wasn't the least interested in doing the pretty socially – smiling and chatting, careful not to overstep the mark with any of the marriageable misses, partnering them in the dances. It was all a dead bore. And, at present, his mind was engrossed with far more important concerns.

He wasn't at all sure he hadn't overstepped the mark with Kit. She hadn't come to the meeting last night, the first meeting she had missed. He'd turned the event to good account by referring to her grandfather's influence. But, deep down, he suspected it was his influence that was to blame. Why she would take exception to his caresses, explicit though they'd been, he couldn't imagine.

She was a mature woman and, although she clearly liked to play games as many women did, her actions, her movements, the strength and wildness of her response, all testified to her knowledge of how such games inevitably ended. After her actions on the yacht, and at the Blackbird, it was difficult to doubt her willingness to pursue that inevitable ending with him. But he couldn't think of any other reason why she'd have stayed away last night.

The idea that she was a tease who didn't pay up he discounted; no woman who was as hot as Kit would draw back from the culminating scene. And even if she was that sort, he'd no intention of letting her shortchange him.

"What are you going to wear?"

George's question dragged Jack's mind from his preoccupation. "Wear?" He frowned. "I must have a domino lying about somewhere."

"You haven't read this, have you?" George dropped the

invitation onto the desk. "It clearly states a proper costume is mandatory. No dominos allowed."

"Damn!" Jack read the invitation, his lip curling in disgust. "You know what this means? A string of shepherdesses and Dresden milkmaids, all either hitting you over the head with their crooks or knocking your shins with their pails."

George laughed and settled in a chair opposite the desk. "It won't be that bad."

Jack raised a cynical brow. "What are you going as?"

George flushed. "Harlequin." Jack laughed. George looked pained. "I'm told it's one of the sacrifices I must make in light of my soon-to-be-wedded state."

"Thank God I'm not engaged!" Jack stared at the invitation again. Then a slow smile, one George was well acquainted with, broke across his face.

"What are you going to do?" George asked, trepidation shading his tone.

"Well – it's perfectly obvious, isn't it?" Jack sat back, pleasurable anticipation gleaming in his eyes. "They're expecting me to turn up, disguised but still recognizable, prime fodder for their matrimonial cannons, right?"

George nodded.

"Did I tell you I've heard, from an unimpeachable source, that Lady Marchmont herself has me in her sights, for some nameless protégé?"

George shook his head.

"Well, she has. It occurs to me that if I'm to attend this event at all, it had best be in a disguise which will not be readily penetrated. If I can pull that off, I'll be able to reconnoiter the field without giving away my dispositions. I'll go as Captain Jack, pirate and smuggler, leader of the Hunstanton Gang."

George appeared skeptical. "What about your hair?"

"There's a wig of my grandfather's about somewhere. With that taken care of, I should be able to pass muster undetected, don't you think?"

At Jack's inquiring look, George nodded dully. With his hair covered, Jack's height was unusual but not distinctive. However . . . George eyed the figure behind the desk. There weren't many men in North Norfolk built like Jack, but he knew better than to quibble. Jack would do what Jack would do, regardless of such minor difficulties. The success of his disguise would depend on how observant the females of the district were. And most hadn't seen Jack in ten and more years.

"Who knows?" Jack mused. "One of these females might actually suit me."

George stared. "You mean you're seriously considering marrying?" His tone was several degrees past incredulous.

Jack waved one hand languidly, as if the subject was not of much importance. "I'll have to sometime, for an heir if nothing else. But don't get the idea I'm all that keen to follow your lead. A dashed risky business, marriage, by all accounts."

George relaxed, then took the opportunity provided by this rare allusion to a topic that Jack more normally eschewed to ask: "What sort of wife are you imagining for yourself?"

"Me?" Jack's eyes flew wide. He considered. "She'd have to be able to support the position – be acceptable as Lady Hendon and the mother of my heir and all that."

"Naturally."

"Beyond that . . ." Jack shrugged, then grinned. "I suppose it'd make life easier if she was at least passably good-looking and could string a conversation along over the breakfast cups. Aside from that, all I'd ask is that she keep out of what are purely my concerns."

"Ah," said George, looking skeptical. "Which concerns are those?"

"If you imagine I'm going to settle to monogamous wedded bliss with a woman who's only passably good-looking, you're wrong." Jack's acerbity was marked. "I've never understood all the fuss about fidelity and marriage. As far as I can see, the two don't necessarily connect."

George's lips thinned, but he knew better than to lecture Jack on that subject. "But you don't have a mistress at present."

Jack's smile was blinding. "Not just at the moment, no. But I've a candidate in mind who'll fill the position admirably." His silver-grey gaze grew distant as his thoughts dwelled on Kit's delicate curves.

George humphed and fell silent.

"Anyway," Jack said, shaking free of his reverie, "any wife of mine would have to understand she'd have no influence in such areas of my life." With Kit as his mistress, he couldn't imagine even wanting a wife. He certainly wouldn't want one to warm his bed – Kit would do that very nicely.

Chapter 14

Noise, laughter, and the distant scrape of a violin greeted Kit as she strolled up the steps of Marchmont Hall. At the door, the butler stood, sharp eyes searching each guest for the required sprig of laurel. Drawing abreast of him, Kit smiled and raised her gloved fingers to the leaves thrust through the buttonhole in her lapel.

The butler bowed. Kit inclined her head, pleased that the retainer had not recognized her. He'd seen her frequently enough in her skirts to be a reasonable test case. Confidence brimming, she sauntered to the wide double doors that gave onto the ballroom, pausing at the last to check that her plain black mask was in place, shading her eyes as well as covering her telltale mouth and chin.

As soon as she crossed the threshold, she was conscious of being examined by a large number of eyes. Her confidence wavered, then surged when no one looked more than puzzled. They couldn't place the elegant stripling, of course. Calmly, as if considering the attention only her due, Kit strolled into the crowd milling about the dance floor. She'd had Elmina recut a cast-off evening coat belonging to her cousin Geoffrey, deepest midnight blue, and had bullied her elderly maid into creating a pair of buff inexpressibles that clung to her long limbs as if molded to them. Her blue-and-gold waistcoat had once been a brocaded underskirt; it was cut long to cover the anatomical inadequacies otherwise revealed by the tight breeches. Her snowy white cravat, borrowed from Spencer's collection, was tied in a fair imitation of the Oriental style. The brown wig had been the biggest challenge; she'd found a whole trunk of them in the attic and had spent hours making her selection, then recutting the curls to a more modern style. All in all, she felt no little pride in her disguise.

Her principal objective was to locate Lord Hendon amid the guests. She'd imagined she'd find him being lionized by the local ladies, but a quick survey of the room brought no such interesting specimen to light. Lady Dersingham was by the musicians' dais, Lady Gresham was seated not far from the door, and Lady Marchmont was hovering as close as she could to the portal; all three were obviously keeping watch.

Kit grinned beneath her mask. She was one their ladyships would be keen to identify; their other prime target would be her quarry. Convinced Lord Hendon had not yet arrived, Kit circulated among the guests, keeping a weather eye on one or another of her three well-wishers at all times. She was sure they'd react when the new High Commissioner darkened the doorway.

To her mind, this opportunity to evaluate Lord Hendon was unparalleled and unlikely to be repeated. She intended to study the man behind the title, and, if the façade looked promising, to investigate further. Disguised as she was, there were any number of conversational gambits with which she could engage the new High Commissioner.

Kit glimpsed Amy in her Columbine costume at the

other end of the room and headed in that direction. She passed Spencer, talking farming with Amy's father, and carefully avoided his attention. She'd convinced him to come alone in his carriage, on the grounds that she needed to arrive without his very identifying escort to remain incognito. Thinking she meant to hoodwink Amy and their ladyships, he'd agreed readily enough, assuming that she'd use the smaller carriage. Instead, she'd ridden here on Delia. She'd never brought Delia to Marchmont Hall before, so the grooms had not recognized the mare.

The Marchmont Hall ballroom was long and narrow. Kit sauntered through the crowd, nodding here and there at people she knew, delighting in their confusion. Throughout, she kept mum. Those who knew her might recognize the husky quality of her voice and be sufficiently shrewd to think the unthinkable. She was perfectly aware her enterprise was scandalous in the extreme, but she'd no intention of being within Marchmont Hall when the time came to unmask.

As she drew closer to the musicians' raised dais, she heard them tuning their instruments.

"You there, young man!"

Kit turned and beheld her hostess bearing down on her, a plain girl in tow. Holding her breath, Kit bowed, praying her mask hadn't slipped.

"I haven't the faintest notion who you are, dear boy, but you can dance, can't you?"

Kit nodded, too relieved that Lady Marchmont hadn't recognized her to realize the wisdom of denying that accomplishment.

"Good! You can partner this fair shepherdess then."

Lady Marchmont held out the young girl's gloved hand. Smoothly, Kit took it and bowed low. "Charmed," she murmured, wondering frantically whether she could remember how to reverse the steps she'd been accustomed to performing automatically for the past six years.

The shepherdess curtsied. Behind her mask, Kit frowned critically. The girl wobbled too much – she should practice in front of a mirror.

Lady Marchmont sighed with relief and, with a farewell pat on Kit's arm, left them in search of other suitable gentlemen to pair with single girls.

To Kit's relief, the music started immediately, rendering conversation unnecessary. She and the shepherdess took their places in the nearest set and the ordeal began. By the first turn, Kit realized the cotillion was more of an ordeal for the shepherdess than herself. Kit had taught her youngest two male cousins to dance, so was acquainted with the gentleman's movements. Knowing the lady's movements by heart made it easy enough to remember and match the appropriate position. Her confidence grew with every step. The shepherdess, in contrast, was a bundle of nerves, unraveling steadily.

When, through hesitation, the girl nearly slipped, Kit spoke as encouragingly as she could: "Relax. You're doing it quite well, but you'll improve if you don't tense so."

A strained smile that was more like a grimace was her reward.

With an inward sigh, Kit set herself to calm the girl and instill a bit of confidence. She succeeded sufficiently well for the shepherdess to smile normally by the end of the measure and thank her effusively.

From the other side of the room, Jack surveyed the dancers: He'd arrived fifteen minutes earlier, rigged out in his "poor country squire togs," a black half mask and a brown tie wig. For the first three minutes, all had gone well. After that, the

156

evening had headed downhill. First, Lord Marchmont had recognized him, how he'd no idea. His host had immediately borne him off to present him to his wife. Unfortunately, she'd been standing with three other local ladies. He was now on nodding terms with the ladies Gresham, Dersingham, and Falworth.

Lady Marchmont had iced his cake with an arch pronouncement that she'd "someone" she most particularly wished him to meet. He'd suppressed a shudder, intensified by the gleam he saw in the other ladies' eyes. They were all in league to leg-shackle him to some damn drab. Sheer panic had come to his rescue. He'd charmed his way from their sides and gone immediately in search of refreshment, remembering just in time to redevelop his limp. At least it provided an excuse not to dance. Strong liquor was what he'd needed to regain his equilibrium. Matthew had gone alone to the Blackbird, to line up their next cargo. Jack wished he was with him, with a tankard of their abominable home brew in front of him.

In the alcove off the ballroom where the drinks were set forth, he'd come upon George, a decidedly glum Harlequin. At sight of him, he'd uttered a hoot of laughter, for which George repaid him with a scowl.

"I know it looks damn stupid, but what could I do?"

"Call off the engagement?"

George threw him a withering look, then added: "Not that I'm not sure it constitutes sufficient cause."

Jack thumped him on the shoulder. "Never mind your troubles – mine are worse."

George studied the grim set of his lips. "They recognized you?"

Reaching for a brandy, Jack nodded. "Virtually immediately. God only knows what gave me away."

George opened his mouth to tell him but never got the chance.

"Christ Almighty!" Jack choked on his brandy. Abruptly, he swung away from the ballroom. "What the bloody hell's Kit doing here?"

Frowning, George looked over the guests. "Where?"

"Dancing, would you believe! With a shepherdess in pale pink – third set from the door."

George located the slender youth dipping through the last moves of the cotillion. "You sure that's Kit?'

Jack swallowed his "Of course I'm damned sure, I'd know her legs anywhere" and substituted a curt, "Positive."

George studied the figure across the room. "A wig?"

"And his Sunday best," said Jack, risking a quick glance at the ballroom. The last thing he wanted was for Kit to see him. If the Lord Lieutenant could recognize him immediately, it was certain Kit would. But she knew him as Captain Jack.

"Maybe Spencer brought him?"

"Like hell! More likely the young devil decided to come and see how the other half lives."

George grinned. "Well, it's safe enough. He'll just have to leave before the unmasking and no one will be any the wiser."

"But *he'll* be a whole lot wiser if he sets eyes on either you or me."

George's indulgent smile faded. "Oh."

"Indeed. So how do we remove Kit from this charming little gathering without creating a scene?"

They both sipped their brandies and considered the problem. Jack kept his back to the room; George, far less recognizable in his Harlequin suit, maintained a watchful eye on Kit.

158

"He's left his partner and is moving down the room."

"Is your fiancée here?" Jack asked. "Can you get her to take a note to Kit?"

George nodded. Jack pulled out a small tablet and pencil. After a moment's hesitation, he scribbled a few words, then carefully folded and refolded the note. "That should do it." He handed the square to George. "If I'm not back by the time for unmasking, make my excuses."

Jack put his empty glass back on the table and turned to leave.

Appalled, George barred the way. "What the hell should I say? This ball was all but organized for you."

Jack smiled grimly. "Tell them I was called away to deal with a case of mistaken identity."

Disentangling herself from the shepherdess's clinging adoration, Kit beat a hasty retreat, heading for the corner where she'd last seen Amy. When she got there, Amy was nowhere in sight. Drifting back along the room, Kit kept a wary eye out for the shepherdess and Lady Marchmont.

In the end, it was Amy who found her.

"Excuse me."

Kit swung about – Amy's Columbine mask met her eyes. Beneath her own far more concealing mask, Kit smiled in delight and bowed elegantly.

She straightened and saw a look of confusion in Amy's clear eyes.

"I've been asked to deliver this note to you – *Kit!*"

Kit grabbed Amy's arm and squeezed it warningly. "Keep your voice down, you goose! What gave me away?"

"Your eyes, mostly. But there was something else – something about your height and size and the way you hold your hands, I think." Amy's gaze wandered over Kit's sartorial

159

perfection, then dropped to the slim legs perfectly revealed by the clinging knee breeches and clocked stockings. "Oh, Kit!"

Kit felt a twinge of guilt at Amy's shocked whisper. "Yes, well, that's why no one must know who I am. And for goodness sake, don't color up so, or people will think I'm making improper suggestions!"

Amy giggled.

"And you can't take my arm, either, or come too close. Please think, Amy," Kit pleaded, "or you'll land me in the suds."

Amy dutifully tried to remember that Kit was a youth. "It's very hard when I've known you all my life and know you're not a boy."

"Where's this note?" Kit lifted the small white square from Amy's palm and unfolded it. She read the short message three times before she could believe her eyes.

Kit, Meet me on the terrace as soon as possible. Jack

"Who gave you this?" Kit looked at Amy.

Amy looked back. George had impressed on her she was not to tell the slim youth who had given her the note – but did George know the slim youth was Kit? She frowned. "Don't you know who it's from?"

"Yes. But I wondered who gave it to you – did you recognize him?"

Amy blinked. "It was passed on. I don't have any idea who wrote it." That, at least, was the truth.

Too caught up in the startling discovery that Jack was somewhere near, probably among the guests, Kit missed the less than direct nature of Amy's answer. Forgetting her own instructions, she put a hand on Amy's arm. "Amy, you must promise you'll tell no one of my disguise."

Amy promptly reassured her on that score.

"And I won't, of course, be here for the unmasking. Can you tell Lady Marchmont – and Spencer, too – that I was here, but that I felt unwell and returned home? Tell Spencer I didn't want to spoil his evening." Kit grinned wryly; if she stayed for the unmasking, she'd definitely ruin Spencer's night.

"But what about the note?" asked Amy.

"Oh, that." Kit stuffed the white paper into her pocket. "It's nothing. Just a joke – from someone else who recognized me."

"Oh." Amy eyed Kit and wondered. The male disguise was almost perfect – if she'd had such difficulty recognizing Kit, who else would?

"And now, Amy dearest, we must part or people will start to wonder."

"You won't do anything scandalous, will you?"

Kit repressed the urge to give Amy a hug. "Of course, I won't. Why, I'm doing everything possible to avoid such an outcome." With a twinkle in her eye, Kit bowed.

With a look that stated she found the act of attending a ball in male attire inconsistent with avoiding scandal, Amy curtsied and reluctantly moved away.

Kit took refuge behind a large palm by the side of the ballroom. Caution dictated she avoid Jack whenever possible, but was it possible? Or wise? If she didn't appear on the terrace, he was perfectly capable of appearing in the ballroom, by her side, in a decidedly devilish mood. No – it was the lesser of two evils, but the terrace it would have to be. After all, what could he possibly do to her on the Lord Lieutenant's terrace?

She scanned the crowd, studying men of Jack's height. There were a few who fit that criterion, but none was Jack. She wondered what mad start had brought him to the ball.

Unobtrusively, she made her way to where long windows opened onto the terrace that ran the length of the house.

The night air was crisp, refreshing after the stuffiness of the close-packed humanity within. Kit drew a deep breath, then looked about her. On the terrace, he'd said, but where on such a long terrace?

There were a few couples taking the air. None spared a glance for the slim youth in the midnight blue coat. Kit strolled the flags, looking at the sky, ostensibly taking a breather from the bustle inside. Then she saw Jack, a dim shadow sitting on the balustrade at the far end.

"What the hell are you doing here?" she hissed as she drew near. He was sitting with his back propped against the wall, one booted foot swinging.

Jack, who had watched her approach, was taken aback. "What am I doing here? What the devil are you doing here, you dim-witted whelp?"

Kit noted the dangerous glitter in the eyes watching her through the slits in his simple black mask. She put up her chin. "That's none of your affair. And I asked first."

Under his breath, Jack swore. He hadn't given his excuse for being at the ball a single thought, so fixated had he been on the necessity of removing Kit from this place of revelations. "I'm here for the same reason you are."

Kit bit back a laugh. The idea of Jack, in disguise, looking over a potential bride from among the local gentry was distinctly humorous. "How did you recognize me?"

Jack's lips twisted in a mocking smile. "Let's just say I'm particularly well acquainted with your manly physique."

Kit's chin rose along with her blush. "What did you want to see me about?"

Jack blinked. What the hell did she imagine he wanted to see her about? "I wanted to make sure that, having now

162

seen how the other half comports itself, you'll realize the wisdom of making yourself scarce, before someone stumbles on your identity."

Behind her mask, Kit's frown was black. The man was insufferable. Who did he think he was, to hand her thinly veiled orders? "I'm perfectly capable of taking care of myself, thank you."

Her clipped tone convinced Jack she was not about to take his suggestion to heart. With an exasperated sigh, he got to his feet. "What sort of chaos do you think you'd cause if that wig slipped loose during one of the dances?" Jack took a step toward her but stopped when she backed away. A quick glance along the terrace revealed a single couple, physically entwined, at the opposite end.

Kit considered insisting Jack sit down again but doubted he'd oblige. He was very good at giving orders and highly resistant to taking any. And in the moonlight on the terrace, his height and bulk were intimidating. Particularly when she didn't want to do what he clearly wanted her to do. She took another step back.

"The ball's over for you, Kit. Time to go home."

Kit took a third step back, then judged the distance between them sufficient to allow her to say: "I've no intention of leaving yet. The person –"

Her words were cut off when Jack's hand clamped over her mouth. In the same instant, his other arm wrapped about her waist and lifted her from her feet. She hadn't even seen him move yet he was now behind her, carrying her to the balustrade. Kit struggled frantically to no effect.

Jack sat on the balustrade, Kit held on his lap, then rolled over the edge. He landed upright in the flower bed six feet below the terrace, Kit safe before him.

Seething with fury, Kit waited for him to release her.

163

When he did, she spun on him. "You misbegotten oaf! How dare you –"

To her surprise, a large hand helped her spin until she was facing away from him again. Her words were cut off again, this time by her own mask, untied, folded then retied over her mouth. Kit's scream of rage was muffled by the black felt. She turned about again, her hands automatically reaching for the mask to drag it away, but Jack moved with her, remaining behind her. He caught her hands in his, his long fingers closing viselike about her wrists, pulling them down and behind her. In stunned disbelief, Kit felt material, Jack's neckerchief most probably, tighten about her wrists, securing them behind her back. Her temper exploded in a series of protests, none of which made it past the gag.

Jack appeared before her. Through the slits in his mask. his eyes gleamed. "You should be on your most ladylike behavior at a ball, you know."

Another volley of muffled protests greeted the sally. With a chuckle, Jack stooped; suddenly, Kit found herself looking down on Lady Marchmont's ruined petunias from a height of four feet. With Kit hoisted over his shoulder like a sack of potatoes, her legs secured under one muscular arm, Jack headed away from the house. Kit's muffled grumbles ceased abruptly when he ran his free hand over the ripe curves of her bottom, nicely positioned for his attentions. A fraught silence ensued. Giving the firm mounds a fond pat, Jack grinned and strode on.

He headed into the shrubbery at the end of the lawn. Taking a path enclosed by high hedges, he cast about for a niche to stow his booty. The walk ended in a fan-shaped bay just beyond the intersection with two other paths. A stone bench with a carved back stood in the bay. Behind it, between the curved hedge and the bench back, Jack found the perfect place to leave his unwilling companion.

Before he lowered Kit, he undid his belt, wrapped it about her knees, and cinched it tight. Then he shrugged her off his shoulder and into his arms.

Kit glared up into his face, silently fuming, her brain seething with the epithets she wished she could hurl at him.

Jack grinned and sat her on the bench. He pulled off his mask and tucked it into his pocket. "I'll have to leave you while I arrange our transportation. How did you get here? You may as well tell me – I'll find out soon enough."

Kit stared back at him.

Jack guessed. "Delia?"

Reluctantly, Kit nodded. A look in the stable would tell him as much.

"Right."

Jack picked her up, and Kit realized just where he was going to leave her. She struggled and shook her head violently, but Jack took no notice. Then she was laid out, full-length on her side, in the shadowy recess behind the bench.

Jack leaned over her. "If you keep quiet, no one will disturb you."

What about spiders? was Kit's agonized thought. She put every ounce of pleading she possessed into her eyes, but Jack didn't notice.

Unperturbed, he added: "I'll be back soon." Then he disappeared from sight.

Kit lay still and pondered her state. Disbelief was her predominant emotion. She was being kidnapped! Kidnapped from the Lord Lieutenant's ball by a man she wasn't at all sure she could trust. He thought she'd muff her lines and bring disaster on her head and, in typically high-handed fashion, had decided to remove her for her own good. There was no doubt in her mind that was how Jack saw it; his actions didn't really surprise her. What did worry her, what was looming as a potential source of panic in her brain, was what he intended doing with her.

Where was he taking her? And what would he do when they got there?

Such questions were not conducive to lying calmly in the dark while being kidnapped. That knowing hand on her bottom had sent a most peculiar thrill all the way to her toes.

In an effort to quell her rising hysteria, Kit forced herself to consider why Jack had been present at the ball. He'd said for the same reason as she. Presumably he'd meant he was here for a lark, just to see how the nobs lived. She could imagine he might do that, just for a laugh – the smugglers' leader at the Lord Lieutenant's ball.

In the shadows before the stable, Jack paused to take stock. Only two grooms sat in the puddle of light thrown by a lamp just inside the open door. The visiting coachmen, his own thankfully included, would be in the kitchen, enjoying themselves. All he had to do was pray that the groom who'd relieved Kit of Delia wasn't one of the two left to mind the stables.

"You two! My horse, quickly." Jack strode forward, habitual command coloring his words.

"Your horse, sir?" The men rose to their feet uncertainly.

"Yes, my horse, dammit! The black Arab."

"Yes sir. Right away, sir."

The alacrity with which the two scrambled up and made their way down the boxes told Jack his prayers had been answered. Delia, however, did not approve of the fumbling attempts of the grooms to saddle her. Jack pushed past them. "Here. Let me."

He'd handled Delia often enough for her to accept his ministrations. As soon as she was saddled, Jack led her to the yard. With a last prayer that Delia would not balk at carrying his weight and the grooms would not notice the stirrups were too short for him, Jack swung into the saddle.

The gods were smiling. Delia sidled and snorted but responded to the rein. With a dismissive nod to the grooms, Jack cantered her out of the yard. As soon as he was out of sight of the stables, he turned the mare toward the shrubbery.

The first intimation Kit had that she was not alone was a soft giggle, followed by a low, feminine moan. She froze. An instant later, silk skirts rustled as a woman sank onto the stone bench.

"Darling! You really are *too* impetuous." The unknown female was a shady figure, the moonlight fitfully glinting on blond curls and bare shoulders.

"Impetuous?" A man sat beside the woman. His tone suggested pique, rather than pride. "How would you describe your own behavior, making sheep's eyes at that devil Hendon?"

Kit's brows rose. *Devil?*

"Really, Harold! How common. I was doing no such thing. You're just jealous."

"Jealous?" Harold's voice rose.

"Yes, jealous," came the reply. "Just because Lord Hendon's got the most *wonderful* shoulders."

"I don't think it was the man's *shoulders* that impressed you, my dear."

"Don't be crude, Harold." A pause ensued, broken by the

woman. "Mind you, I daresay Lord Hendon's equally impressive in other departments."

A growl of frustration came from Harold, and the two silhouettes above Kit fused.

Kit lay in her nook and tried to ignore the snuffles and slurps and funny little moans that came from the couple on the bench. It was enough to put anyone off the business for life. She turned to a contemplation of the new vision of Lord Hendon that was forming in her mind. Perhaps she'd been hasty in thinking him a fusty old crock. Certainly, a devil with impressive shoulders and equally impressive other parts did not fit the image she'd constructed. And the woman on the bench sounded as if she had the experience to know of what she spoke.

Perhaps she should give Lord Hendon a closer look. That had, after all, been her aim in coming to the ball, even if she hadn't had much hope of him then. Now – who knew? But Jack would soon be back, determined to take her away. Recalling that she'd yet to satisfy herself as to where Jack was taking her, Kit tested the bonds at her wrists. They gave not at all. She could moan and attract the attention of the couple on the bench, assuming she could make them understand it was not them doing the moaning, but the idea of the explanations she'd face defeated that thought.

Really, if there was any justice in the world, Lord Hendon would stumble upon her and rescue her from Jack and his altogether frightening propensities. Resigned, Kit stared at the small section of sky she could see and wished the couple on the bench would go away.

"Who's that coming?" The woman's voice held a note of panic.

"Where?" The same panic echoed in Harold's tone.

"From the side. See – there."

A long pause ensued. All three figures in the alcove held their breath. Then, "Dammit! It's Hendon." Harold rose and drew the woman to her feet.

"Perhaps we ought to wait for him – he might be lost."

Harold snorted in disgust. "All you females are the same. You'd crawl all over him if he gave you half a chance. But we can't let him catch us together, and how would you explain being here alone? Come on!"

The two figures departed, and Kit was alone.

Lord Hendon was close, but she couldn't even get to her feet. The chances of anyone walking up and looking over the back of the bench to find her were negligible. Kit closed her eyes in exasperation and swore beneath her gag.

Two minutes later, the hedge rustled. Kit opened her eyes to see Jack leaning over her. He lifted her from her bed, then propped her against his hip and bent down to undo his belt. Her legs free, Kit sank onto the bench.

While Jack replaced his belt, Kit stared about her, looking down each of the three paths leading from the bench. Where had Lord Hendon gone?

"Who are you looking for?" Jack asked, puzzled by her obvious search.

Kit glared at him.

With a lopsided grin, Jack reached for the ties of her mask.

Freed of her gag, Kit moistened her lips and glanced around once more. "There was a couple here, sitting on the bench. They left a few minutes ago because they saw Lord Hendon coming. Did you see him?"

Jack's stomach muscles clenched. He shook his head slowly and answered truthfully, "No. I didn't see him." What was it that made him so easy to recognize? The wig covered his hair and he hadn't even been limping.

He watched as Kit glanced around again. What was her interest in Lord Hendon? Had she heard the descriptions and been tantalized? Jack hid a smirk. If that was so, it might make telling her the truth later much easier. Taking her arm, he drew her to her feet. "Come on. I've got Delia"

They walked through the extensive shrubbery, Jack's hand on Kit's elbow. He didn't release her hands – he didn't fancy finding out what retribution she might visit on him if she had the chance.

Kit walked beside him, her insides in a most peculiar knot. The hold on her arm was proprietory, a feeling intensified by the fact that her hands were still tied. She didn't bother asking to be untied. He'd do it if he wished, and she wasn't going to give him the joy of refusing her.

Delia was tethered to a branch just beyond the last hedge. Jack walked Kit to the mare's side, then, to her relief, stepped behind her and untied her hands.

Her relief was short-lived. He untied only one hand, then brought both in front of her and lashed them together again.

"What on earth . . .?" Kit's incredulous protest hung in the dark.

"You can't ride with your hands tied behind you."

"I can't ride with my hands tied, period."

Jack's lips quirked. "You didn't think I was going to put you on Delia and let you loose, did you?"

Kit swallowed. She hadn't thought that, no. But she wasn't at all sure what he was going to do.

"If I did," Jack continued, untying Delia's reins, "you'd be back at the ball as fast as Delia can go."

Kit could hardly deny that; she kept silent.

Jack pulled off his wig and stuffed it in the saddle pocket. "Up you go." The mare's reins in his hand, he lifted Kit up.

Kit swung her leg over and settled, then realized the stirrups had been lengthened. She stared at Jack. "We can't both ride – she'll never handle the weight."

"She will. We won't get above a canter, if that. Shift forward."

For an instant, Kit stared mutinously at him, but when he planted his foot in the stirrup, she realized that if she didn't do as he said, she'd be squashed. Slammed from behind – again. Even so, although she moved forward until the pommel pressed into her belly, it was a tight fit. Delia sidled but accepted them both. Jack, with his far greater weight, sank into the saddle seat proper and settled his feet in the stirrups. He lifted her, then resettled her against him a more comfortable position but one every bit as unnerving as she'd feared.

Jack touched the mare's sides and Delia set off. Kit was too fine a rider for him to risk letting her have her feet in the stirrups. Which meant he'd have to endure her curves, riding in front of him, moving against him with every stride the mare took.

Within minutes, his patience was under threat. His jaw ached, a dull echo of the far more potent ache throbbing in his loins. The rubbing rhythm of Kit's firm bottom transformed mere arousal to rock-hard rigidity and reduced his resolution to almost nothing. Jack gritted his teeth harder; there was nothing else he could do. She was an itch he couldn't yet scratch.

Which, for a confirmed rake, was an agonizingly painful predicament.

Chapter 15

In the dark, Kit blushed and wished her mask was still on. With every step Delia took, the rigid column of Jack's manhood pressed into her back. No thought of teasing him entered her head. Instead, she fervently prayed he wouldn't think of teasing *her*. In a fever of irritation at an opportunity lost – when would she get a chance to size up Lord Hendon again? – compounded by the inevitable effect of Jack so close and her consequent fear of what might transpire, Kit fidgeted, wriggled, and squirmed in a hopeless endeavor to move farther away from him. "Damn it, woman, stay still!" Jack's growl was every bit as intimidating as the pressure in her back. Kit froze, but within seconds she was uncomfortable again. She had to get her mind off the physical plane. "Where are we going?" They were skirting Marchmont Hall in a northwesterly direction; they could be headed anywhere.

"Cranmer."

"Oh."

Jack frowned. Was that disappointment he heard in her husky voice? Perhaps he should change his plans and take her to the cottage instead. Was she ready to give over her games and take him on? The last question dampened his ardor. Despite her relative calm, he didn't think she was particularly pleased at being removed from the ball. A few more nights would dim the memory sufficiently. Two nights, to be precise.

Kit tried to stay still, but her mind wouldn't let go of the fascinating subject of Jack's anatomy. She wondered if Lord Hendon was better equipped and wished the woman in the shrubbery had been more explicit. Her own experience in the matter was all but nonexistent. But the insistent pressure in the small of her back provoked the most intense speculation.

Luckily for her peace of mind, recollection of Lord Hendon, that unattained object of her daringly scandalous escapade, rekindled her ire. Her brilliandy conceived and faultlessly executed plan to gain firsthand knowledge of his elusive lordship was ending in ignominious retreat, before her quarry had even been sighted. The thought lowered Kit's spirits dramatically. For a full mile, she sat engulfed in a mood perilously close to a petulant sulk.

Jack was taking her home. Gratitude was not the predominant emotion coursing through her veins. What right had he to interfere?

Abruptly, Kit sat bolt upright. No matter what rationale he gave, Jack had no right to meddle in her affairs. Yet here she was, being taken home like a wayward child who'd been caught watching the adults at play. And she'd let him! What was the matter with her? She'd never let anyone, even Spencer, treat her with such high-handedness.

"You really are an arrogant swine!" she exclaimed.

Jerked from salacious dreams, Jack didn't trust his ears. "I beg your pardon?"

"You heard me. If you had any real concern for my welfare, you'd turn Delia around this instant and take me back to the ball. Only now it's too late," Kit ended lamely. "There won't be enough time before the unmasking."

"Time for what?" Jack was puzzled. If she hadn't gone to the ball for a lark, what possible reason could she have?

"I wanted to meet someone – to see what he's like – but you kidnapped me before I got the chance!"

The aggrieved note in Kit's voice was genuine enough to touch a chord of sympathy. And awaken Jack's curiosity.

"You were waiting for a man? Who?"

Beneath her breath, Kit swore. Damn! How had that slipped out?

Despite her surge of temper-assisted courage, Kit hadn't lost her wits. "Never mind – no one you'd know."

"Try me."

Kit's senses pricked. Jack's deep voice was rapidly developing that tone of command she found particularly difficult to resist. "I assure you he's someone with whom you're definitely *not* on a first-name basis."

Jack's attention had focused dramatically. What man had Kit been waiting for and, more importantly, why? What reason could a woman of her ilk have for looking over a man incognito? The answer was so glaringly obvious that Jack wondered why he hadn't thought of it the instant he'd laid eyes on her in the ballroom. Kit, more than twenty if experience was any guide, had recently returned from London where doubtless her life had been rather fuller. Particulariy with respect to male company. She had no lover at present – a fact he'd bet his entire estate on – and was on the lookout for a local candidate. Obviously, she had someone in mind. Someone other than himself.

Then her preoccupation in the shrubbery flooded his

mind with a radiant light. "You were waiting for Lord Hendon."

At the bald statement, Kit pulled a horrendous face. "What if I was? It's no concern of yours."

Hysterical laughter bubbled behind Jack's lips; manfully, he swallowed it. Christ – this mission was descending into farce! Should he tell her? What if she didn't believe him? A strong possibility, he had to admit, and one he couldn't readily overcome. *Convincing* her might jeopardize his mission. *Telling* her might jeopardize his mission. Hell! He was going to have to convince her he was a better lover than his reputation made him out to be.

A sudden vision of what his fate might have been, if he hadn't been previously acquainted with Kit and had remained at the ball, threatened his composure. Reappearing in North Norfolk as himself looked set to be even more dangerous than assuming the guise of a smugglers' leader. The local ladies were stalking him with a venegance – on both sides of the blanket. He could have ended with Kit as his mistress and Lady Marchmont's drab protégé as a wife!

Jack's eyes narrowed. There was every possibility that scenario would still come to pass, but it would be on his terms, not theirs.

A disgusted snort brought his attention back to the slight figure before him. He felt the warmth radiating from her body, separated from his by a handbreadth. Only by exercising the most severe discipline had he resisted the temptation to pull her back against him, curving her body into his.

"Thanks to you, I'll probably never get another chance!" Disgruntled, Kit shifted and immediately remembered what was pressing against her back. Her temper overcame her maidenly reticence. "Damn it! Can't you stop that? Make it go away or something?"

She twisted about to try and get a look at the offending article. Jack's hands clamped about her shoulders and forcibly restrained her.

There was a distinct edge to his words. "There is a way to make it go away. If you don't sit still, you'll be providing it."

The raw desire in his voice petrified Kit into abject obedience. Inwardly, she railed. What was it about Jack that gave him this strange power over her? Not even the most ardent of London's rakes had made her feel like mesmerized prey about to be devoured, inch by slow inch. Her skin was alive, nerve endings flickering in fevered anticipation. He was her predator; every time he threatened, she froze. As if immobility could protect her from his strike! Her instinctive response was so illogical, she'd have laughed if she could have eased the knots in her stomach long enough to do so.

Jack stared at the back of Kit's wig, his frown only partly due to physical discomfort. He could hardly miss the effect his words had had – Kit sat as rigid as a poker, all her alluring warmth gone, an icily disapproving aura cloaking her slender frame. Inwardly, he swore. He wished she'd stop vacillating – first hot, then cold; steamy one minute, frigid the next. Every time he alluded to their inevitable intimacy, she pokered up. Maidenly virtue was certainly not the cause. Which left the irritating conclusion that her strange behavior was her idea of playing vixenish games.

Jack's eyes narrowed. "A word of advice – if you wish to secure Lord Hendon as your protector" – what a joke – she was going to have him as her protector regardless – "you'd be better served by curbing your hoity ways, dropping your manipulative playacting and relying on your *beaux yeux* to take the trick."

Kit's jaw dropped.

It wasn't the shock of why he thought she was interested in Lord Hendon that held her in raging silence – after her initial surprise that struck her as exquisitely funny. But that he had the nerve to suggest the effect he had on her was assumed, presumably to attract him, to suggest that she was *manipulative*, sent her temper into orbit. Her larynx seized; her fingers curled into claws. She'd seen manipulative females aplenty in London – tizzy, dim-witted women with more hair than wit. And she'd laughed over their theatrical and frequently transparent antics with her cousins. To be classed with their kind was the lowest form of insult.

"My manipulative propensities?" she inquired silkily, as soon as she'd regained control of her voice. Her tone would have sent Spencer for the brandy, but Jack had yet to experience her temper unleashed. "That, my good man, is certainly a case of the pot calling the kettle black."

My good man? Jack's scowl was as black as the night sky. "What the devil do you mean by that?" Had he said hoity? The damned woman ought to be on the stage. Now she was pulling rank on him like a bloody duchess!

To Kit's ears, Jack's growl was pure music. She was spoiling for an argument with him, infuriatingly arrogant oaf that he was. "I mean," she said, enunciating carefully, "it hasn't escaped my notice that anytime I'm in danger of winning a point, you wield that . . . that thing between your legs like a bloody sword of Damocles!"

Jack choked. "Winning points? Is that what you call your little exhibition on the yacht the other night?"

Kit shrugged. "That was just curiosity."

"*Curiosity?*" Jack hauled on the reins and brought Delia to a halt. "When you'd been waggling your tail at me for weeks?"

"*Oh!*" Kit shifted about to half face him. "I only did that because you were acting like a solid lump of cold stone. And you call *me* manipulative? Huh!"

Jack had had enough. How could he argue when all she had to do to demolish his arguments was wiggle her hips? He swung his leg over Delia's neck, taking Kit's along with it. Together, they slid to the ground.

Kit shook off his restraining hand and rounded on him. "When it comes to being manipulative, I'm a babe in the woods compared to you! You pretended to be totally indifferent to me, just so I'd feel piqued enough to try to capture your interest. I'm not manipulative – you are!"

Her accusation passed Jack by. One of her phrases had lodged in his brain, overwhelming it, obscuring all rational thought.

"Indifferent?" Jack stared at her. How the hell did she think he could possibly *pretend* to be indifferent to her? He hurt like hell, and she accused him of . . . He reached for her hands, still bound together with his neckerchief. "Does *that* feel indifferent?"

Kit's gasp at her first overt contact with an aroused male member never made it past her lips. Fascination smothered it. Between her hands, Jack's manhood pulsed, radiating heat through the corded stuff of his breeches. It felt hard, ridged, and curiously alive. Involuntarily, her slender fingers curled around it.

It was Jack who gasped. Unprepared for the outcome of his wild and undisciplined action, let alone her totally unexpected response, he closed his eyes and let his head fall back, hands fisting at his sides while he fought for control. In dawning wonder, Kit glanced up and saw the effect of her touch. Maidenly modesty did not rear its head as, her eyes straining to catch any change in his expression, she slowly slid her fingers up the long shaft until her questing fingertips found the smooth, rounded head.

She heard Jack's breath catch, saw the tension that already held him tighten its grip. His breathing faltered. Instinctively, she reversed direction, following the rigid rod down to its source amid flesh much softer. Her fingers discovered the round fruit within the soft pouches; she felt them tighten.

The groan Jack gave delighted her, thrilled her. Then he moved.

Jack gripped her shoulders between his hands. His mouth found hers unerringly, all manner of wildness unleashed by her bold touch. One arm slid around her back to gather her to him. The other hand slid into her curls, dislodging her wig. It fell to the ground, a pool of shadow in the moonlight, ignored by them both.

For the life of him, Jack couldn't regain control. Years of rakish plunder had hardened his heart; he was always in control of his senses, not the other way around. But her blatant yet oddly innocent touch had reached deep, to find something buried beneath layers of sophistication and stroke it to life, something buried so long ago he'd forgotten how it felt to be totally consumed by passion.

Urgency coursed through his veins. Experience told him the woman in his arms was far from the same state. He bent his considerable talents to rectifying the situation.

Kit was stunned. She couldn't move; her arms were trapped between their bodies, her hands still pressed intimately against him. But she'd forgotten all that. Her lips were on fire. And the heat came from him. She tried to appease the demand in the hard, hot lips pressed to hers; her lips softened but that wasn't enough. Then his tongue flicked along the swollen contours, and she shuddered and yielded the prize he sought.

She expected to be revolted, as she had been before. Instead, as his tongue stroked hers, flames flickered to life, warming her from within. His slow, sensuous plundering of her mouth shook her, draining the strength from her limbs. She wanted desperately to hang on to him but couldn't.

Totally engrossed in her responses, Jack sensed her need. He raised his head and thanked heaven for instinct. Distracted by their argument, he hadn't paid any attention to their direction, yet he'd stopped Delia beneath the spreading branches of a tree, shielded from any chance observer. Disengaging from Kit, he stepped back, lifting her tied hands around his neck. He straightened and pulled her hard against him.

Kit had no time for thought. No sooner had she been released than she was trapped again, this time breast to chest, pressed firmly against Jack from shoulder to thigh. His lips recaptured hers, and his tongue took up where it had left off, frazzling her defenses.

Defenses? What a joke! Her head was swimming, but her body seemed alive. Alive as it had never been before. Kit felt Jack's arms ease from about her and wondered at the warping of her senses. She couldn't see, she couldn't hear. She couldn't have strung two coherent words together. But she could certainly feel. His large hands came to rest just behind her shoulders. For one unnerving moment, she thought he intended to end the kiss. A shudder of relief ran through her as his palms swept her back, down over her waist, tracing her curves with authority. When his hands cradled her bottom, her fevered flesh burned.

With a low growl of satisfaction, Jack shifted his hold and lifted her, taking two steps to set her back against the trunk of the tree, bringing her head level with his. He let her slide slowly down until her feet just touched the ground, one of his thighs wedged firmly between hers.

Fire raged through Kit, leaving her scorched, parched, thirsty. Her lips clung to his, as if the passion in his kiss was her only salvation. Little rivers of flame ran through her veins, pooling in liquid fire between her thighs. She pressed her thighs hard against the muscular column between them but could find, no relief. The flames flared briefly, then faded to a glow.

Then Jack's lips left hers. Too weak to complain, she let her head fall back, surprised at the soft moan that escaped her.

"Breathe out."

Without thought, Kit complied.

"More."

With a deft wiggle, Jack freed Kit's breasts from their bands. Her startled gasp was cut off as his lips returned to hers. Her mouth opened to his penetration, a honey-sweet cavern yielded like an offering. He might be in the grip of a raging lust unlike any other he'd ever experienced, but he still took time to savor her while his hands freed her shirt from the waistband, pushing the sides of her coat and waistcoat wide apart, baring her breasts for his ministrations. When his hand closed about one delectable globe, he felt a shudder of pure pleasure pass through her and knew she was his.

Kit was entirely beyond thought, her mind overwhelmed with feeling. Jack's confident possession of her breast brought a murmur of denial to her lips, but he ignored it. She ignored it, too, as his fingers sought her tightening nipple and caressed it to aching hardness. He seemed to know just what her flesh required, far more certainly than she did. When he turned his attention to her other breast, she pressed the soft mound into his palm, seeking relief from the driving need for satisfaction.

Jack drew back slightly, the better to view his conquests. The ivory skin of her breasts sheened like silk beneath his hands; it felt like satin. The rosy peaks were tight little nubs, dusky against the ivory. She had beautiful breasts, not overly large but firm and perfectly rounded. One strawberry-tipped peak beckoned; he dipped his head to taste it, drawing the succulent fruit into his mouth, swirling his tongue about the sensitive tip.

Kit lost the fight to stifle her gasps. Her fingers tangled in Jack's hair, pulling long strands free of the riband at his neck. He suckled, and her fingers tightened on his skull. God! She hadn't known she could *feel* so intensely. Her breathing was ragged, desperate yet disregarded. Feeling was all.

Desire drumming heavy in his veins, Jack released her breast. His lips returned to hers while his fingers sought her waistband.

Relief flooded Kit. Jack seemed content to nibble tantalizingly at her lips, allowing her mind to struggle free of the drugging effect of his kisses. She tried to ignore the peculiar hot ache deep within her, called to life by his passion, quietly building even though his own ardor seemed to have abated. Thank goodness he'd stopped! Her sense of right and wrong was hopelessly compromised.

What had Amy said? The kiss had come first – Jack had certainly cleared that hurdle. She'd willingly prop up the tree for the rest of the night if he'd only continue kissing her as before, deep, hot, and searing. What happened next? Her breasts – Amy had been right about that, too. Jack's hands on her breasts had been a purely sensual experience; she now understood that hitherto inexplicable female tendency to allow men to fondle their breasts. Kit shuddered at the memory of Jack's mouth on her nipple. Desperate to remember the next stage in Amy's scheme of loving, she pushed aside the recollection. What came next?

Whatever it was, Kit doubted she should wait to see if Jack would attempt it. Even her wilder self agreed it was time to take her newfound knowledge and run. In between savoring the heady taste of her teacher, warm, male, and aroused, she fought to regain some degree of control, some power to act. Jack had already gone too far, but at least he'd ceased his scandalously bold caresses. He'd drawn her into deep waters; it was time to retreat to safer shores.

With an effort, Kit gathered her wits and drew her lips from Jack's light, lingering kiss. He let her go without complaint, his head immediately dipping to her breast, tracing a path of fire to one burgeoning nipple.

Kit shook her head; words of firm denial formed on her lips.

They exploded in a long-drawn, half-sighed "*Ja-ack!*" of protest as she felt his palm flatten possessively over her naked stomach.

Kit's eyes flew wide. While she'd been gathering her wits, he'd been opening her breeches! Jack suckled on one nipple, and her fingers clenched in his hair, holding his head to her breast as her hips tilted into his shockingly intimate touch.

And then things got worse.

His long fingers slipped into the silky curls between her thighs.

Kit moaned and struggled to find the strength to break free of the conflagration of her senses. He was igniting it, and she couldn't stop the flames. She didn't even want to anymore.

But she had to make him stop.

His fingers parted her soft flesh and pressed gently.

Kit forgot about stopping. Pleasure streaked through her, sharp and tangible. His fingers set up a deliberate circular motion, first one way, then the other. His lips pulled hard on her nipple and a bolt of white-hot desire shot from her breast to the point where his fingers pulsed flame through her flesh.

His name was on her lips, a soft sigh he didn't mistake. Kit felt the low rumble of his satisfaction. Then his lips returned to hers. It never entered her head to deny him – she welcomed him, lips parting to receive him. She felt his weight as he pressed against her, the hard muscles of his chest comforting her aching breasts.

The material of her breeches strained across her hips as his hand pressed between her thighs. Mindlessly, she parted them further, wordlessly inviting the intimate contact. When one long finger slid slowly into her, she shuddered. Amy's words blossomed in her brain. Hot and wet. Kit knew then. She was hot and wet. Hot and wet for Jack.

Her every sense was centered on his finger, on his slow, inexorable invasion. Kit felt molten, her nerves liquefied. Heat beat in steady pulses through her. She tried to break free of his kiss, to draw breath, but he wouldn't allow it. Instead, his tongue set up a slow, repetitive dance of thrust and retreat. Inside her, his finger picked up the rhythm.

Beyond thought, beyond any sense of shame, Kit responded to the building beat, her body twisting and lifting in his intimate embrace, opening to his deepening caress.

Having made certain of his victory, Jack turned his mind to its accomplishment. And hit a snag. Several snags.

Three seconds of rational thought were sufficient to make clear the enormity of his problems. The ground about them was uneven and strewn with flints – an impossible proposition, even if they had a blanket, which they didn't. He didn't know what sort of tree they were under, but its bark was thick, rough, and sharp. If he took her against it, it would shred her soft skin. But the truly insurmountable difficulty he faced was her breeches. Tight-fitting inexpressibles, they clung to her skin as if she'd been poured into them. He was well accustomed to getting himself out of such attire – they peeled off his form readily enough. They didn't peel off Kit at all. He'd opened the flap to caress her. Now he needed far greater access, but try as he might, no amount of tugging seemed to shift them from her curvaceous hips.

Jack moaned deep in his throat and slanted his mouth over Kit's, deepening the kiss in an effort to deny the truth. Dammit! She was so hot – hot and ready for him. His finger slid effortlessly along her heated channel, slick with the evidence of her arousal. The urge to scorch himself in that slippery heat was overwhelming.

He was too well acquainted with the female body to miss her increasing tension. He didn't have time to stop and get her to assist; he couldn't afford to let her cool. He'd pushed her well along the route to fulfillment – impossible to draw back now.

Frustrated beyond measure, pulled by an urgency outside his control, Jack released his manhood. It sprang free, erect, engorged. He withdrew his hand from between Kit's thighs, ignoring her helpless moan. With a yank, he gained as much leeway as her tight breeches would allow. It wasn't enough.

With an anguished groan, Jack slipped his throbbing staff into the furnace between her silken thighs. If that was to be the only piece of heaven offered him that night, he was in too great a need to scorn it.

Kit groaned into his mouth. She had no doubt what the pressure that had replaced his hand was. But she didn't care. No – she did care – she wanted it there. Even more – she wanted him inside her. He drew back and thrust into the soft hollow between her thighs. In their curious, fully upright position, he could not penetrate her, yet she felt the swollen head of his staff nudge her soft center. Instinctively, she clamped tight about his hard smoothness, dragging her lips free to draw a shuddering breath.

Jack's head was bowed, his temple pressed to her curls, his breathing harsh in her ear. Kit felt him withdraw. She moaned her disapproval and tilted her hips, trying to draw him back. To her relief, he returned, his hips thrusting, the rigid column of his manhood parting her slick, swollen flesh and nudging deeper, the sudden friction sending shafts of pure delight coursing through her. With his next thrust, a furnace opened deep. Kit's hands clenched in Jack's hair; her body strained against his.

Then it happened.

Ripples of tension gripped her, surrounding and compressing her heat until it exploded, sending molten waves of sensation surging along every vein. Indescribable excitement gripped her, and her soul burned, consuming her overloaded senses. Caught on the crest of their passion, abandoned to feeling, she clung to Jack, his name soundless on her lips.

The flames fell and spread their heat through her flesh. Kit tilted her hips, instinctively seeking his fulfillment as part of hers.

Equally instinctively, Jack took the extra inch she offered him to penetrate more deeply into her slick heat. He gasped as the scalding softness of her swollen flesh engulfed him. Yet the ultimate caress of her body remained beyond his

186

reach. His muscles quivered as frustration fleetingly impinged on rampant desire. His chest labored as he struggled for control. The hot honey of her passion poured over him; the faint, pulsing ripples of her release caressed him. Jack forgot about control. He withdrew and thrust again, over and over. The wave of his release hit him, crashing him into pleasured oblivion.

He'd missed seeing her eyes when she'd climaxed.

Jack's first thought on recovering from his exertions seemed perfectly rational. Next time, he'd make sure he satisfied his curiosity. Right now, he was too pleased with himself to allow any quibbles to dim his mood. Despite the limitations, the experience had been one to remember.

He glanced down at Kit. The aftershocks of her remarkable climax had died, but she was still dazed. Aware of the etiquette demanded of such intimate moments, even in such extraordinary circumstances, Jack carefully withdrew from the soft hollow between her thighs.

Kit's consciousness made contact with reality as Jack settled her coat lapels in place. She stiffened, her eyes blinking wide. Had she dreamed it?

One glance at Jack's face dispelled that faint hope. His lips looked as if they couldn't stop smiling. Smugly. Kit felt faint. Her clothes were back in place, fastened, all except her bands, which he'd left about her waist.

She tried to ignore the dampness between her thighs.

Luckily, Jack took charge – without being asked, naturally. He settled her on Delia and then they were heading westward once more, at a walk.

The walls of Cranmer Hall were taking shape on the horizon before Kit came to grips with what had happened. She and Jack had been intimate. The thought sent her mind into a dizzying panic, only slightly ameliorated by the startling conclusion that, despite all, she was still a virgin. He hadn't breached her, of that she was certain. Years before, her grandmother had instructed her in the bald facts of wifely duty; Kit had felt no pain or discomfort – not the slightest. Neither had she felt any awkwardness or shyness in letting Jack caress her as he had, shockingly intimate though that had been, nor of letting him push that thing of his between her thighs – not at the time. Now, she was positively sunk in guilt, wallowing in the outraged modesty she hadn't felt while in his arms, kissed into complaisance. How could she have let it happen?

Easily, came the languid reply. *And you'd do it again, and more, if he wanted you.*

Kit smothered her groan and leaned her head back against Jack's shoulder, too exhausted to deny her wilder self's outrageous assertion. At least the comfort of her riding position had improved. Jack had untied her hands – afterward, damn him. There'd been moments under that tree when she'd have killed to have her hands free. Now they rested, crossed, on the pommel while Jack managed the reins. Her body fit snugly into his, the curve of her back settled into his midriff, his thighs on either side of hers, supporting her. The pressure in his loins had disappeared; she'd apparently been successful in taking care of that. There was nothing in their contact to cause alarm. She could fall asleep, if she wished.

Delia plodded on.

"Which way to the stables?"

Jack's quiet whisper brought Kit blinking awake. Familiar landmarks rose out of the dark. They were in a dip just behind the Hall. For a moment, she leaned against Jack's chest, savoring the hard warmth, wishing irrationally that his arms would come around and hold her. At the thought, panic pushed her upright. "I take Delia in through the paddock. I have to jump the fence."

The figure behind her was still, then said, "All right. I'll leave you here."

One hard hand closed on her waist. Kit stiffened, but Jack just needed her as balance as he swung down from the saddle. He handed her the reins. "Wait while I adjust the stirrups."

Shortening the straps so the stirrups sat once more in the groove they'd worn in the thick leather, Jack forced his mind to function – not an easy task in its present, slightly intoxicated state. If he was any judge of such experiences, what had happened beneath the tree should whet the appetite of a woman who was currently forced to a proscribed existence.

Yet there was something in Kit's response that warned him not to take her for granted. Her silence could simply be due to tiredness; her climax had been particularly strong. But there was more to it than that. Perhaps she was piqued he'd found her so easy to tame? Safely hidden by the dark, Jack grinned fleetingly. He had a premonition that she might be reluctant to yield more than she had already, not without a further concession from him. And at present he couldn't offer her anything, not even his name.

Whatever, two nights from now she would spend some time in his bed. And he'd stake his hard-won reputation that afterward, she wouldn't walk away from him with her pert nose in the air.

Jack straightened and pulled his wig from the saddle pocket. He stepped back. "I'll see you tomorrow at the Old Barn."

Excuses jostled on Kit's tongue, but she swallowed them.

Four weeks she'd agreed to – four weeks he'd get. With a curt nod, she wheeled Delia and put her over the fence.

Cantering up the steep paddock to the stable, Kit resisted the temptation to look back. He'd be standing where she'd left him, hands on hips, watching her. She'd turn up tomorrow, and if they were doing a cargo, the night after that. But from then on, she'd give Captain Jack a wide berth. Distance was imperative. She knew the dangers now; there could be no excuse.

When the dark cavern of the stable had swallowed Kit, Jack turned and headed north. The moon sailed free of its fettering clouds and lit his way. Miles ahead, Castle Hendon awaited its master, his bed fitted with silk sheets, cool and unwarmed. Jack's lips quirked. He had an ambition to see Kit writhing in ecstasy on that bed, her curls a flaming aureole about her head, those other curls he'd touched but hadn't seen, burning him. He'd counted the nights ever since he'd first touched her and known his senses weren't playing him false. Now, she was damn near an obsession.

As his swinging stride ate the miles, his mind remained on the woman who'd captured his senses. She'd never be just another mistress – those who'd come before her had never intrigued him as she did. From her, he wanted much more than mere physical gratification, despite that every time he set eyes on her he was driven by a primal urge to bury himself in her heat. The need to possess her went much further than that.

He wanted to bring her to climax again and again. He wanted her cries of satisfaction to ring in his ears. He needed to know she was close and safe at all times.

Jack frowned. He'd never felt like that about a woman before.

Chapter 16

The slap of the waves against the fishing boat's hull was drowned by the roar of the surf. Thigh deep in the tide, Jack flexed his shoulders, then reached for the barrel Noah held out. With the keg balanced on his shoulder, he waded to the shore, to where the ponies were being loaded.

Jack waited for the men lashing the barrels to the ponies' saddles to take the heavy keg, then turned to survey his enterprise.

They had the routine down pat. Even as he looked, the men in the emptied boats bent to the oars and the six hulls slipped back out through the surf, off to find any fish they could before heading home. The last kegs were being lashed in place, then the parcels of lace, stacked against a rock nearby, would be balanced on top and secured.

As the lace was brought up, Jack let his gaze rise to the cliff overlooking the beach. He'd stationed Kit on the eastern point, but had no idea where she actually was. Doubtless the stubborn woman had made good her threat and moved farther west. She'd attended the meeting in the Old Barn the previous night, slipping in late to stand in the shadows at the back. Immediately after he'd finished detailing tonight's run, she'd vanished.

He hadn't been surprised. But he'd be damned if he let her escape him tonight.

Two miles to the west, Kit halted Delia She'd gone far enough. Time to turn back if she was to meet Jack at the cliff top as ordered. But still she sat, staring, unseeing, westward.

Her stomach was tied in knots. Her nerves wouldn't settle, fluttering like butterflies every time Jack's image hove on her mental horizon. His ideas for tonight, as far as she'd allow herself to imagine them, were pure madness, but what she could do to avoid them was more than she could fathom.

She would have to see him, that much was plain. Was there any chance she could talk her way free of his "later"? His words on the ride back from the ill-fated masquerade made it clear he'd read her teasing as encouragement. Kit grimaced. She simply hadn't realized how much she affected him. Whatever his reasons for reticence, she'd fallen into the trap.

With a tight little sigh, she plotted her course. She would have to explain. As a gently reared woman, she couldn't – simply could not – consider the alternative.

Light drizzle started to fall, misting Delia's breath. Kit's fingers were tightening on the reins to draw the mare about when she heard a jingle.

Followed by another.

Her senses pricked. The hairs on her nape rose. She'd heard that sound before. The heavier clink of a stirrup confirmed her deductions. An instant later she saw them, a whole troop, advancing at a steady canter.

Kit didn't wait to see more. She took the first path she found down to the sands and let Delia's reins fall. Her cheeks stung by the flying black mane, she clung to the mare's neck as the sand sped beneath the black hooves.

Automatically checking the ropes holding the precious cargo in place, Jack passed down the pony train. He'd made sure Kit wouldn't disappear like a wraith the instant the last pony gained the cliff top by the simple expedient of ordering her to meet him at the head of the path up from the beach – in the presence of half a dozen men. She wasn't a fool. She wouldn't risk the instant suspicion that failure to comply with such explicit orders would generate.

He was nearing the end of the pony train, and the men at its head were already mounting, when the reverberation of flying hooves on firm-packed sand brought him instantly alert.

Out of the night, a black horse materialized. Kit. Riding hard. From the west.

By the time she was slowing, so as not to spook the ponies, Jack was already running to the head of the train, where Matthew waited, mounted, Champion's reins in his hand. The big stallion was shifting, excited by the precipitous arrival of the mare, his huge hooves stamping the sand. Jack threw himself into the saddle as Kit pulled up before him, Delia pawing the air.

"Revenue. From Hunstanton," Kit gasped. "But they're still a mile or more away."

Jack stared at her. A mile or more? She'd been reinterpreting his orders with a vengeance! He shook off the urge to shake her – he'd deal with her insubordination later and enjoy it all the more.

He turned to Shep. "Stow the stuff in the old crypt. Then

clear everyone. You're in charge." The train had been intended for the Old Barn, but that was impossible now. Kit had given them one chance to get safely away; they had to take it. "The four of us" – his nod indicated Matthew and George as well as Kit – "will draw the Revenue off toward Holme. With luck, they won't even know you exist."

Shep nodded his understanding. A minute later, the train moved off, disappearing into the dunes cloaking the eastern headland. They'd go carefully, wending their way under maximum cover close by Brancaster before slipping south to the ruined church. Jack turned to Kit. "Where, exactly?"

"On the cliff, riding close to the edge."

Her voice, strained with excitement, showed an alarming tendency to rise through the register. Jack hoped George wouldn't hear it. "Stay by me," he growled, praying she'd have the sense to do so.

He touched his heels to Champion's sides and the stallion was off, heading for the path to the cliff top. Delia followed, with Matthew's and George's mounts close behind. They swung inland to slip into the protection of the belt of trees running parallel to the cliff's edge, a hundred yards or more from it. They didn't have to go far to find the Revenue.

In the shadow of a fir, Jack stood by Champion's head, his hand clamped over the grey's nose to stifle any revealing whinny, and watched the Revenue men under his command thunder past like a herd of cattle without thought for stealth or strategy. He shook his head in disbelief and exchanged a pained look with George. As soon as the squad had passed, they remounted.

A sudden hoot from beside her startled Kit as she was settling her boot in the stirrup. She sat bolt upright, only to hear a long-drawn birdcall answer from a few feet away. Then Jack struck his knife blade to his belt buckle, muttering unintelligibly. George and Matthew responded similarly. Kit stared at them.

The retreating drum of the hooves of the Revenue's horses came to a sudden, somewhat confused halt. Matthew and George continued with their noises while Jack urged Champion to the edge of the trees. The mufffled din continued until Jack turned and hissed: "Here they come."

George and Matthew held silent, watching Jack's upraised hand. Then his hand dropped. "Now!"

Amid cries of "The Revenue!" they spilled from the trees, heading west. Jack glanced about to find Delia's black head level with his knee, Kit crouched low over the mare's neck. His teeth gleamed in a smile. It felt good to be flying before the wind with her at his side.

They made as much noise as a fox hunt in full cry. Initially. When it was clear all the Revenue Officers were in dogged pursuit, floundering behind them, Jack pulled up in the lee of a small hill. Matthew and George brought their mounts to plunging halts beside him; Kit drew Delia to a slow halt some yards farther on. Her muffler had slipped slightly; she didn't want George or Matthew to see her face. The drizzle was intensifying into rain. A drip from the damp curls clinging to her forehead coursed down to the tip of her nose. Raising her head, she looked east. Low clouds, purple and black, scudded before the freshening wind.

Jack's voice reached her. "We'll split up. Kit and I have the faster horses. You two head south. When it's safe, you can separate and go home."

"Which way will you head?" George shook the water from his hat and crammed it back on.

Jack's smile was confident. "We'll head west on the beach. It won't take long to lose them."

With a nod, George turned and, followed by Matthew,

slipped into the trees lining the road on the south. They couldn't head off until the Revenue were drawn away – the fields were too open and clearly visible from the road.

The squad of Revenue men were still out of sight on the other side of the hill. Jack nudged Champion close to Delia. "There's a path to the beach over there." He pointed. Kit squinted through the rain. "Where that bush hangs over the cliff. Take it. I'll follow in a moment."

Kit resisted the impulse to say she'd wait. His tone was not one to question. She kicked Delia to a canter, swiftly crossing the open area to the cliff's edge. At the head of the path, she paused to look behind her. The Revenue came around the hill and saw them – she at the cliff, Jack riding hard toward her. He'd dallied to make sure the troop didn't miss them. With a howl, the Revenue took the bait. Kit sent Delia to the sands, reaching the foot of the path as Champion landed with a slithering thump a few yards away. She'd forgotten that trick of his.

"West!"

At the bellowed order, Kit turned Delia's head in that direction and dropped the reins. Primed by the tension, the mare obediently went straight to a full gallop, leaving Champion in her wake. Kit grinned through the raindrops streaking her face. Soon enough, the thud of Champion's hooves settled to a steady beat just behind her, keeping pace between her and their pursuers.

Behind Kit, Jack watched her flying coattails, marveling at the effortless ease of her performance. He'd never seen anyone ride better – together, she and Delia were sheer magic in motion. She held the mare to a long-strided gallop, a touch of pace in reserve. Jack glanced behind him. The Revenue were dwindling shapes on the sand, outdistanced and outclassed.

Jack looked forward, opening his mouth to yell to Kit to turn for the cliff. A blur of movement at the top of the path, the last path before they passed onto the west arm of the anvil-shaped headland above Brancaster, caught his eye. He shook the water from his eyes and stared through the rain.

Hell and confound the man! Tonkin had not only disobeyed orders and come east, but he'd had the sense to split his men into two. He and Kit weren't leading the Revenue west – they were being herded west. Tonkin's plan was obvious – push them onto the narrow western headland, then trap them there, a solid cordon of Revenue Officers between them and the safety of the mainland.

Kit, too, had seen the men on the cliff; slowing, she glanced behind her. Champion did not pause; Jack took him forward to keep pace between Delia and the cliff. "Keep on!" he yelled in answer to the question in Kit's eyes.

"But –"

"I know! Just keep going west."

Kit glared but did as he said. The man was mad – all very well to keep on, but soon they'd run out of land. She could just make out the place ahead where the cliff abruptly ended. There was only sea beyond it.

Unconcerned by such matters, Jack kept Champion at a full gallop and pondered his new insight into Sergeant Tonkin. Obviously, he'd underestimated the man. He still found it hard to believe Tonkin had had wit enough to devise a trap, let alone put it into practice. It wasn't going to work, of course – but what could one expect? Tonkin's net had a very large hole which was one hole too many to trap Captain Jack.

A crack of thunder came out of the east. The heavens opened; rain hit their backs in a drenching downpour. Jack laughed, exhilaration coursing through him. The rain would hinder Tonkin; it would be morning before the sodden Revenue men could be sure the prey had flown their coop.

Kit heard his laughter and stared.

Jack caught her look and grinned. They were still riding hard directly west. The tide was flowing in fast, eating away the beach. On their left, the cliff swept up to a rocky outcrop, then fell to a rock-strewn point. The beach ran out. Kit pulled up. Champion slowed, then was turned toward the rocks.

"Come on." Jack led, setting Champion to pick his way across the rocky point, waves washing over his heavy hooves. Delia followed, hooves daintily clopping.

Around the point lay a small, sandy cove. Beyond, sweeping southeastward, the beaches on the southern side of the headland gleamed, a pale path leading back to the mainland. But the Revenue would be skulking somewhere in the murk, waiting.

In the lee of the cliffs, the rain fell less heavily. Jack pulled up in the cove; Kit halted Delia alongside Champion. She sat catching her breath, staring through the rain at the headland on the opposite side of the small bay.

"Well? Are you ready?"

Kit blinked and turned to Jack. "Ready?" The sight of his smile, a melding of excitement, laughter and pure devilry, set her nerves atingle. She followed his gaze to the other side of the bay. "You're joking." She made the words a statement.

"Why? You're already soaked to the skin – what's a little more water?"

He was right, of course; she couldn't get any wetter. There was, however, one problem. "I can't swim."

It was Jack's turn to stare, memories of their night of near disaster on the yacht vivid in his mind. In a few pithy phrases, he disabused her mind of any claim to sanity, adding his opinion of witless women who went on boats when they couldn't swim. Kit listened calmly, well acquainted with the argument – it was Spencer's standard answer to her desire to sail. "Yes, but what are we going to do now?" she asked, when Jack ground to a halt.

Jack scowled, narrowed eyes fixed on the far shore. Then he nudged Champion closer to Delia. Kit felt his hands close about her waist.

"Come here."

She didn't have much choice. Jack lifted her across and perched her on Champion's saddle in front of him. It was a tight fit; Kit felt the butt of Jack's saddle pistol press into one thigh. He took Delia's reins and tied them to a ring on the back of Champion's saddle, then his belt was in his hands. "Hold still." Peering at her waist, he threaded his belt through hers.

"What are you doing?" Kit twisted about, trying to see.

"Dammit, woman! Hold still. You can wriggle your hips all you like later but not now!"

The muttered words reduced Kit to frozen obedience. Later. With all the excitement, she'd forgotten his fixation about later. She swallowed. The moment hardly seemed ripe to start a discussion on that subject. He'd been half-aroused before she'd wriggled; now . . .

"I'm just making a loop so I can catch hold of you if you slip off."

The observation did nothing for Kit's confidence. "If I slip off?"

Jack straightened before she could think of any other route of escape. "Hold tight to the pommel. I'll swim alongside once we're in the water." With that, he set his heels to Champion's sides.

Both horses took to the water as if swimming across bays in the dead of night was a part of their daily routine. Kit envied them their dull brains. Hers was frantic. She clung to the pommel, both hands frozen and fused to the smooth outcrop. As the first wave lapped her legs, she felt Jack's comforting bulk, warm and solid behind her, evaporate. Swallowing her protest, she turned her head and found him bobbing in the water alongside her.

"Lean forward as if you were riding hard."

Kit obeyed, relieved to feel the weight of his hand in the small of her back.

A moment later, a wave crashed over her, drenching her with icy water. She shrieked and came up sputtering. Instantly, Jack was beside her, his face alongside hers, his arm over her back, one large hand spread over her ribs, and her breast. "Sssh. It's all right. I won't let you go."

The reassurance in his tone washed through her. Kit relaxed enough to register the position of his hand but was in no mood to protest. If she could have got any closer to him she would have, regardless of any retribution later.

The tide rushed through the narrow neck and into the bay. It carried them forward like flotsam and, in a short time, disgorged them on the sands of the mainland. As soon as Champion's hooves scraped the bottom, Jack swung up behind Kit. She heaved a sigh of relief and decided not to take exception to the muscular arm that wound about her waist, pulling her back tightly, tucking her into safety against him.

Jack countered the stallion's surge up the beach, holding him back until the mare's shorter legs reached the sand. As soon as they left the surf, he pushed Champion into a canter, heading for the closest path off the sand and the relative safety of the trees.

Kit held her peace and waited for Jack to come to a halt and set her down. But he didn't. Instead he steered Champion straight through the trees bordering the cliff and struck south through the teeming rain. Disoriented, Kit took a few minutes to work out where he was headed. Then her eyes flew wide. He was taking her straight to the cottage!

"Jack! Stop! Er . . ." Kit struggled to think of a pressing reason for a sudden departure, but her mind froze.

Champion's stride didn't falter. "You've got to get out of those clothes as soon as possible," Jack said.

Paralysis set in. Why as soon as possible? Wouldn't some other time do? For the life of her Kit couldn't think of any words to counter his firm assertion. She decided to ignore it. "I can ride perfectly well. Just stop and let me get on Delia."

The only answer he gave was to turn Champion onto the road to Holme. A few minutes later, they reached the path that led south to the cottage. Fear loosened Kit's tongue.

"Jack –"

"Dammit, woman! You're soaked. You can't ride all the way to Cranmer like that. And in case you hadn't noticed, the storm's about to break."

Kit hadn't noticed. A quick glance around his shoulder showed thunderheads lowering through the gloom. Even as she watched, a bolt of lightning streaked earthward. Kit stopped arguing and snuggled back into the warmth of Jack's chest. She hated thunderstorms; more importantly, so did Delia. Yet the mare seemed unperturbed, pacing steadily beside Champion. Perhaps she should ask Jack to ride home with her. No – they might have to stop under a tree.

There was no denying she could not afford a chill she couldn't explain. But what on earth was she to do when she got to the cottage? The thought focused her mind on what had hitherto proved the most reliable reflection of Jack's state of mind. To her surprise, she couldn't feel anything – there was none of the firm pressure she'd come to recognize, despite the fact that she was wedged more tightly against him than ever before. What was wrong?

Then the import of his words registered. He'd only meant she had to get out of her wet clothes, not that . . . Kit blushed. To her shame, she realized she felt no relief at her discovery, only the most intense disappointment. The truth hit her, impossible to deny. Her blush deepened.

Why not admit you wouldn't mind trying it with him? What have you got to lose? Only your virginity – and who are you saving that for? You know Jack would never hurt you – a bruise or two maybe, but nothing intentional. You'll be safe with him. Why not take the plunge? And what more perfect night for it – you know you hate trying to sleep during storms.

Kit remained silent, battling her demons.

Despite her beliefs, Jack's mind was well and truly occupied with her forthcoming seduction. But he was freezing, too. They both needed to get out of the rain-soaked wind whipping across the land. The double meaning in his first statement had been entirely intentional – he couldn't have planned this night better. He was looking forward to peeling Kit's wet clothes from her and, after that, he knew just how to warm them both. What he was planning would eradicate any residual chill.

There was no better way to while away a storm.

Chapter 17

The cottage loomed out of the dark, squat and solid, tucked into the protection of the bank behind it. Jack rode straight to the stable. He dismounted, then lifted Kit down. "Go in. The fire should be lit; there's wood beside it and towels in the wardrobe. I'll take care of Delia."

Kit stared through the darkness but couldn't make out his expression. Dully, she nodded and headed for the cottage door. His last comment was obviously intended to let her know she'd have time to get undressed and dried before he came in. Doubtless there'd be a robe or something in the wardrobe for her to wrap herself in. Presumably, getting into her breeches the other night had slaked Jack's lust, at least for the present. Either that, or the drenching had doused his ardor. Kit grimaced and reached for the latch.

The main room was lit by the red glow of a smoldering log. With a sigh, Kit fell to her knees on the mat in front of the fireplace. The wood was in a basket to one side. She laid logs on the flames, then sat back and watched them catch. The warmth slowly thawed her chilled muscles. With another sigh, she struggled to her feet.

There were towels on the top shelf of the wardrobe. Kit drew down an armful of blessedly dry linen and went to the fire. Leaving the pile on the end of the bed, she spread one towel on the mat, then pulled up a chair and proceeded to struggle out of her wet clothes. Hat, muffler, and coat she draped on the chair. She sat and pulled off her boots, then knelt on one end of the towel and, after one wary glance at the door, pulled her shirt over her head.

It was a battle to free her shoulders and arms, but eventually she managed it. Her bands were even more trouble, with the knot pulled tight and the sodden material clinging to her skin. She ran through her repertoire of curses before the knot finally gave way. It was a relief to unwind the yards of material and free her breasts.

Kit dropped the long band on the towel and sat back on her heels, letting the fire chase away her chills. Reaching back, she tugged a towel from the pile. Bending forward, she draped the towel over her neck, running the ends over her curls, scattering droplets into the fire. Once her hair had stopped dripping, she dried her arms and back, then started on her breasts.

The door opened.

Kit turned with a gasp, the towel clutched to her chest.

Jack stood in the doorway, looking for all the world as if he'd just forgotten what he'd come in to do. A deceptive expression. He'd come in to seduce Kit Cranmer, and there wasn't anything capable of making him forget that. His stunned look was due to the vision before him – Kit, bare to the waist, kneeling before his fire, her curls burnished by the flames. Kit, with wide eyes darkening from amethyst to violet, the towel clutched to her chest totally failing to conceal the twin peaks of her breasts jutting provocatively on either side, the long line of her legs revealed by her wet breeches.

Slowly, Jack shut the door, his eyes never leaving the woman silhouetted by the flames. Without turning, he slid the bolt home. He crossed to the table and laid his pistol down before shrugging out of his coat.

Held immobile by his silver gaze, Kit watched, helplessly transfixed. When he pulled his shirt over his head, she blinked free only to be mesmerized by the play of light over the muscles of his chest. She didn't notice him pause to release his hair, but it was swinging free, brown streaked with gold, brushing his shoulders, when he knelt on the towel beside her.

His hands closed on her bare shoulders. Gently, he drew her to face him.

Kit looked deep into eyes of brightest silver burnished with passion. Desire burned, a steady flame in their depths. Her mouth went dry. She shuddered, swept by a force beyond her experience.

Jack watched burgeoning passion turn Kit's eyes to glowing purple. When her tongue came out to moisten her lips, he judged it safe to reach for the towel. She relinquished it without protest. He glanced down at the treasure now completely revealed and watched as, caressed by his ardent gaze, her nipples crinkled tight.

With a slow smile of satisfaction, and anticipation, Jack returned his gaze to her face, noting her wide eyes and the lips already parted for his kiss.

Kit could barely breathe as Jack brought his hands up, skimming the contours of her neck, to cradle her face, his long fingers sliding into her curls. For a moment, he paused, his eyes holding hers, an unanswered question in their silvered depths.

She wanted this, she realized. Every bit as much as he did. In that instant, Kit made her decision. She put aside all the precepts of twenty-two years of training and reached for her heart's desire.

As Jack bent his head, she rose on her knees to meet him.

Jack took her mouth in a burning kiss, slanting his head as she opened to his penetration. Kit braced her hands against his upper chest and leaned into his caress. In seconds, her blood was alight, ignited by his fire.

Thank God her hands were free – free to roam the warm expanse of male skin, to caress the bands of hard muscle, to tangle in the springy brown hair. Kit's questing fingers found a hidden nipple. To her delight, she felt it harden to her touch. Hands spread, she explored the ridges of muscle above his waist before moving on to his broad back. Her hands found water. He was still wet.

Kit drew back from their duel of tongues. Jack's brow quirked. He reached for her, but she stayed him, one small hand braced against his chest as she reached for a towel.

A droplet of water fell from his hair and trickled, unheeded, down his chest. Kit saw it. She smiled, then leaned forward and licked it off. Jack shuddered and closed his eyes, his hands fisting by his sides.

Kit's seductive smile grew. She set to work drying his chest, working the towel in small circles, moving with a deliberate lack of haste. She stood and moved behind him to towel his back.

Jack sat on his heels and let her, held in thrall by her sensuous attentions. The tantalizing play of the towel would have melted a statue. Or at least sent it up in flames. His body was nearing that state.

When she reappeared before him, he caught her hands and drew her down to her knees again, taking the towel and tossing it aside. But he didn't pull her into his arms. He reached for her breasts, taking one luscious mound in each hand, squeezing gently, then circling the taut nipples with his thumbs.

Kit's eyes closed. She swayed toward Jack, her senses overloaded.

Jack kissed her, letting his hands drop to her waist. She was going too fast – he wanted to spin out her time as long as he possibly could. He didn't want her reaching her peak just yet – he had other plans.

The kiss slowed Kit down, easing her from a full boil to a bubbling simmer. Instinctively, she realized Jack wanted her in that state. She didn't know why, but conundrums were beyond her. His hands had moved to the fastenings of her breeches. The wet fabric trapped the buttons. It took the combined efforts of them both to win through. Once the flap was open, Jack eased the breeches down, running his hands over the cool skin of her buttocks.

Kit wriggled her hips free of the clinging folds, thanking all her angels that her riding breeches were not as tight as her inexpressibles. If she'd been wearing them tonight, she felt sure he'd have ripped them from her. At Jack's urging, she stood. He drew the breeches to her feet and helped her from them. But before she could sink to her knees again, his hands fastened about her hips, holding her where she was, totally naked before him.

For one long moment, Jack surveyed her beauty. Then he bent his head to pay homage.

Kit's gasp when his lips burned her navel echoed in the quiet room. Her fingers threaded into his hair; her hands clutched his head. She felt the thrust of his tongue, languid and rhythmic, and her flesh caught fire. When his lips finally moved on, her sigh filled the room.

She waited to be released, but Jack hadn't finished. His tongue explored the curve of her hip. Kit felt his hands shift down and around until each large palm cupped a firm buttock. His fingers gripped her, holding her prisoner. She smiled – she wasn't about to try to escape.

Then he shifted, settling lower on his knees. His lips dipped downward. And inward.

"*Jack!*" Kit's shocked protest ended in a whimper of pleasure. Her knees lost all ability to support her, but Jack held her steady as his lips closed over the bright curls at the apex of her thighs and his tongue probed the soft flesh they concealed.

Kit swayed, eyes closed. She'd wanted him at her feet, but this wasn't what she'd meant. *This* was beyond scandalous – it was a damned sight beyond anything Amy could even dream. Kit shuddered, and her head fell back. Her mind fragmented. Jack shifted his hold and lifted her left leg, hooking her knee over his shoulder, trailing hot kisses back up the satiny flesh of her inner thigh before settling to plunder her softness with the same unrelenting thoroughness he'd used earlier on her mouth.

Kit couldn't think. Her entire consciousness was centered on that point where Jack's hot mouth and even hotter tongue were drawing an answering heat from her. Her hands dropped to his shoulders, her nails sinking deep in convulsive reaction.

Concentrating on every spasm of her response, Jack knew when she approached the point beyond which her climax would become unavoidable. He changed tack, drawing her back from the brink, letting the flames he'd fanned die to a smolder before patiently stoking them to a blaze once more. From nibbling kisses about the curl-covered mound, he progressed to a slow exploration of the heated flesh that surrounded the entrance to her secret cave.

He had her balanced perfectly; her knee on his shoulder

let him steady her with that hand alone, leaving his left hand free to caress her bottom. Her skin was damp, but not from the rain. His hand skimmed one ripe hemisphere, then his fingers sought the cleft between, sliding down to find the spot where a little pressure went a long way. Kit's shuddering gasp told him he'd found it. He moved her knee, opening her fully, pausing to circle the swollen bud of her passion with his tongue before plundering the delights of her honey-filled cave.

He wondered how long she could take it. How long could he?

Sensation after sensation crashed through Kit. She felt battered by the volleys of passion rocketing along her veins. Hypersensitized, she was agonizingly aware of every erotic move Jack made. Wantonly, she abandoned herself to delight, reveling in the shocking intimacy. Again and again, he brought her to the point where she could sense those odd ripples of tension building within her. Then his attention would wander, slowing her down when she wanted to rush headlong to her fate. When he did it again, she moaned her displeasure. She struggled in his hold. "Damn you, Jack!" But she couldn't tell him to stop; she didn't know what she wanted.

But she was quite sure he did. She heard his deep chuckle, and felt its reverberations through her hands. He drew back to look up at her, his eyes alight with a searing silver flame. "Had enough?"

"Yes – no!" Kit glared as best she could, but it was a weak effort.

Jack laughed and let her knee down. He got to his feet and Kit swayed into him. His lips found hers and she tasted her nectar on his lips and tongue. The flames started to build again.

Then Jack drew away. Kit slumped against him, too weak to protest. He held her, his hands roaming her silken back, marveling at the texture of her skin. She was well and truly primed, ready to explode. And, thank Christ, he was still in control. God knew how long that would last.

Kit moaned her disapproval and lifted her face for his kiss. Jack obliged but kept the kiss light. He disengaged, and his lips brushed hers. "I take it that means you want me inside you?"

Kit blinked.

She couldn't believe her ears. After what he'd just done to her – after what she'd just let him do to her – he wanted her to say it. Aloud. She set her lips mutinously.

He raised his brows.

"Yes, damn you! I want you to put that bloody sword of yours inside me. All right?"

Jack crowed once in triumph, then swept her up into his arms. "Far be it from me to disappoint a lady." In two strides, he reached the bed. It wasn't his bed at the Castle, with its silken sheets, but it would do for now. The wind howled about the eaves as he laid Kit down, pulling the covers from under her. They wouldn't need them for an hour or two.

Deposited in the middle of the bed, Kit fought an automatic urge to cover her nakedness. But Jack's hungry gaze dispelled her inhibitions. She stretched, catlike, settling herself on the pillows, and watched him undress.

His boots came off first, then he stood and peeled off his wet breeches. Kit's heart leapt to her mouth when she saw what she'd previously only felt. Jack reached for a towel and dried his legs. When he turned his attention to what hung between them, Kit's mouth went dry. It had to be impossible, surely? But it was patently obvious that Jack had been accommodated by other women, although she couldn't imagine how.

A log settled in the hearth, sending sparks flying, recalling Jack to his duties as host. Dropping the towel, he crouched to tend the fire.

Kit drew a deep breath, then another. It would work – he knew what he was doing, even if she didn't. He wouldn't hurt her, she knew that. How was it going to feel, having that pushed inside her?

She forced her mind to other things – to the sheen of the flames on his skin, to the sculpted muscle covering his large frame. Her gaze was drawn to a number of scars scattered randomly over him. One in particular held her attention, a long gash on the inside of his left knee, highlighted by the flames as he stood and turned toward her.

His weight bowed the bed, rolling her into his arms. Kit lost all hope of retaining any degree of lucidity the instant his lips met hers.

Jack savored the taste of her, relishing the ardor he sensed beneath her calm. She'd cooled somewhat, but all that meant was that he'd have the pleasure of stoking her flames yet again. Regardless of her previous experience, he had every intention of making sure this was one night, one time, one man she'd never forget. He set his mind and his hands to the task.

His knowing fingers searched and found all her points of passion, those particular areas where she was most sensitive. The lower curve of her buttocks quickly became his favorite – she heated in an instant at the lightest caress. Anything more definite brought a moan to her lips. Satisfied she was safe from any chill, Jack gathered her to him, pressing her slim length to him, from shoulder to knee. But before he could roll her beneath him, he was seduced

211

by the sensation of hot silken skin sliding sensuously over him.

Kit responded instinctively to the novel texture of Jack's body. She'd never felt anything like it before. Consumed by curiosity, she rubbed her soft thighs against his rough hardness, marveling at the friction of his hair against her skin, at the contrast between his lean muscle and her yielding flesh.

She sensed the hiatus in Jack's attention and assumed it was her turn to explore. She'd made her decision; there was no reason to shortchange herself. Whatever penance she'd pay would be the same. Opening her eyes, she spread her hands across his chest and wondered at the width of the muscles that spanned it. She glanced into Jack's face and found his eyes shut, his jaw set, his lips thin.

Smiling, she moved her hands lower and watched the tension in his face, his whole frame, grow. Tentatively, she reached for him, taking him between her hands as she had two nights before. Her fingers moved up the throbbing shaft and found the rounded head. A bead of moisture clung to her fingers.

Jack's control snapped. He forgot all thoughts of slow mutual torture, consumed by the need to douse the flames she'd set raging through him. His heat needed hers to come to fruition. In one smooth move, he pulled her beneath him, coming over her to settle on his elbows.

Kit's gasp was lost as Jack's mouth took hers in a relentless plunder of her senses. His fingers laced through her curls, holding her head steady while he ravished her mouth, sending heated longing down every nerve. His hips were heavy on hers, pressing her into the bed. She welcomed his weight and wanted more but he ignored her tugging. She felt him shift slightly, then his hand slipped between them to expertly caress the soft flesh between her thighs. Kit moaned and opened to his fingers, her breath catching as they slid slowly into her. She felt his thumb flick against her and sparks flew. The furnace deep within her ignited.

His hand withdrew and she frowned and shook her head, too breathless to find words to protest. She writhed, searching mindlessly for fulfillment. Then she felt his thighs press heavily between hers, nudging them farther apart. Smooth, hard pressure eased her aching flesh.

That was what she wanted. Kit moaned and tilted her hips in instinctive invitation.

Despite the mists of lust clouding his mind, Jack's faculties still functioned. They registered the unexpected tension in the ligaments of Kit's thighs and passed the information on.

With an effort, Jack drew his lips from Kit's. His head bowed, he drew a deep breath, then shook his head to clear it of the irritating niggle that was threatening to spoil his evening. But that only made the evidence more obvious. Dammit! It was as if she'd never spread her legs before. He frowned, and Kit moaned impatiently. Jack shook aside his ridiculous fancy. The woman writhing in urgent entreaty beneath him had most assuredly been this way before. He flexed his hips and entered her, slowly, letting her heat welcome him, the slickness of her arousal smoothing his way.

Three inches in, the truth hit him like a sledgehammer.

Jack froze. In stunned disbelief, he stared at the woman lying naked in his arms, her creamy skin flushed with passion, her features rapt, her mind centered on the place where their bodies joined. He could feel her tightening about him, even though he was barely inside her.

"Christ!" Jack dropped his head, his jaw resting on her cheekbone.

Kit opened her eyes, bewildered and bemused.

Jack didn't look at her. He couldn't. "Kit, are you a virgin?"

Her silence was answer enough, but he needed to hear it, incontrovertible, from her lips. "Dammit, woman! Are you?"

Kit's soft "Yes," was drowned by Jack's groan. She felt him tense; his body went rigid. Then, slowly, he drew away.

The effort nearly killed him, but Jack forced his body to compliance. He pulled out of her clinging heat, then abruptly sat up and swung his feet to the floor. He dropped his head in his hands, shutting out the temptation to look at her. If he did, he'd lose the battle with his body, which was already in flaming rebellion.

He had to think. It wasn't just that she was a virgin and he'd long ago given up deflowering the little dears. There was something more significant about the fact. With a groan, he struggled to summon his wits from their preoccupation with attaining a goal he was no longer sure it was safe to gain.

Kit frowned at the broad back, which was all of Jack she could see. Something had given her away, but with passion beating steady in her veins, she was in no mood to pander to any peculiar rakish whim. She'd learned from her cousins that virgins were not the favored fare of rakes, the consensus being that experienced women gave better value besides being free of potential complications. It was too bad if Jack subscribed to such nonsense. He'd brought her this far; she'd be damned if she'd leave his bed untried.

When he gave no sign of coming to his senses and instantly returning to her arms, Kit sat up. Apparently, if she wished to get his mind back where she wanted it, and his body along with it, she was going to have to make her wishes plain.

She came up on her knees on the bed close behind him.

Slowly, she placed her hands on his back, spreading the fingers wide, then sliding them around, pushing under his arms until she'd reached as far as she could. She clung to him, pressing her breasts, her hips, against his back, her fingers sinking into the deep muscles of his chest.

Jack stiffened. His head came up; his hands dropped, clenched, to his knees.

Kit nuzzled his neck, and whispered softly in his ear. "Jack? Please? Someone has to do it. I want it to be you."

The thought that this was the first time in his entire career he'd felt at a disadvantage in a bedroom floated through Jack's fevered brain. He couldn't think with her so close, in her present state. There was something important about her being a virgin that he should have grasped, but the elusive fact slipped further away as Kit laid her cheek against his shoulder.

"Jack? Please?"

What man of flesh and blood could resist such a plea? He certainly couldn't.

With a sigh of defeat, Jack pushed aside the disturbing conviction that he was about to commit an irrevocable act which would seal his fate forever, and turned. Kit was right behind him, waiting, her expression anxious.

Her heart in her mouth, Kit met Jack's gaze, smoldering silver fire. Would he? When his eyes held hers, as if trying to see beyond the passion of the moment, her confidence faltered. Her arms dropped to her sides. The silver gaze fell to her parted lips, then to her breasts, rising and falling rapidly, and finally, to the auburn curls between her widespread thighs.

Jack groaned and took her to the sheets, turning her into his arms. "Hell only knows, Kit Cranmer, but you're the most wanton virgin I've ever known."

It was the last lucid thought either of them had. Their lips met in a frenzy of need, too long denied to be gentle. The fire of their passion engulfed them, obliterating any lingering reservations. When Jack swung over her, Kit accepted his weight eagerly, her hands kneading his back in frantic entreaty.

Eyes closed, savoring the feel of her slim body arching against his, Jack grimaced. She was going to try his control as it had never been tried before. Bend your knees up. It'll make it easier.

Kit complied with the rough command, too far gone in longing to be concerned over the intimate and vulnerable position. She felt his fingers part her, then hardness, smooth and solid, entered her. The pressure built as he pushed farther, inexorably inward, forcing her heated flesh to yield him passage. There was no pain, but she felt the tension when he abutted the barrier that marked her incontrovertibly virgin. To her dismay, he pulled back. Kit clamped her muscles tight to hold him within her.

Braced above her, he gave a chuckle that changed halfway through to a groan. Relax.

Passion permitted her a spurt of resentment. Relax? He might have done this countless times before, but he knew she was a novice. Did he have any idea what it felt like to have him invading her body in such an intimate way? At the thought, Kit pressed her head back into the pillow. She moaned, with relief, with anticipation, as she felt him return, surging up to the barrier, only to stop and retreat again.

Gradually, as he repeated the motion, Kit caught his rhythm. Instinctively, she matched it, tightening as he withdrew, relaxing as he entered. Even through her slickness she could feel the friction in her flesh. A flame of a different sort grew steadily, ripples of tension concealed within it.

Jack's groan was encouraging. He dropped from his elbows, the pressure of his chest soothing her aching breasts. Kit hugged him to her. Her lips sought his, every bit as fervent as he. Her breath was suspended when his tongue delved deep. The sensation that streaked through her was quite different now that he was inside her. Her tension built. She felt her body arch hard against his, her hips lifting, searching. One large hand pushed under her until it cradled her buttocks. At the limit of his next outward movement, the long fingers slipped between her thighs, to the point of their union. And pressed.

Kit came off the bed, arching wildly in the grip of a passion she'd no hope of controlling. In desperate need of air, she dragged her lips from Jack's, pressing her head back into the pillows. She felt him thrust powerfully and a fiery pain flared inside. Her fingers dug into his back as he plunged deep into her body. Abruptly, the pain of his invasion disappeared in an explosion of delicious release, her tension peaking and overflowing in intense ripples through her straining muscles, the flames he'd stoked transforrning pain to pleasure.

It took some minutes before Kit's mind registered anything beyond the warmth left behind by the flames. They continued to flicker, drawing her back to reality and the fact that Jack was holding still, his cheek pressed hard against her hair, his breathing a ragged, desperate sound by her ear. Her senses returned and she felt the steady throb of him, deep against her womb.

It was torture of the most exquisite sort, but Jack held still, every muscle clenched with the effort. He should have expected it. The damn woman had done everything she could to bring him low so of course she'd climax at just that moment. As their heartbeats mingled, the tension of her release dwindled. Her body's instinctive response to his invasion subsided as her muscles adapted to the novelty of having him buried inside her. When her hips tilted slightly, experimentally, as if to draw him deeper, he released the breath he'd been holding and started to move.

Kit responded immediately, caught by the discovery of how easily he rode her now that there was no barrier holding him back. His lips returned to hers and she accepted his kiss eagerly, her body straining against his as sensation washed through her. The tight buds of her nipples brushed his chest, over and over. With something very like awe, she felt that odd tension burgeoning once more, swelling and growing and expanding within her.

Jack released her lips, his breathing labored. His thrusts rocked her; she urged him on, her hips meeting his, her hands urgent on his back.

"*Jack!*" Kit's breath caught on a sob.

Her second climax overtook her, hurling her into the limbo of lovers. She was deaf to Jack's triumphant shout as he followed her.

Firelight filled the room with shifting shadows, gilding the heavy musculature of Jack's back as he stood at the end of the bed and stared, frowning, at the woman curled naked under the sheet.

The vision of how she'd looked, sprawled, sated and at peace beneath him, shook him. It took no effort to conjure up the rosy-tipped breasts, firm and proud, the tiny waist and those hips that had defeated him under the tree. And her legs – long and slender, thighs firm and strong from riding. She'd given him the ride of his life. He glanced down, and was relieved to see the memory hadn't stirred him beyond mild interest. She was exhausted – more from her own excesses than his. He'd no plans to mount her again that night.

Jack took a long sip of brandy from the glass in his hand. She'd fallen asleep virtually instantaneously the first time. He'd held her cradled in his arms, tired but not ready to sleep, prey to an emotion he couldn't define. He'd forgotten it when she'd stirred. Her lids had fluttered, then opened wide, the amethyst eyes large and shining. He'd been watching, interested to see her reaction. Having been in the same position often before, he'd been prepared for anything from shocked reproaches to smug self-satisfaction. He hadn't been prepared for the smile of dazzling beauty that had lit her face, or the warm tenderness in her eyes. And even less prepared for the kiss she'd bestowed on him.

His body had reacted with a vengeance. His control in abeyance, he'd been unable to rein in the passion that had flared. When her fingers had touched him, stroked him, he'd been rigid and ready for her. He'd heard her chuckle, delighted with his response as she continued to caress him.

"You fool! You'll be sore enough as it is."

She'd only laughed, a low, husky, mind-numbing sound that had frazzled his good intentions. "I'm not sore at all."

He'd lain on his back and tried to ignore her. She'd come over him, her breasts brushing his chest, to kiss him long and lingeringly, exploring his mouth as he had hers. His control had been in tatters by the time she'd drawn back to whisper against his lips: "I want you Jack. Inside me. Now."

How he'd remained still in the face of such an invitation he'd never know. But she hadn't been defeated. "I'm hot and wet for you, Jack. See?" And the brazen woman had caught his hand and guided his fingers to where her warm honey was spilling onto her thighs.

With a groan, he'd delved deep and heard her breath

catch. An instant later, he'd rolled her onto her back and, with one powerful thrust, had sheathed himself to the hilt in her welcoming warmth. And it hadn't stopped there.

He'd tried to remind himself she was new to the game but her responses drove him far beyond rational thought. However hard he pushed her, she met him and urged him on, matching his passion with hers. Of her own volition, she'd wrapped her long legs about his waist, opening to him completely. As her tension had mounted a second time he'd remembered what he'd promised himself.

"Open your eyes." Thankfully, she'd responded to his gravelly command, ground out through clenched teeth. His next thrust had sent her spiraling over the precipice. As her lids drooped, he'd closed his own eyes in satisfaction. Her eyes had gone black.

Sensing that her release had been total, he'd opened her even wider and thrust deeply, seeking his own ticket to heaven in her fire. He'd found it.

When next he'd been able to sense anything, he'd felt her soft breath on his cheek. She'd fallen asleep while he was still inside her, a small, satisfied smile on her lips. Feeling ridiculously pleased with himself, he'd held her close and turned to his side, careful not to disturb their union. He'd surrendered to sleep, feeling her heartbeat in his veins.

He'd woken ten minutes ago. After gathering his wits, he'd carefully unwound their tangled limbs and pulled the sheets over her. Then headed for the brandy.

The intensity of his satisfaction was one thing. What was much more worrying was this other feeling, an irrational emotion which the events of the night had caused to grow alarmingly. Her whispered plea had been his undoing, in more ways than one.

Jack snorted and sipped his brandy, raising his head to

listen to the storm as it swept past. The wind was still howling; the rain was still drumming against the shutters. There'd been a number of cracks of thunder; from them, he judged the worst was past. Outside. Inside, he was far from convinced Kit's seduction was the end of anything. It felt much more like a beginning.

His eyes traced the curves concealed beneath the sheet. If it'd just been lust, all would be well, but what he felt for the damn woman went far beyond that. Jack grimaced. No doubt George could define the emotion for him, but he, of his own volition, wasn't ready to do so yet. He didn't trust the feeling – he'd wait to see what came next. Who knew how she'd behave tomorrow – she'd been one surprise after another thus far.

With a sigh, Jack drained the glass and replaced it on the table. He stoked the fire, then joined Kit between the sheets. She stirred and, in her sleep, snuggled closer. Jack smiled and turned on his side, drawing her to him, curving her back into his chest. He heard her contented sigh as she settled under his arm. At least he wouldn't have to spend any more nights following her home through the dark.

Chapter 18

Dawn was painting the sky when Kit rode up the paddock at the back of the Cranmer Hall stables. She dismounted and led Delia inside, then unsaddled the mare and rubbed her down. Delia had survived the storm, safe in her stall beside Champion. As for herself, Kit wasn't so sure.

She couldn't even remember any thunder, let alone the panic that usually attacked her at such times. What she could remember had kept her cheeks rosy all the way home from the cottage.

The weight of Jack's arm across her waist had penetrated her doze and brought her fully awake. She'd spent minutes in stunned recollection, as the events of the night had replayed in her brain. Jack had been sound asleep beside her. She'd edged from under his arm, conscious of a reluctance to leave his safe warmth yet quite sure she wouldn't want to be there when he awoke.

With a last pat for Delia, Kit left the stables. The morning-room windows which gave onto the terrace had long been her favored route for clandestine excursions. Minutes later, she was safe in her chamber. She discarded her clothes, a simple matter now that they were dry. She'd dressed in silent haste, petrified lest Jack should hear her and wake up. But he'd slumbered on, a smile she'd long remember on his lips.

She'd remember his lips for a long time, too. Kit blushed and clambered into her bed. Damn the man – she'd wanted to be initiated, but had he needed to go so far? She couldn't even think of the experience without blushing. She'd have to get over it, or Amy would become suspicious. The idea of confiding in Amy surfaced, only to be discarded. Amy would be horrified. Scandalized by her wildness. But then, Amy was marrying for love. She, Kit, was not marrying at all.

Kit pulled the covers to her chin and turned on her side, conscious of the empty bed behind her and annoyed at herself for it. She'd have to put the entire episode from her mind or even Spencer would notice. She wasn't up to analyzing how she felt and what her conclusions on the activity were – she'd do that some other time, when she could think straight again.

She closed her eyes, determined to find slumber. She'd learned what she'd wanted to know – Jack had been a thorough teacher. Her curiosity had been well and truly satisfied. She was free and unfettered. She was no longer in charge of smugglers; she no longer needed to appear at their runs to be a redundant lookout. All was well in the world.

Why couldn't she sleep?

Seven miles to the north, Jack came awake and instantly knew he was alone. He sat up and scanned the room, then, his privacy confirmed, fell back to the pillows, a puzzled frown on his face. Had he dreamed it?

A glance to the left revealed two bright strands of curling

red hair, lying in an indentation in the pillow. Jack picked them up; the dim light filtering through the shutters struck red glints from their surface. Memories flooded him. One brow quirked upward. He lifted the sheet and looked down to where a few flecks of reddish brown stained the cream sheets.

No, he hadn't dreamed it. Once his mission was complete, he'd build on the start he'd made last night.

Jack groaned. Who was he fooling? His mission might take months. He couldn't possibly wait that long; after last night, he sincerely doubted she could. Not that she'd know that, but she'd find out soon enough. He might as well face it – for good or ill, Kit Cranmer and his mission looked set to stay entangled, certainly for the forseeable future.

His glance strayed to the bright strands wrapped around his fingers. He should, of course, feel irritated. But irritation was not what he felt.

Four days later, irritation was very close to his surface. He'd spent his Saturday and Sunday in a peculiar daze. On both nights, he'd gone to the cottage, but Kit hadn't shown up. He'd relieved his frustrations by visiting the Revenue Office at Hunstanton on Monday and making Sergeant Tonkin's life miserable. His questions had been phrased in an idle way, concealing the fact that he was intimately acquainted with Tonkin's unsuccessful attempt to trap his "big gang." He'd made Tonkin squirm, then later felt guilty. The man was a blot on the landscape, but in this instance he'd only been doing his job.

Jack had ridden to the Monday meeting at the Old Barn, silently rehearsing the words he intended to burn Kit's ears with, when they repaired to the cottage afterward. She hadn't shown her face.

What annoyed him most was that he actually felt hurt by her nonappearance. And the emotional hurt was much worse than the physical manifestation. At least, thanks to her earlier antics, he'd got used to that.

Now, he stood on the sands in the lee of the cliff and waited for his first "human cargo" to come ashore. He forced his mind back to the present, slamming a mental door against all thoughts of a redheaded houri in breeches. He glanced up at the cliff. Joe was on watch, but Jack doubted Sergeant Tonkin would try his luck quite so soon after his last dismal failure.

The first boat came in, swiftly followed by three more. A cargo of kegs and one man. He was in the first boat, a slight figure muffled to the eyes in an old greatcoat. Matthew, beside Jack, snorted at the sight.

Jack grimaced. "I know, you old warhorse – I'd like to get my hands around his throat, too. But he won't escape."

Matthew shifted, checking their surroundings. "D'ye think Major Smeaton'll have reached London by now?"

"George won't have dallied on the road. He should have passed the news on by now. There will be a welcome awaiting this one when he gets to London. A welcome he wasn't counting on."

"Why can't we just stop him here?"

"Because we need to know who he's meeting in London." Jack started down the beach. Reluctantly, Matthew followed.

Jack paid little attention to the spy, which gave the spy equally little chance of studying him. His disguise was good but not perfect; he'd no idea who the man was or what his station in life might be. A fellow officer, or the personal servant of a fellow officer, might well recognize him, or at least realize there was something a little odd about the

Hunstanton Gang's leader. Jack busied himself with his material cargo and ignored the man.

The spy was put on a pony, and Shep and two of the older members of the gang set out to deliver him to the ruins of Creake Abbey. From there, he'd be spirited to London, the Admiralty's tracker on his tail.

Satisfied that all had gone smoothly, Jack followed the kegs to the Old Barn. They'd be taken to the abbey the following night. After the men had dispersed, he and Matthew rode to the cottage. From the first, he'd made a point of changing his clothes and his identity at the old fishing cottage; tonight, he had another reason for calling in. He didn't have much hope Kit would appear, but he wouldn't be able to sleep, alone between his silk sheets, if he didn't check.

The cottage was empty.

Lord Hendon rode home to his castle, cursing all red-headed houris.

There was no moon on Wednesday night. Astride Delia, Kit sat concealed in the deepest shadows under the trees in front of Jack's cottage and waited for him to return from the Blackbird. She'd determined not to come near him. Nothing could have got her to the cottage again – nothing except the news that the Hunstanton Gang had run a "human cargo" last night.

The past five days seemed an eon in time. She'd been consumed by an odd restlessness that increased daily. Doubtless the effect of delayed guilt. It had even disturbed her sleep. She didn't need to convince herself of the threat Jack represented. He was a smuggler – not of her class, hardly an acceptable suitor. The events of Friday night were burned into her brain; the effects were burned into her flesh. She'd wanted to know – now she knew. But that didn't mean she could turn her back on Spencer and all he represented. She was a gentlewoman, no matter how much that sometimes irked. After the night of the storm, Jack was not just forbidden fruit – he was danger personified.

So she'd stayed away from the Monday night meeting but had dropped by the little fishing village this afternoon. Noah and the others had been there. Without hesitation, they'd filled her in on the previous night's activities.

Their lack of loyalty to their country didn't overly surprise her. She doubted that, living isolated as they did, they understood the implication of "human cargo." Jack hadn't spelled it out for them. But nothing could convince her Jack didn't have a military background. There was no possibility he didn't comprehend the significance of the men he was smuggling into the country.

Delia shifted. Kit sighed. She shouldn't have come – she didn't want to be here. But she couldn't let "human cargoes" be run and not do something about it. If she could make Jack stop, she would. If not . . . She'd think about that later.

A jingle of harness came to her ears, carried clearly over the silent fields. It was five minutes before they came into view, coming up the track from the northern coast, Matthew, George, and Jack. Kit held her breath.

They were walking their horses toward the small stable when Jack realized Kit was close. Or rather, Champion sensed Delia's presence and showed every sign of refusing to go into the stable without his lady love. Jack dismounted and took hold of the stallion's bridle above the bit. "Matthew, I'll be here for a while. You go on home."

With a mumbled "Aye," Matthew turned his horse and headed south for the Castle.

Jack turned to George, who was eyeing him suspiciously.

Captain Jack's devilish smile appeared. "I'd ask you in, but I suspect I've got company."

George looked down on him, his expression resigned. Jack knew he'd never ask who the company was. George didn't approve of his rakish ways.

"I take it you're sure you can handle this company alone?"

Jack's smile deepened. "Quite sure."

"That's what I thought." George pulled his chesnut about, then paused to add: "One day, Jack, you'll get bitten. I just hope I'm around when it happens, to say 'serves you right.'"

Jack laughed; George touched his heels to his horse and departed.

Jack noted the direction of Champion's fixed stare but didn't follow it. Instead, he spoke sternly to the horse. The stallion tossed his grey head at the rebuke but consented to be led to his stable. Jack unsaddled the great beast and rubbed him down in record time.

He'd expected Kit to appear as soon as the others left. When she didn't, Jack went back to stand in front of the cottage, wondering if Champion could have been mistaken.

From the shadows of the trees, Kit watched him. Up to the time he'd arrived, her course had been clear. But the sight of him had awoken memories of that stormy night in the cottage, reducing her to vacillating nervousness. Perhaps she'd do better to meet him in daylight?

Convinced by the pricking of his own senses that Champion hadn't been mistaken, Jack lost patience. He stood in the doorway of the cottage, hands on hips, and faced the trees across the clearing. "Come out, Kit. I've no intention of playing hide-and-seek in the dark."

The subtle threat in his tone made up Kit's mind for her.

Reluctantly, she nudged Delia out of the trees. Suddenly remembering she'd no idea what Jack had made of her absence, she reined in. But she'd already gone too far. Jack stepped forward and caught Delia's bridle. The next instant, Kit felt his hands at her waist. She bit back a protest which wouldn't have been listened to anyway, too stunned by the force of her reaction to his touch to do anything more than summon up her defenses. Things were more serious than she'd thought; she'd have to ensure she didn't give herself away.

To her relief, Jack released her immediately. Without a word, he led Delia to the stable. Uncertain of her welcome and a host of related matters, Kit followed.

Jack hadn't noticed her reaction, for the simple reason he'd been too busy registering the violence of his own feelings. He'd never known a woman to affect him as Kit did. It was novel, unnerving and bloody annoying to boot. He hurt like hell in two entirely different places. He intended to see she eased at least one of the ills she'd inflicted on him – the more accessible one. The other he wasn't sure even she could cure.

Delia went readily into the stall next to Champion. Jack unsaddled her and rubbed her down. He was aware of Kit hovering at the stable door but ignored her as best he could. If he acknowledged her presence, she'd be on her back in the hay inside of a minute.

When she saw Jack unsaddling Delia, Kit sought for words to protest – she wasn't staying long. None came. In fact, she was seriously wondering if it was safe to talk to Jack at all. There was a certain tension in the large frame, a tension that was making her decidedly uneasy.

Before she'd time to think of anything to the point, Jack finished with Delia and strode out of the stable. "Come on."

To her annoyance, Kit found herself scurrying in his wake as he strode to the cottage door. He went through and held it open for her. Firelight cast a rosy glow through the room. Summoning what dignity she could, Kit sauntered to the table and dropped her hat on a chair. She was unwinding her muffler when the sound of the bolt on the door falling home set every nerve quivering. Her senses in turmoil, she forced herself to continue with her task, folding the muffler and placing it by her hat. Then she turned to face him.

Only to find he was right behind her. She turned into his arms and his lips came down on hers. Her moan of protest turned to a moan of desire, then faded to a whimper of pleasure as his tongue touched hers. Incapable of resisting, Kit placed her hands on Jack's shoulders and gave herself up to his embrace. She remembered her mission – to make him see sense, to promise not to run more spies – but she wouldn't be able to do anything until his passionate welcome came to an end. She might as well enjoy it until then. Besides which, thinking while Jack's lips were on hers, while his tongue played havoc with her senses, was well-nigh impossible.

Thinking was certainly not on Jack's agenda. What need was there for thought? He didn't even need to rein in his desire – she'd already given herself to him. His expertise as a lover would take care of her needs. His most urgent thought, the only one left in his brain, was to satisfy his needs. The primal lust he'd denied for too long, which she'd fed then let go hungry for five days and four nights, was on the rampage and had to be assuaged.

The softening of her body against his, her surrender implied, was all he waited for.

Kit felt his body envelop her, his hard heat both reassuring and exciting. His hands shifted and he backed her up until the table pressed against her thighs. Even in her semidrugged state, intoxicated with the taste of his passion, some small part of her brain was awake enough to register alarm. But before she could think, Jack's hands shifted. To her breasts, bound beneath her bands. Instantly, Kit felt discomfort which rapidly turned to pain. Her breasts swelled at Jack's touch; the bands cut into her soft flesh.

Luckily, Jack understood the source of her sudden gasp. He yanked her shirt free of her breeches and pushed it high to expose the linen bands. Kit lifted her arm so he could get at the knot. In a moment, it was undone; seconds later, the bands hit the floor and she breathed again.

Then Jack's lips found her nipple and her diaphragm seized. A sound halfway between a moan and a gasp was torn from her lips. As his tongue rasped her sensitive flesh, Kit arched into his hands. They fastened about her waist and he lifted her, setting her bottom on the table's edge, moving with her so that he stood between her wide-spread thighs.

The vulnerability of her position convinced Kit that Jack's welcome was not going to end with a kiss, or even with a caress, no matter how intimate. She wasn't entirely sure how he'd do it, but she knew what he intended.

A thrill of sheer delight coursed through her. She shuddered, and knew it drove him on. His lips returned to hers, his tongue instigating a duel of desire. She participated fully, all thought of her purpose drowned beneath the passion that flooded her. Wrapping her arms tight about his neck, she pressed her body to his. She could feel the evidence of his desire, pulsing hard and insistent against the softness of her belly.

When Jack's hands went to her knees, then skimmed the long muscles of her thighs back to her hips, Kit's stomach clenched in anticipation. One hand slid between her thighs to cup the mound between, long fingers stroking her through the stuff of her breeches. Kit moaned her displeasure, the sound trapped between them. A familiar heat was beating steady in her veins, a void had opened up deep inside. She needed him to fill her.

She felt Jack's knowing chuckle, then his hands moved to the buttons of her breeches. For the life of her, Kit couldn't imagine what he was about. Why not just take her to the bed? But she wasn't about to start an argument. With the flap open, his hands eased the garment over her hips. He lifted her, tipping her backward on the table, stepping back to draw the breeches to her boots. The boots pulled off easily; the breeches followed, leaving her naked from the waist down, her shirt pushed up to expose her breasts. Leaning back on her elbows, Kit blushed. But she forgot her inhibitions the instant her gaze collided with Jack's. Silver flames smoldered in his eyes. Sparks of pure passion lit their depths.

Kit watched him straighten, her breath caught in her throat, the sensation of being about to be devoured creeping over her. She shuddered in delicious anticipation and held out one arm to him. He smiled, supremely male, and closed the distance between them, his hands on the buttons of his corded breeches. As he stepped between her thighs, spreading them wide, his manhood sprang free, engorged and fully erect.

Kit's eyes flew wide, her mind seized, her heartbeat thundered in her ears. He was going to take her here and now – *on the table.*

She didn't have time for so much as a squawk. Jack's hands fastened about her hips and he drove into her. Kit's mind clenched in expectation of pain. There was none. Instead, her body welcomed him, arching, drawing him deeper. As Jack withdrew then thrust into her again, seating himself firmly within her, Kit felt the slipperiness that had eased his passage.

She'd been ready for him. She'd wanted him, and her body had known it. He'd known it.

Kit's eyes glazed as Jack's thrusts settled to a steady pounding. This was different from last time. The urgency coursing his veins communicated itself to her. She responded instinctively, lifting her hips, tilting them to draw him deeper still. She felt his fingers tighten about her hips. Her lids fell as she eased from her elbows to lie back on the table, her hands fastening on Jack's forearms, her fingers digging into muscles that flexed as he held her immobile against his repeated invasions.

The fever inside her burgeoned and grew, rapidly overtaking all other sensations. Her whole being was focused on his possession of her, complete and devastating as it was.

"Lift your legs."

Kit wrapped them about his waist.

Jack groaned and drove into her, wanting every fraction of an inch of penetration he could get. Her body welcomed him with heat and yet more heat, her muscles clenching about him in time with his thrusts.

A blinding explosion rocked Kit. Her body arched; her nails dug deep into Jack's arms. His response was to lean forward and take one nipple into his mouth. He suckled and she cried out. The waves of sensation abruptly intensified, breaking in a glorious climax to flow as molten passion through her veins. Her throbbing contractions continued long after. They were still with her when Jack reached his own release, spilling his seed deep within her.

Jack drew a shuddering breath and looked down at Kit, spread in wanton abandon before him. She was barely conscious, lying back on the table, struggling to breathe as he was, waiting for some measure of physical ability to return.

He couldn't resist a smug smile, but it turned to a half grimace as reality intruded. Five days had passed before she'd returned to his side. Once he touched her, she was his, but out of his reach, she was clearly one of those females with a very long fuse. There were ways to shorten that fuse, things he could do to ensure she burned with a passion to match his, not only in intensity, but in frequency, too. He didn't know where their lives were headed, only that they'd remain inextricably entwined, and, at least for him, the ties went deep. Strengthening the ties that held her to him seemed a good idea.

Kit lay still and waited for Jack to do something. She wasn't capable of doing anything herself. Her extended climax had drained her, physically and mentally. She remembered she'd come here to talk but couldn't recall any pressing urgency about the matter. While her flesh still throbbed and he remained inside her, she couldn't even recall what her point had been.

When he eased from her, Kit opened her eyes. From under weighted lids, she watched as he discarded his clothes. Naked, he came to her, a smile of male triumph on his lips, the expression echoed in his silver eyes. She suspected she should take exception but could only manage a weary smile.

"Come on. Up with you."

Jack caught her hands and drew her to sit on the edge of the table. While he divested her of her coat and pulled her shirt over her head, Kit wondered how she'd ever be able to face him across this particular table again. All he'd have to do was look at its surface and she'd curl up with embarassment.

To her relief, he swung her up in his arms and headed for the bed, presumably understanding that her legs were as incapacitated as her brain. Kit sighed contentedly when Jack laid her between the sheets. She curled into his arms, entirely at peace.

Beds she could cope with. Tables were something else again.

Chapter 19

It was a perfect summer night, the air soft and balmy. Kit stood beside Delia close by the cliff, waiting for Captain Jack. A sickle moon rode the purple skies, shedding just enough light to distinguish the huddled shapes a few yards away as men, rather than rocks. Their muffled conversation drifted past Kit's ears.

Facing the waves, Kit registered their regular ebb and flow, a parody of her confusion. Jack had unleashed all manner of wild longings; they sent her surging forward to some unknown fate. A deep-seated acknowledgment of what was due her position, her loyalty to Spencer, drew her back. Wednesday night had been a disaster. Kit's lips lifted in a self-deprecatory smile. A delicious disaster, but a disaster nonetheless. She'd intended to convince Jack of the folly of running "human cargoes." Instead, she'd been convinced of the folly of self-delusion.

No one, not even Amy, had warned her of the fever in her flesh. Of the aching void that, now the way was open, seemed to have grown within her. Her mind longed to recapture that moment of completeness. Her body yearned for the flame to transform her fever to consuming passion. She'd sensed it even after that first night at the cottage – a restlessness, a need she'd tried to ignore and had done her best to stifle. Wednesday night had left her with no alternative but to admit her addiction to Jack's loving.

Delia shifted, blowing low. Kit peered down the beach but could see nothing. She'd intended to bring up the subject of the spies once she'd recovered from Jack's amorous welcome. But he'd never let her recover. He'd stirred her awake far too soon; rational conversation had not been his aim. The night had dissolved into an orgy of mutual satisfaction. She couldn't deny she'd enjoyed it – her pleasure had been his command.

With a grimace, Kit shifted her stance. She might revel in Jack's attentions, but she wasn't about to let passion rule her life. Yet the niggling suspicion that Jack had *intended* Wednesday night, certainly the latter half of it, that he'd planned and executed their play like some campaign, had remained, a shadow in her mind. At dawn, he'd helped her dress, his touch deeply unsettling, then he'd saddled Delia. He'd told her of tonight's run, making it unnecessary for her to attend the meeting last night in the Old Barn.

Naturally, she hadn't gone, knowing that if she did show her face, she'd be admitting to him her addiction to his company. Instead, she'd gone early to bed. But not to sleep. Half the night had passed in tossing and turning, the fever burning slow and steady and unfulfilled.

Had he purposely drugged her with passion?

The broad shoulders of her nemesis hove into view. Kit watched as he rode up on Champion, George and Matthew, as ever, in attendance. Jack's silver-grey gaze swept her, the comprehensive glance followed by a fleeting smile. He dismounted, and the men milled about him.

Kit waited until the men moved to their positions, George and Matthew with them, before stepping forward. "Where do you want me tonight?"

Immediately, she bit her tongue. Jack had been glancing down the beach; at her words, his head swung about, an arrested expression on his face. For one fractured minute, she thought he'd answer with the words in his mind.

Jack was sorely tempted. The sound of her husky tones confidently voicing such a query sent a spasm of sheer desire through his veins. But he clamped a lid on that particular pot and set it aside to simmer. A slow, infinitely devilish smile twisted his lips. "I'll think about it for the next hour or two. I'll tell you my decision later – at the cottage."

Kit wished she could say something to wipe the smug expression from his face.

"But for now," Jack continued, suddenly brisk, "I need you on lookout. Wherever you like, since you won't obey my orders."

Kit tilted her chin. She turned and set her foot in her stirrup, pointedly getting on with her business.

The large hand that caressed her bottom shattered her complacency. After one leisurely circuit, it boosted her up to her saddle. Kit landed with a gasp. In daylight, her glare would have fried him. In moonlight, he stood, hands on hips, a patronizing expression on his face and gave her back arrogant stare for stare.

Sheer fury seared Kit's veins. She clamped her lips shut and hauled on Delia's reins. If she gave vent to her feelings here and now, her disguise would be blown past redemption.

Once on the cliff, she found a position overlooking Jack's operations and dismounted. Too furious to sit still, she paced back and forth, twitching her gloves between her hands, her gaze on the beach, her temper on the boil.

Exclamations crowded her brain. *How dare he?* seemed far too mild. Besides, she knew how he dared – he knew damn well she wasn't strong enough to withstand attack on that front, damn his silver eyes! If she didn't need to know about the spies, she'd never come near him again. But she'd been through all the arguments, assessed all the alternatives. Until she had some facts, a run date for instance, there was no point in revealing her masquerade. If Spencer heard of it, he'd forbid her to continue, and then they'd never stop the spies.

Anger was not the only emotion coursing through her. Kit shivered with reaction. Damn the man – if she'd needed any confirmation he'd planned Wednesday night's activities, that knowing caress had provided it. He'd purposely lit the fires of sensual pleasure in her flesh, so it would take just a caress to stir them to life. Kit ground her teeth and kicked a rock out of her way.

He was too damned sure of himself! He was too damned sure of her.

The run proceeded smoothly, as all Jack's enterprises did. Kit watched, mulling over that fact. Jack's cottage was on Lord Hendon's land. And Lord Hendon had conveniently sent Sergeant Osborne to patrol the Sheringham beaches and Sergeant Tonkin to watch the shores of the Wash. A cynic might imagine there was a connection.

Kit snorted. The only real connection would be that Lord Hendon, like all the surrounding gentry, tolerated the smugglers. But not the spies. On that point, Jack had stepped beyond the line.

As the ponies headed for the cliff, Kit rose and caught Delia's trailing reins. She mounted and urged the mare into the trees lining the first field. From there, she watched until the last of the pack train emerged from the cliff path. Then, before the grey stallion appeared, Kit turned Delia's head for Cranmer Hall and dropped her hands.

She kept the mare to a steady gallop, the black hooves eating the miles. When the shadow of the Hall loomed out of the dark, Kit uttered a small whoop and sent Delia flying over the stable paddock fence.

Safe home. She'd escaped Jack's trap, for one night at least. A fever might be the price she'd have to pay, but she'd pay gladly. Aside from anything else, it was safer this way.

Jack and his swaggering arrogance could spend the night alone.

On Sunday afternoon, after spending a virtuous morning at church, then presiding over the luncheon table, Kit sat Delia in the shadow of the trees facing Jack's cottage, her confidence at an all-time low. Distrustful of her reasons for being there, uncertain of her chances of success, she bit her lip and eyed the closed door. There was nothing to tell her if the cottage was inhabited or not.

If she sat still for long and Champion was in the stable, the stallion would sense Delia's presence and neigh, destroying any advantage surprise might otherwise give her. If she sat still for much longer, her courage would desert her and she'd turn tail for home. Kit directed Delia in an arc about the clearing. She approached the stable and dismounted, then led Delia inside.

Champion's huge grey rump loomed out of the dimness.

Kit stopped, not sure if she felt relieved, excited, or dismayed. The stallion's head came around; Kit took Delia to the stall alongside. After tethering the mare, she debated whether to unsaddle or not. In the end, she did, refusing to acknowledge the action implied anything at all about her intentions, much less her hopes. She rubbed the mare down, ears pricked to detect any sound of approaching danger.

She knew why she was there – she needed to mend her fences with Jack; he was her only reliable source of information on the spies. Her wilder self jeered; Kit strangled it. There might be other reasons she'd ridden this way, but she wasn't ready to acknowledge them – not in daylight. Her innards were in a dreadful state; trepidation walked her nerves. She'd never felt like this before, not even when admitting to riding Spencer's favorite stallion at the age of ten. Spencer's rages had no power to make her quiver. The thought of how Jack would look when next she saw him, in a few minutes, did.

How would he welcome her this time?

The thought stopped her in her tracks as she headed for the stable door. She almost turned back to resaddle Delia. But her reason for being here resurfaced. She couldn't walk away from "human cargo." Kit set her jaw. With a determined stride, she made for the cottage door.

Kit paused with her hand on the latch, swept by the sense of being about to enter a potentially dangerous animal's lair. The cold iron of the latch sent a thrill through her fingers. Her whole being vibrated with anticipation. In truth, she wasn't sure where the danger lay – with him? Or with herself?

Inside the cottage, Jack lay sprawled on his back in the middle of the bed, his hands locked behind his head. He stared at the ceiling.

How long would it be before it got to her? How long before she came to find him?

He gave a disgruntled snort; his brows lowered. When he'd embarked on his scheme to embed passionate longing firmly beneath Kit's satiny skin, he'd overlooked the inevitable effect such an undertaking would have on his own lustful appetites. Since Wednesday night, he'd been ravenous. And, thanks to Kit, he hadn't been able to sate his hunger. No other woman would do. He'd retired to the cottage, to brood on his desire.

He wanted *her* – Kit – the redheaded houri in breeches.

When he stroked her, she purred. When he mounted her, she arched wildly. And later, when their passion was spent, she curled into his side like a small cream-and-ginger cat. His very own kitten.

His very own pedigree kitten. When it came to making love, she was an aristocrat, no matter what her breeding. Her performances to date had been eye-opening, particularly to one of his experience. He'd thought he'd known all there was to know of women; she'd proved him wrong. The feigned responses of the gilded whores of the *ton* had always bored him. Kit' s naturalness, her sincere enjoyment of their play despite the underlying prudery behind her occasional shocked protests, entranced him. He'd been able to turn her protests into moans with satisfying regularity.

With a stifled groan, Jack stretched his arms and legs, trying to ease the tension locked in the heavy muscles. His frown convened to a scowl. Twenty-four hours had been too long for him – seventy-two had been hell. The fact that she could deal with this particular disease better than he could was a severe blow to his male pride.

The latch on the door eased upward.

Instantly, Jack was alert, half-sitting before his mind took control and stilled his instinctive reaction. His impulse was to cross silently to stand behind the door. But if his visitor was Kit, he might scare her witless by appearing beside her so unexpectedly.

The door swung slowly inward. The shadow of a slender figure, topped by a tricorne, fell on the floor. Jack relaxed. He permitted himself a smug smile, then the memory of the past seventy-two hours intruded. He'd no guarantee she'd come to alleviate his discomfort. His expression bland, he settled back on the pillows.

Kit scanned the area revealed by the open door. Jack was not at the table. Swallowing her nervousness, she took a deep breath and stepped over the threshold. She paused by the door, one hand on the edge of the worn wooden panel and forced herself to look at the bed.

There he lay, sprawled full-length on the covers, arrogant male inscribed on every line of his tautly muscled frame. Watching her. With a distinctly predatory gleam in his silver eyes.

Kit's breath suspended; her mouth went dry. She felt her eyes grow larger and larger.

Jack read her state in her eyes and knew precisely why she'd come. The news sent his senses soaring, but he clamped down on them before they addled his wits. His body had tensed with the instinctive urge to rise and go to her, to sweep her into his arms and crush her lips, her breasts, her hips, to his. But if he did, what would happen next?

The door was midway between the bed and the table, not particularly close to either. Judging by his last effort in welcoming her, they'd probably end up on the floor. While he had nothing against *al fresco* intercourse, he hadn't been particularly proud of his lack of control in taking her on the table. He didn't know what she'd made of the experience, but he'd seen the red patches on her buttocks later. And felt hideously guilty. Too often he'd ended up giving her bruises, however unintentionally. Some like the marks his fingers left in the soft curves of her hips were unavoidable given she bruised easily. But he didn't need to add to them through lack of thought.

"Bolt the door." He tried to keep the raw passion pulsing his veins from coloring his tone and only partially succeeded.

Kit's eyes grew rounder still. Her limbs felt heavy as her gaze trapped in Jack's silver stare, she moved slowly to obey. Her fingers fumbled and she dragged her eyes from his. The bolt slid home with a metallic thud. Slowly, she turned back to face him, expecting to see him rising.

He hadn't moved. "Come here."

Kit considered that carefully. She might be mesmerized; she wasn't witless. But she was caught, very firmly, in the sensual web he'd woven with such consumate skill, her pulse already increasing in anticipation of what was to come. Acknowledging the inevitable, she placed one foot before the other. Slowly, warily, she approached the bed.

"Stop." The gravelly command halted her a yard from the end of the bed. "Take off your hat and coat."

Kit's stomach contracted. She pulled off her hat and dropped it, then shrugged off her coat and let it slide to the floor. As the silver gaze dropped from her face to sweep her figure, Kit felt the embers of her passion glow.

"Take off those damned breeches."

Kit's embers burst into flame. She stared at Jack, shocked and tantalized by his suggestion.

Jack clenched every muscle in an effort to remain prone on the bed. Kit's eyes glowed violet, purple sparks of passion striking from their depths. He wasn't the least surprised to see her fingers move to the buttons which secured the drab breeches. He watched the slim digits work the buttons free. Then, slowly, she peeled back the flap, revealing an expanse of creamy stomach with a riot of red curls at its base.

Kit moved in a dream, sundered from reality. She saw the tension in Jack's frame increase and reveled in her power. Moving with deliberate slowness, she inched the garment off her hips, balancing on one foot to draw off her boot. When the second boot was off, she lifted first one leg then the other free of her breeches. She sent them to join her coat, then turned to pose, weight on one leg, the other knee bent inward, facing Jack.

He hadn't moved, but she could feel the effort it was costing him to remain where he was.

"Lift your shirt and free your breasts." Rigid with need, Jack forced the command from between clenched teeth. His eyes were glued to the rich bounty thus far revealed; his mouth was dry with anticipation of the revelations to come.

Wondering why he hadn't told her to take her shirt off, Kit obeyed the command literally, assuming there was some pertinent point she'd yet to comprehend behind it. She thought for a moment, then artfully rolled the front of her shirt up until she could hold the folds between her teeth. A sudden shift of the body in the bed told her the impulse was worth following. To her relief, the knot gave easily. She unwound the band. Slowly. The long strip went about her five times. She released her shirt just before the band dropped. Her breasts sprang free, proudly erect, semiobscured behind fine linen.

Jack swallowed a groan. His fingers, locked behind his head, clenched, biting into the backs of his hands. He couldn't imagine where she'd learned her tricks; the idea that they were instinctive started to unravel his much tried control. To gain a little time, and strength, he examined the figure before him critically. Light streamed through the window on the other side of the cottage. Kit stood directly between the bed and the window; he had an unimpeded view of her silhouette. Lingeringly, he examined every curve, knowing his gaze was heating her. The thought of what that meant forced him to speak. "Come and kneel on the bed beside me."

Without haste, Kit obeyed, climbing onto the horsehair mattress to sit on her knees by his side. In that position her shirt covered her legs, giving her a modicum of relief from Jack's ardent gaze. He wasn't wearing a coat. His shirt was not of the same fine quality as hers; the muscles of his chest and arms showed as rounded ridges beneath its surface. Her gaze skimmed his chest, then dropped to where his shirt disappeared into the waistband of his breeches. She couldn't miss the bulge just below.

Jack saw the direction of her gaze. He kept his hands locked safely behind his head and fought to control his breathing. "Undress me."

Kit's eyes flew to his, startled conjecture in their purpled depths. Her lips parted but no protest came. Instead, she seemed to consider the idea; Jack wondered what form of slow torture she was planning.

Beneath her stunned surprise, Kit was aware of growing excitement. Never having attempted such an undertaking before, she took a minute to work out her approach.

Jack held his breath when she shifted, pressing her hands, palms flat, against his chest. She swung over him, straddling him.

Boldly, Kit settled her bottom on his thighs. She heard his indrawn breath and felt the sudden leaping of the rigid rod half-trapped beneath her. She shuffled forward, pressing herself against him, protected from instant retribution by the material of his breeches. She glanced up; Jack's eyes

246

were tight shut. A muscle flickered along his clenched jaw. With a smile of feminine triumph, Kit set to work, pulling his shirt from his breeches, tugging his arms from behind his head, eventually tugging him into a half-sit to drag the shirt off over his head.

Freed of his shirt, Jack fell back on the pillows, in pain, but eager to see how she'd manage the rest.

Flinging the shirt aside, Kit turned her attention to his waistband. It was the work of a moment to wriggle the buttons free. She laid the flap open and gazed down in awe at the prize revealed. Thick as her wrist, engorged and empurpled, Jack's staff pulsed against the hair curling over the solid wall of his abdomen. Without thinking, Kit's fingers moved to touch it, to caress it.

Jack groaned, unable to keep the sound back. He shut his eyes, not wanting to see what she might do next. The soft caress of her lips sent him rigid; the wet sweep of her tongue, inexpert but guided by unerring instinct, broke his control. It was impossible to lie still in the face of such provocation. But he managed to keep his hands from tangling in her curls and guiding her lips to where his throbbing flesh most wanted to feel them. Instead, he forced his hands to his hips, easing his breeches down. With his help, she managed the task efficiently, sliding down the bed to pull off his boots and free his legs.

Kit slipped from the bed, Jack's breeches in her fingers, and turned to survey her handiwork. Naked, displayed for her delectation, Jack was nothing short of magnificent. Not for the life of her could she keep the smile from her face.

"Come back here."

Kit's eyes flew to Jack's. What she saw in the silvered depths sent a thrill of sheer desire streaking through her. With unfeigned eagerness, she resumed her position at his side, gently simmering, intrigued to discover what next he had in mind.

Jack's mind wasn't functioning with its customary clarity. It was overheated. He watched Kit climb back on the bed, her bright eyes drifting down his torso. She knelt on her shirt and it drew taut, outlining the tight crescents of her nipples before she pulled it free. It would be easy enough to roll her beneath him and sheath himself in her heat, but in the past seventy-two hours, his imagination had been working overtime; he'd an ambition to turn some of his dreams to reality. But did he have sufficient willpower to do it?

"Ride me."

The command jerked Kit from her rapt contemplation. *Ride him?*

Jack read her question in her startled eyes, deep-hued violet and darkening rapidly. Despite the effort it cost him he smiled. "When I mount you, I do all the hard work. This time, it's your turn."

Kit simply stared, trying to make sense of his words. Then she glanced down to where his member angled upward from its curly nest.

"Here. I'll show you." Jack caught her hands and drew her over him. "Straddle me like before."

Kit did, and nearly shot from the bed when she felt his staff leap under her. She froze, her weight steady against him, her thighs spread, her knees on either side of his hips. Breathless, she waited, stunned by the sense of vulnerability that washed over her.

Rigid with effort, Jack forced every muscle in his body to absolute obedience. A single upward thrust would sink his staff into her, hard against the source of the heat pouring over him from between her widespread thighs. But aside from the fact that he knew he might hurt her by such an aggressive entry in this position, she'd tensed and was probably dry.

He drew a ragged breath and avoided looking at the juncture of her thighs, where the head of his manhood nestled amidst her flaming curls. He eased his convulsive grip on her hands and raised them, placing them on the pillow, one above each of his shoulders. Another deep breath allowed him to run his hands back along her arms to curve about her shoulders. "Lean forward and kiss me."

Kit did as she was told, intrigued by this latest twist in his game. It started off as he'd said, with her kissing him, but he quickly took over, his fingers tangling in her curls, holding her head steady while his tongue plundered the soft cavern of her mouth. She made no protest at the change. Her furnace was alight; she needed to find the path to his flame.

Jack lowered his hands from Kit's head to her shoulders, then set them to mold her body as he wished, bringing her up on her hands and knees over him. He drew his lips from hers and urged her forward so he could take one shirt-veiled nipple into his mouth. Kit's gasp urged him on. He licked the material until it clung to the ripe peak then drew the turgid flesh deep into his mouth. He suckled and Kit moaned, her body spasming in response. Her eyes were closed, her lips parted. Jack switched to her other breast and repeated the exercise.

Kit moaned with each successive onslaught on her senses. An urgent ache had developed between her thighs. She longed to ease it; she knew how. But Jack relentlessly stoked her fire, apparently unaware of her need.

"Jack!" Kit put all the longing she could into the syllable. Instantly, she felt his hands pushing aside her shirt to reach between her thighs. She sighed in relief when first one long finger, then two, slid into her. The fingers moved and she gasped, concentrating on their probing. They settled to a rhythm she recognized; she matched it. Jack's mouth continued on her breasts, his tongue laving the sensitized peaks, sending streams of fire coursing down her veins.

Jack waited until her gasps were quick and uneven, until her hips were pressing against his hand, her body seeking greater satisfaction. Her honey poured over his fingers as he drew them from her. "Now take me inside you."

The growled command was barely discernable but Kit heard and needed no further urging. She edged back, to where his member waited, throbbing with the desire to ease her need. She lowered herself onto it, tilting her hips to catch its head, drawing it into her. As soon as she felt him enter her, Kit sank back, taking him fully in one smooth movement.

Jack couldn't breathe. He grabbed her hips and raised her slightly. Immediately, Kit took the initiative, rising until he felt sure he'd lose her clinging heat, only to impale herself more deeply on the downward stroke. Once he was sure she was in control, Jack drew a ragged breath and refocused his attention on her breasts, warm and ripe beneath the tantalizing film of her shirt.

Kit savored the sensation of being in complete control, able to slide his strength into her at whatever pace she desired. She spread her thighs wide and took him deep; she experimented, clenching her muscles tight about him, closing her thighs to minimize penetration.

She felt Jack's hands close about her breasts, one hand covering each ripe mound, squeezing in rhythm with her ride. His fingers found her nipples. Then he started rocking his hips against hers, driving into her as she descended. Abruptly, Kit understood the purpose of her shirt. The edge floated on her thighs, rising and falling as she did, bringing home to her the view Jack would have if he was watching their bodies merge.

As she felt her fires coalescing, pooling into the conflagration that would ultimately consume her senses, Kit forced her eyes open. Jack was watching. Avidly.

With a groan she closed her eyes. Her head dropped back as the fires raged. She tightened her body, trying to hold back the inevitable, to prolong the sweet agony for just a little longer.

Jack wasn't up to prolonging anything. The sensual sight of their bodies fusing, of his staff driving into her, slickly penetrating her fevered body, was not designed to stave off consummation. He felt her body clench against release, tightening about him. He let go of her breasts and gripped her hips, holding her immobile. Drinking in the sight, he drove deeply into her.

That was all it took.

They climaxed together, gasping, their eyes open, gazes locked, their souls as fused as their bodies.

Kit's release swept her, draining her of all strength. She slumped forward and Jack gathered her to him, settling her legs so she lay on top of him, tucking her head under his chin.

She fell asleep with his arms about her.

When Kit awoke, they were lying entangled under the covers. She couldn't remember being moved, but Jack now lay sleeping beside her, one arm tucked protectively about her. Kit smiled sleepily, feeling the steady beat of his heart against her cheek. She was warm and secure, sated and content. Which was more than she'd been able to say since Wednesday night.

She squinted over the bedclothes at the window; the pink tinge of sunset was coloring the sky. It was nearly time to leave.

Memories of her recent activities drifted through her brain. She stifled a delighted giggle, then sobered. If she'd learned anything from today's episode, it was that she couldn't live without Jack. The fire in her veins was a drug she could no longer face the day without. Only he could stoke the blaze.

But Jack was smuggling spies.

Kit snuggled closer to his comforting warmth. She knew, beyond all doubt, that he was not personally involved with the spying. He was just misguided, believing it no different than smuggling brandy. She'd have to ensure, next time, that she explained it to him fully. It was up to her to make him see sense.

She had to succeed. There were three lives depending on it – Julian's, Jack's, and hers. Kit sighed. She'd speak to him about it next time she came. There was no point in spoiling the moment now.

Carefully, she eased from Jack's side, only to have him draw her back, his arm heavy in sleep. Kit glanced at the window. Perhaps it wasn't that late. She wriggled against Jack, rising up to find his lips with hers. And set about kissing him awake.

Chapter 20

The stars fell from Kit's eyes on Monday night. She'd decided to attend the meeting at the Old Barn. Although she no longer felt compelled to join the smugglers on their runs, she needed to see Jack, to try to learn more about his views on "human cargoes." When better to lead the conversation in that direction than on the slow ride back to the cottage after the meeting? She held few illusions as to how much rational discussion they'd engage in once they entered the cottage. But he'd only run one "human cargo" in the last two months; she had time, she felt, to pursue his conversion at a leisurely pace.

The meeting had already started when she got there. She slipped into the protective shadows at the back of the barn and found a dusty crate to perch on. Some noticed her furtive entrance; a few nodded an acknowledgment before returning their attention to Jack, standing in the cone of weak light shed by a single lamp.

Kit saw his grey eyes sweep her, but Jack's recitation of detail never faltered. He was midway through describing a cargo to be brought in the next night on the beaches east of

Holme. Kit listened with half an ear, fascinated by the way the lamplight gilded the odd streaks in his hair.

Jack turned to address Shep. "You and Johnny collect the passenger from Creake at dusk. Bring him direct to the beach."

Kit froze.

Shep nodded; Jack turned to Noah. "Come in and pick him up. Your boat should be the last to the ship. Transfer him and get the last of the goods."

"Aye." Noah ducked his head.

"That's it, then." Jack scanned the faces, all weather-worn, most expressionless. "We'll meet again Thursday as usual."

With grunts and nods, the band dispersed, unobtrusively slipping into the night in twos and threes. The lamp was hauled down and extinguished.

Still Kit sat her crate, head down, her face hidden by the brim of her tricorne. Jack eyed her silent-figure. His misgivings grew. What the devil was wrong now? He'd expected her to arrive, but her pensiveness was unsettling. Eagerness was what he'd been expecting after her efforts of Sunday afternoon.

George and Matthew joined him by the now open door.

"I'm heading straight home." George spoke in a subdued tone, clearly aware Kit was behind in the gloom. He raised a questioning brow.

Jack's jaw set. He nodded decisively. George slipped into the night.

"You'd best be on your way, too."

"Aye." Matthew went without question. Jack watched him mount and head south, through the shielding trees and into the fields beyond.

In the darkness behind Jack, Kit struggled to bring some

order to her mind. Jack must have known about this latest "human cargo" since his visit to the Blackbird last Wednesday. Although she'd spent all Wednesday night and Sunday afternoon by his side, he'd not mentioned the fact. He'd not even alluded to it. So much for her ideas of learning of the spies ahead of time. Now, she'd less than twenty-four hours to make a decision and act.

When the silence of the barn remained unbroken, Jack turned and paced inside. He stopped where the moonlight ran out, and looked to where he knew Kit still sat. "What is it?"

At his impatient tone, Kit bristled, a fact Jack missed in the dark. Realizing her advantage, she took a long moment to weigh her strategy. She'd intended dissuading Jack from his treasonous enterprise; it was still worth a try. But the drafty barn, with its loose boards and warped doors, was no place to have a discussion on treason, particularly not with the person you suspected of committing it. "I need to talk with you."

Hands on hips, Jack glared into the dark. Talk? Was she up to her tricks again? He was getting damned tired of her changes in mood. He'd thought, after Sunday, that their relationship had got itself on an even keel – that she'd accepted her position as his mistress. Admittedly, she didn't know whose mistress she was, but he didn't think she'd jib at the change from smuggler to lord of the castle. He didn't think she'd jib, period.

Then he remembered she'd been watching him avidly when she'd first come in. Her attitude had changed later. An inkling of his problem blossomed in Jack's brain. "If you want to talk, it'd better be back at the cottage."

Kit stood and walked forward.

Jack heard her. He turned and strode to the door, not

255

looking back to see if she was following. He went to where Champion stood tethered under a gnarled fir and vaulted into the saddle. He nudged the stallion into a canter, ignoring the horse's reluctance. Champion's gait didn't flow freely until halfway across the first field, when Delia drew alongside.

Jack rode in silence, his eyes probing the shadows ahead, his mind firmly fixed on the woman by his side. Why should she get her inexpressibles in a twist over him smuggling spies? Did she even know they were spies? The road appeared ahead, and he turned Champion onto the beaten surface.

Edging Delia up alongside Champion, Kit glanced at Jack's stern profile. It wasn't encouraging. Far from dampening her determination, the observation strengthened her resolution. Matthew was Jack's servant, George a too-close friend; neither had shown the slightest ability to influence Jack. Clearly, it was time someone forced him to consider his conscience. She didn't expect him to like the fact she intended to be that someone, but male arrogance was no excuse. She'd tell him what she thought regardless of what he felt.

They turned south and walked their mounts up the winding path to the top of the rise. Kit watched as Jack peered down, automatically ensuring that they hadn't been followed. The path below remained clear. She saw Jack grimace before he turned Champion's head for the cottage. Setting Delia in Champion's wake, she fell to organizing her arguments.

Jack dismounted before the stable and led Champion in. Kit did likewise, taking Delia to the neighboring stall. Having decided on her route of attack, she went straight to the point. "You do know the men you bring in and take out are spies, don't you?"

Jack's answer was to thump his saddle down on top of the partition between the stalls. Kit stared into the gloom. So he was going to be difficult. "You've been in the army, haven't you? You must know what sort of information's going out with your 'human cargoes.'"

When silence prevailed, Kit dropped her saddle on the partition and leaned on it to add: "You must have known men who died over there. How can you help the enemy kill more of our soldiers?"

In the dark, Jack closed his eyes against the memories her words unleashed. Known men who'd died? He'd had an entire troop die about him, blown to hell by cannon and grapeshot. He'd only escaped because a charger harnessed to one of the guns he'd been trying to reposition had fallen on him. And because Matthew, against all odds, had found him amidst the bloody carnage of the retreat.

Champion shifted, nudging him back to the present. Unclenching his fingers, he grabbed a handful of straw and fell to brushing the glossy grey coat. He had to keep moving, to keep doing, letting her words, however undeserved, wash over him. If he reacted, the truth would tumble out, and, God knew, the game they were playing was too dangerous for that.

When Kit realized she wasn't going to get any verbal reaction, she plowed on, determined to make Jack see the error of his ways. "Just because you survived with a whole skin doesn't mean you can forget about it."

Jack paused and considered telling her just how little he'd forgotten. Instead, he forced himself to continue mutely grooming Champion.

Kit glared in his direction, uncertain whether he could see her or not. She grasped some straw and started to brush Delia. "Smuggling's one thing. It might be against the law, but it's only dishonest. It's more than dishonest to make money from selling military information. From selling other men's lives. It's treason!"

Jack's brows rose. She should be in politics. He'd finished rubbing Champion down. He dropped the straw and headed for the door. As he crossed the front of the cottage, he heard a muffled oath from the stable. As he went through the doorway, he heard Kit's footsteps following. Jack headed straight for the keg on the sideboard.

Kit followed him into the room, slamming the door behind her. "Well, whatever . . ." Her voice died as she blinked into the black void left once the door had shut. She heard a muttered curse, then a boot hit a chair leg. An instant later, a match scraped, then soft light flared. Jack adjusted the wick, until the lamp threw just enough light to see by. Then he grabbed his glass, half-filled with brandy, and dropped into the chair on the other side of the table, his long legs stretched before him, his eyes broodingly watching her.

"Whatever," Kit reiterated firmly, trying to ignore all that lounging masculinity, "you can't continue to run your 'human cargoes.' They may pay well, but you're running too great a risk." She glared at the figure across the table, as inanimate as the chair he occupied. In the low light, she could barely make out his features, much less his expression. "What sort of leader knowingly exposes his men to such dangers?"

Jack shifted as her words pricked him. He prided himself on taking care of those in his command.

Kit sensed her advantage and pounced. "Smuggling's a transportable offense; treason's a hanging matter. You're deliberately leading these men, who don't know enough to understand the risks, to court death." When no response came, she lost her temper. "Dammit! They've got families dependent on them! If they're taken and hanged, who's going to look after them?"

Jack's chair crashed to the floor, overturned as he surged to his feet. Kit's nerves jangled. She took an instinctive step back.

"What the hell would you know of taking care of anyone? Taking responsibility for anything? You're a *woman*, dammit!"

The outburst hauled Jack to his senses. Of course she was a woman. Of course she knew nothing of leading and the consequent worries. He should know better than to let a woman's words get under his skin. He frowned and took another sip of his brandy, holding her silent with a glower. What he couldn't fathom, what he should pay more attention to understanding, was why she was so opposed to him running spies. In his experience, women of her ilk cared little for such abstract matters. Whoever heard of a lowborn mistress lecturing her aristocratic lover on the morality of political intrigue?

With an effort, Kit shook free of Jack's intimidating stare and glared back. Setting her hands on her hips, she opened her mouth to put him right on the role of women.

Jack got in first, one long finger stabbing the air for emphasis. "You're a woman. You're not the leader of a gang of smugglers – you played at being a lad in charge of a small group, but that's all." His empty glass hit the table. He placed both hands beside it and leaned forward. "If I hadn't come along and relieved you of command, you'd have sunk without trace long since. You know nothing – *nothing* – of leading men."

Kit's eyes sparked violet daggers; her lips parted on words of rebuttal.

Jack was in no mood to give her a chance. "*And* if you've any notion on lecturing me on the matter, I suggest you keep your ill-advised opinions to yourself!"

Fury surged through Kit's veins, cindering her innate caution. Her eyes narrowed. "I see." She studied the large form, bent intimidatingly over the table, the very table where she'd lain, sprawled in wanton abandon, five nights before, with him, erect, engorged, between her wide-spread thighs.

Kit blinked and shook aside the unhelpful memory. She rushed into speech. "In that case, I'll have to take . . ." Some sixth sense made her pause. She looked into the grey eyes watching her. Caution caught her tongue.

"Have to take . . .?"

Jack's soft prompt rang alarm bells in Kit's brain. Desperation came to her rescue. She put up her chin, cloaking her sudden uncertainty in truculence. "Take what steps I can to see that you don't get caught." Racked by nerves, she resettled her muffler. It was time for her to leave.

A cold calm descended on Jack, leaving little room for emotion. He saw straight through her obfuscation. "You mean to warn the authorities of our activities."

The statement brought Kit's head up so fast, she'd no time to wipe the truth from her eyes. The moment hung suspended between them, her silence confirming his conjecture more completely than any confession.

Realizing the trap she'd fallen into, Kit blushed. Denial was pointless, so she took the other tack. "If you continue to run spies, you leave me little choice."

"Whom do you plan to convince? Spencer?" Jack moved, smoothly, to come around the table.

Her mind on his words, Kit shrugged, raising her brows noncommittally. "Perhaps. Maybe I'll look up Lord Hendon – it's his responsibility, after all."

She swung to face Jack. And found him on the same side of the table and advancing slowly. Her heart leapt to her throat. She recalled the time on the Marchmont Hall terrace when she'd underestimated his speed. Cautiously, she backed away.

Her eyes rose to meet his. She read his intent in the darkened grey that had swallowed all trace of silver. "What do you think you're doing?" Irritation colored her tone. How like him to decide to play physical just now.

Despite his years of training, Jack couldn't stop himself from admiring the threat she posed. Satisfied he could reach the door before she could, he stopped with two yards between them and met her aggravated amethyst gaze. "I'm afraid, sweetheart, that you can't expect to leave just yet. Not after this little talk of ours." Jack couldn't keep a smile from twisting his lips as his mind assembled the rest of his plan. "You must see that I can't have you scurrying off to Lord Hendon." Heaven help him if she did!

Warily, Kit eyed the distance between them and decided it was enough. Despite his words, there was no overt threat in his tone or his stance. "And how were you planning to stop me? Wouldn't it be easier to just stop running spies?"

Jack's gilded head shook a decided negative. "As far as I can see," he said, "the best thing I can do is keep you here."

"I won't stay, and you know you sleep soundly."

Jack raised a brow but didn't attempt to deny it. "You'll stay if I tie your hands to the headboard." When Kit's eyes widened, he added: "Remember the last time I had you with your hands tied? This time, I'll have you flat on your back in the middle of my bed."

Desire flickered hungrily in Kit's belly. She ignored it, blinking to dispel the images conjured up by his words, by his deepening tones. "There'll be a fuss if I disappear. They'll search the county."

"Perhaps. But I can assure you they won't search here."

His glib certainty struck Kit between the eyes. A conglomeration of disjointed facts fell into place. She stared at Jack. "You're in league with Lord Hendon."

Her tone of amazed discovery halted Jack; her words sent a thrill of expectation through, him. She was so close to the truth. Would she guess the rest? If she did, what would she think?

It was his turn to be too slow with his denial to disguise the truth. Instead, he shrugged. "What if I am? There's no need for you to spend any of your time considering the subject. I've much more urgent matters for your attention." With that growled declaration of intent, Jack stepped forward.

Kit immediately backed away, her eyes wide. He was mad – she'd thought it often enough. "Jack!"

Jack took no notice of her imperious warning.

Kit drew a deep breath. And dashed for the door.

She'd taken no more than two steps before she felt the air at her back stir. With a shriek, she veered away from the door. Jack's body rushed past her, slamming against the wooden panels. Kit heard the bolt fall home.

Wild-eyed, Kit scanned the room and saw Jack's sword propped against the wardrobe. Her heart thudding, she grabbed it up and whirled, wrenching the gleaming blade from the scabbard. She presented it, a lethal silver scythe transcribing a protective arc before her.

Jack froze, well out of her range. Inwardly, he cursed. Matthew had found the sword thrust to the back of the wardrobe. He'd taken it out and cleaned it before grinding the edge to exquisite sharpness. Apparently, he'd left it out in the belief his master should carry it.

Instead, his master, in full possession of his senses, now wished the sword he'd carried for ten years and more at the devil. If it'd been any other woman, he'd have walked calmly forward and taken it. But even though Kit had to use both hands to keep the blade balanced, Jack didn't make the mistake of thinking she couldn't use it. He didn't for a moment believe she'd run him through, but by the time she realized that, her stroke might be too advanced to stop, given her unfamiliarity with that particular blade, weighted for slashing swings, not thrust and parry. She might not kill him, but she could do serious damage. Even more frightening was the possibility she might get hurt herself.

That thought forced Jack to move cautiously. His gaze locked with Kit's, steadying, trying to will some of his calm into the frightened violet eyes. He wasn't sure how far she was from real panic, but he didn't think she'd hand over the sword, not after his threats. Slowly, he edged around the bed, away from her. Her eyes followed, intent on his movement, clearly puzzled by it.

Her breathing was too fast. Kit tried to contain her panic, but she was no longer sure of anything. She frowned when Jack stopped on the opposite side of the bed. What was he up to? She couldn't make for the door, he was far too fast for that. The corner of the room was just a step away; she'd already backed as far as she could into its protection.

Jack moved so fast Kit barely saw the blur. One moment he was standing still, feet apart, hands relaxed by his sides. The next, he'd grabbed the covers and whipped them over the sword, following them over the bed to wrench the blade from her hands. Over her shriek, Kit heard the muffled thud as the sword hit the ground, flung out of harm's way. Jack's arms closed about her, an oddly protective trap.

Struggling made no impression. Her legs were pressed

against the bed, then she was toppled onto it. Kit's breath was knocked out of her when Jack landed on top of her. He used his body to subdue her struggles, his legs trapping hers, his hips weighting hers down, long fingers holding her head, gradually exerting pressure until she kept still. Half-smothered by his chest, Kit had to wait until he shifted to look down at her before opening her mouth to blister his ears. But no sound escaped her. Instead, his mouth found hers and his tongue filled the void with brandy-coated fire.

One by one, Kit felt her muscles give up the fight, relaxing as his intoxicating taste filled her senses, warming her from the inside out. The scandalous idea of being tied to his bedhead took on a rosy glow. As the insidious effect spread, her beleaguered mind summoned its last defenses. It couldn't happen. But she'd only have one chance to change her fate.

For one long moment, Kit flowed with the tide, then, abruptly, she threw every muscle against him, pushing hard to dislodge him and roll his weight from her.

Jack was taken aback by the force of her shove. But, instead of suppressing it by sheer weight, he decided to roll with her push and bring her up over him. Fully atop her, he couldn't reach that particular area of her buttocks that always proved so helpfully arousing. Reversing their positions was an excellent idea. He rolled, pulling her with him.

His head hit the bedend, concealed beneath the disarranged sheets.

Kit knew the instant he lost consciousness. His lips left hers, his fingers slid from her hair. She stared down into his face, oddly stripped of emotion, relaxed and at peace. In panic, she wriggled off him. She placed a hand on his chest and breathed a sigh of relief when she felt his heart beating steadily. Puzzled, she felt under his head and found the rounded wood of the bedend. The mystery solved, she sat up and tugged him farther onto the bed, then fetched a pillow to cradle his head.

Kit sat and frowned at her threat removed. How long would he remain unconscious? Reflecting that his skull had shown every indication of being thick, she decided a tactical withdrawal was her only option. She'd tried her best to make him see sense; his actions, his words, left her no alternative but to act.

Late-afternoon sunlight spilled through the cottage door, glimmering along the gilt edges of the playing cards Jack shuffled back and forth. His long fingers re-formed the pack, then briskly set them out.

Jack grimaced at the hand. All very well to play at Patience; he was desperately short of the commodity. But, despite the promptings of his wilder self, there was blessedly little he could do. When he'd woken in the dead of night to find himself alone, nursing a sore skull, he'd initially thought Kit had coshed him. Then the final moments of their tussle had cleared in his painful head and he'd worked it out. Small comfort that had been. She'd stated, categorically, that she was going to cause him heaps of trouble.

Irritation itched; he shook aside his thoughts and stared at the cards.

What would she do? He didn't feel qualified to guess, given he still couldn't fathom her peculiar intensity over the spies. She'd threatened to go to Lord Hendon. He'd considered that long and hard, eventually quitting home immediately after breakfast, leaving his butler, Lovis, with a most peculiar set of instructions. Luckily, Lovis knew him well enough not to feel the remotest surprise. Hopefully, no other redheaded woman would call unattended on Lord Hendon.

Driven by a growing sense of unease, he'd gone to Hunstanton and put Tonkin through his paces. His message ought to have been clear, but Tonkin's interest in his "big gang" had grown to an obsession. Regardless of orders, Jack didn't trust the old bruiser an inch. He didn't think Tonkin trusted him, either. The man wasn't stupid, just an incompetent bully. He'd left Hunstanton even more disturbed than before.

The feeling that had taken root in his gut was all too familiar. Years of campaigning, both overtly and covertly, had instilled a watchfulness, a finely honed sixth sense, always on the alert for danger. With the steady drub of Champion's hooves filling his ears, he'd headed for the cottage, watching the storm gathering on his horizon swell and grow, knowing it would soon unleash its fury, wreaking havoc with his well-laid plans. And feeling totally impotent in the face of impending disaster.

But he was used to meeting that particular challenge and had long since perfected the mental and physical discipline needed to see any storm through.

However, the fact that Kit was enmeshed in the danger, up to her pretty neck, set a worried edge on his nervous energy. Theoretically, he should have already taken steps to nullify the threat she posed. In reality, there seemed little he could do without further jeopardizing his mission. Forced to spend the hours until the run in idle isolation, he'd had time to consider his options. The only one with any real merit was kidnapping. He'd have to be careful not to be seen by any on the Cranmer estate, but he could keep her here, in safety and comfort, for a week or so, until the worst was past. If the mission dragged on, as it quite possibly would, he'd move her up to the Castle once the first hue and cry had died. There, safety and comfort, both hers and his, would be assured. She'd be his prisoner, but after the first inevitable fury, he didn't think she'd mind. He'd ensure she was occupied.

The idea of having time to get to know Kit, of having the leisure to learn why she thought as she did, felt as she did, blossomed before him. Jack forgot his cards, mesmerized by a sudden glimpse into a future he'd never previously found attractive. Women, he'd always firmly believed, had but one real role in life – to pander to their man's wishes. An aristocratic wife – his, for instance – would bear his children and manage his households, act as his hostess and support his position socially. Beyond that, she figured in his mind much as Matthew or Lovis did. His many mistresses had had but one sphere of responsibility – the bedroom – where they'd spent the majority of time flat on their backs, efficiently catering to his needs. The only communication he recalled having with them was by way of soft moans and groans and funny little gasps. He'd never been interested in what they'd thought. Not on any subject.

Absentmindedly gathering the cards, Jack refocused his abstracted gaze. The more he thought of it, the more benefits he saw in kidnapping Kit. After tonight, assuming they both survived the coming storm, he'd act.

Spencer, of course, would have to be told. He couldn't steal away the old man's granddaughter, whom he clearly cared for, and leave him to grieve unnecessarily. It would mean overturning one of his golden rules – he'd never, not even as a child, told people more than they'd needed to know, a habit that had stood him in good stead over the years. But he couldn't have Spencer on his conscience any more than he could tolerate Kit continuing her dangerous crusade.

At the thought of her, his redheaded houri, a stern frown

settled over his face. He hadn't asked to feel about her as he did, but there was no point in denying it. She was more than the latest in a long line; he cared for her in ways he couldn't remember caring for anyone else in his life. Once he had her safe, he'd drum into her red head just what the upshot of that was. She would have to mend her ways – no more dangerous escapades.

Would she be silly enough to try to turn some of the men against him? Jack shuddered. There was no value in torturing himself. Shutting out his imaginary horrors, he purposefully reshuffled the cards.

Ten minutes later, the peace of sunset was interrupted by the steady clop of hooves, approaching from the east. Jack raised his head to listen. Both the confident pace and the direction suggested George had come to their rendezvous early. A glimpse of sleek chestnut hide crossing the clearing brought a half smile to Jack's face. He needed distraction. George came through the door, his face set in disapproving lines.

Jack's smile of welcome faded. His brows rose.

George halted before the table, his gaze steady on Jack's grey eyes. Then he glanced at the keg on the sideboard. "Is there anything in that?"

With a grunt, Jack rose and fetched a glass. After a second's hesitation, he took a glass for himself and half filled both. Was this the start of his storm?

George drew up a chair to the table and dropped into it.

Placing one glass before George, Jack eyed his serious face. He resumed his seat. "Well? You'd better tell me before Matthew gets here."

George took a sip and glanced at the open door. He got up, shut it, then paced back to the table. He put his glass down, but remained standing. "I went to see Amy this afternoon."

When George fell into a pensive daze and yielded nothing further, Jack couldn't resist. "She wants to call off the wedding?"

George flushed and frowned. "Of course not! For God's sake, be sensible. This is serious."

Jack duly composed his features. George grimaced and continued: "When I was leaving, I got talking to Jeffries, Gresham's head groom. The man's a mine of information on horses."

Jack's stomach clenched, but his expression remained undisturbed.

George's gaze leveled. "We were talking of bloodlines in the district. He mentioned a black Arab mare, finicky and highbred. According to Jeffries, she belongs to one of Amy's friends."

"Amy's friend?" Jack blinked and the veils fell. He knew, then, what was coming. He should have guessed; there'd been enough inconsistencies in her performance. If he hadn't been so besotted with her, doubtless he'd have unmasked her long ago. The idea that some part of him had known, but he hadn't wanted to face the truth, he buried deep.

"Amy's bosom-bow," George confirmed, his voice heavy with disapproval. "Miss Kathryn Cramner. Known as Kit to her intimates." George slumped into his chair. "She's Christopher Cranmer's daughter, Spencer's grandchild." George studied Jack's face. "His legitimate granddaughter."

Spencer's legitimate granddaughter. The thought reeled through Jack's brain in dizzying splendor. Stunned shock vied with disbelief, before both gave way to an overwhelming urge to lay hold of Kit and shake the damned woman as she deserved. How *dared* she take such scandalous risks? Clearly, Spencer had no control over her. Jack made a mental note to be sure the full magnitude of her sins was made clear to his redheaded houri in breeches – not that she'd get a chance to wear breeches again. She'd have to learn to take very good care – of herself, of her reputation. As Lord Hendon, he'd every right to ensure the future Lady Hendon played safe.

For that, of course, was the crowning glory of George's revelations. As Miss Kathryn Cranmer, Kit was more than eligible for the vacant post of Lady Hendon. And after their recent activities, there was no possibility he'd let her slip through his net. He had her right where he wanted her – in more ways than one. After tonight's run, he'd call on Spencer. Between them, they'd settle the future of one red-headed houri.

A smile of pleasant anticipation suffused Jack's face.

George saw it and sighed heavily. "From that besotted look, I take it affairs between you and Kit have gone a lot farther than I'd feel happy about?"

Jack grinned beatifically.

"Christ!" George ran one hand through his dark hair. "Stop grinning. What the hell do you plan to do about it?"

Jack blinked. His grin faded. "Don't be a fool. I'll marry the damned woman, of course."

George just stared, too astounded to say anything.

Jack swallowed his irritation that George should have entertained any other option. That George had thought *he'd* entertain any other option. It was all Kit's fault. Any woman running about in breeches was fair game. At least only George knew who she was. Then it hit him. "When did you guess she was a woman?"

George blinked, then shrugged. "A week or so ago."

Puzzled, Jack asked: "What gave her away?" He'd thought Kit's disguise particularly good.

"You, mostly," George absentmindedly replied.

"What do you mean – me?"

Jack's aggressive tone recaptured George's attention. Briefly, he grinned. "The way you behaved toward Kit led to only one conclusion. Which I'll be bound the rest of the Gang jumped to. Matthew and I know you rather better. Which made us wonder about Kit."

"Humph!" Jack took a swig of his brandy. Had any of the others guessed? Now she'd assumed the title of his future wife, he felt much more critical of Kit's wildness. He wasn't at all sure he approved of her having the nerve to do such outrageous things. It didn't auger well for a peaceful married life.

Jack glanced up to find the shadows deepening. The run was scheduled for immediately after nightfall. He hoped Kit would turn up. Now that he understood what a prize she was, he wanted her safe in his keeping. Quite how he'd handle her return to Cranmer and the inevitable interview with Spencer he hadn't yet decided. But he wanted her with him tonight.

He wanted to give her a piece of his mind, apologize, propose, and make love to her.

The order was beyond him; he'd leave that in the hands of the gods.

Chapter 21

A brisk northeasterly was whipping along the cliffs by the time Kit reached the coast. Dark clouds scudded before the moon. In the fitful light, she found the Hunstanton Gang already unloading their boats, the ponies lined up on the sands. The surf ran high; the crash of waves cloaked the scene in noise. As she watched, a light drizzle started to fall.

Squinting through the damp veil, Kit spotted Jack's look-out. The man was perched on a hillock commanding a fair view of the area. Her approach had been screened by wind-twisted trees, but he'd be unlikely to miss any larger mass of horsemen.

Staring at the boats, Kit picked out the figure of Captain Jack, tall and broad-shouldered, wading through the surf, a keg under each arm. The sight brought no comfort to her tortured brain.

What was she to do? Last night had passed in agonized self-argument as she sifted the possibilities, considered every avenue. In the end, everything had hinged on one point – did she really believe Jack was involved in spying himself? The answer was a definite, unshakable, albeit unsubstantiated,

No. Given that, she'd concluded that speaking to Lord Hendon was the only safe way forward.

Jack had admitted a connection with the High Commissioner, one that presumably involved supplying brandy to the Castle cellars. Hopefully, his powerful benefactor would be able to succeed where she had failed and force sense through Jack's skull. She couldn't believe Lord Hendon would condone smuggling spies; she felt confident she could make him understand that Jack was not personally involved, just misguided.

But Lord Hendon had not been at home. She'd whipped up her courage and gone to the Castle on her afternoon ride. The head groom had been apologetic. Lord Hendon had left the house early; it was not known when he'd return.

She'd gone back to Cramner even more worried than when she'd set out. She'd have to make sure she spoke to Lord Hendon soon, or her courage would desert her. Or Jack would catch her and tie her to his headboard.

His threat had forced her to face reality. Ever since their liaison had gone beyond the innocent, she'd been battling her conscience. Guilt now sat on her shoulders, a heavy and constant weight. She'd lost all chance of making a respectable match, a fact that caused her no regret, but she knew how saddened Spencer would be if he ever learned of it. Jack's hold over her, over her senses, was strong, but she was too wise to let it go on. Disaster skulked the hedges of that road – she knew it well enough.

So here she was, watching over Jack's operations in the hope of following the next spy he brought in. If she could find the next connection, she could give that to Lord Hendon as a place where official scrutiny could start, avoiding any mention of Jack and the Hunstanton Gang. It was one thing to hold to the high road and condemn men for running spies. It was another to betray men she knew to the hangman. She couldn't do it.

There were some among the Gang she wouldn't trust an inch, but they were not true villains. Misled, badly influenced, they might commit foul deeds, but ever since she'd known them they'd behaved as reasonable beings, if not honest ones. They'd done nothing to deserve death. Other than assist the spies.

The drizzle intensified. A raindrop slid under her tricorne and coursed sluggishly down her neck. Kit shifted and glanced west, toward Holme.

The sight that met her eyes tensed every muscle. Delia, alerted, lifted her head to stare at a small troop of Revenue Officers picking their way along the cliffs. Another hundred yards and they'd see the activity on the beach.

Strangling her curses, Kit swung to stare at Jack's lookout. Surely he could see them? A small spurt of flame was her answer, followed by the noise of a shot, instantly drowned by the waves' roar. She heard the shot, but it was immediately apparent that neither Jack and his men, nor the Revenue troop, had. Both parties proceeded as before, unperturbed.

"Oh, God." Kit sat Delia in an agony of indecision. There was no way the lookout, scrambling from his perch, could get close enough to warn the men on the beach before the Revenue were upon them. Men on foot stood no chance against mounted troops armed with sabers and pistols. Her choice was clear. She could warn the Gang, or sit and watch their destruction.

Delia broke from the cover of the trees and went straight to the head of the nearest cliff path. In seconds, they were down, then flying over the sands toward the men by the boats.

Jack took another keg from Noah and waded slowly ashore. The tide was running high, the sands shifting underfoot.

Spray and spume blotted out the cliffs; the roar of the waves drowned all other sounds. But the frown on Jack's face was not due to the conditions. He was worried about Kit.

Not even George knew of her threat to disrupt the Gang's activities; that information put her life in too much danger to be shared, even with his closest friend. But the sense that a storm was edging closer, that fate was closing in, on him and on her, was intensifying with each passing hour. And he didn't know where she was, much less what she was doing.

Matthew had arrived from the Castle with the disturbing news that she'd been there, but slipped through his net. The fact that she'd had the strength of purpose to try to see Lord Hendon was causing him grave concern. Unable to see the High Commissioner, would she take her information elsewhere? Jack hefted the keg to the back of a pony, wishing he could shrug off his worries as easily.

A black blur at the edge of his vision had him swinging around. He recognized Kit instantly. Equally instant came recognition of the reason for her speed. The storm was about to break.

His bellowed command saw all hands double pace, securing the last of the kegs, men scrambling aboard the lead ponies. The desperate struggle to clear the beach was already under way as he and George ran to the end of the line, to where Kit would pull up.

Kit saw them waiting, Jack's hands open at his sides, ready to catch Delia's bridle and quiet the excited mare. Abruptly, she pulled up ten yards away, out of their reach.

Jack swore and stepped forward.

Instantly, Kit pulled Delia back on her haunches, sharp black hooves flailing the air. When Jack stopped, she let Delia down but kept the reins tight. "Revenue. Only six.

They'll be around the bluff any minute!" She had to scream over the sound of the waves.

Jack nodded curtly. "Go east!"

If there was any question as to the absolute nature of the bellowed command, his arm, pointing toward Brancaster, dispelled it. But Kit could see they'd never make it off the beach in time; the Revenue were too close.

A cry on the wind drew all eyes to the bluff. The troopers came tumbling over the ridge, their horses slithering through the sand dunes.

Kit looked back at the smugglers. The boats were pulling out; the ponies were almost ready to go. Matthew had left to get the horses. Five minutes would see them all safe. Her eyes locked with Jack's. He read her decision in that instant and lunged for her reins. Kit moved faster. She sprang Delia. West.

"Christ!" George joined Jack, staring aghast at Kit's dwindling figure. "She'll never make it!"

"She will," Jack ground out. "She has to," he added under his breath.

The black streak that was Kit hugged the line of the waves, as far from the cliff as possible. The troopers saw her flying toward them and checked at the cliff foot. When it became clear she would pass them by, they milled uncertainly, then, with a bellow to stand, they set off to intercept her. But they'd misjudged Delia's speed and left it too late. Kit swept past and on toward Holme. With cries and curses, the Revenue charged in pursuit.

Biting back a curse, Jack swung and roared his orders, setting the men on their way. Soon, he and George were the only ones left standing. Matthew arrived with the horses; vaulting to the saddle, Jack yelled: "She'll have to go inland before Holme." Then Champion surged.

Jack leaned over Champion's neck, holding the grey to a wicked pace, trying, over the pounding of his heart, to take stock. Had Kit tipped off the Revenue, then changed her mind at the last minute?

The thought twisted through him, a sour serpent sowing seeds of doubt. Abruptly, he shook it aside. Kit had drawn the Revenue off at her own expense and was now in considerable danger. He'd concentrate on saving her satin hide first; learning the truth could come later.

Jack forced his mind to business. Kit was not well-versed in pursuit and evasion; on the other hand, Delia was the fastest thing on four legs this side of the Channel. But Holme, on its rocky promontory that blocked the beach, was close; Kit could not lose the Revenue before running out of beach. She'd have to go inland, taking to the fields or heading on to the west coast.

The drizzle intensified. Jack welcomed the sting of rain on his face. He swore, volubly, comprehensively, his gut clenched, the chill of doom in his veins. They'd started well behind the Revenue. When they sighted the promontory, the beach between them was deserted. Jack rode to where a well-worn cliff path led up from the beach. He drew rein where the path narrowed as it turned up the cliff. The sand was freshly and deeply churned. Jack drew his pistol and signaled to George and Matthew before sending Champion quietly up the path. There was no one at the top. Jack dismounted and studied the ground; George and Matthew rode in wide arcs.

"This way," George called softly. "Looks like the whole troop."

Jack remounted and walked Champion to view the barren stretch of track leading west. When he raised his head, his expression was grim. Kit had taken her pursuers as far from the Hunstanton Gang's field of operations as possible. She was making for the beach north of Hunstanton, to head south along the wide stretches of pale sand at a pace the Revenue could never match. Doubtless, she thought to come up to the cliffs somewhere near Heacham or Snettisham, to disappear into the fields and coppices of the Cranmer estate.

It was a good plan, as far as it went. There was just one snag. With his sense of doom pressing blackly upon him, Jack prayed that, for the first time in his life, his premonition would be wrong.

Without a word, he set his heels to Champion's sides.

Far ahead, on the pale swathes of sand lapped by the waves of the Wash, Kit hugged Delia's neck and flew before the wind. Once she was sure the Revenue had followed her, she'd watched her pace, holding back so they remained in sight, held firm to their purpose by her bobbing figure for-ever before them. She'd had to pull up on the cliff top near Holme, letting them get close enough to see her clearly. Like obedient puppies, they'd followed, noses glued to her trail as she'd led them onto the beach above Hunstanton. Now that they were too far from Brancaster to give Jack and his crew any trouble, she was intent on losing them and heading for the safety of home.

Delia's long stride ate the miles. Kit saw the indentation that marked the track up to Heacham just ahead. She checked Delia and looked behind her.

There was no sign of her pursuers.

Kit threw back her head and laughed, exhilaration pumping through her veins. Her laughter echoed back from the cliffs, startling her into silence. Here in the Wash, the waves were far gentler cousins of the surf pounding the north coast. All was relatively silent, relatively serene.

Shaking off a shiver of apprehension, Kit sent Delia toward the track to Heacham.

She'd almost reached the foot of the track when a horde of horsemen broke cover, pouring over the cliff, another group of Revenue men, barking orders she barely heard. A spurt of flame glowed in the night.

A searing pain tore through her left shoulder.

Delia reared. Instinctively, Kit wrenched her south. The mare went straight to a gallop; the reins slack, Delia lengthened her stride, quickly travelling beyond pistol range. The Revenue Officers howled in pursuit.

Kit was deaf to their noise.

Grimly, she hung on, her fingers laced into Delia's mane, the stringy black hair whipping her cheek as she laid her head against the glossy neck. Delia's hooves pounded the sand, carrying her southward.

Jack, George, and Matthew caught up with the small Revenue troop on the beach south of Hunstanton. The Officers had given up the unequal chase. They milled about, disgruntled and disappointed, then re-formed and headed for the track up from the beach.

Concealed in the shadows of the cliff, Jack heaved a sigh of relief.

A shot rang out, echoing eerily over the water.

Jack's blood chilled. Under his breath, he swore. Kit had been hit – he was sure of it.

The Revenue troop also heard the shot. Instead of heading for home, they wheeled and cantered along the sands. Once they gained sufficient lead, Jack gave the signal to follow.

Battling faintness and a white haze of pain, Kit struggled to focus on what she should do. The hot agony in her shoulder was draining her strength. If she stayed on the sands, Delia would keep on until she fell from the saddle. As each stride the mare took pushed fiery needles into her shoulder, that wouldn't be long delayed. And then the Revenue would have her.

Spencer's image rose in her mind; Kit gritted her teeth. She had to get off the beach.

As if in answer to her prayer, the small track leading up the cliffs to Snettisham appeared before her. Gasping with the effort, Kit turned Delia into the narrow opening. The mare took the climb without further direction.

Waves of cold darkness welled about her; Kit fought them back. She rode with knees and hands, the reins dangling uselessly about Delia's neck. It was all Kit could do to discern the direction of the quarries and head Delia toward them.

In her wake, her pursuers came on, noisily clamoring for her blood, all but baying their enthusiasm.

A cold, shrouding mist closed in. Kit hugged Delia's glossy neck, her cheek against the warm wet hide. She tugged her muffler away from her dry lips and struggled to draw breath. Even that hurt.

The mouth of the quarries loomed out of the dark. Obedient to her weak tug, Delia slowed. Using her knees, Kit guided the mare into the quarries. If she could rest for a while and gather her strength, then Cranmer was not far away.

Delia walked among the jumbled rocks, hoofbeats muffled by the matted grass covering the disused tracks. Kit's cheek rose and fell with each stride. There was blackness all around, cold and deep, empty and painless. She could feel it enshrouding her. Kit focused on the black gloss of Delia's hide. Black rushed in and filled her senses. Black engulfed her. Black.

*

The scene Jack, George, and Matthew finally came upon was farcical. The Revenue troop had kept to the beach as far as the Heacham trail, then had gone up to the cliff top and continued south; they had followed quietly. The noise emanating from Snettisham drove them to pull away and enter the tiny village from the east, keeping within cover.

The place was in an uproar. The villagers had been woken and turned out of their houses; a large troop of Revenue men was searching the premises.

Jack, George and Matthew sat their mounts in stunned disbelief. One glance was enough to convince them that Kit and Delia were not present. With a contemptuous snort, Jack pulled Champion about. They retreated to a shadowy coppice separated by a field from the activity around Snettisham.

George drew his chestnut up beside Champion. "She must have got away."

Jack sat still and tried to believe it, waiting for the explanation to unlock the vise that fear had clamped about his heart. Finally, he sighed. "Possibly. You two go home. I'll check if she's got back to Cranmer."

George shook his head. "No. We'll stick with you until all's clear. How will you know if she's already got in?"

"There's a way into the stables. If Delia's there, Kit's home." The memory of how the mare had stayed by Kit when he'd brought her down on the sands so many moons ago was reassuring. "Delia won't leave Kit."

George grunted, turning his horse toward Cranmer Hall.

Reaching the stables was no problem; ascertaining Delia's presence in the dark took much longer. Twenty minutes after he'd left them, Jack rejoined George and Matthew outside the stable paddock, his grim face telling them his news.

"Not there?" George asked.

Jack shook his head.

"You think she's been shot?" It was Matthew, lugubrious as ever, who put their thoughts into words.

Jack drew a tense breath, then let out a short sigh. "Yes. If not, she'd be here."

"She lost them at Snettisham, so presumably she's somewhere between there and here."

George jumped when Jack thumped his shoulder.

"That's it!" Jack hissed. "Snettisham quarries. That's where she'll have gone to earth."

As they swung up to their saddles, George grimaced. Snettisham quarries were enormous, new digs jostling with old. Neither he nor Jack knew them well; Snettisham was too far from Castle Hendon to have been one of their playgrounds. Not so for the Cranmers; Snettisham was on their doorstep. Finding an injured Cranmer in the quarries was going to take time, time Kit might not have.

George had reckoned without Champion. They returned to Snettisham to find the Revenue gone and the village quiet. At the mouth of the quarries, Jack let Champion have his head. The big grey ambled forward, stopping now and then to snuff the air. George wondered at Jack's patience, then caught a glimpse of his face. Jack was wound tight, more tense and grim than George had ever seen him.

Champion led them deep into a section of old diggings. Suddenly, the stallion surged. Jack drew rein, holding the grey back. Sliding to the ground, Jack quieted the great beast and signaled for George and Matthew to dismount. Puzzled, they did, then they heard the muttering coming from around the next bend in the track.

Matthew took the horses, nodding at Jack's silent direction to muzzle Champion. George followed Jack to the bend in the track.

His saddle pistol in one hand, Jack stood in the shadow of a rock and eased forward until he could see the next stretch. Moonlight silvered the hunched shoulders of Sergeant Tonkin, shuffling along, eyes on the ground, his mount ambling disinterestedly behind him.

"I swear we hit 'im. Can't be wrong. *Must've* at least winged 'im."

Still muttering. Tonkin followed the track on. A large opening to one side drew his attention. Abruptly he stopped muttering and disappeared through it.

Jack and George slid silently in his wake.

A clearing lay before them. At the far end, the entrance to an old tunnel loomed like the black mouth of hell. Before it, as black as the blackest shadow, stood Delia, head up, ears pricked. At Delia's feet lay a rumpled form, stretched out and silent.

"I knew it!" Tonkin crowed. He dropped his reins and raced forward. Delia shied; Tonkin waved his hands to ward off the skittish animal. Reaching the still figure, he grabbed the old tricorne and tugged it off.

Moonlight played on a pale face, haloed in red curls.

Tonkin stared. "Well, I'll be damned!"

With that, he slipped into peaceful oblivion, rendered insensible by the impact of Jack's pistol butt on the back of his skull.

Swearing, Jack shoved Tonkin aside and fell on his knees beside Kit. With fingers that shook, he searched for the pulse at her throat. The beat was there, weak but steady. Jack drew a ragged breath. Briefly, he closed his eyes, opening them as George knelt on Kit's other side. She was lying on her stomach; with George's help, Jack turned her onto her back.

"Christ!" George blanched. The front of Kit's shirt was

283

soaked in blood. The hole in her shoulder still bled slug-gishly.

Jack gritted his teeth against the cold spreading through him; chill fingers clutched his heart. His face a stony mask, he lifted Kit's coat from the wound, fighting to conquer his shock and respond professionally. He had tended wounded soldiers often enough; the wound was serious but not nec-essarily fatal. However, the ball had lodged deep in Kit's soft flesh.

Turning, Jack called Matthew. "Go for Dr. Thrushborne. I don't care what you have to do but get him to Cranmer Hall as fast as possible."

Matthew grunted and went.

Jack and George packed the wound, padding it with the sleeves torn from their shirts and securing it with their neck-erchiefs. Kit had already lost a dangerous amount of blood.

"What now?" George sat back on his heels.

"We take her to Cranmer. Thrushborne can be trusted." Jack rose and clicked his fingers at Delia. The mare hesi-tated, then slowly approached. "I'll have to tell Spencer the truth."

"All of the truth?" George clambered to his feet. "Is that wise?"

Jack rubbed a fist across his forehead and tried to think. "Probably not. I'll tell him as much as I have to. Enough to explain things." He tied Delia's reins to Champion's saddle.

"What about Tonkin? He saw too much."

Jack cast a malevolent glance at the Sergeant's inanimate form. "Much as I'd like to remove him from this earth, his disappearance would cause too many ripples." His jaw set. "We'll have to convince him he was mistaken."

George said no more; stooping, he lifted Kit into his arms.

Jack swung up to Champion's saddle, then, leaning down, took Kit's limp form from George. Carefully, he cradled her against his chest, tucking her head into his shoulder. He looked at George, a worried frown on his face. "I'll need you to get into Cranmer. After that, you'd better go home." A weak, weary smile, a parody of Captain Jack's usual ebullience, showed through his concern, then faded. "I've enough to answer for without you added to the bill."

Chapter 22

The ride to Cranmer Hall was the longest two miles Jack had ever traveled. Kit remained unconscious, a minor mercy. To have her severely wounded was bad enough; to be forced to watch her bear the pain would have been torture. His guilt ran deep, increasing with every stride Champion took. His fear for Kit was far worse, dragging at his mind, threatening to cloak reason with black despair.

At least he now knew she hadn't betrayed them. If Tonkin had received word that his "big gang" was running a cargo that night, the whole Hunstanton Office would have been on the northern beaches. Instead, it seemed he'd set a small troop to patrol the area of his obsession. They'd just struck lucky.

Cranmer Hall rose out of the dark. Kit's home slumbered amid darkened gardens, peaceful and secure. Jack stopped before the front steps. With Kit in his arms, he slid from the saddle. George tied his chestnut to a bush by the drive, then hurried to catch Champion's reins.

"Once I'm inside, take him around to the stables before you go."

George nodded and led the grey aside.

Jack climbed the steps and waited before the heavy oak doors for George to join him. When he did, Jack, his face impassive, nodded at the large brass knocker in the middle of the door. "Wake them up."

George grimaced and did. The pounding brought footsteps flying. Bolts were thrown back; the heavy doors swung inward. George melted into the shadows at the bottom of the steps. Jack strode boldly over the threshold.

"Your mistress has had an accident." Jack searched the four shocked male faces before him, settling on the oldest and most dignified as being the best candidate for Cranmer's butler: "I'm Lord Hendon. Wake Lord Cranmer immediately. Tell him his granddaughter has been wounded. I'll explain as soon as I've taken her upstairs. Which is her room?" During this exchange, he walked confidently toward the stairs. Turning back, brows lifting impatiently, he prayed the butler would hold true to his profession and not panic.

Jenkins rose to the challenge. "Yes, m'lord." He drew a deep breath. "Henry here will show you Miss Kathryn's room. I'll send up her maid immediately."

Jack nodded, relieved he wouldn't have to deal with dithering servants. "I've sent my man for Dr. Thrushborne. He should arrive soon." He started up the stairs, Henry hurrying ahead, holding a candelabrum aloft to light the way.

Jenkins followed. "Very good, m'lord. I'll have one of the men watch out for him. I'll inform Lord Cranmer of the matter directly."

Jack nodded and followed Henry down a dark corridor deep into one of the wings. The footman stopped by a door near its end and set it wide.

Worried by the chilled dampness of Kit's clothes, Jack's

eyes went immediately to the fireplace. "Get the fire going. Fast as you can."

"Yes, m'lord." Henry bent to the task.

Jack crossed to the four-poster bed. Kneeling on the white coverlet, he gently placed Kit upon it, carefully easing his arms from under her then arranging the pillows beneath her head, pulling the bolster around to cushion her injured shoulder. Then he stood back.

And tried to hold his thoughts at bay. He'd experienced war firsthand; he'd nearly perished twice. But the mind-numbing fear that threatened to possess him now was beyond anything he'd previously felt. The idea that Kit might not live he blanked from his mind; that was a possibility he could not face. Drawing an unsteady breath, he fought to focus his mind on the here and now, on the tasks immediately before him. The next hours would be crucial. Kit had to live. And she had to be protected from the consequences of her actions. First things first. He had to get her out of her wet clothes.

Jack turned to survey Henry's handiwork. The fire blazed in the grate, throwing light and warmth into the room. "Good. Now go shake that maid awake."

Henry's eyes grew round. "Elmina?"

Jack frowned. "Miss Kathryn's maid." He nodded a curt dismissal, wondering what was wrong with Elmina.

Henry swallowed and looked doubtful, but went.

Jack paced before the fire, rubbing sensation and strength back into his arms. When Elmina failed to materialize, he swore and returned to Kit's side. Carefully, he untied their makeshift bandage. The wound had stopped bleeding. He started the difficult task of easing Kit from her wet clothes.

He'd removed her coat and was fumbling with the laces

of her shirt when the door behind him opened and shut. Quick footsteps and stiffly swishing skirts approached.

"*Mon Dieu! Ma pauvre petite! Qu'est-ce qui s'est passé?*"

Jack blinked at the torrent of French that followed hard on the heels of that beginning. He stared at the small dark-haired woman who appeared on the other side of the bed to lean over Kit, laying a hand on her forehead. Then she noticed what he was doing and slapped furiously at his hands.

Jack recoiled from the ferocious attack and her equally ferocious words. Glancing toward the end of the bed, he saw two young maids hovering uncertainly. From their blank looks, Jack surmised they couldn't understand French. The virago, presumably Elmina, was dividing her time between verbally wringing her hands over Kit and hurling insults at him. What loosely translated as "blackguard" and "moun-tebank" were the least of them.

When Elmina bustled around and tried to shoo him from the room, Jack came to his senses. "*Silence!*" He spoke smoothly in French. "Cease your wailing, woman! We need to get her into something dry immediately." Jack leaned back over Kit and started on her laces again. His idiomatic French had set Elmina back on her heels. "We'll need bandages and hot water. Can you manage that?"

His sarcasm flicked Elmina to attention. She drew a ful-minating breath; Jack looked at her and imperiously lifted one brow. Elmina's glance fell to the still figure on the bed, then she swung about and addressed the two maids. "Ella – get all the old sheets you can find. Ask Mrs. Fogg. Emily – run to the kitchen and fetch the kettle. And tell Cook to pre-pare some gruel."

Jack shook his head. "She won't be able to eat. Not until we get the bullet out of her."

"*Mon Dieu*! It's still there?"

The last lace unraveled. Jack looked up into Elmina's black eyes, pieces of coal in a face pale with anxiety. Despite her sprightly movements, she was a lot older than he'd expected. And, judging from her tirade, hellishly protective of Kit. How had his kitten escaped this mother cat? "Your mistress is lucky to be alive. She's going to need help to stay alive. Now help me get this off her." He pulled his sharp knife from its sheath in his boot and quickly slit the shirt. "Come around here. Bring that towel with you."

Picking up the small towel lying folded on Kit's washstand, Elmina hurried to obey. Jack freed the wound of torn fragments of shirt, then covered the angry flesh with the towel. "Help me ease off this sleeve."

With Elmina's help, the sleeve was removed without jarring the wound. Picking up his knife, Jack reached for Kit's wet bands.

"*Monsieur!*"

Jack all but snarled. "What now?"

Elmina's eyes were huge black orbs. Under Jack's glare she clenched her hands tight. "*Monsieur*, it is not proper that you should be here. I will take care of her."

Proper? Jack closed his eyes in frustration. Neither he nor Kit possessed a proper bone in their bodies. He opened his eyes. "Damnation, woman! I've seen every square inch of skin your *pauvre petite* possesses. Right now, I'm trying to ensure that she lives. The proprieties be damned!"

He'd spoken in English. Elmina took a moment or two to catch up. By then, Jack had expertly slid the knife between Kit's breasts and slit the bands.

Elmina's "*Sacre Dieu!*" was a weak effort as, grudgingly, she gave up her fight. Muttered references to the madness of the English, and the shocking want of delicacy displayed by unnamed peers, punctuated the next ten minutes.

The hot water and bandages arrived. Jack watched Elmina bathe the wound. The maid's hands were steady, her touch sure. When the ugly hole had been cleansed, he helped her tie a wad of torn sheeting over it. Kit's breathing had improved, but her complexion remained alarmingly pallid.

Jack left Elmina in charge with strict instructions to be called immediately should Kit regain consciousness or Dr. Thrushborne appear. In the corridor outside Kit's room, he slumped against the wall and shut his eyes. For one instant. despair overwhelmed him – Kit lay so very still, her skin so very cold. Her breathing was the only sign of life. Even if the wound didn't kill her, in her weakened state, an inflammation of the lungs might.

He tried to imagine his life without her – and couldn't. Abruptly, he opened his eyes and pushed away from the wall. Kit wasn't dead yet. If she could fight, he'd be by her side.

His face grave, Jack went to face Spencer.

Jenkins was waiting at the top of the stairs. "Lord Cranmer's in his chamber, m'lord. If you'll follow me?"

A weary grin twisted Jack's lips. The formal phrasing seemed out of place. He suspected he looked like a disreputable gypsy. And he was on his way to tell one of his father's closest friends that he'd seduced his granddaughter.

Spencer's rooms were in the opposite wing. Jenkins knocked, then held the door wide. Jack drew a deep breath and entered.

The dark was dispelled by a single lamp, turned low, set on a table in the center of the large room. In the uncertain light beyond, Jack saw the man he'd met in King's Lynn months before. Swathed in a dressing robe, Spencer sat in an armchair. The mane of white hair was the same; the shaggy brows overhanging his deep-set eyes had not changed. But the anxiety in the pale eyes was new, etching lines about the firm lips, deepening the shadows in the sunken cheeks.

Held by Spencer' s gaze, Jack paused just inside the pool of lamplight, aware of Spencer stiffening as he took in his odd attire. Abruptly, Spencer raised a hand and dismissed the small man hovering at his side.

As the door closed, Spencer lifted his chin aggressively. "Well? What have Kathryn – and you – been up to?"

Feeling as if he was facing a court-martial, Jack clamped a lid on his natural arrogance and replied simply and straightforwardly. "I'm afraid Kit and I have become rather closer than is acceptable. In short, I seduced her. The only fact I can proffer in my defense is that I didn't know at the time she was your granddaughter."

Spencer snorted incredulously. "You didn't recognize the coloring?"

Jack inclined his head. "I knew she was a Cranmer but . . ." He shrugged. "There were other possibilities."

Spencer's gaze was sharp. "Led you to believe she was something she's not, did she?"

Jack hesitated.

"You may as well give me the whole of it," declared Spencer. "I'm not likely to faint from the shock. Told you she was illegitimate, did she?"

Jack grimaced, remembering that first night, so long ago. "Let's just say that when I made my supposition plain, she didn't correct me. I'd hardly expected your granddaughter to be riding the countryside alone at night in breeches."

Spencer sighed deeply. Slowly, his head sank. For a long

moment, he stared into space, then in a gruff voice he muttered: "My fault – no denying it. I should never have let her grow so damned wild."

Minutes ticked by; Spencer seemed sunk in abstracted gloom. Jack waited, not sure what was going through the old man's mind. Then Spencer shook his head and looked him straight in the eye. "No sense in wailing over past history. You say you seduced her. What do you plan to do about it, heh?"

Jack's lips twisted wryly. "I'll marry her, of course."

"Damn right you will!" Spencer's shrewd eyes narrowed. "Think you'll enjoy it – being married to a wildcat?"

Briefly, Jack smiled. "I'm looking forward to it."

Spencer snorted and waved him to a chair. "You don't seem overly put out by the fall of the cards. But Jenkins said something about Kit's being hurt. What's happened?"

Jack drew an armchair to the table and sat, using the moments to assemble the essential elements of his tale. "Kit and I have been meeting by night at the old fishing cottage on the north boundary of my land."

Spencer nodded. "Aye. I know it. Used to go fishing with your father from there."

"I was on my way there tonight when I heard a commotion. Shots and horsemen. I went to investigate. From the cliffs I saw a chase on the sands – the Revenue following a horseman. Only the horseman was Kit."

"*They shot her?*" Spencer's incredulous question hung in the air. The sudden rigidity in his large frame was alarming.

"She's all right," Jack hastened to reassure him. "The bullet's lodged in her left shoulder but too high to be fatal. I've sent for Thrushborne. He'll dig it out, and she should be fine." Jack prayed that was true.

"I'll have their hides! I'll see them swing from their own

gibbets! I'll . . ." Spencer ground to a halt, his face purpling with rage.

"I rather think we should tread warily, sir." Jack's quiet tone had the desired effect. Spencer turned on him.

"D'ye mean to say you'll let the bastards get away with putting a damned hole in your future wife?" Spencer's wild eyes dared him to confess to such weakness.

"Ah – but you see, that's just the point." Jack held Spencer's gaze. "They don't know they shot my future wife."

The silence that followed was broken by a creak as Spencer sank back in his chair.

Jack examined his hands. "All in all, I'd rather the authorities were not made aware that my future wife rides wild through the night dressed for all the world as a man."

Eventually, Spencer sighed deeply. "Very well. Handle it your way. God knows, I've never been much good at hauling on Kit's reins. Perchance you'll have more success."

Recalling that he'd not succeeded in retiring Young Kit as he'd planned, Jack wasn't overly confident on that point. "There's a complication." Spencer's head came up, reminding Jack forcibly of an old bull about to charge. "Tonkin, the sergeant at Hunstanton, saw Kit without the hat and muffler she uses to conceal her face. He got a good look at her before I deprived him of his wits. When he comes to his senses, he'll be around here as fast as he can."

The look on Spencer's face suggested he'd like to lock Tonkin in a dungeon and be done with it. Grudgingly, he asked: "So what do we do?"

"He'll come asking questions, wanting to see Kit. The last person he'll expect to see will be me. He needs my permission to go any farther than questions. The story we'll tell is that I had dinner here this evening, with you and your granddaughter – a very private celebration of our betrothal. I remained until quite late, discussing the arrangements with Kit and you. Your health is uncertain, so the wedding will be a small affair, to be held as soon as possible."

Spencer's expression turned grim, but he said nothing. Jack continued: "Tomorrow morning, I'll call early to see you alone, to discuss the settlements. That's my reason for being here when Tonkin arrives."

"What if he insists on seeing Kit?"

"I doubt he'll insist, not if I'm here. But if he does, Kit will have gone to visit the Greshams, to tell her friend Amy the news."

Spencer nodded slowly, mulling over the plan.

The door opened and Jenkins entered. "Dr. Thrushborne's arrived, m'lord. He's asking for Lord Hendon."

Jack rose. Spencer started to rise with obvious difficulty; Jack waved him back. "Kit's unconscious at the moment – there's nothing you can do." As Spencer sank back, softly wheezing, Jack added: "I'll come and tell you what Thrushborne says."

His face pale, his lips pinched, Spencer nodded. Jack returned the nod, then strode back to Kit's chamber.

God – let her live!

Telling Spencer had been bad enough; he shared some part of the blame for Kit's wildness. But Jack couldn't excuse his own behavior; he should have acted earlier, more decisively, more effectively. He should have taken better care of her. At least Thrushborne was here. He had been treating Hendons and Cranmers for decades. He could be relied on not to talk. So far, so good. But there was a long way to go before they were out of the woods.

Jack entered Kit's room without knocking. A small black whirlwind descended on him.

"Out! *Monsieur* we do not need you! You will be in the way. You'll –"

"Elmina, do stop that. I asked Lord Hendon to come." Dr. Thrushborne's mild tones halted Elmina in mid-stride. Jack sidestepped about her. Thrushborne was wiping his hands on a clean towel. Beyond him, his intruments were laid out on a table drawn up by the bed.

Thrushborne regarded Jack. He waved at Kit's still form and raised an inquiring brow. "I gather you know this lady rather well?"

Jack didn't bother answering. "Will she live?" It was the only question he was interested in.

Thrushborne's brows rose. "Oh, yes. I should think so. She's a healthy young woman, as you doubtless know. She'll do well enough, once we get that lump of metal out of her."

Jack suspected Thrushborne was enjoying himself. It wasn't often he had a Hendon at his mercy. But Jack couldn't drag his gaze from the still figure on the bed. He didn't care about anything – anyone – else.

Thrushborne cleared his throat. "I'll need you to hold her while I pull the bullet out. She's barely unconscious, but I don't want to give her a sedative yet."

Jack nodded, steeling his nerves for the coming ordeal. He obeyed Thrushborne's orders implicitly, trying not to bruise Kit as he held her right shoulder and leaned on her left arrn to immobilize her. When the doctor's forceps probed deep, she gasped and struggled, furiously trying to pull away. Her whimpers shredded Jack's nerves. When tears welled beneath her closed lids and a choked sob escaped her, his stomach clenched. Gritting his teeth, Jack mentally ran through every curse he'd ever learned – and concentrated on obeying orders. Elmina hovered, murmuring soothingly, holding Kit's head through the worst, bathing her forehead with lavender water. As far as Jack could tell, Kit was oblivious to all but the pain.

Finally, Thrushborne straightened, flourishing his forceps. "Got it!" He beamed, then, dropping the forceps in a basin, gave his attention to staunching the blood, flowing freely again.

By the time Kit was bandaged and dosed with laudanum, Jack felt dizzy and weak.

About to leave, Thrushborne turned to him. "I take it I haven't seen anything at all of Miss Kathryn?"

Gathering his wits, Jack shook his head. "No. You were called to see Spencer."

The doctor frowned. "My housekeeper saw your servant come for me – why was that?"

"I was here when Spencer was taken badly and sent Matthew, rather than one of the Cranmer staff."

Thrushborne nodded briskly. "I'll call again in the morning – to see Spencer."

With a weary but grateful half smile, Jack shook hands. Thrushborne departed; Elmina followed, taking the bloody rags to be burned. Alone with Kit, Jack stretched, easing his aching back. He'd have to see Spencer and make sure the servants, both here and at Castle Hendon, understood their story sufficiently well to play their parts. He didn't doubt they'd do it. The Hendons and Cranmers were served by locals whose families lived and worked on the estates; all would rally to the cause. Tonkin was thoroughly disliked by all who knew him; the Revenue in general were favorites with no one. With care and forethought, all would be well. With a long-drawn sigh, Jack turned to the bed.

Kit lay stretched out primly, not wantonly asprawl as he was used to seeing her. It would be some time before he saw her like that again. How long? Three weeks, maybe four?

Jack contemplated the wait, by dint of sheer determination holding back the thought that he might never see her like that again. She would live – she had to. He couldn't live without her. The space beside her looked inviting, but Spencer was waiting, and Elmina would soon be back. With a wrenching sigh, Jack gazed down at the silent beauty. Her chest rose and fell beneath the sheet, her breathing shallow but steady. Jack put out a hand to brush a silky curl from her smooth brow, then bent to gently kiss her pale lips.

He dragged himself away. Elmina had said she'd watch Kit for what was left of the night, and Spencer was still waiting.

"Sergeant Tonkin, my lord." Jenkins held the library door wide, an expression of supercilious condescension on his face.

Stepping over the threshold, Sergeant Tonkin hesitated, his regulation hat clutched in his hands. Spying Spencer behind the desk, Tonkin headed in that direction, his stride firmly confident.

Spencer watched him approach, an expression of calm boredom on his aristocratic features. From an armchair halfway down the long room, Jack studied Tonkin's face. The sergeant hadn't seen him, so focused was he on his goal. An air of smug belligerence hung about Tonkin as he halted on the rug before the desk and saluted.

"My lord," Tonkin began. "I was a-wondering if I might have a word with Miss Cranmer, sir."

Spencer's shaggy brows lowered. "With my granddaughter? What for?"

The barked question, so direct, made Tonkin blink. He shifted his weight. "We have reason to believe, m'lord, that Miss Cranmer might be able to help us with our investigations."

"How the devil do you suppose Kathryn could know anything of your business?"

Tonkin stiffened. He shot Spencer a swift glance, then puffed out his chest. In a pretentious tone, he stated: "Some of my men were chasing a smugglers' leader last night. The man . . . that is, this leader . . . was shot. I found the fellow – the leader – in the quarries."

"So?" Spencer's gaze turned impatient. "If you've got the man, what's the problem?"

Tonkin colored. With one finger, he tugged at his collar. "But we haven't got him – that's to say, this leader."

"*You haven't?*" Spencer leaned forward. "The man was wounded and you let him get away?"

Watching, Jack sensed the moment when Tonkin's obsession came to his rescue. Instead of wilting under the heat of Spencer's glare, his backbone straightened like a poker, his beady eyes suddenly intent. "Before others of the gang knocked me out, I managed to get a good look at the fellow's – that is . . ." Gritting his teeth, Tonkin drew a deep breath then continued: "I got a good look at the leader's face. Red curls, my lord," Tonkin pronounced with relish. "And a pate, delicate-looking face with a small pointy chin." When Spencer merely looked blank, Tonkin added: "A *female* face, my lord."

Silence filled the library.

When Spencer frowned, Tonkin nodded decisively. "Exactly, m'lord. If I hadn't seen it with me own two eyes, I'd have laughed the idea aside, too."

Spencer's expression turned openly puzzled. "But I still don't see, Sergeant, what this has to do with my granddaughter. You can't seriously imagine she'll be able to help you?"

Tonkin's face fell; a second later, crafty suspicion gleamed in his small eyes. He opened his mouth.

Jack smoothly intervened. "I really think, Sergeant, that you'll have to explain why you imagine Miss Cranmer would be more help to you in identifying and locating a Cranmer . . . connection than Lord Cranmer himself. I must tell you such matters are not normally the province of the ladies."

Tonkin whirled, his expression, unguarded for an instant a medley of fury and rampant suspicion. With the next breath, his unlovely mask fell back into place; he drew himself up and saluted. "Good morning, m'lord. Didn't see you there, sir." Then the implication of Jack's words registered. "*Connection*, m'lord?"

Jack raised a bored brow.

Visibly girding his loins, Tonkin shook his head. "No, sir." Chin up, at attention, he spoke to the air above Jack's head. "I know what I saw, sir. This woman rode a magnificent black horse. I saw with my own eyes the hole my men blew in her shoulder." Tonkin pressed his lips tightly together against the impulse to explain *whose* shoulder; meeting his eyes, Jack understood. Fanatical determination flared in those beady orbs as Tonkin, his chin pugnaciously square, glanced sideways at Spencer.

Jack smothered the urge to strangle the man. "Perhaps, Sergeant, if you'd tell us exactly what happened, his lordship might be able to clarify matters for you?"

Tonkin hesitated, eyes going from Jack to Spencer and back again before, very slowly, he nodded. And determinedly began his tale.

In her bed abovestairs, Kit lay flat on her back and tried to remember how she'd got there. Her shoulder was on fire; one minute she felt flushed, the next as cold as ice. Eyes closed against the light, she heard the door open and shut.

"Sergeant Tonkin's 'ere, miss." Kit identified the whisperer as Emily, one of the upstairs maids. "Jenkins just showed 'im into the library."

"This is the Revenue man, yes?" Elmina answered from the direction of the fireplace. Kit frowned. The Revenue? *Here?*

"He's a terrible bully, that one," Emily explained. "He's asking to see Miss Kathryn. Jenkins said as he'd seen her face."

Elmina's response was dismissive. "His lordship will take care of it. And Lord Hendon is there, too, is he not? Rest assured, all will be well."

"Elmina!" Kit struggled onto her good elbow, wincing at the pain in her left shoulder. Her weak call brought both Elmina and Emily rushing to the bed. "Get me my dove grey gown. Quickly."

Her face a mask of horror, Elmina remained rooted to the spot. "No, no, *petite!* You are much too weak to get up! You will reopen your wound."

"If I don't go down and let Tonkin see me, I might not live to heal anyway." Gritting her teeth, Kit managed to sit on the edge of the bed. Suddenly, she remembered all too well. Closing her eyes, she willed her dizziness away. "Dammit, Elmina! Don't argue – or I'll do it myself."

The threat worked, as it usually did; muttering, Elmina hurried to the wardrobe. Returning within minutes with the grey dress and Kit's underclothes, she ventured: "Lord Hendon is downstairs."

"So I heard." Kit looked at her clothes and wondered how she was going to cope. Lifting her left arm was to be avoided at all costs. She was wearing a fine linen nightgown with a high frilly neck. She'd chosen the grey gown because of its neckline, round and high enough to conceal her bandages. If she wore the dress on top of the nightgown, hopefully Tonkin wouldn't notice.

Battling dizziness, she stood; in a voice devoid of all unnecessary strength, she directed Elmina in helping her into the dress and easing the bodice up over her injured shoulder. She felt weak as a newborn kitten – just standing was an effort. While Elmina quickly laced the gown, Kit considered what might be transpiring downstairs. If Tonkin had seen her face, she doubted he'd go away without laying eyes on her. She hoped Spencer wouldn't lose his temper before she got down. The most puzzling aspect was why the elusive High Commisioner had chosen this particular day to pay a morning visit. Perhaps, if she could think straight enough, she might be able to enlist his aid in getting rid of Tonkin. Then, later, she could tell him about Jack and ask for his help in that matter, too.

How she was to manage that with Spencer looking on was beyond her at present. She'd worry about that once Tonkin was gone.

Elmina finished lacing the dress and hurried to get Kit's brushes. Kit looked down. The room swayed and she quickly raised her head. Fixing her gaze on her mirror across the room, she tried a step or two. It was going to be dicey, but she'd do it if it killed her. Her chin went up. She hadn't done anything she was ashamed of; she wasn't going to let a bully of a sergeant drag the Cranmer name through the mud.

Downstairs, Tonkin was struggling to keep his head above water. At Jack's artful prompting, he'd explained what had happened, in detail. When retold in such a way, his night's efforts lost much of their glory.

With that accomplished, Jack sat back and calmly

engaged Spencer in a detailed discussion of all the Cranmer "connections" currently known. Throughout, he kept a careful eye on Tonkin, noting the sergeant's rising impatience – and his increasing irritation. Despite being subjected to considerable discouragement, Tonkin wasn't about to let go. When Spencer came to the end of the list of his sons' acknowledged bastards, Jack quietly put in: "But I believe the Sergeant said the face he saw was distinctly feminine. Is that right, Tonkin?"

Tonkin blinked, then nodded eagerly. "Yessir, your lordship. A woman's face, it was."

Spencer frowned, then shook his head. "Can't think of any male Cranmer with effeminate looks."

"I hesitate to suggest it," Jack said, "but could it possibly have been a female relative?" He could almost hear Tonkin's satisfied sigh.

"Aren't any," Spencer decisively replied. "Only girl in the family's Kathryn and stands to reason couldn't be her."

With a fleeting smile, Jack nodded in agreement.

Tonkin's face was a study in dismay. "Pardon me, your lordship, but why's that?"

Spencer frowned at him. "Why's what, Sergeant?"

Tonkin gritted his teeth. "Why *couldn't* it be Miss Cranmer, m'lord?"

As one, Jack and Spencer stared at him, then both erupted into laughter. Tonkin reddened; he looked from one to the other, ugly suspicion gathering in his eyes.

Spencer recovered first, waving his hand to and fro. "A rich jest, Sergeant, but I can assure you my granddaughter does not consort with smugglers."

Tonkin reacted as if slapped.

"I think, perhaps," put in Jack, sensing Tonkin's swelling belligerence, "that the Sergeant might as well know – just so

303

he can accept Miss Cranmer's innocence as proven fact, my lord – that Miss Cranmer had dinner with both you and myself last night. We sat late, Miss Cramner with us, discussing the details of our impending nuptials."

Jack smiled at Tonkin, the very picture of helpful assurrance.

"Nuptials?" Tonkin stared.

"Precisely." Jack adjusted the cuff of one sleeve. "Miss Cranmer and I will shortly be married. The announcement will be made in the next day or so." Jack smiled again, openly confident. "You can be one of the first to wish us happy, Tonkin."

"Er . . . yes, of course. That is . . . I hope you'll be very happy, sir . . ." Tonkin faltered to a halt.

The door behind him opened.

The three men turned. Three pairs of eyes fastened on the slim grey figure who appeared in the doorway; shock registered, in equal measure, on all three faces.

Kit saw it and glided forward, filling the telltale void. "Good morning, Grandfather." She crossed to Spencer's side. Placing her right hand on his shoulder, she planted a dutiful kiss on his cheek, grateful that impassivity had dropped like a veil over his features. Straightening, denying the wave of dizzying pain that threatened to engulf her, she looked directly at Tonkin. "I heard Sergeant Tonkin was asking after me. How can I help you, Sergeant?"

It was a bold move. Jack held his breath, wondering if Tonkin could see how pale she was. To him, her condition was obvious, but apparently Tonkin had never set eyes on Kit before last night. His heart in his mouth, Jack willed his muscles to relax. He'd shot to his feet the instant Kit had appeared; only by the most supreme effort had he stifled the overwhelming urge to go to her side. How on earth she'd got

304

dressed and downstairs was a wonder; how long she'd remain on her feet was a major concern. She'd seen him as she'd entered. As her gaze had passed over him, he'd seen the shock of recognition flare beneath the haze of pain.

Sergeant Tonkin simply stared, speechless. His gaze flicked to Jack, then to Spencer, then, surreptitiously, he darted a glance at Kit, dwelling on her left shoulder.

Aware of his scrutiny, Kit held herself erect, her expression relaxed and open, waiting for Tonkin to state his business. Her grasp on Spencer's shoulder was nothing less than a death grip; luckily, Spencer had put up his hand to cover hers, the warmth of his large palm imparting strength and support enough to anchor her to consciousness. Kit drew on it unashamedly.

From where she stood, Kit could see Spencer's expression, arrogantly supercilious as he stared at Tonkin. A peculiar hiatus held them all.

Jack broke it, strolling casually forward to Kit's side.

The instant he moved, he drew Kit's gaze. Lips slightly parted to ease her increasingly painful breathing, Kit watched him approach. Her wits were slowing, becoming more sluggish. They'd said Lord Hendon was with Spencer. There was no one else in the room except Jack. And it *was* Jack, for all that he was far more elegantly dressed than she'd ever seen him, moving with a languid grace she recognized instantly. The man approaching her was a rake of the first order, one who'd learned his recreational habits in the hothouse of the *ton*. The man approaching her was Jack. Confusion welled; Kit resisted the urge to close her eyes against it.

Jack stopped by her side; she looked into his eyes and saw his concern and his strength. He reached for her right hand, lifting it from Spencer's shoulder. She let him, relief spreading through her at the comfort in his touch. His other arm slid about her waist, a very real support.

Aware of the picture he was creating for Tonkin, Jack raised Kit's fingers to his lips. "The sergeant thought he saw you last night, my dear. Your grandfather and I were just explaining that he must have been mistaken." Jack smiled reassuringly into wide amethyst eyes, hazed and dull with pain. "You'll be pleased to know I've given you an alibi. Even one so earnest as Sergeant Tonkin will have to accept that while you were having dinner with me, and later discussing our wedding, you couldn't possibly have been simultaneously riding the hills."

"Oh?" It was no effort to infuse the syllable with bewilderment. Kit dragged her eyes from Jack's to gaze in confusion at Sergeant Tonkin. Dinner? Wedding? Her faintness intensified. The arm about her waist tightened possessively, protectively.

Kit's obvious confusion dispelled the last vestige of Tonkin's certainty. Jack could see it in his eyes, in the sudden slackness of his features. The pugnacity that had kept him going drained away, leaving him off-balance.

Swallowing, Tonkin half saluted. "I can see as you don't know nothing about it, miss." He glanced warily at Jack, then Spencer. "If it's all right with you, my lords, I'll be on my way."

Jack nodded; Spencer simply glared.

With a last salute, Tonkin turned and quickly left the room.

As soon as the door shut, Spencer turned in his chair, anxiety and relief flooding out in a fiercely whispered: "And what's the meaning of all this, miss?"

Kit didn't answer. As the door clicked shut, she'd leaned back against Jack's arm and shut her eyes. The willpower that had kept her going abruptly faded. She felt Jack's arms close about her. She was safe; they were all safe.

She heard Spencer's question as if from a distance, muffled by cold mists. With a little sigh, she surrendered to the oblivion that beckoned, beyond pain, beyond confusion.

Chapter 23

During the next week, the servants of Cranmer Hall and Castle Hendon struggled to preserve a facade of normality in the absence of their masters. Lord Cranmer was seriously ill and took to his bed. Miss Kathryn Cranmer stayed by his bedside, unable because of the exigencies of her nursing to see anyone. Lord Hendon was as mysteriously elusive as ever.

Behind the scenes, Spencer remained in his rooms, too worried to be of much practical use. Jack spent most of his time with Kit, helping to nurse her. Her shoulder wound healed well, but in her weakened state the cold she'd caught in the quarries rapidly developed into something worse. As the week progressed, Kit's fever mounted. Only Jack had the strength to hold her easily, to cajole and if necessary force her to drink the drafts the doctor prepared. Only his voice penetrated the fogs Kit wandered through, dazed, weak, and confused.

Dr. Thrushborne called every morning and afternoon, worried by Kit's state. "It's the combination of things," he explained to Jack. "The chill coming on top of a massive loss of blood. All we can do is keep her warm and quiet and let Nature work for us."

Two grim days later, he answered an exhausted Jack's unvoiced question: "The fact she's still with us is the brightest sign. She's a slip of a thing, but all the Cranmers are as stubborn as hell. I don't think she plans to leave us just yet."

Jack couldn't even summon a smile. His world centered on the room at the end of the wing. Other than an obligatory visit to Hunstanton to follow up Tonkin's suspicions, and an equally obligatory appearance at the church at Docking on Sunday, he'd not left the Hall. Matthew acted as his go-between, relaying his orders to Castle Hendon and supplying him with clothes, as well as taking messages to George, who'd temporarily assumed the leadership of the Gang. The bed in the room next to Kit's had been made up, so he could grab a few hours' sleep whenever exhaustion forced him to yield his place to Elmina.

It wasn't that he distrusted Elmina; he'd learned she'd been maid to Kit's mother and had been with her *petite* since her birth. However, like Spencer, she was incapable of exerting any control over her erstwhile charge. On the second night, he'd fallen into exhausted slumber, stretched, fully dressed, on the bed next door. He'd been awoken by a high-pitched altercation. In Kit's room, he'd come upon the staggering sight of Kit, out of bed, rummaging through her wardrobe, while Elmina remonstrated helplessly. He'd walked in and picked Kit up, ignoring her struggles and the curses she'd laid about his ears. He'd discovered she was fluent in two languages.

Even when he'd put her back in bed, she'd fought him, but eventually yielded to his greater strength. Delirious, she hadn't known who he was; her confusion that someone existed who could deny her had been obvious. The conviction that his kitten had gone her own way ever since she'd set foot from her cradle took firm root in Jack's mind.

And when her fever mounted, draining what little strength she still possessed, leaving him to watch, impotent, as death fought to claim her, he made a solemn vow that if she was spared, he'd keep her safe for the rest of her life. Without her, his life would be worthless – he knew that now. His vulnerability angered him, but he couldn't deny it. Nor could he walk away from his own part in her ill-fated masquerade. When all this was over, she'd be his responsibility – a responsibility he'd take more seriously than any other in his life.

For Kit, the week passed in a peculiar haze, lucid moments submerged in mists of confusion. Her body went from chilled shivering to heated dampness; her brain hurt dreadfully whenever she tried to think. Throughout it all, she was aware of a protective presence at her side, of a rock which remained steady within her whirling world. In the few scattered moments when she was fully conscious, she recognized that presence as Jack. Why he was in her bedroom was beyond her; she could only be grateful.

The end came abruptly.

She opened her eyes in the early dawn and the world had stopped spinning. She saw Jack, sleeping, slumped in an armchair facing the bed. Smiling, she wriggled to turn over, the better to appreciate the unexpected sight. A dull ache in her left shoulder stopped her. Frowning, she relived the night on the beach and her race from the Revenue. She'd been shot but had reached the quarries. After that came – nothing. Jack must have found her and brought her home.

Smiling at his evident concern, for it must have been that which had driven him to stay overnight, braving Spencer's wrath, Kit stumbled on her first difficulty. How had Jack convinced Spencer to allow him to stay, not just at the Hall, but in her room? She tried to concentrate, but her mind wasn't up to it. An elusive recollection niggled. Sergeant Tonkin was caught up in it somewhere; perhaps she'd been conscious for a time at the quarries and had overheard the sergeant and his men? Kit frowned, then mentally shrugged. No doubt it would come back to her.

Thoughts of Spencer reminded her she should go and reassure him as soon as possible; she knew how he fretted when she was hurt. Kit flexed her shoulder. She squinted down; all she could see was bandage. She felt nothing more than a mild ache.

Her gaze rested on Jack's sleeping figure, drinking in the familiar features like a soothing draft. His cheekbones and brow seemed more angular than she recalled. The normally smooth planes of his cheeks were roughened by stubble. He looked thoroughly rumpled, nothing like her last image of him. Kit frowned. Again, that elusive memory flitted past, tantalizingly insubstantial. She grimaced and shook her head. Her lids were heavy. It was too early to get up. Besides, Jack was still sleeping and looked like he needed the rest. Perhaps she should nap, just until he awoke?

Lips curved? she drifted back to sleep.

The sensation of being stared at penetrated Jack's slumber. Opening his eyes, he looked straight into shocked amethyst. Kit was awake and staring at him as if she'd seen a ghost. The look on her face told him he didn't need to worry about how to remind her of the scene in Spencer's library.

"Lord Hendon?" The weakness in her voice owed more to shock than illness. Suddenly, purple flares erupted in her violet eyes. "*You're Lord Hendon!*"

Jack winced at the accusation. He sat up and rubbed his

311

hands over his face. It was just like her to return to the living with a rush. All his notions of gently explaining matters to a meek and confused woman went out the window. Kit was awake, alive and well, and in full command of her senses. And she hadn't changed one bit.

Kit jumped when Jack's hands dropped from his face to slap the arms of the chair. He surged to his feet, grinning inanely, his expression a mixture of joy, delight, and unadulterated relief. Before she could gather her wits, she'd been scooped from her bed and, in a tangle of sheets, deposited in his lap. Then he kissed her.

To Jack, Kit's lips, warm and sweet, tasted better than ambrosia. Stubbornly, she kept them locked against him. She struggled, but it was a weak effort – he felt perfectly justified in ignoring it.

Kit tried to protest, but her mumbles fell on deaf ears. She was confused and angry – and she intended telling him about it before he stole her wits. But it was already too late. A familiar warmth was spreading through her. She clamped her lips tight shut, only to feel her body respond shamefully to his nearness. Of their own volition, her lips parted, eager to yield him the prize he sought. Kit gave up. She wound her arms about his neck and returned his kiss with all the fervor of a woman too long denied.

It felt like heaven to be with him again.

Jack shifted his hold and Kit winced. He raised his head immediately. "Damn! I forgot about your shoulder."

"Forget my shoulder." Kit drew his head back to hers, but it was clear she'd unintentionally brought him to his senses. When he drew away again, she let him go.

Jack looked deep into Kit's eyes and wondered just how much she'd remembered. Whatever the answer now was the time to tell her of their betrothal. Lifting her he placed her back on the bed, plumping up the pillows at her back and tucking the coverlet about her. Kit accepted his ministrations, her expression turning suspicious.

Should he return to the formality of the chair? Jack temporized and sat on the bed, one of Kit's hands in his. He glanced into her eyes and squared his shoulders. Proposing would have been a damn sight easier. "As you've realized, I'm Lord Hendon."

"Not Captain Jack?"

"That, too," he admitted. "Lord Hendon is Captain Jack."

"When did you realize who I was?"

"The evening before you were shot." Memory stirred and Jack rose to pace the room. "I recognized you as a Cranmer at the outset, but I thought you one of the family's by-blows – as you well know." He shot an accusing glance at Kit. She met it with bland innocence. "That afternoon, George came to see me. He'd been visiting Amy –"

"Amy?" Kit stared.

Jack stopped and considered, but Kit's mind made the jump without further assistance.

"George is George Smeaton?"

Jack nodded. "We grew up together."

Kit tried to juggle the pieces of the jigsaw that were falling into her hands.

"The Greshams' groom told George who the black Arab mare belonged to. George came and told me."

Kit's mind was racing, filling in gaps, recalling snippets here and there. One particularly disturbing fragment was rapidly growing in importance. "My memory is still a little hazy," she began, "but I seem to recall some mention of a wedding?" She tried to make the question as innocuous as such a question could be. When Jack's brows rose arrogantly, her heart stood still.

"Naturally, in the circumstances, we'll be married." Neither his tone nor the glint in his grey eyes suggested there was any alternative.

Kit blinked. "Married?" Just like that? To a man like Jack? Worse – to a *lord* like Jack. Merciful heavens! She'd never be able to call her soul her own. "Just a minute." She tried to keep her voice even. "I'm not quite clear on what happened. When did we become betrothed?"

"As far as I'm concerned," Jack growled, his eyes gleaming, "we became betrothed when you begged me to take your maidenhead."

"Ah." Kit's eyes glazed. Arguing that point was impossible. She tried a different tack. "When did this idea of marriage enter your head?"

Frowning, Jack tried to gauge her direction, wary of answering in the wrong way.

"After you'd found out who I was?"

Jack scowled.

Which was answer enough for Kit. "If you've determined on marriage purely to save my reputation, you can forget it." She sat up. "I'd already decided not to marry, so there's really no need for any charade."

The idea that she was rejecting him held Jack speechless for all of ten seconds. "Charade?" he growled. "Charade be damned! If you've a dislike of marriage – though what you can know of the matter defies me – you should have remembered that *before* you gave yourself to me. *You* offered – *I* accepted. It's too late for second thoughts." Hands on hips, he glowered at Kit. "And in case it hasn't sunk in yet, let me tell you that women of your station can't go about giving themselves to men like me and expect to get let off the hook!"

Kit's eyes blazed. "Dammit! There's no sense in marrying me if you don't want to!"

Jack nearly choked. "What's wanting got to do with it? Of course I want to marry you!"

The statement, uttered at half bellow, stopped them both in their tracks.

Turning it over in his mind, Jack decided there was nothing he wished to add. He had to marry. He wanted to marry Kit. In fact, as far as he was concerned, they were married already. He just had to get her to agree.

Kit watched him, a considering frown on her face. Lord Hendon was fast becoming a far greater threat to her future than Captain Jack had ever been. Jack was an arrogant rogue, who could send her senses spinning with a single caress and was quite prepared to tie her up and carry her off if she didn't obey his orders. But she'd been in no danger of having to marry Captain Jack. Lord Hendon had all Jack's attributes, if anything, in greater measure. While Jack might bellow to overcome any resistance, Lord Hendon, she suspected, would simply raise one of those supercilious eyebrows and people would fall over themselves to obey. Kit swallowed a snort. And he expected her to marry him?

She glanced up, into his silver-grey eyes, and saw something in their shimmering depths which made her throat contract. The implication of his watchful silence broke over her.

He wanted her to marry him. He wanted her.

Abruptly, Kit threw off the bedclothes and swung her legs over the side of the bed. She'd forgotten that curious sense of being stalked. Right now, she'd prefer to be a moving target.

"Stay in bed, Kit."

The undisguised command flicked Kit on the raw. She threw Jack a fulminating glance, but before she could take up her verbal cudgels, he was speaking again. "Dr.

315

Thrushborne will be here soon, as he has been every morning for the past week."

"Week?" Kit stared. It couldn't have been that long. "What day is it?"

Jack had to think before answering: "Tuesday."

"God lord! I've lost a week!"

"You nearly lost your *life*."

The deliberate tones jerked Kit back to full awareness. Jack had drawn closer. He stooped and scooped her legs in one arm and toppled her back on her pillows tucking her legs under the covers.

"No more games, Kit. For God's sake, stay in bed and do whatever Thrushborne says. The story we've put about –"

While Jack sat beside her and filled her in on their tale, Kit struggled to regain some sense of reality, some semblance of normality. But nothing seemed the same anymore.

Jack came to the end of his tale. "Elmina will be here soon, and I should return to Castle Hendon. I'll be back this evening." He rose, wondering what more he could say. He wasn't sure if she'd accepted their marriage as inescapable fact; he hadn't yet told her how soon it would be. But it was high time someone took charge of Kit Cranmer; he was that someone.

Kit couldn't clear her brow of the frown, born of puzzlement and uncertainty, that had settled there. She glanced up at Jack, towering over her. To her surprise, his long slow smile transformed his face. Swiftly, he bent to run his lips along her forehead, easing the tension. Then, his fingers tipped up her face and his lips touched hers in a kiss of warmth and promise.

With a flick of her curls he was gone.

Kit sank back onto her pillows with a groan. She needed to think.

But the time to think was hard to find.

Elmina entered the room before Jack could have reached the top of the stairs. Intrigued by her maid's apparent acceptance of a man in her life, Kit couldn't resist a few leading questions. What she learned left her even more adrift than before. It seemed that during her illness, Jack had taken over – taken *her* over – with Spencer's and everyone else's blessing.

Before she could decide what she felt about that, Spencer himself appeared. That interview was more painful than she'd anticipated. It very quickly became clear that Spencer blamed himself for her wildness, a fact which irritated Kit immensely. Her wildness was her cross to bear – it didn't owe its existence to anyone else; no one else was to blame. She'd always loved Spencer precisely because he'd never sought to draw rein on her. In her rush to reassure him, she found herself accepting her impending marriage with glib serenity. She convinced Spencer. When he left, much happier than when he'd entered, she was left wondering if she could convince herself.

Dr. Thrushborne was the next to cross her threshold. He was thrilled to find her awake and lucid. He examined her wound and declared it healing well. Pleased, he congratulated her on her forthcoming nuptials, teasing her on the anticipated date of her first confinement. As he was a favorite, Kit let him off with a glare.

In reply to her query, he agreed she could leave her bed, on condition she remained within the house and took care not to overtax herself.

Which was why, when Lady Gresham and Amy arrived that afternoon, she was lying on the *chaise* in the back parlor.

"Amy!" Kit sat up with a start, simultaneously remembering her wound and that she'd no idea how much Amy

317

knew. Did George confide in Amy? Kit hesitated, just long enough for Lady Gresham to sweep in.

"Don't get up, Kit, dear." Her ladyship bent, offering a cheek for Kit to kiss. "The whole county knows how pressed you've been with Spencer so ill. I take it he's improved?"

Kit nodded, fervently hoping Spencer was still keeping to his rooms. "Greatly improved, I'm pleased to say." That, at least, was the truth.

While Lady Gresham settled her skirts in an armchair, Kit smiled at Amy, still wondering, but her friend only returned the smile gaily, apparently oblivious to any deeper currents. Perhaps George was as secretive as Jack.

"Well!" Lady Gresham smiled beatifically. "We called last week and again yesterday, as I hope they've told you. The first was simply to see how you were coping but, of course, we heard your news on Sunday and simply couldn't wait to congratulate you."

Kit tried to disguise her stare. What news? Sunday? The suspicion she'd just set foot in one of Jack's webs grew. "It was such a shock to hear the banns read out." Amy put a hand on Kit's arm. "Lord Hendon made your excuses quite beautifully, didn't he, Mama?"

"So accomplished," sighed Lady Gresharn. "And so thrillingly handsome. Why – he's his father all over again."

Kit waited for the room to stop whirling. She could have told her ladyship just how accomplished Lord Hendon was – and how thrilling his handsomeness could be. "What was his father like?" She asked the question to gain time to gather her scattered wits and shackle her temper. If she screamed, she'd never be able to explain it.

But *banns?* Damn it, how had he managed that?

Her ladyship's reminiscences on the previous Lord Hendon were tame compared to what Kit knew of the present incumbent. But by the time Lady Gresham had recalled to whom she was speaking and curtailed her ramblings, Kit was in command of herself once more.

The rest of their visit was spent in joyous discussion of her wedding, on which subject Kit invented freely. What else could she do? She could hardly tell Lady Gresham that the banns had been read without her consent. Even if she did, they'd probably put the outburst down to exhaustion consequent on nursing Spencer. And no matter how angry Jack made her, she wasn't about to deny a betrothal. He'd made it perfectly plain how he saw that point. No – she was trapped. She might as well smile and enjoy it.

When she finally found solitude, in the peace of the gazebo with the red banners of sunset flying the sky, that attitude was close to the summation of her thoughts. She'd little choice but to marry Jack, Lord Hendon. Short of creating an almighty scandal, there was nothing she could do to avoid it. She'd made her decisions – her own mistakes; this was where they'd landed her.

Would marrying Jack be such a black fate? Settling on the seat, Kit couldn't suppress a smile. The prospect of being Lady Hendon was not entirely grim. Her physical satisfaction was guaranteed. Jack was a magnificent lover. Moreover, he seemed very interested in teaching her all she would ever wish to know. But she was not a dim-witted miss, entranced by a handsome face. She knew Jack too well. His autocratic tendencies, his habit of command, his determination to have things his own way – all these she'd recognized from the first. They'd been bad enough in Captain Jack but in Lord Hendon, her husband, they could well prove overwhelming.

That was what worried her.

Kit crossed her arms on the sill, sinking her chin into her

sleeve. Her stomach knotted every time she tried to imagine how Jack would behave once they were married. In recent years, her freedom had become precious. As her husband, Jack would have more right to control her than anyone had ever had. And he'd served notice on her freedom – if not directly, then indirectly. Marriage to him would leave her with only as much freedom as he deigned to allow her. Could she tolerate such a situation?

Thoughts of Amy surfaced, bringing their childhood vow to mind. She'd marry for love or not at all. Did she love Jack?

Kit's brow creased. How to tell? She'd never been in love before – but she'd never felt for a man what she did for Jack. Was that love?

With a disgusted snort, she shrugged the question aside. It was irrelevant. She was marrying Jack.

Did he love her?

An even greater imponderable but far more to the point. He wanted her – not for a moment did she doubt that. But love? He wasn't the sort to make such an admission of weakness. That was how many men saw love, and who was she to deny it? Every time she thought of Jack, every time he kissed her, she felt weak. But the idea of Jack reduced by love to a weak-kneed state was simply too much to swallow.

Could she make him love her? He might be in love with her, but how would she ever know if he could never bring himself to admit it? Could she *make* him admit it?

A challenge, that.

Kit's brows rose. Maybe that was how she should approach this marriage – as a challenge. One to be grasped and made into what she wanted it to be. And before she'd finished, she'd make sure she heard him say he loved her. The gentle breeze had turned cool, wafting the last of the perfume from the roses. Kit stared at the full blooms as they merged with the dusk. It was nearly time for dinner – time to go in and face her future.

A smile twisted Kit's lips. Undoubtedly, running in Jack's harness was going to try her temper to the limit. But there'd be compensations – she was determined to claim them.

"I might have guessed."

Startled, Kit swung about. Jack lounged in the doorway of the gazebo, his shoulders propped against the frame. With the last of the light behind him, she couldn't be sure of his expression.

"Elmina said Thrushborne told you to stay inside the house."

Kit's natural instinct was to ask who dared question her. But Jack's tone was not aggressive – was, in fact, close to tentative, as if he didn't know how she'd respond. Kit held her own features to impassivity as she rapidly considered her options. If she was to live with this man for the rest of her life, she'd do well to start practicing a little tact. According to Lady Gresham, a little of that commodity could go a long way in domestic affairs.

"I was miles away," she said, and watched his jaw harden in an effort to stifle his demand to be told what she'd been thinking of. Kit bowed her head to hide her smile. "It's getting rather chilly. I was about to go in."

She made to rise, and, instantly, he was there, by her side. Kit was glad to let him take her hand. She made no demur when his other arm slipped supportively about her waist. It was, she decided, quite pleasant to be treated like porcelain – at least, by Jack. As they walked through the darkened garden, whiffs of sandalwood mixed with the floral fragrance. That was something she should have picked up. An aroma of sandalwood had clung to Captain Jack, yet it was a rich man's scent. But the fragrance was so familiar, it hadn't registered as odd.

The warmth of the large body so close to hers was both comforting and distracting. Even in her weakened state, she could still feel the excitement his presence generated, setting her pulse beating in double time. She felt his gaze, still worried, scan her face. His arm tightened, almost imperceptibly. Kit knew that if she glanced up, he would pull her to him and kiss her.

She kept her gaze level. She wasn't ready for that yet. When he kissed her, she lost her wits. She became his, and he could do anything with her he wished. She needed time to adjust to the fact that in three weeks, that would be her permanent state.

As she went up the steps on Jack's arm, Kit wondered if she would be strong enough to be Lady Hendon – and still be herself.

Chapter 24

The wedding of Jonathon, Lord Hendon, and Miss Kathryn Cranmer was the highlight of the year in that part of Norfolk. Women from miles about crowded the yard of the tiny church in Docking that had served the Cranmers and Hendons for centuries. Maids from the surrounding houses jostled with farmers' wives, vying for vantage points from which to Ooh and Aah. All agreed that the bridegroom could not have been more handsome, in his bottle green coat and ivory inexpressibles, his brown hair, tied back in a black riband, glinting in the sunlight. He arrived commendably early and disappeared into the church, accompanied by his friend, Mr. George Smeaton of Smeaton Hall.

The subsequent interval was easily filled with satisfying gossip. The groom, with his military career as well as his natural heritage as a Hendon, provided much of the fare. The only stories known of Miss Kathryn dated from schoolroom days. While these were wild enough to satisfy the most avid gossip, all agreed the lady must have left such scandalous doings behind her. When she was handed down from the Cranmer coach, a slender figure in a cloud of ivory lace, beaded with pearls, the breath caught in every throat, only to be let out, a moment later, in the most satisfied of communal sighs.

The murmur which rose from the congregation behind him told Jack that Kit had arrived. He turned, slowly, and looked down the aisle. She'd paused just inside the church while a teary Elmina resettled her long train. As he watched, Kit started her walk toward him, her hand steady on Spencer's arm. Behind her veil, she was smiling serenely, her chin tilted at that particular angle he knew so well. As she neared the end of her walk to his side, Jack met her gaze. His lips curved in a slow smile, quite impossible to deny. She looked superb. There were pearls about her throat, others dangled from her ears. Pearl rosettes held the heavy train on her shoulders. Even the headdress that held her delicate veil in place was composed of pearls. None, in his eyes, could vie with the pearl the dress contained.

The service was short and simple. Neither of the chief participants had any difficulty with their vows, uttering them in firm accents perfectly audible to the many guests squeezed into the church.

And then they were running the gamut of well-wishers, lining their route to the Hendon barouche. Jack handed Kit in, then jumped in behind her. "To the Hall, Matthew."

To Kit's astonishment, the coachman's head turned to reveal Matthew's lugubrious features. "Aye," he chuckled. He nodded a welcome in her direction before giving the horses the office. A pair of high-stepping bays, they quickly drew the carriage free of the crowd.

Bowling along the country lanes, through shadows shot with sunlight, they had little chance to talk, too occupied with acknowledging the waves and wishes of tenants and other locals lining the way. Only when the carriage turned into the long Cranmer Hall drive did Jack get a chance to settle back and cast a knowledgeable eye over his bride's gown.

"How did you manage that?" It occurred to him that the gown was a feat bordering on a miracle, given the short notice she'd had.

"It was my mother's." Kit glanced down at a lace sleeve, closed with pearl buttons. "She was particularly fond of pearls."

Jack's lips twitched. He hadn't associated his Kit with anything so feminine as jewelry. He wondered how she'd look in the Hendon emeralds. They were somewhere in the Castle. He'd hunt them out and take them to London to be cleaned and reset; their present heavily ornate settings would not suit Kit's delicate beauty.

They'd decided on a ceremony late in the day, to be followed by a banquet and ball. As the evening wore on, Jack sat at the high table and watched his wife enchant their acquaintances. There was, he reflected, nothing to complain of in Kit's social graces. Ever since that evening when he'd found her in the gazebo, she'd behaved perfectly. Her demeanor had supported the fiction of their arranged marriage; even the most sharp-eyed observer could find no inconsistency in her manner. So successful had she been in projecting the image of a woman well pleased that Spencer now behaved as if the arrangement had always been in the wind. She was confident and serene; while her attitude held no overt maidenly modesty, neither did it suggest she was aware of her husband in any intimate way.

All of which, of course, was the most complete humbug. But only he knew that the elegant Lady Hendon stiffened slightly whenever he was near, clamping a stubborn hold

325

over her normal responses to him. Only he was aware that she avoided meeting his eyes, using every feminine wile under the sun to accomplish that feat.

He wondered whether she knew what she was doing.

Since that night in the gazebo, he'd not so much as kissed her. She hadn't given him a chance, and, wise enough to guess at her lack of enthusiasm for their union and the reasons behind it, he hadn't gone out of his way to create one. Time enough, he'd reasoned, to reel her in once they were married.

Now they were married, and he was rapidly losing patience.

He hadn't anticipated her degree of social confidence, either. He'd expected her to need help in taking up the role of Lady Hendon. Instead, the mantle had settled easily on her slim shoulders. He now understood why their story of an arranged marriage had been accepted so readily by their neighbors. Kit was the perfect candidate, one who, to all intents and purposes, could be said to have been bred for the position. Her six years in London were the icing on the cake. Aside from anything else, the fact she'd survived those years *virgo intacta* was the ultimate assurance she was not one of those women he mentally stigmatized as the gilded whores of the *ton*.

All in all, there was nothing in her manner or morals he wished to change. It was the distance she seemed intent on preserving between them that he could not abide.

Vignettes of memory, drawn from the hours they'd spent in the cottage, flashed through Jack's mind. With a smothered curse, he stifled them. He took another sip of brandy and watched his wife go down the dance with some local squire. She must know he liked her as she was – would she try to pretend that all the wildness had gone out of her, that by marrying her he'd tamed her?

326

Jack's lips twisted in a slow smile. If she thought that, she was in for a surprise. She might try to play the merely dutiful wife, but her fires ran deep. And he knew how to ignite them. Jack glanced at his watch. It was early, but not too early. And who was to gainsay him?

He raised his head and looked over the crowd to where Elmina sat by the door. She saw his nod and slipped away. Excusing himself to Amy, who was seated beside him in deep conversation with George, Jack rose and stepped from the dais.

Kit laughed at yet another weak joke elliptically alluding to her husband's sexual prowess and expertly turned the conversation into safer channels. There'd been more than one moment that evening when she'd been sorely tempted to let loose the reins of her temper and give her teasing companions the facts. In truth, the facts were far more torrid than anything they imagined.

The music ceased, and she thanked Major Satterthwaite before moving off down the room. Within minutes, she was surrounded by a party of the district's dames, the ladies Gresham, Marchmont, and Dersingham among them. Their talk was serious, revolving about the redecoration of Castle Hendon. Kit listened with half an ear, making the appropriate noises in the right places. She'd perfected the art of polite conversation during her stay in London. It was a prerequisite for retaining one's sanity in the ballrooms of the *ton*. At least the ladies' conversation was not peppered with allusions to the coming night's activities. Every teasing comment simply added to her nervousness, which in turn increased her irritation with her own irrationality.

Why on earth should she feel nervous over what was to come? What could Jack possibly do to her – with her – that he hadn't already done? Images of them, in various positions in the cottage, rose to torment her. Kit smiled and nodded at Lady Dersingham, and wondered whether her fever had truly addled her wits.

Then she saw him approaching through the crowd, stopping to chat here and there as people claimed his attention. But his silver-grey eyes were on her. Her breathing suspended. That familiar sensation of being stalked blossomed in Kit's midriff. No, it wasn't the fever that had addled her brain.

Kit wrenched her eyes from her approaching fate, fixing them on the mild features of Lady Gresham, and desperately tried to think of a reason why it was too early to leave for home. For Castle Hendon.

The instant Jack joined the group, she knew it was hopeless. All the ladies, *grandes dames* every one, positively melted at the first sound of his deep voice. She didn't bother trying evasion. Instead, she raised her chin and nodded polite acquiescence to his suggestion that they leave. "Yes, of course. I'll change my clothes."

With that, she escaped upstairs, not bothering to haul Amy from George's side.

In her bedroom, a surprise awaited her. Instead of the new carriage dress she'd ordered Elmina to lay out, her maid was smoothing the full skirts of a magnificent emerald velvet riding habit.

"Where did that come from?" Kit shut the door and went to the bed.

"Lord Hendon sent it for you, *ma petite*. He said you should wear it. Is it not enchanting?"

Kit examined the severe lines of the habit and could not disagree. Her mind raced, considering the implications. Her initial impulse was to refuse to wear clothes her husband

328

had decreed she should wear. But impulse was tempered by caution. A habit meant horses. Kit slipped the heavy ivory wedding dress from her shoulders and Elmina eased it over her hips. Freed of her petticoats, Kit sat before her dressing table while Elmina pulled the pins from her headdress.

She hadn't discussed how they were to travel to Castle Hendon, leaving Jack to deal with that as his prerogative. She'd imagined they'd go in the barouche. The riding habit said otherwise.

Suddenly enthusiastic, Kit hurried Elmina. A wild ride through the night was just what she needed to dispel her silly trepidation. The knots in her stomach would disappear once they were flying over the fields.

Pirouetting in front of her long mirror, Kit was pleased to approve of her husband's taste. How had he known? A wry smile twisted her lips. Not only had Jack known she'd prefer to ride, he'd known she'd never refuse to wear the habit in such circumstances. As she'd once remarked, when it came to manipulation, he was a master.

When she appeared at the top of the stairs, it seemed that all of Norfolk had gathered in the front hall. Buoyed by the knowledge that she looked her best, Kit beamed upon them all. As she descended the stairs, an avenue opened from their foot, through the throng, to where Jack waited for her by the door. Even from that distance, Kit caught the glint in his eyes as they swept over her, appreciation glowing in their depths. Pride was etched in every line of his face.

She must have responded to the wishes of those lining her route for they seemed happy enough, but Kit was unaware of anything beyond Jack. He held out one hand as she approached and she slipped her fingers into his, dimly aware of the cheers that rose about them. Then Jack's fingers tightened about hers and he drew her out onto the porch.

Some had noticed her dress and started whispering. The whispers turned to exclamations when the crowd, pushing through the door behind them, saw the two horses Matthew held prancing in the moonlight. Delia was a shifting black shadow, highlighted by the white flowers someone had plaited into her mane; beside her, Champion's hide gleamed palely.

Kit turned to Jack.

He lifted one quizzical brow. "Are you game, my lady?"

Kit laughed, her nervousness drowned by excitement. Smiling, Jack led her down the steps and across to the horses. He lifted her to her sidesaddle before swinging up to Champion's broad back.

Only Spencer approached them, all others too wary of the sharp hooves striking sparks from the flinty drive. He came between them, reaching up to squeeze Kit's hand before placing it on her pommel with a valedictory pat. Then he turned to Jack. "Take care of her, m'boy."

Jack smiled. "I will." And that, he thought, as he wheeled Champion, was a vow every bit as binding as the ones he'd given earlier that day.

The horses needed no urging to leave the noisy crowd behind. Well matched for pace, they fell to the task of covering the five miles to Castle Hendon with highbred ease. Jack felt no urge to converse as the miles disappeared beneath the heavy hooves. One glance at Kit's face had told him his bright idea had been a master stroke.

His lips curved. In his present state, being forced to traverse the eight miles of road between Cranmer Hall and Castle Hendon in a closed carriage with Kit, knowing they'd have to appear before the Castle staff immediately upon their arrival, would have been nothing less than torture.

Riding was far safer.

Beside him, Kit gloried in the rush of wind on her face. The regular thud of Delia's hooves steadied her skittering pulse until it beat to the same racing rhythm. There was excitement in the air, and a sense of pleasure shared. She slanted a glance at Jack, then looked ahead, smiling.

They sped through the night, the moon's luminescence spilling softly over them, lighting their way. For Kit, the black mass of Castle Hendon appeared before them too soon, bringing her respite from jangling nerves to an end. Grooms came running. Jack lifted her down before the steps leading up to the huge oak doors of her new horne.

Her feet touched the ground, then she was swung up into Jack's arms.

Kit bit back a squeal and glared at him.

Jack grinned and carried her up the steps and through the open door.

Kit blinked in the glare of lights that greeted them. As Jack set her on her feet, she adjusted her features and smoothly moved into the business of greeting her new staff.

She vaguely remembered Lovis from her single visit as a child. Jack hadn't been at home at the time. Many of the other staff had family at Cranmer, so her progress down the long line was punctuated by explanatory histories. When she reached the end and acknowledged the bob of the sleepy scullery maid, Kit heard Jack's deep voice just behind her.

"Lovis, perhaps you'd show Lady Hendon to her room?"

Lovis bowed deeply. "Very good, m'lord."

Kit hid a nervous grin, realizing there was a tradition to be upheld. Lovis led the way, positively steeped in ceremony. Kit followed him up the wide curving staircase. When she reached the bend, she was relieved to see her husband still at its foot, conversing with one of the male staff – the head groom, as far as she recalled. The thought that he would doubtless give her time to soothe her frazzled nerves before coming to her eased her skittish pulse.

Please, God, let it be slow and steady. Too often, their first encounters resembled a clash of the furies.

The chamber Lovis led her to was enormous. Castle Hendon had grown up about a medieval donjon. Looking about her, Kit surmised her room might well have been part of the donjon's main hall. The walls were of solid stone, papered and painted over, the doors and windows set into their thickness. Extensive reworking had enlarged the windows; Kit felt sure that when she drew the curtains the next morning, the views the Castle was famed for would greet her eyes. Her sleepy, sated eyes.

With a start, Kit fell to examining the furnishings. They were exquisite, every one. She stopped by the four-poster bed. It was huge, covered in pale green satin, the Hendon arms carved in the headboard.

Kit wondered what the pale satin would feel like against her skin.

Abruptly, she remembered she had no clothes with her. In a panic, she flew to the massive mahogany armoire, pulling open doors and drawers. She found a complete wardrobe – dresses, underwear, accessories – all put carefully away, as if she'd always lived here. But none of them were hers. Her luggage was somewhere between Cranmer and Castle Hendon, with Elmina.

Puzzled, she drew forth a fine voile nightdress. Shaking out its folds, she held up the almost transparent garment. That her husband had chosen this wardrobe – for her – was instantly apparent.

Muttering an imprecation against all rakes, Kit bundled the shocking nightgown into a ball and crammed it back in the drawer. Her fingers pulled at the next fold of material. They couldn't all be like that, surely?

"What are you doing?"

Kit jumped and whirled to face her husband. To her surprise, he was not where she expected – at the door from the corridor – but lounged against another door she'd yet to investigate. Presumably, it led to his apartments. Kit swallowed nervously. The smile on Jack's face sent the butterflies that had taken up residence in her stomach into a frenzy.

"Er . . ." *Think, dimwit!* "I was looking for a nightdress."

As she watched Jack's smile widen, Kit could have bitten her tongue.

"You won't need one." Jack pushed away from the door and started toward her, his smile growing more devilish with every stride. "I'll keep you warm."

"Er . . . yes. Jack, stop!" Kit held up her hand in panic. "Shouldn't you send for a maid?"

The witless question had the desired effect. It pulled him up short. It also brought a frown to his face and darkened his eyes.

Jack stopped in the middle of his wife's bedroom and placed his hands on his hips, the better to intimidate her into dropping her silly pose. He'd had enough. "What the devil's the matter with you, woman? In case you've forgotten, I'm perfectly qualified to undress you. I hardly need a maid to show me how." With that statement of intent, he stepped purposefully forward but stopped when he saw sheer alarm flare in Kit's eyes.

What was the matter with her? Kit wished she knew. If he'd come to her as Captain Jack, she'd have been in his arms in a trice. Making love to Captain Jack had been easy. With Captain Jack there hadn't been a tomorrow.

But there was no way she could possibly confuse the man

standing in the middle of her bedroom with Captain Jack. The physical manifestations were the same, but there the similarity ended. This was Lord Hendon, her husband. The superb cut of his coat, the fine linen of his shirt, the gleaming hair neatly confined, and especially the sapphire signet ring glinting on his right hand, all underlined the essential difference. This was the man she'd married, vowed to honor and obey. This was the man who as of this evening was all things to her. The man who now had legal rights over her far beyond those any other had ever had. Her mind was not capable of equating making love to this man with making love to Captain Jack.

It simply wasn't the same. *He* wasn't the same. Kit drew a shuddering breath. No matter what he thought, she'd never made love to him before.

Jack watched the expressions flit across her pale face and his confusion grew. She couldn't possibly be nervous, but he hadn't previously thought her such an accomplished actress. Her eyes were enormous pools of fright, skittering and restless. Her fingers were clenched so tightly on the door of the wardrobe her knuckles showed white. When a shiver of apprehension flickered over her skin, he gave up the fight against incredulity.

She *was* nervous.

"Hell!" Jack turned toward the bed, running one hand through his hair, disarranging it. Absentmindedly, he tugged at the black riband and freed the long locks, dropping the riband on the floor. He shot a glance at Kit, all but petrified by the wardrobe. If she was nervous, he hoped she'd keep her gaze level, and not let it drop to the bulge he was well aware was distorting the perfect cut of his inexpressibles. Hell and the devil! This looked set to be a long-drawn act, and he wasn't at all sure he was up to it.

"Come here." He struggled to soften the raw desire in his growl and only partly succeeded.

Kit's alarm flared again, but when he held out his hand, imperiously beckoning her forward, she hesitated, then came to his side, slipping a trembling hand into his. Smoothly, Jack drew her into his arms, turning to clasp her fully to him.

"Relax." He breathed the command into the soft curls by her ear. Now that he had his hands on her, he didn't need any further confirmation of her state. She was wound tight, quivering with tension. He wasn't fool enough to ask for explanations. Instead, his lips found the pulse point beneath her ear.

Kit shivered and wondered how she was to obey that order. His lips traveled her jaw, placing gentle kisses along the curve. Reassured she was not about to be devoured, she leaned into the warmth of his embrace, yielding her mouth to his expert attentions.

When her lips parted automatically to receive him, Jack clamped an iron hold on his reactions. What sort of hell on earth had he landed himself in this time? Not only did she need to be wooed gently, but her responses were ingrained, a natural part of her that he'd taken care, in their earlier engagements, to encourage. Now they looked set to drive him to the brink of madness. Every time he thought he had their relationship pegged, she invented a new twist to torment him. Mentally gritting his teeth, Jack set about the task of seducing his wife.

Unaware of the trouble she was causing, Kit felt the knots in her stomach ease as Jack's hands commenced a leisurely exploration of her fully clothed form, his tongue probing the soft contours of her mouth unhurriedly, as if he was willing to spend all night in such intoxicating play. She knew he wouldn't, but it was a comforting sensation. The kiss deepened by almost imperceptible degrees, his caresses becoming increasingly intimate until she was warmed through. She was glad to slip her arms free of her jacket. Snuggling closer, she pressed her tingling breasts to his chest. His hands roamed her back, molding her to him until her thighs were wedged firmly against his. The evidence of his desire pressed strongly against her stomach. Kit felt a familiar ache grow inside.

What followed was a carefully orchestrated journey into delight. Throughout, Jack held tight to the reins of his desire, not relinquishing his grip even when Kit lay naked beneath him, gasping with desire, her thighs spread, her hips tilting in unmistakable invitation. He sank into her welcoming heat, his jaw clenched with the effort to remain in control, determined that, whatever the cost, she'd have a night of loving she'd never forget.

He filled her and Kit sighed deeply. She closed her eyes, savoring the sensation of being so thoroughly possessed. Her skin was alive, her swollen breasts ached, her body yearned for completion. When Jack moved within her, she bit her lip and held still, sensing his strength, his hardness, his unrelenting need. Then she moved with him, letting her own need flower, feeding and assuaging his. She wrapped her arms about him, wound her legs about his hips, and let the dance consume them. Their bodies strove, intimately locked, heated and slick. As the glory drew nearer, Kit gasped and surrendered – to passion's flames, to mind-numbing delight, to incandescent sensation.

When, at last, they lay spent in each other's arms, and Jack felt the last of Kit's sweet spasms fade as her breathing slowed into blissfully sated slumber, triumphant possessiveness streaked through him.

She was his. He'd recaptured his wild woman. He'd never let go of her again.

With a sigh of contentment, deepened by the glow of achievement, of satisfaction in a job well-done, Jack turned on his side, taking Kit with him, carefully resettling her against him.

Halfway back from paradise, Kit felt his weight shift but was too deeply sated to protest. She'd forgotten what it was like – to lose her wits, to surrender her senses to the conflagration of their desire. Slow and steady she'd wanted; slow and steady she'd got. Jack's loving was a potent brew; she was addicted beyond recall. There was no hope of denying it, so she might as well accept it as her lot.

Who knew what lay in store – for her, for him? After tonight, whatever happened, she'd have to face it acknowledging that, for her, only one man held the power to open the doors of paradise.

Her husband. Jack – Lord Hendon.

Chapter 25

The next morning, Kit entered the breakfast parlor already flustered by the lateness of the hour. It was not her habit to keep servants waiting on her but she'd slept in, drained by Jack's method of waking her.

Instantly meeting her husband's all-too-knowing gaze, and his slow smile, did nothing for her composure. Drawing dignity about her as best she could, she busied herself at the sideboard, praying the blush she could feel warming her cheeks wasn't visible to the reprobate at the end of the table.

She'd thought he'd have left the house by now – doing whatever it was that gentlemen did – but she'd donned a new morning gown just in case. The delicate primrose shade was a favorite – she hoped he appreciated it. He was looking as hideously handsome as ever, lounging in his chair, long fingers crooked about the handle of a cup, yesterday's paper spread before him.

Her plate in her hands, Kit turned. The question of where to sit was answered by Lovis, who held the chair at the other end of the table. Ignoring her husband, Kit sat and picked up her fork. From the corner of her eye, she saw Lovis dismissed by a languid gesture.

Jack waited until the door closed behind his butler to remark: "I'm glad to see your appetite's returned."

Kit glanced down at her plate, seeing for the first time the mound of rice pie she'd piled on it, two kippers nestling on one side with a serving of kidney and bacon on the other. A slice of ham was laid atop, a dob of pickle in the middle. Head on one side, she considered the sight before replying: "Well, I'm hungry." It was his fault she was. How dare he tease her about it?

"Quite so."

Kit glanced up in time to catch his proprietary gloat before Jack substituted a more innocent expression. Her eyes narrowed. She wished she could say something, do something, to wash the smug glint from his eyes.

When she continued to stare, Jack's brows rose in deceptive candor. "You'll need to keep up your strength," he offered. "I suspect you'll find the role of Lady Hendon unexpectedly tiring."

Warning flames flickered at the back of Kit's glare. Jack laughed and, setting down his cup, rose, coming around the table to stand by her side. "I hadn't intended to leave you so soon, but I'm afraid I have to hie off to inspect some fields. I'll be back by midday."

Kit remembered her morning engagement and bit back her request to go with him. She looked up at him, her expression blank. "Mrs. Miles is to show me over the house this morning. No doubt I'll be so entralled I won't even notice your absence."

Jack tried to keep his lips straight and failed woefully. A rumbling chuckle escaped him. He put out one finger and wound it in the curls by Kit's ear. Then he bent his head and whispered: "Never mind. Why not use the time to consider the more interesting aspects of Lady Hendon's duties? Perhaps, when I get back, we could discuss those?"

Kit stiffened. He couldn't mean . . .?

Jack's fingers drifted down the sensitive skin beneath her ear. His lips followed, leaving a tickling trail of nibbling kisses. Before she could gather her wits, he tipped her chin up, kissed her full on the lips, and was gone.

Stifling a most unladylike curse, Kit wriggled her shoulders to dispel the delicious shiver he'd sent rippling down her spine, drew a deep breath, and applied herself to her breakfast.

Her morning went in the inescapable task of being ceremonially inducted into the workings of Castle Hendon. The staff was pleasant, clearly pleased to find a local filling Lady Hendon's shoes. The business of running a household was second nature to Kit – a legacy from her grandmother. She dealt with the staff with an innate confidence that had the inevitable result. By midday, the domestic reins were firmly in her hands.

Jack was not at the luncheon table; Lovis confirmed he'd not yet returned. Used to solitude, Kit walked the extensive gardens, then, tiring of such tame exercise, went upstairs to change into her new riding habit. The day was fine, the breeze beckoned – what better way to spend an afternoon than riding her husband's lands?

The stables were large, set around two interconnecting yards. Kit wandered along the rows of stalls, searching for Delia's black hide. The head groom came out of the second courtyard. Catching sight of her, he hurried over, doffing his cap as he came.

"Good afternoon, ma'am."

Kit waited for him to ask if he could help her. When he

simply stood, plainly nervous, twisting his hat in his hands, she took pity on him. "I'd like my horse, please. The black mare."

To her surprise, the man subjected his hat to a further twist and looked even more uncomfortable. Kit frowned, a nasty suspicion displacing her good humor. "Where is Delia?"

"The master said to put her in the back paddock, my lady."

Kit put her hands on her hips. "Where is this back paddock?"

The groom waved in a southerly direction. "Over the hills a-way."

Too far to walk. Before Kit could ask her next question, the groom added: "The master said she was only to be brought up at his orders, ma'am."

Inwardly, Kit seethed. There was no point haranguing the groom; he was only obeying orders. The person she wanted to harangue, *needed* to harangue, was the giver of those orders. Abruptly, she turned on her heel. "Send word to me the moment Lord Hendon returns."

"Begging your pardon, ma'am but he came in not ten minutes ago."

Kit's eyes glittered. "Thank you – Martins, isn't it?"

The groom bowed.

Kit rewarded him with a stiff smile and marched back to the house.

She found Jack in the library. She sailed into the room and waited until she heard Lovis shut the door before advancing on her husband. He was standing behind his desk, a sheet of paper in his hand. Noting the arrested look in his eyes, she realized any attempt to hide her anger would be wasted. She drew breath, only to have him seize the initiative.

"I'm sorry I wasn't back for lunch. How did your tour with Mrs. Miles go?" Jack dropped his list on the blotter and came around the desk.

Thrown by the mild question, Kit blinked, then realized Jack was advancing on her. He was going to kiss her. Nimble-footed, she stepped around a chair. "Er . . . fine. What have you done with my horse?"

His flanking attack defeated, Jack halted and faced her guns. He contemplated her belligerent stance, muted in effect by her retreat behind the chair. "I've had her put in a paddock large enough for her to stretch her legs."

"She stretches her legs often enough. I ride her every day."

"Past tense."

Kit frowned. "I beg your pardon?"

"You *rode* her every day."

When no further explanation was forthcoming, Kit gritted her teeth and asked: "Just what are you trying to say?"

"As of now, you ride Delia only when I ride with you. Other than Champion, there's no beast in Norfolk that can keep up with that black streak you call a horse. I won't saddle my grooms with the responsibility of trying to keep you in sight. Hence, you ride with me, or accept a meeker mount and take a groom with you."

Kit had never known exactly what *flabbergasted* felt like. Now, she knew. She was so angry, she couldn't even decide which point to attack first.

The obvious riposte – that Delia was her horse – had an equally obvious answer. As his wife, all her property was his. But his dictates were outrageous. Kit's eyes glittered dangerously. "Jonathon," she said, using his given name for the first time since their wedding vows, "I've been riding since I could walk. In the country, I've ridden alone all my life. I will not –"

342

"Be continuing in such unacceptable style."

Kit bit her tongue to keep from screaming. The unemotional statement sounded far more ominous than Spencer's ranting ever had. She drew a deep breath and forced her tone to a reasonable pitch. "Everyone around about knows I ride alone. They think nothing of it. On Delia, I'm perfectly safe. As you've just pointed out, no one can catch me. None of our neighbors would feel the least bit scandalized to see me riding alone."

"None of our neighbors would imagine I'd allow you to do so."

It was an effort, but Kit swallowed the curse that rose to her lips. Her husband's calm gaze hadn't wavered. He was watching her, politely attentive but with the cool certainty that he'd be the victor in this little contretemps stamped all over his arrogant face. This was the side of Jack she didn't know but had surmised must exist; this was Jonathon.

Kit tried a different tack. "Why?"

Explaining was not his style, but in this case, Jack knew the ground to be firm beneath his feet. She was new to his bridle; it wouldn't hurt to give his reasons. "Firstly, as Lady Hendon, your behavior will be taken as a standard for others to follow, a status not accorded Miss Kathryn Cranmer but a point I'm sure Lady Marchmont and company would quickly make clear to you if I did not." He paused to let the implication of that sink in. Strolling toward the chair behind which Kit had taken refuge, he continued: "There's also the fact that your safety is of prime concern to me." Another pause enabled him to trap her gaze in his. "And I don't consider riding the countryside alone a suitably safe pastime for my wife."

Was he really just concerned for her welfare? Kit opened her mouth, but Jack held up a hand to stop her.

"Spare me your arguments, Kit. I won't change my mind. Spencer let you ride alone for far longer than was acceptable. He'd be the first to admit it." Kit stiffened as Jack's gaze slowly traveled the length of her slim frame. A subtle smile twisted his lips. "You're not a child anymore, my dear. You are, in fact, a most delectable plum. One I've no intention of letting any other man taste."

One arrogant brow lifted, inviting her comment. Kit bit her lip, then blurted out: "If I were in breeches, no man would look twice at me."

She shifted uneasily as she watched Jack's smile grow. It wasn't entirely encouraging, for it didn't reach his eyes.

"If I ever come upon Lady Hendon in breeches, do you know what I'll do?"

The soft, velvety tones transfixed Kit. She felt her eyes grow round, trapped in her husband's gaze. Little flames flickered deep. Slowly, all but mesmerized, Kit shook her head.

"Wherever we are, indoors or out, I'll take great delight in removing said breeches from her."

Kit swallowed.

"And then –"

"Jack!" Kit scowled. "Stop it! You're just trying to scare me."

Jack's brows flew. He reached out and, to Kit's surprise, pushed the chair from between them. She hadn't realized he was so close. Before she could react, he caught her elbows and pulled her to him. Trapped within the circle of his arms, Kit looked into his face, her pulse accelerating. A peculiarly devilish look had settled over his features. "Am I?"

For the life of her, Kit couldn't decide if he or not.

"Try me, by all means, if you doubt it."

The invitation was accompanied by a look which made

Kit vow not to call his bluff. She became engrossed in smoothing his lapel. "But I need the exercise."

Even as the plaintive words escaped her lips, Kit realized her error. Her eyes flew wide; there was no way she would risk looking up.

A nerve-stretching pause ensued. "Really?" came the mild reply.

Kit wasn't about to answer.

"I'll bear that in mind, my dear. I'm sure I can devise any number of novel ways to exercise you."

Kit didn't doubt it. The tremor in the deep voice suggested he didn't either. A maxim of Lady Gresham's recurred in her mind. *When all else fails, try cajoling.* She looked up. "Jack —"

But he shook his head. "Give over, Kit. I won't change my mind."

Kit stared into his perfectly serious eyes and knew it was beyond her powers to sway him. With a sigh of exasperation, of deep frustration, she grimaced at him.

He kissed her pouting lips. And kept kissing them until she yielded. Feeling her wits slip their moorings, Kit summoned enough will for one mental curse against masterful men, before settling down to enjoy one.

For the rest of that day, she maintained an attitude that was the very essence of wifely complaisance. Her halo positively glowed. Her husband had insisted — she'd desisted. If she couldn't win the bout, she was detemined to make the most of her defeat. Unfortunately, Jack showed every sign of being overly understanding. When he used her new-found meekness to trap her into agreeing to retire early, Kit rapidly reverted to her usual argumentative self. Only by then it was too late.

She had her revenge two days later, when the question of

her visiting the shops in Lynn arose. It quickly became clear that Jack was not enamored of the idea of her being simultaneously out of his sight and off Hendon lands. She simply shrugged. "If you want to come with me, I've no objection." She kept her eyes, wide and innocent, on the gloves she was buttoning up. "But I hadn't imagined you sitting in on all the visits I'll have to pay in a few weeks. Not but what the ladies would be only too pleased to see you."

She won her carriage by default. But when she descended the front steps on her husband's arm, it was to see, not one, but two footmen waiting in attendance. She hesitated only a moment, taken aback by the sight but, by now, too wise not to accept the better part of victory with good grace. The footmen dogged her steps throughout her expedition.

Despite such adjustments, the end of their first week of married life arrived without major drama. Settled in an armchair before the fire in the library, Kit yawned and gave in to one of her favorite fascinations, studying the way her husband's brown hair glinted gold in lamplight. He was seated at the huge desk placed across one corner of the room, going through a ledger. Their interactions had fallen into a routine, a fact for which she was grateful. After so many years essentially alone, she found it reassuring to know when Jack would be with her and when her mind would be free to deal with the more mundane of Lady Hendon's duties. To her surprise, she was fast coming to the conclusion that married life would suit her after all.

Her days tended to start at dawn, although she'd not yet managed to leave her bed before nine. Her previous habit of riding before breakfast had died a death, thanks to Jack's amorous inclinations. He still rode early, though how he managed it was beyond her. After the shortest of recuperative naps, he'd be up and about while she lay sprawled under her green satin coverlet, her limbs weighted with delicious languor, utterly incapable of moving, let alone thinking. After bathing, dressing, and breakfasting, usually alone, she would check with Mrs. Miles and issue her orders for the day. The time before luncheon was easily filled with trips to the stillroom, the laundry, the kitchen or the gardens. Jack usually joined her for luncheon, after which, on all but one day, he made himself available to escort her on a ride. She'd accepted his offers with alacrity, thankful not to have to forgo her daily round with Delia.

On the afternoon he'd been detained at Hunstanton, she'd swallowed her pride and asked for the mare he'd chosen as Delia's substitute to be saddled. Escorted by a senior groom, she'd set out for Gresham Manor.

As newlyweds, their first weeks would be theirs, to settle into married life without distraction. But after that, the bride visits would start. And the dinners. Kit knew what to expect; the prospect held no terrors for her, but she did wonder how her socially ept but reluctant husband would cope.

Her visit with Amy had been relaxing but had highlighted the truth of Jack's warning that her status as Lady Hendon was a far cry from the importance of one Miss Cranmer. The idea of taking precedence over Lady Gresham required some adjustment. Her ladyship commented favorably on the correctness of her escort. Kit bit her tongue. Amy was dying to hear her private news, but Lady Gresham, also curious, did not leave them alone. Kit departed the Manor with the definite impression that she'd disappointed her friends by remaining essentially herself, rather than being visibly transformed in some miraculous way by her husband's legendary skills.

She'd ridden back to Castle Hendon chuckling all the way, much to the confusion of her groom.

The fire crackled and hissed as a drop of rain found its way down the chimney. Kit stifled another yawn. Of all the times in their day, the evenings were the most peaceful. Until they went upstairs to her bedroom. But even there, the atmosphere had calmed. The tenor of their lovemaking had changed; knowing there was nothing to keep them from spending however many hours they wished on the road to paradise, Jack seemed content to keep progress as slow as she wished, spinning out their time in that bliss-filled world. His touch was exquisite, his timing faultless. Each night there were new doors to open, new avenues to explore. Each led to the same peak, beyond which lay a selfless void of indescribable sensation. Her delight in learning the pathways of pleasure was unfeigned; he was a patient teacher.

Kit sighed and smiled at his bent head.

She was eagerly awaiting her next lesson.

A boom of thunder shook Kit awake. She curled tight and clutched the covers over her ears, but still the reverberations echoed through her bones. Then she remembered she was a married woman and reached for her husband. Her groping hand met empty air. There was nobody in the bed beside her.

Kit sat up and stared, first at the rumpled sheets, then about the empty room. Lightning lit the chamber, a bright beam shafting through a chink in the curtains. Kit flinched. Where was Jack when she needed him?

The following thunderclap propelled her to her feet. She snatched up the scandalous silk negligee Jack had insisted she wear so he could enjoy divesting her of it, and wrapped its gossamer folds about her, cinching the tie tight. With a determined frown, Kit made for a door beyond which she'd yet to explore – the one that led to Jack's rooms. Whatever his reasons for going to his own bed on this of all nights, she intended making it perfectly plain that during thunderstorms, his place was by her side.

As she'd suspected, the door led to the master bedroom. If her room was large, Jack's was enormous. And equally empty. Kit stared into the shadowy corners, then sank onto the bed as realization struck.

Lord Hendon is Captain Jack.

In the upheavals of the past weeks, she'd completely forgotten that fact. After recovering from her wound, she'd tacitly accepted that becoming Lady Hendon meant no more smuggling. She was convinced Lord Hendon would see it that way. She'd put all thought of the Hunstanton Gang from her. But, apparently, Captain Jack intended to go his own road, regardless.

Oblivious of the storm raging outside, Kit sat on Jack's bed and struggled to make sense of the facts in her hands. It was no use – they simply did not form a coherent whole. When the cold penetrated her thin gown, she crawled to the pillows and drew the coverlet about her. Lord Hendon had been appointed as High Commissioner specifically to stop the smuggling of spies. The same Lord Hendon, in his guise as Captain Jack, was actively engaged in smuggling spies. Despite his total disinterest in the subject, she'd gleaned sufficient snippets to confirm her vague notion that the same Lord Hendon had a war record – an exemplary war record. In fact, according to Matthew, he was a damned hero. So what the hell was he doing smuggling spies?

With a frustrated growl, Kit thumped the pillow and laid her head down. She was missing bits of this jigsaw. Jack, damn his hide, was playing some deep game.

Sleep tugged at her lids and she yawned. She could understand why he hadn't told her before. But she wasn't a smuggler anymore – she was his wife. Why shouldn't he tell her now? With a little nod, Kit settled her chin deeper into the pillow and closed her eyes. She'd stay here until he did.

The bed curtains stirred in the current of air as the door opened and shut. Kit came awake with a start. Her eyes adjusted to the dark, she instantly espied her husband's large form as he crossed the room to the washstand.

He hadn't seen her in the shadows of the bed.

Kit watched as he stripped off his shirt, then grabbed a towel and dried his hair. She tuned her senses to the night sounds; the storm had eased; it was raining. As Jack passed the towel over his shoulders and chest, Kit realized he must be soaked. He sat on a chair and, with an effort, pulled off his boots. When he stood, bending to place the boots aside she asked: "What was the cargo tonight? Brandy or lace?"

She saw every muscle in his large frame tense, then relax. Slowly, Jack straightened and looked directly at her. Kit held her breath. The silence was so deep she could hear the rain spattering the window panes.

"Brandy."

Kit hugged her knees. "Nothing else?" she inquired innocently.

Jack didn't answer. Her presence in his room at this particular moment had not been part of his plan. Just as it formed no part of his plan to satisfy her curiosity about Captain Jack's nocturnal adventures. From Spencer, he had learned about her cousin Julian; he now understood her interest in stopping the spies. A praiseworthy ideal for the High Commissioner's lady. But telling her anything at all was out of the question.

This was the woman who'd blithely accepted a position as leader of a smuggling gang, the same woman who on more than one occasion had disobeyed his explicit orders. Even hinting at the truth was too dangerous.

Intent on getting warm as quickly as possible, Jack peeled off his sodden breeches, leaving them in a heap on the floor. He toweled his legs and cast a considering glance at the bed. Now she was here . . .

Kit tried to ignore the tingle of anticipation that flickered along her nerves. "Jack, what's – *Oh!*"

She bit back a squeal as Jack landed on the bed beside her. He wrestled the covers away from her. The thin film of her negligee was summarily dispensed with before he rolled her beneath him. His lips found hers as her hands, and the rest of her, made contact with his naked body. After a blood-stirring duel of tongues, Kit drew back to gasp: "You dolt! You're freezing! You'll catch your death of cold." His skin was iced, all except one part of him, which was already basking in the heat at the juncture of her thighs.

"Not if you warm me up."

Kit gasped as she felt one large hand slip beneath her bottom, tilting her hips, opening her to his invasion. She felt his spine slowly flex. Hard as steel, smooth as silk, he entered her. Kit gasped again, her body arching in instinctive welcome.

His lips sought hers. They moved together, Kit following his lead, rising to his thrusts, stoking the flames higher until they broke in a molten wave, sending heated pleasure coursing through them.

Later, he moved off her, drawing her about so she lay curled with her back to him. He settled his larger body around hers and immediately fell deeply asleep.

Snuggled beneath a heavy arm and halfway to sleep herself, Kit grimaced. Marriage to Lord Hendon had changed nothing. When it came to smuggling, he was Captain Jack. And Captain Jack kept his own counsel.

Chapter 26

Why wouldn't he tell her? Kit cantered up the Gresham's drive with that refrain ringing in her ears. She'd not seen her aggravating husband since dawn when, after exhausting her thoroughly, he'd carried her back to her bed. She vaguely recalled him saying something about inspecting his coverts. She wasn't deceived. He'd purposely found some activity to keep him out all day so she couldn't pursue her questions. Doubtless, he thought time would blunt her curiosity.

With a snort, Kit slid from the saddle without waiting for the assistance of her groom. "Is the family in, Jeffries?"

"Lord Gresham's off to Lynn, miss – I mean, your ladyship." Jeffries smiled as he took her bridle. "Lady Gresham took the carriage out an hour ago. But Miss Amy's inside."

"Good!" Kit stalked to the house and entered by the morning room windows.

Amy was there, idly plying her needle. She jumped up as soon as she saw Kit. "Oh, good. Mama's gone to Lady Dersingham's. Now we can talk." Then Amy noticed Kit's high color and the brisk way she stripped off her gloves. Her eyes widened. "What's the matter?"

"That damned husband of mine's as close as an oyster!" Kit flung her gloves onto a table and fell to pacing the room, her long swinging strides more suited to Young Kit than Lady Hendon.

"What do you mean?" Frowning, Amy sank back onto the *chaise*.

Kit glanced her way. Amy knew nothing of her husband's alias but the need to unburden herself was strong. "What do you think of a gentleman who refuses to tell his wife," Kit paused, searching for words, "the details of a transaction he's involved in, when he knows she's interested and it would not be a . . . a breach of confidence or any such thing?"

Amy blinked. "Why do you want to know about Jonathon's business?"

The simple question sent Kit's temper into orbit. With a frustrated growl, she went about the room again, struggling for calm. Why did she want to know what Jack was up to? Because she did. While she'd been Young Kit and he Captain Jack, she'd felt a part of his adventures. She couldn't – wouldn't – accept that being his wife meant she had to remain distanced from what affected him most nearly. Besides which, if she knew what he was up to, she was sure she could help.

She stopped in front of Amy. "Let's just say that not knowing is driving me crazy. Besides which," she added, kicking her skirts out of the way to pace again, "there are reasons of . . . of honor which say he should tell me. If he had *any* gentlemanly instincts, he would."

Amy looked stunned – and thoroughly confused. "Do you mean that Jonathon's not truly the gentleman?"

It was Kit's turn to blink. "Of course not!" She frowned at Amy. "That wasn't what I meant."

Amy eyed Kit with affectionate understanding and patted the *chaise*. "Do sit down, Kit – you're making me dizzy. Now tell me – is it really as exciting as they say?"

The point of the question missed Kit entirely. She dropped into a chair opposite Amy and frowned. "Is what so exciting?"

"You know." Amy's slight blush jolted Kit's mind into the right rut.

"Oh, that." Kit waved dismissively, then abruptly changed her mind. She wagged a knowledgeable finger at Amy. "You know, you didn't have the half of it when you told me all that stuff about getting hot and wet."

"Oh?" Amy sat straighter.

"No," Kit affirmed. "It's much worse than that."

When Kit fell into a reverie and said nothing further, Amy glared. "Kit! You can't just stop there. I told you all I know – now it's your turn. I'm marrying George next month. It's your duty to tell me so I'll know what to expect."

Kit considered; she decided her vocabulary wasn't up to it. "Do you mean to tell me your George hasn't gone beyond a kiss and a fondle?"

"Of course not." Amy's expression held more disgruntled disgust than shock. "Jonathon didn't go any farther with you before your marriage, did he?"

Kit's eyes glazed. "Our relationship didn't develop along quite the same lines as yours and George's." Her voice sounded strangled. Memories of how far Jack had gone threatened to overcome her. Even if she gave Amy an edited version, it would shock her to the core. "I'm sorry, Amy, but I can't explain. Why don't you press George for further details? Here he comes now."

Through the morning room windows she could see George striding up from the stables. He reached the windows

355

and checked at the sight of her. Then, smoothly, he entered and greeted Amy, bowing over her hand before raising it to his lips.

Watching closely, Kit noted the glow that infused Amy's face and the brightness in her eyes. When his eyes met Amy's, George's face softened; as his lips brushed Amy's fingers, his eyes remained on hers. The warm affection in his gaze was fully returned by Amy. Kit felt uncomfortably *de trop.*

Releasing Amy with understated reluctance, George turned to Kit and took her hand in greeting. "Kit."

She returned his nod graciously. They'd met only twice since she'd dropped the guise of Young Kit – once at the wedding, once at their belated betrothal dinner. She'd always had the distinct impression that George disapproved of her wild ways far more strongly than Jack did. "Amy and I were discussing the merits of a husband being open with his wife." Kit kept her gaze innocent and unthreatening. "Perhaps, in the interests of a well-rounded argument, you could give us your views on the matter."

George raised his brows, his expression growing wary. "I suspect it depends very much on the nature of the relationship, don't you think?" With a smile for Amy, George sat on the *chaise* beside her.

"True," Kit acknowledged. "But given the relationship was right, the husband's willingness to confide is the next hurdle, don't you think? What reasons could a man have for keeping secrets from his wife?"

Their next half hour was spent in a peculiar three-way conversation. George and Kit traded oblique references to Jack's reticence, none of which Amy understood. Amy, for her part, urged Kit to unburden herself and explain her problem more fully – an undertaking George endeavored to discourage. In between, all three traded local gossip, and George managed to discuss the details of their wedding, which he'd come to the Manor to clarify.

Sensing the currents between Amy and George, suppressed in her presence, Kit rose and picked up her gloves. "I must be going. I feel sure my husband won't approve of my being out after dark."

With that acerbic comment, she embraced Amy fondly, nodded to George, and sailed from the room.

Amy watched her go, sighed – then went straight into George's arms. They closed about her; she and George exchanged a warm and unrestrained kiss. Then Amy pulled back with a sigh. "I'm worried about Kit. She's troubled by something – something serious." She met George's gaze. "I don't like to think of her riding alone in such a mood."

George grimaced. "Kit's a big girl."

Amy pressed closer. "Yes, but . . ." The eyes that met George's twinkled. "And Mama will be home any minute."

George sighed. "Very well." He kissed Amy again, then set her from him. "But I'll expect a reward next time I call."

"You may claim it with my blessing," Amy declared. "Just as long as Mama is out."

George grinned, more than a touch wickedly. "I'll be back." With a wave, he headed for the stables.

He caught up with Kit as she left the stables, mounted on a chestnut mare. George stared. "Where's Delia?"

For one fractured moment, Kit thought she'd erupt in flames. Her glance seared George. "Don't ask!" She swung the chestnut toward the drive.

"Wait!" George called. "I'll ride part of the way with you."

When he rode out a minute later, Kit was schooling the mare in prancing circles, her groom watching from a

357

distance. She fell in beside George; together they headed north and west.

George glanced at Kit. "I take it Jack hasn't explained about the smuggling?"

Kit narrowed her eyes. "Explanations do not seem to be his strong point."

George chuckled. When Kit glared, he explained: "You don't know how true that is. Neither explanations nor excuses are part of Jack's makeup. They weren't characteristics of his father's either."

Kit frowned. "Someone once said he was 'Hendonish.' Is that what that means?"

George grinned. "If it was a woman who said it, not entirely, but it's not unrelated to what I'm trying to say. Jack's a born leader – all Hendons have been for generations. He's used to being the one who makes the decisions. He knows what he wants, what needs to be done, and he gives orders to make it happen. He doesn't expect to have to explain his actions and doesn't relish being asked to do so."

"That much, I'd gathered."

George glanced at Kit's disgruntled expression. "If it's any consolation, despite the fact Matthew and I have known him for most of his life, and shared most of it, too, we received not the smallest word of explanation for your inclusion in the Gang. He didn't even tell us you were a woman."

They rode on in silence, Kit considering George's words. His confidence did, in fact, ease some of the frustration dragging at her heart. Clearly, her husband was an autocrat of long standing; if George was right, a hereditary one. Equally clearly, none of those close to him had made the slightest push to influence his high-handed ways. The determination to make him change his attitude, at least with respect to her, grew with every short stride her meek chestnut took.

The fork that led to Smeaton Hall appeared ahead. Kit drew rein. "You know the truth about the smuggling, don't you?"

Pulling up beside her, George sighed. "Yes, but I can't tell you. Jack's my superior in this. I can't speak without his approval."

Kit nodded and held out her hand. "Thank you."

George met her eyes, then squeezed her fingers encouragingly. "He'll tell you in the end."

Kit nodded. "I know. When it's over."

George could only grin. He bowed and they parted, understanding each other rather better than before.

Kit stared at the packages on the carriage seat opposite. Had she bought enough? She'd come to Lynn to get some cambric. After last night, she'd decided that cambric shirts would be much more sensible for Jack to wear around the estate. He'd spent all yesterday helping thin coppices. She hadn't known but should have guessed he'd be the sort of landowner who got off his horse, took off his coat, rolled up his sleeves, and helped his men. She'd come upon him entirely unintentionally, when, just before changing for dinner, she'd gone into his room in search of the sash that went with her silk negligee. It had been missing ever since the storm, three nights before. A groan emanating from the room beyond had drawn her to the open door.

The room had been fitted out as a bathing chamber, with a huge copper tub in the center. Jack had just sunk into the steaming water. He was facing away from her and as he bent forward to rest his head on his knees, she saw his back. It was covered with scratches.

"What on earth have you been doing?"

359

She'd strode forward, entirely forgetting her sash, oblivious of Matthew standing to one side.

Water had hit the floor as Jack swiveled, then he'd grimaced and leaned back in the tub, settling his head on the raised edge. "Falling through brambles." A wave of his hand had sent Matthew from the room, a fact of which she should have taken more notice.

She'd stood by the tub, hands on hips, and examined all of her husband that she could see. Jack opened his eyes and squinted up at her through the steam. "You'll be pleased to know it's only my back."

At his grin, she'd humphed. "Lean forward and let me see."

She'd had to nag but in the end, he'd let her examine his wounds. Some of the scratches were deep and had bled, but none qualified as serious.

"Seeing you're here, you may as well minister to my injuries." He'd held out the sponge.

She'd pulled a face and taken the bait.

She should, of course, have guessed which track his mind had taken. But it hadn't occurred to her that the tub was big enough for them both. And she'd certainly never imagined it was possible to perform the contortions they had within its slippery confines.

Yet another novel experience her husband had introduced her to.

Kit shook aside the distracting memory. She counted the ells of material again and wished she'd brought Elmina. Still, Lynn wasn't so far that she couldn't come again if they needed more. Kit turned to the window, to call to Josh the coachman that they could leave, when her gaze alighted on a natty trilby, entirely out of place in provincial Lynn.

360

Intrigued, she drew closer to the glass to view the body beneath the hat. "Good Lord!" Kit stared, seeing a ghost.

It was Belville – Lord George Belville.

Kit blinked, then stared again. The four years since he'd been a suitor for her hand had not treated him kindly. He still possessed a large, strong-boned frame, but his face was more fleshy and his girth had increased dramatically. His skin bore the pasty complexion of one who spent too much time in the gaming room. Features Kit remembered as finely chiseled had been coarsened by drink and general decadence, until he was but a bloated caricature of the man she'd nearly agreed to wed.

A cold shiver touched Kit's nape and spread over her shoulders. Keeping within the shadows of the carriage, she watched as her erstwhile suitor strolled across the square to the King's Arms, Lynn's most comfortable inn. Belville was addicted to town pursuits. What was he doing here?

At the door of the inn, Belville paused. He glanced about, studying all those his pale gaze could find. Then, slowly, he entered the inn and shut the door behind him.

Frowning, Kit sank back against the squabs. Then, shifting to the other side of the carriage, she called to Josh to take her home. For some reason, she was sure she didn't want Belville to see her. He represented part of her history that was no longer relevant; she didn't intend to let him cloud her present happiness.

As the carriage rumbled out onto the open road, Kit's frown deepened. Belville was nothing but a government official – he couldn't harm her. So why did she feel so threatened?

Kit was already in bed when Jack entered her room that night.

He paused in the doorway, studying her pensive face.

What was she planning now? His gaze dwelled on the halo of curls, on the full lips and delicate features, before sweeping over the alluring figure outlined in ivory silk. She hadn't seen him yet; her nipples were soft rose circles at the peaks of her full breasts. Her arms were bare, as ivory as her nightgown and equally silky. The simple sheath clung to her curves, highlighting the indentation that marked her tiny waist before flaring over her luscious hips. The triangle of red curls at the apex of her thighs was just visible through the sheer material. The long sweep of her sleek thighs led to dimpled knees, peeking from the folds of the gown. Below her well-turned calves, her tiny feet were tinted a delicate pink. Slowly, Jack let his gaze travel upward once more. His lower chest contracted; a familiar tightening in his groin suggested full arousal was not far off. With a wry grin, he moved slowly into the room. It was comforting to know that these days, satisfaction was readily available. And guaranteed. It was, he felt, one of the less well publicized benefits of marriage.

As he circled the room snuffing candles and opening the curtains, he wondered again what devilry his wild woman was hatching. For once, her mind was definitely not on him.

"I went into Lynn today."

"Oh?" Jack paused in the act of snuffing the last candle in the candelabrum.

"Mmm." Kit looked around and located him, standing with the silver snuffer in one hand, the strong planes of his face lit by the single flame, his gilded hair winking wickedly in the golden light. "I saw Lord Belville."

"Who's Lord Belville?"

An impish grin twisted Kit's lips. "You could say he was an old flame."

Jack frowned and doused the candle, leaving the room lit

by the wavering light of Kit's bedside candle and the moonlight streaming in. Laying the snuffer down, he walked to the bed. "What do you mean – an old flame?"

Inwardly, Kit was delighted with his raspy growl, but she needed no demonstration of Jack's possessiveness. She immediately dismissed the idea of making him jealous. But she was truly puzzled by Belville's presence and felt Jack should hear of her tenuous connection with that questionable peer from her, rather than from Belville. "When I was eighteen, I nearly accepted a proposal of marriage from him."

Jack tugged the sash of his midnight blue robe open and shrugged the silk from his shoulders. Kit's mouth went dry as her eyes disobeyed all injunctions and roamed his large and very aroused body, caressing each and every muscle, homing in on the promise of pleasure soon to be enjoyed. She fervently hoped her mention of Belville was not going to mar that pleasure.

But Jack's "Tell me," uttered as he stretched out on the bed beside her, was encouraging.

Kit moistened her lips and tried to drag her eyes up to his face and her wits back from whence they'd wandered. She fastened her gaze on Jack' s silver eyes, gleaming under heavy lids. "Did I tell you my uncles and aunts kidnapped me and took me to London to be married for their convenience?"

Jack's lips twitched. He shook his head. "Lie back, close your eyes, and start at the beginning."

Kit drew an unsteady breath and did as she was told. His voice had dropped to a husky growl. She commenced her story with her grandmother's death and her removal from Cranmer Hall. She felt Jack shift and come up on one elbow beside her. As she reached London, she felt a tug loosen the first of the silk bows that held her nightgown closed.

Her narrative faltered. Her lids flickered.

"Keep your eyes shut. Go on."

Another unsteady breath was necessary before she could. Slowly, her story unfolded, kept moving by Jack's rumbling prompts. Equally slowly, her nightgown was opened all the way down to her feet. She'd got to refusing her first suitor when she felt the bow on each shoulder give way. A second later, the two halves of her nightgown were lifted from her.

Kit's voice suspended. She was lying naked beside her husband.

"What happened then?"

"Ah . . ." It was an effort to collect her wits but, falteringly, she took up her tale. Jack's fingertips touched her, tracing patterns over her skin. His lips followed the trails they'd laid, but his body, his limbs, never touched her. It was like being made love to by a ghost. Soon, her nipples were hard crests atop her swollen breasts. Her stomach was as tight as a drum. Her skin was a mass of sensitized nerves, flickering in anticipation of his next touch.

Kit had no idea how coherent she was, but Jack seemed to follow her tale. His voice, deep and vibrating with passion, urged her on whenever she failed. But when his lips touched her navel and his fingers grazed her thighs, she gave up.

Resisting the temptation to open her eyes, she replied to his "And?" with a simple, "Jack, I can't think, lying here like this."

"Turn over then."

She was halfway over before her mind focused. She hesitated, and would have turned back to ask why, but two large hands fastened about her hips and helped her onto her stomach. Resigned, Kit settled her cheek into her pillow, feeling the sensuous slide of silk and satin beneath her, the coolness soothing her aching breasts and that other ache buried in the soft fullness of her belly. Air played over the heated contours of her back. Jack still lay beside her, not touching her at all.

Assuming that after her protest he'd remain that way, Kit took up her story. She made it to Belville's offer before Jack's palm made contact with her bottom. Moving in slow, sensuous circles, barely touching, his hand stroked her body to instant life.

"Jack!" Kit's eyes flew open. She tried to turn, but Jack leaned over her, his chest angled across her back.

"What happened next?" His lips were at her nape.

In a garbled rush, Kit babbled the tale of her eavesdropping, barely aware of what she said. Jack's hand continued its gentle stroking, extending his area of attentions to the sensitive backs of her thighs. As she recounted her ultimate refusal of Belville's offer, she felt Jack's other hand slip beneath her to close possessively about one breast. Kit moaned softly. The hand on her bottom paused, poised on the fullest point in the curve. The fingers about her breast squeezed gently. Kit felt her body tense; her thighs parted slightly. Jack's hand slipped between, nudging them farther apart. Kit's tension wound tighter. A long finger slid effortlessly into her.

"*Oooh!*" A delicious shudder wracked her as the soft, long-drawn moan left her lips. The finger probed deeply. Kit bit her lip to stifle the moans of surrender that welled in her throat. A second finger joined the first and she gasped.

"Tell me again – what does Belville do?"

What was left of Kit's mind reeled. She told him, as quickly as she could, as completely as she could, her mind centered on his fingers, sliding easily in and out of her body, delving deep one minute, twirling about the next. She got to the end an instant before her vocal cords seized. "Jack!" His name was all she could manage in her need, her voice low and weak.

He heard her. His fingers left her. To her surprise, Kit felt her hips being lifted and a pillow stuffed under her stomach. Jack's weight pressed against her, then she felt the pressure build between her thighs.

He came into her with a rush. Her mind disintegrated. She gasped, with shock. He held still for a few moments, allowing her to grow accustomed to this latest variation, to get used to the sensation of fullness and the deep penetration he'd achieved. Then he started to move.

Kit soon caught the rhythm, riding his downward thrusts before twisting her hips upward to capture and hold him, before he drew back again. He rode her long, he rode her hard, each deep, controlled stroke sending her closer to ecstasy; she writhed beneath him, wordlessly begging for more. When the final all-consuming wave of passion caught them and flung them clear, exhausted, wrung out, and deliriously sated, Jack collapsed on top of her. His lips caressed her earlobe, before, chuckling, he lifted away and dropped to the bed beside her once more.

"Kitten, if you were any wilder, I'd have to tie you up."

Moonlight patterned the floor of Kit's bedroom when Jack woke from his sated slumber. He lay still, savoring the deep contentment of the moment, the warmth of the silken limbs entwined with his. Kit's breath was a butterfly's kiss on his collarbone. He resisted the temptation to tighten his arms about her.

The long-case clock in the corridor struck eleven.

Jack stifled a sigh and carefully disengaged from Kit's embrace. He slipped from her warm bed and found his robe on the floor. Shrugging into it, he paused, looking down on his sleeping wife. Then, a smile on his lips, he turned toward his room.

The instant the door to Jack's room shut behind him, Kit opened her eyes. She blinked rapidly, then sat up, shivering when the cold found her naked shoulders. She dragged the coverlet to her chin and listened.

The heavy tock of the clock was the only sound to reach her straining ears.

Quickly, she slipped from the bed and made for her wardrobe. She'd need to hurry if she was to have any hope of following her husband to his rendezvous.

Chapter 27

The soft shush of the waves on Brancaster beach filled Jack's ears. Leaning against a rock, he looked across the moonlit sands. In the lee of the cliff, Champion snorted, unhappy at being tied next to Matthew's gelding. The rest of the Gang had yet to arrive; the boats weren't due for another hour.

Crossing his arms over his chest, Jack settled down to wait. The memory of the silken limbs he'd left so reluctantly warmed him. She was a passionate woman, his kitten. She'd succeeded in dramatically altering his view of marriage. Before she'd burst into his life, the urge to settle down and manage his inheritance had been driven more by duty than desire. Now, there was nothing he wanted more than to devote his energies to being the lord of Castle Hendon, to watching his children grow, and to taking delight in his wife. He'd no doubt she'd keep him amused – in the bedroom and out of it. Once this mission was finished, he'd be free to follow his own road. Now, thanks to his wild woman, he knew where that road was headed.

His thoughts of Kit reminded him of Lord Belville. He wasn't sure why she'd mentioned him. He'd never met the man; the only piece of her information that had interested him had been Belville's connection with Whitehall. As for the rest, Kit was his now, and that was that.

A cloud of salt spray, whipped by the freshening wind, drifted past. Jack frowned. Could Belville be part of the network that he, George, and countless other careful hands had been slowly unraveling? It was possible.

After months of careful, cautious work, they were nearing the end of their trail. Originally, his mission had been merely to block the routes by which spies were smuggled out of Norfolk. But his success in becoming the leader of the Hunstanton Gang, and then monopolizing the trade in "human cargo," had made Whitehall more ambitious.

Despite having closed the spy-smuggling routes operating out of Sussex and Kent, the government had failed to identify at least one of the principal sources. Which meant there were still traitors sending information out of London. But the plans for Wellington's summer maneuvers were too vital to risk their falling into French hands. So Jack, George, and a select group of others had been summoned from their military postings and asked to sell out of the services to take up civilian appointments under the control of Lord Whitley, the Home Office Undersecretary responsible for internal security.

When the first of the incoming spies the Hunstanton Gang had passed on had reached London and led them to the next connection, the government had moved cautiously. While one group of officers tracked the London courier back to his source, presumably buried somewhere in the British military establishment, the government had decided to turn the route Jack now controlled to their own ends. Sir Anthony Blake, alias Antoine Balzac, had been the spy they'd "smuggled" to France the night Kit had been shot.

Instead of the real plans for Wellington's coming campaign, he'd carried information put together by a conglomerate of officers who'd seen active service only a short time before. The information had been accurate enough to pass the scrutiny of the French receivers. The government had already seen evidence that the false trails were being followed, translated into field movements that would help rather than hinder the duke's forces.

That sort of return was worth a great deal of risk. The number of lives saved would be enormous. So they'd decided to chance a final hand, a last throw of the dice.

Anthony was to carry another packet of information into France, but this time, he would bargain for information in return – information on who the London traitor was. On his last visit, he'd made contact with a French liaison officer who had a great liking for cognac. The man knew the details of the entire English operation. Anthony was sure he could extract at least a clue.

The government now needed that clue. The courier they'd been following in London had been killed in a tavern brawl. The unexpected setback had been disheartening, but all concerned were now even more determined to identify the traitors still remaining. Even if he learned no names, if Anthony could discover how many traitors were left within the military establishment, tonight's mission would be worth the risk.

Hoofbeats, muffled by the sand, approached. Jack recognized George's chestnut. At sight of the figure on the second horse, Jack grinned and straightened. When the horses pulled up beside him, he caught the newcomer's bridle. "Ho, Tony! Ready for another bout of *la vie française*?"

Sir Anthony Blake grinned and dismounted. Another of Lord Whitley's select crew, he was the scion of an ancient English house, but half-French. He'd learned French at his mother's knee and had absorbed the full range of French mannerisms and characteristic Gallic gestures. In addition, he was slim and elegant with black hair and black eyes. He looked French. His ability to pass as French had yielded considerable benefits to His Majesty's government over the many years of war with France. Anthony's black eyes gleamed. "Ready as I'll ever be. Any developments?"

Jack waited until George and Anthony tethered their mounts and rejoined him before answering Anthony's question. "Nothing's happened to change your direction. But I've just learned that a gentleman connected with Whitehall has been seen in these parts. Do you know anything of a Lord Belville?"

Anthony frowned. His estates were in Devon; London was no more his cup of tea than Jack's or George's. "If I'm thinking of the right man, he's a nasty bit of work. Got a position somewhere in the long corridors on the strength of his pater's influence. Unsavory reputation socially, but nothing in it that would interest us."

Jack grimaced. "That's much as I'd imagined. Still, if he's poking his nose about without good reason, I'll follow it up."

The three of them fell to discussing the details of Antoine's trip.

"I'll play it safe and take the usual route back unless there's good reason to do otherwise."

Jack nodded. "Here comes our little troop." The members of the Hunstanton Gang were gathering. "God only knows how they'll react when they learn they've been doing their bit for Mother England." With a wry grin, Jack moved forward to take command.

Above him, hidden by a spiky tussock close by the cliff's edge, Kit frowned. Who was the third man?

She'd had a time following her husband, the short strides of her obedient little mare no match for either Champion or Matthew's black. The need to wait until they were clear of the stables before entering to saddle her mount had meant she'd left the Castle well behind them. But, courtesy of the moon and the elevation of her husband's home, she'd seen enough to realize they were making for the cottage. She'd drawn into the trees surrounding it only minutes before Jack had reemerged in his Captain Jack costume. She'd thanked her stars she hadn't been riding Delia then. Champion had no interest in the chestnut mare; he'd obeyed Jack's instruction without hesitation. She'd dropped behind again on the ride to the coast, and had had to cast about to find their position on the sands. She'd been surprised to find no one else there.

Then George and his companion had arrived. There was something about the way the unknown man held himself, the way he conversed with Jack and George, that disallowed any idea he was a new recruit for the Gang.

Kit saw Joe split from the knot of men around Jack and head toward the cliffs. Jack's lookout. There was a small knoll a few feet from the cliff, about fifty yards from where she was crouching. Once on it, Joe would be able to see her clearly. As Joe started up the cliff path, Kit scrambled along the edge until she found a deeply shadowed crevice. There were tussocks growing from the walls every few feet. The area at the bottom looked sandy. With a last glance to where her mare was concealed in a stand of trees, Kit went over the edge.

She dropped to the sand and wiped her hands on her breeches, then slid to the end of the shadows. Glancing left, she saw the run in full swing. Immediately before her were the horses, Champion and three others, tethered under the overhang of the cliff. Beyond them lay a section of dunes, heavily covered with clumps of sea grass. Kit slipped out and around the horses, patting Champion's great nose on the way. She gained the dunes and worked her way cautiously forward, until she was mere yards from where Jack and George stood, their mysterious visitor between them.

The run was a small one, leaving Jack and George with nothing to do but watch.

Kit glanced back at the cliff. She couldn't see Joe, but if he came to the cliff's edge, he'd spot her immediately. Not that she was frightened of being discovered. Jack had drummed into his men's heads that on no account were they to shoot or knife anybody. The most she had to fear was being locked in her room in Castle Hendon. And learning what Jack would do on finding her in breeches. Kit shook aside the distracting thought and focused on her husband and his associates. Unfortunately, they said nothing.

When the last boat was being unloaded, Jack turned and nodded to Anthony. "Good luck."

Anthony ducked his head but gave no word in answer. He strode down the beach on the first stage of his journey into danger.

Jack watched him go, watched the boat disappear into the surf to make contact with the ship standing offshore. Then he gave the final orders to clear the beach, sending the cargo on to the old crypt. Both he and George lingered on the sands, strangely tied to the fate of their friend. Matthew ambled the beach before them, patiently waiting.

Behind them, Kit lay burrowed in the sand, thoroughly perplexed. Why "Good luck"? And why was she so sure Jack would have shaken the man's hand, but had stopped himself from doing so? She'd sensed his intent quite clearly. Yet, from everything she'd been able to see, the man was French.

She bit her lip, then shook her head. She simply could not believe Jack was smuggling spies. Damn the man – why couldn't he relieve her of this miserable uncertainty? It was all his fault. Her peace of mind was in tatters purely because he had a constitutional objection to being understood!

Suppressing a snort, Kit glanced back over her shoulder. And froze.

A few feet away, so close his grey shadow almost touched her, stood the hulking figure of a man. A scream of fright stuck in her throat. Her wide eyes took in a heavy frame and fleshy jowls. The man was staring at Jack and George, still watching the waves some fifteen feet ahead, presenting her with a haughty profile. He was oblivious of her, prone almost at his feet. Moonlight glinted on the long barrels of the pistols he carried.

The man was Lord Belville.

Kit couldn't breathe.

"We may as well go."

Jack's voice cut through the frozen moment. It brought Belville to life. He stepped forward, passing Kit, still lying immobile, to drop the last few feet to the sand. Another step took him clear of the dunes to face Jack and George as they turned toward the horses, Matthew a few steps behind them.

"Not so fast, gentlemen."

Jack pulled up, startled by the appearance of an armed stranger from dunes he had every right to expect were safe. Where the hell was his lookout?

As if reading his mind. Belville's lips twisted in an unpleasant smile. "I'm afraid your lookout met with a fatal accident." He glanced at the fingers of his right hand, closed about a pistol butt. "Slitting a throat is silent, but such a messy business."

Kit felt her blood run cold. She saw the expression on Jack's face harden. *Oh, God!* If she didn't do something, he would be shot! Pressing her fingers to her lips, she struggled to think.

Thankfully, Belville seemed inclined to conversation. "I must admit that when our courier died in that brawl, we originally believed it simply bad luck. However, when we had no further approaches from our French comrades, when, in fact, they suggested they no longer needed our services, we thought an investigation was in order." Belville rolled the syllables from his tongue, his genial manner counteracted by the menace of the pistols in his hands. "Perhaps," he suggested, "given the trouble you've put me to, you'd like to explain just who you are and who you're working for? Before I put a bullet into each of you."

Kit wished him luck. She couldn't believe Jack would tell him anything, even under such pressure, but she wasn't about to wait to find out. She'd remembered Jack's saddle pistol. Pray God he kept it loaded. As she wriggled back through the dunes, she heard her husband's voice.

"You're Lord George Belville, I take it?"

Kit wondered what her erstwhile suitor would make of that. She hurried toward the horses, protected from sight by the dunes.

His gaze steady on Lord Belville's malevolent eyes, Jack inwardly cursed himself for a fool. He should have taken the time to learn why Kit had wanted to tell him about Belville. She'd been uneasy enough to mention him in the first place. He should have trusted her instinct. Now Joe was dead. And God knew how he, and George and Matthew, were going to get out of this without ending in the same state.

"How do you know who I am?" Belville's honeyed tones had become a snarl.

"You've been identified by someone with a direct connection to the High Commissioner. You could say that person has his lordship's ear."

Jack heard George, beside him, choke. Carefully, he weighed up the odds. They weren't encouraging. Belville had only two pistols, but he could see the butt of a smaller gun glinting in the man's waistband. Presumably, he also had a knife somewhere about him. Even if he missed one shot – and why should he, he'd plenty of room and they'd no cover – he'd still have a weight advantage over either George or Matthew in a knife fight.

Keep talking and pray for a miracle seemed the best bet.

"Who is this person? This intimate of the High Commissioner's?"

Jack's brows flew. "Ah – now that would be telling secrets, wouldn't it?"

Belville leveled his pistols. "I don't believe there is such a person."

Jack shrugged. "But how did I know you? We haven't met before."

The barrels wavered. Belville stared, eyes narrowing. "Who are you?"

Out of sight and sound, Kit's fingers closed about the small pistol tucked into the pocket in Champion's saddle. She let out a sigh of relief. If only she could get back in time.

As she scurried into the dunes, she heard Belville's voice, angry and demanding. Clearly, he hadn't liked being known. Jack's voice answered, smooth and confident, which only seemed to wind Belville's spring tighter. Kit forced herself to take care twisting through the dunes, praying her husband's glib tongue wouldn't get him shot before she made it back.

"Let's just say I'm someone with an interest in the traffic." Jack kept his eyes on Belville's. "Perhaps, if we talk, we might discover our interests are complementary?"

Belville frowned, clearly debating the possibility. Then he slowly shook his head. "There's something damned odd about your 'traffic.' You sent a man out tonight – Henry and I would like to know what he was carrying. There's no other traitor in Whitehall bar us – Henry's quite sure of that. Which means you're running a double deal, one which may well rebound on Henry's and my necks." Belville smiled, a chilling sight. "I'm afraid, dear sir, that your days in the profession have come to an end."

So saying, he raised both pistols.

Ten feet behind him, Kit skidded to a soundless halt in the sand, eyes wide and terrified. She jerked Jack's pistol up before her, clutching it in both hands. Screwing her eyes tight shut, she pulled the trigger.

An explosion of sound ricochetted from the cliffs. Both Jack and George rocked back on their heels, expecting to feel the searing pain of a bullet somewhere in their flesh. As the veil of powder smoke drifted past on the breeze, they looked at each other and realized neither had stopped a bullet. Matthew reached them, equally astonished to find both unharmed. In amazement, they all turned to stare at Belville.

His lordship's pasty complexion had paled, a look of incredulity stamped across his fleshy features. Both pistols were smoking but pockmarks in the sand at Jack's and George's feet bore evidence that he'd not raised his weapons far before discharging them.

Bewildered, Jack looked into the man's eyes, only to find

them glazing. As he watched, Belville twisted to the right and collapsed in a heap on the sand.

Facing them stood Kit, now revealed, a smoking pistol in her hands, her eyes enormous pools of shock.

Jack forgot about Belville, about missions and spies. In a split second, he'd covered the space between them and wrapped Kit in his arms, crushing her to him, furious and thankful all at once. "Damn woman!" he said into her curls. "How the hell did you get here?"

He felt weak, shock and relief offsetting his anger that she was there at all. As he reached for the gun, hanging from her limp fingers, he swore softly. "What the hell am I to do with you?"

Kit blinked up at him, thoroughly disoriented. She'd just killed a man. She wriggled in Jack's arms, trying to peer around his shoulders to where George and Matthew were bent over Belville's body. But Jack held her firmly, using his body to shield her. "Be still."

With no alternative, Kit did. Almost immediately waves of nausea swept through her. She paled and swayed into Jack's embrace as faintness dragged at her senses.

"It's all right. Breathe deeply."

Kit heard the words of comfort and did as she was told. Gradually, the world stopped spinning.

Then George was beside them.

Jack held her tight, her face pressed to his chest. Beneath her cheek she could feel his heartbeat, strong and steady, very much alive. Tears started to her eyes. Annoyed at her weakness, Kit blinked them away.

One look at George's face was enough for Jack, but be had to know and Kit had to hear. "Dead?"

George nodded. "Clean through the heart."

Jack stifled a ridiculous urge to ask Kit whether, among

her many odd talents, she included pistol shooting. Even at such close range, a clean shot under pressure took skill. And courage. But he had no doubt of her reserves of that quality.

The resigned overtones in each man's voice brought Kit's head up. She stared at Jack. "Didn't you want him dead?"

To his exasperation, Jack couldn't come up with a convincing affirmative fast enough to allay her suspicions. Instead, her shocked gaze compelled him to stick to something like the truth. "It would have been more help if we could have got him alive, but," he hurried on, "in the circumstances, Matthew, George, and I are perfectly happy to be alive. Don't think we're complaining."

Jack couldn't tell what she was feeling; her eyes reflected a turmoil far deeper than his own. To his relief, George came to his aid.

"Matthew says a body put in here will be taken out to sea."

Jack nodded. A disappearance would be easier all around. Bodies had to be explained, and explaining Belville's would not help their mission.

"Joe – we have to find Joe!"

Kit's voice jerked both her listeners to a sense of their duty.

"No!" came from both of them.

"I'll take you home," Jack continued. "George will deal with Joe."

But Kit drew back as far as he'd let her, shaking her head vehemently. "But he might not . . . No. We have to look now!"

Both men registered the note of hysteria in her voice. They exchanged troubled glances over her head.

"Come on!" Kit was tugging at Jack's arm. "He might be dying while you argue!"

Neither Jack nor George held much hope for Joe but neither felt confident of convincing Kit of the fact he was almost certainly dead already. With a sigh, Jack released her but retained a firm hold on her hand. Together, the three of them mounted to the cliff and approached the hillock.

A pathetic bundle in worn clothes was all that remained of Joe. The sand about was stained with the blood that had poured from the gaping wound in his neck. Kit stared. Then, with a convulsive sob, she buried her face in Jack's shirt.

George checked but there was no vestige of life left in the huddled form.

Kit struggled to draw breath. For weeks, she'd been Jack's lookout, playing smuggler without a care in the world. It had all been a game. But Joe's death was no game. If she'd still been with Jack, she would have died. Instead, Joe had gone. Any possibility of feeling remorse for killing Belville disappeared, run to ground along with Joe's blood. She'd avenged Joe, and for that she was glad.

The sudden rush of emotions weakened her to the point where Jack's arms were the only thing holding her upright. He sensed her draining strength and swore.

To Jack, the sight of his murdered lookout was a scene from a nightmare. Of course, in his worst nightmare, the huddled figure was Kit. The fact that it was Joe who had died muted the shock, but it was still very real. Badly shaken, he swung Kit into his arms, drawing comfort from the warmth in her slim frame.

George looked up. "Matthew and I will sort this out. For the Lord's sake, get her home. And don't leave her alone."

Jack needed no further urging. He carried his silent wife down to the horses and set her on Champion. He swung up behind her and settled her against him. "Where's your horse?"

Kit told him as they negotiated the climb to the cliff. Jack rode to the trees and tied the mare to Champion's saddle before setting a direct course for the Castle. His one aim was to get a brandy into Kit and then get her to bed. She was already shivering. He'd no experience of deep shock in women, but he fully expected her to get worse.

As they traversed the moonlit fields, Kit struggled to find her mental feet. She'd killed a man. No matter how she viewed that fact, she was unable to feel anything like guilt. In the same position, she'd do it again. He'd been about to kill Jack, and that was all that had mattered. As Castle Hendon loomed on the horizon, she accepted reality. Jack was hers – like any female of any species, she'd kill in a loved one's defense.

"We'll have to do something for Joe's family."

The sudden comment brought Jack out of his daze. "Don't worry. I'll deal with it."

"Yes, but . . ." Kit went on, unaware she was babbling all but incoherently.

Jack soothed her with reassurances. Eventually, she quieted, as if her outburst had drained her remaining strength. She sagged against him, comfortingly alive. Jack concentrated on guiding Champion through the darkening fields. His mind was full of conflicting emotions. The moon was setting; it was full dark by the time he clattered into his stables.

He shouted for Martins. The man came at a run, tucking his nightshirt into his breeches. Jack dismounted, then lifted Kit down, ignoring Martins's shocked stare. His wife's breeches were the most minor of the concerns pressing for his attention. He left Martins to deal with the horses and carried Kit to the house. He let them in through a side door. A single candle waited on the table just inside. Jack ignored it. He carried Kit straight to her room.

Once there, he stripped her of her clothes, ignoring her protests, handling her gently, like a child. He grabbed a towel and rubbed her briskly, over every square inch, until she glowed. Kit grumbled and tried to stop him, then gave up and lay still, slowly relaxing under his hands. He left her for a moment, stretched naked on her bed, her coverlet thrown over her. When he returned from his room, he was also naked and carried two glasses of brandy.

Jack slipped under the coverlet, feeling Kit's satin skin warm against his. "Here. Drink this."

He held the glass to her lips and persevered until, under protest, she'd drained it. He drained his own in one gulp and put both glasses on the table. Then he slipped down into the bed beside her, gathering her into his arms.

To his surprise, Kit turned to look up at him. She put up one hand to draw his head down to hers. He kissed her. And went on kissing her as he felt her come alive.

It hadn't been his intention, but when later he lay sated and close to sleep, Kit a warm bundle beside him, he had to admit his wife's timing had not been at fault. Their union had been an affirmation of their need for each other, of the fact that they were both still alive. They'd needed the moment.

Jack yawned and tightened his hold about Kit. There were things he had to think of, before he could yield to sleep. Someone had to take news of Belville's death posthaste to London. It sounded as if "Henry" was Belville's superior in the spying trade, and presumably worked somewhere in Whitehall. Whoever Henry was, they needed to make sure of him before Belville's disappearance tipped him off. Could George go to London? No – whoever went would need to explain Belville's death. He could take responsibility for his wife's actions; no other man could.

He would have to go, and go early.

Jack glanced down at Kit's curly red head, a fuzz in the darkness. He grimaced. She wouldn't be pleased, but there was no help for it.

The vision of her, his smoking pistol in her hand, came back to haunt him. He hadn't known what he'd felt when he'd seen her standing there and realized what she'd done. He still didn't.

No husband should have to go through the traumas she'd put him through. When he returned from London, that was something he *was* going to explain.

Chapter 28

When Kit woke and saw the letter, addressed to her in her husband's scrawl, propped on the pillow beside her, she groaned and closed her eyes. When she opened them again, the letter was still there.

Damn him! What now? Muttering French curses, she sat up and broke the seal.

Her shriek of fury brought Elmina hurrying in. "*Ma petite*! You are ill?"

"I'm not ill – but he will be when I get my hands on the bloody high-and-mighty High Commissioner! How *dare* he leave me like this?"

Kit threw down the letter and flung the covers from her legs, barely noticing her nakedness in her anger. She accepted the gown Elmina, scandalized, threw about her shoulders, shrugging into the silk confection before she realized it was one of those he'd bought her. "What's the use of these things if he's not even here to see them?"

Her furious question was addressed to the ceiling. Elmina left it unanswered.

By the time Kit had bathed and breakfasted, very much

alone, her temper had cooled to an icy rage. She read her husband's letter three more times, then ripped it to shreds.

Determined not to think about it, she tried to submerge herself in her daily routine with varied success. But when evening approached and she was still alone, her distractions became limited. In the end, after a lonely dinner, seated in splendid solitude at the dining table, she retired to the library, to the chair by the fire, to stare broodingly at the vacant chair behind his desk.

It wasn't fair.

She still had very few clues as to his purpose, but her suspicions were mounting. She'd helped him gain control over all the smugglers in the area – she didn't know why he'd needed that but was sure it had been his objective in joining his Gang with her small outfit. Despite her constant requests, he'd refused to divulge his plans. Even when she'd threatened him with exposure, he'd stood firm. Then she'd saved them from the Revenue, nearly dying in the process. Had he weakened? Not a bit!

Kit snorted and shifted in her chair, slipping her feet from her slippers and tucking her cold toes beneath her skirts.

His reaction to the latest developments was all of a piece. He'd hied off to London, to smooth things over regarding Belville's death, so he'd said. Kit's eyes narrowed, her lips twisted cynically. He'd slipped up there. Their story for public consumption was that Belville had disappeared, presumed a victim of the treacherous currents. She wished she knew who Jack was seeing in the capital. Doubtless, they were getting the explanation she'd been denied.

Kit sighed and stretched. The lamps were burning low. She might as well go up to her empty bed. There was no getting away from the fact that her husband simply didn't trust her, was apparently incapable of trusting her.

Full lips drew into a line; amethyst eyes gleamed. Kit put her feet back into her slippers and stood.

Somehow, she was going to have to make clear to her aggravating spouse that his attitude was simply not good enough.

With a determined tread, she headed for bed.

When Sunday dawned, Kit found herself both husbandless and filled with restless energy – the latter a natural consequence of the former. Flinging back the curtains, she looked out on a fairy-tale scene. The green of the fields was dew-drenched, each jeweled blade sparkling under a benevolent sun. There was not a cloud to be seen; the birds sang a serenade of joy to the bluest of skies. A glint appeared in Kit's eye. She hurried to the wardrobe. It would have to be her inexpressibles; Jack had been overly hasty in divesting her of her riding breeches and Elmina had yet to mend them.

Clad as a boy, she slipped from the still sleeping mansion. Saddling the chestnut with her convertible sidesaddle was easy enough. Then she was riding out, quickly, lest the grooms see her, heading south. She reached the paddock where Delia was held. The black mare came racing at her whistle. It was the work of a few minutes to transfer the saddle, then she turned the chestnut loose to graze in unwonted luxury, while she and Delia enjoyed themselves.

She rode straight for the north coast, passing close by the cottage, a black arrow speeding onward. When they pulled up on the cliffs, exhilaration pounded in her veins. She was breathing hard. Laughter bubbled in her throat. Kit held up her hands to the sun and stretched. It was wonderful to be alive.

It would be even more wonderful if her hideously handsome husband was here to enjoy it with her – only he wasn't. Kit pushed that thought, and the annoyance it brought, aside. She cast about for a cliff path.

She rode eastward along the sands, then came up to the cliffs to make her way onto the anvil-shaped headland above Brancaster. Kit let Delia have her head along the pale sands where the Hunstanton Gang had run so many cargoes.

She found the body in the last shallow bay before the eastern point.

Pulling Delia up a few yards away, Kit stared at the sprawled figure at the water's edge. Waves washed over his legs. He'd been thrown up on the beach by the retreating tide. Not a muscle moved; he was as still as death.

His black hair rang a bell.

Carefully, Kit dismounted and approached the body. When it was clear the man was incapable of proving a threat, she turned him on his back. Recognition was instant. The arrogant black brows and aristocratic features of Jack's French spy met her wondering gaze. He was deathly pale but still alive – she could see the pulse beating shallowly at the base of his throat.

What had happened? More importantly, what should she do?

With a strangled sigh, Kit bent over her burden and locked her hands about his arms. She tugged him higher up the beach, to where the waves could no longer reach him. Then she sat down to think.

If he was a French spy, she should hand him over to the Revenue. What would Jack think of that? Not much – he wouldn't be impressed. But surely, as a loyal Englishwoman, that was her duty? Which took precedence – duty to one's husband or duty to one's country? And were they really different, or was that merely an illusion Jack used for his own peculiar ends?

Kit groaned and drove her fingers through her curls. She wished her husband were here, not so he could take control but so she could vent her feelings and give him the piece of her mind he most certainly deserved.

But Jack wasn't here, and she was alone. And his French friend needed help. His body was chilled; from the look of him, he'd been in the water for some time. He looked strong and healthy enough, but was probably exhausted. She needed to get him warm and dry as soon as possible.

Kit considered her options. It was early yet. If she moved him soon, there'd be less chance of anyone seeing him. The cottage was the closest safe place where he could be tended. She stood and examined her patient. Luckily, he was slighter than Jack. She'd found it easy enough to move him up the beach; she could probably support half his weight if necessary.

It took a moment to work out the details. Kit thanked her stars she'd trained Delia to all sorts of tricks. The mare obediently dropped to her knees beside the Frenchman. Kit tugged and pulled and pushed and strained and eventually got him into her saddle, leaning forward over the pommel, his cheek on Delia's neck, his hands trailing the sands on either side of the horse. Satisfied, Kit scrambled on behind, drew a deep breath and gave Delia the signal to stand. She nearly lost him, but at the last moment, managed to haul his weight back onto the mare. Delia stood patiently until she'd settled him once more. Then they set off, as fast as she dared.

Dismounting was rather more rough-and-ready. Kit's arms ached from the strain of holding him on. She slid to the ground, then eased the leaden weight over until, with a swoosh, he left the saddle to end in a sprawled heap before the door. Exasperated with his helplessness, Kit spared a moment to glare at him. She paused to tug him into a more comfortable position before going into the cottage to prepare the bed.

She found an old sheet and spread it on the bed. His clothes would have to come off, but not until she'd used them as handholds to get him up onto the mattress. Returning to her patient, she dragged him inside. Getting him up on the bed was a frustrating struggle, but eventually, he was laid out upon the sheet, long and slim and, Kit had to admit, handsome enough to make her notice.

Jack didn't leave his knives lying about, but his sword still resided in the back of the wardrobe. Kit put it to good use, slicing the Frenchman's clothes from him. She tried not to look as she peeled the material away, turning him over on his stomach as she went and pulling the muddy sheet from under him. There were bruises on his shoulders and arms, as if he'd been in a fight, and one purpling blotch on one hip, as if he'd struck something. She flicked the covers over him and tucked them in.

Glowing with pride in a job well-done, she set about lighting the fire and heating some bricks. Later, when her patient was as warm and dry as she could make him, she made some tea and settled down to wait.

It wasn't long before, thawed by the warmth, he stirred and turned on his back. Kit approached the bed, confidently leaning across to lay a cool hand on his forehead.

Strong fingers encircled her wrist. Heavy lids rose to reveal black eyes, hazed with fever. The man stared wildly up at her, his eyes searching her face. "*Qui est-ce vous êtes?*" The black eyes raked the cottage, then returned to her face. "*Où sont-nous?*"

The questions demanded an answer. Kit gave it in French. "You're quite safe. You must rest." She tried to ease her hand from his hold, but his fingers tightened instead. Irritated by this show of brute male strength when it was least helpful, Kit added with distinct asperity: "If you bruise the goods, Jack won't be pleased."

The mention of her husband's name saw her instantly released. The black eyes scanned her, more confused than ever. "You are . . . acquainted with . . . Captain Jack?"

Kit nodded. "You could say that. I'll get you something to drink."

To her relief, her patient behaved himself although he continued to study her. He drank the weak tea without complaint. Almost immediately, he sank back into sleep. But his rest was disturbed.

Kit bit her lip as she watched him twist in the bed. He was muttering in French. She drew closer, to the foot of the bed. In his present state, she wasn't certain how clear his mind was. Getting too close might not be wise.

Suddenly, he turned on his back and his breathing relaxed. To her surprise, he started speaking quite lucidly in perfect English. "There are *only two* of them – only two more of the bastards left. But Hardinges drank too fast – the cretin passed out before I could get anything more out of him, blast his ignorant hide." He paused, a frown dragging the elegant black brows down. "No. Wait. There was one more clue – though God knows it's not much to go on. Hardinges kept using the phrase 'the sons of dukes.' I think it means one of the two we're after is a duke's son, but I can't be sure. However, I wouldn't have thought Hardinges was given to poetic illusion." A brief smile flickered over the dark face. "Well, Jack m'lad, I'm afraid that's all I could learn. So you'd better get on that grey terror of yours and fly the news back to London. Whatever they do, they'll have to do it fast. The vultures are closing in – they know something's in the wind our side, and they're determined to extract the ore by whatever means possible. If there's a rat still left in our nest, they'll find him." The long speech seemed to have drained the man's strength. After a pause, he asked: "Jack?"

Startled, Kit shook off her daze. "Jack's on his way."

The man sighed and sank deeper into the pillows. His lips formed the word "Good." The next instant he was asleep.

With gentle snores punctuating the stillness, Kit sat and put the latest pieces of the jigsaw of her husband's activities into place. He was the High Commissioner for North Norfolk – he'd been specifically entrusted with stamping out the smuggling of spies. It now appeared as if, not content with chasing spies on this side of the Channel, Jack had been instrumental in sending some of their own to France.

All of which was very well, but why couldn't he have told her?

Kit paced before the fire, shooting glances every now and then at her patient. There was no reason why Jack couldn't have entrusted her with the details of his mission, particularly not after her sterling service to the cause, albeit given in ignorance. It was patently clear that her husband harbored some archaic idea of her place in his life. It was a place she had no intention of being satisfied with.

She wanted to share his life, not forever be a peripheral part of it, an adjunct held at arms' distance by the simple device of information control.

Kit's eyes glittered; her lips thinned. It was time she devoted more of her energies to her husband's education.

It was late morning before she felt comfortable in leaving the Frenchman – who was clearly no Frenchman at all. There was no possiblity of hiding her male garb, so she didn't try. She rode straight to the Castle stables and dismounted elegantly as Martins ran up, his eyes all but popping from his head.

"Take care of Delia, Martins. You can return her to the back paddock later and bring up the chestnut. I'll not be riding again today."

"Yes, ma'am."

Kit marched to the house, stripping off her gloves as she went. Lovis was in the hall when she entered. Kit sent one defiant glance his way. To his credit, not a muscle quivered as he came forward, his stately demeanor unimpaired by a sight which, Kit suspected, sorely tried his conservative soul.

"Lovis, I want to send a message immediately to Mr. Smeaton. I'll write a note; I want one of the men ready to carry it to Smeaton Hall as soon as I've finished."

"Very good, ma'am." Lovis moved to open the library door for her. "Martins's son will be waiting."

Pulling the chair up to her husband's desk, Kit drew a clean sheet of paper toward her. The note to George was easy, suggesting he go immediately to the aid of his "French" friend, whom she'd left in the cottage, somewhat *hors de combat*. She paused, then penned a final sentence.

"*I sure that you, being so much more in Jack's confidence, will know better than I how best to proceed.*"

Kit signed the note with a flourish, a grim smile on her lips. Perhaps it was unfair to make George squirm, but she was beyond feeling amiable toward those who'd helped her husband attain his present state of arrogance. She addressed the missive, confident it would send George posthaste to his friend's help. He could take subsequent responsibility.

She rang the bell and gave the note to Lovis to speed on its way.

For the next twenty minutes, she barely stirred, her mind

engrossed with forming and discarding various options for bringing Jack's shortcomings to his attention.

When it came to it, she could think of only one way to proceed. There was no point in any complex maneuvers – he was far more expert in manipulation than she. In truth, she had little idea of how to go about bringing him to her heels in true feminine fashion. If she went that route, she'd a shrewd suspicion she'd end on her back, beneath him, leaving him as arrogant as ever. And as unwilling as ever to make concessions. The best she could hope to do was to make a statement – something dramatic enough to make him sit up and take notice, something definite enough for him to be forced to at least acknowledge her point of view.

Determination beating steady in her veins, Kit set out another sheet of paper and settled to write a letter to her errant spouse.

Jack arrived home on Monday evening. He'd had to wait until that morning to speak to Lord Whitley. Various schemes were already afoot to flush out the man they believed was Belville's Henry. All that remained was to wait for Anthony's return, to see if there were any more traitors to track down. They were nearly there.

With a deep sigh, Jack climbed the steps to his front door. Lovis opened it to him.

"My lord. Mr. Smeaton asked you be given this the instant you crossed the threshold."

Jack tore open the single sheet. George's writing took a moment to decipher. Then Jack heaved a weary sigh. He hesitated, wondering whether to send a message up to Kit. He wouldn't be back in time for dinner. It was doubtful he'd be back before she was abed. With a slow grin, he went back out the door. Much better to take her by surprise. "I'll return later tonight, Lovis. No need to tell anyone I was here."

At the cottage, he was greeted by a much-improved Sir Anthony. George was not there to hear the recounting of Antoine's adventures; he'd been summoned to a Gresham dinner.

"One of the trials of an affianced man." Grinning, Jack pulled up a chair, straddling it. It transpired that the French had tracked Antoine down, not out of suspicion, but in order to interrogate him in case he knew more than he'd yet revealed. He'd escaped by stowing away aboard a lighter bound for Boston on the other side of the Wash. Unfortunately, it had also turned out to be a smugglers' vessel. Smugglers did not like stowaways; he'd had to fight his way off, throwing himself overboard before they'd skewered him.

Anthony's tale suggested that the French were desperate for information. The news that there were only two traitors left was music to Jack's ears. "We've got them." Quickly, he filled Anthony in on the happenings on the beach after he'd taken ship, referring to Kit only as another member of the Gang.

"George said something about that," Anthony said. "But he said he'd leave it to you to elaborate as you 'had a deeper interest in Belville's death.' What on earth did he mean?"

Jack had the grace to blush. "Don't ask."

Anthony threw him a look of mock surprise. "Keeping secrets from your friends, Jack m'lad, is most unwise."

"You'll meet this secret eventually so I wouldn't repine." At the intrigued look on Anthony's face, Jack continued quickly: "Whitley thinks Belville's Henry, whom we believe is Sir Henry Colebourne, will be behind bars in a few days at most. Which, together with your information, means the end is nigh. We'll have got them all."

Anthony lay back on his pillows with a deep sigh. "However will they get along without us, now we've all sold out?"

"I'm sure they'll manage. Personally, I've got fresh fields to plow, so to speak." Jack's smile of anticipation was transparent.

Anthony's gaze descended from the ceiling to examine the odd sight of Jack's eagerness for civilian life. "I don't suppose," he said, "your newfound liking for peaceful endeavors has anything to do with the redheaded lad who brought me here?" At Jack's arrested expression, Anthony quietly added: "Taken to the other side, Jack?"

Jack bit back a distinctly rude reply. His eyes gleamed. "From which comment I take it my wife was wearing breeches when she brought you here?"

"*Your wife?*" Anthony's exclamation brought on a fit of coughing. When he'd recovered, he lay back on his pillows and fixed Jack with an astonished stare. "Wife?"

Jack nodded, unable to contain his smile. "You've had the pleasure of meeting Kathryn, Lady Hendon, better known as Kit." He paused, then shrugged. "It was she who shot Belville."

"Oh." Anthony struggled to match fact with memory. "How on earth did that slip of a thing get me from the beach to here?"

Jack stood. "Probably sheer determination. It's a quality she has in abundance. I'll leave you now, Tony." He walked forward to drop a hand on Anthony's shoulder. "I'll send Matthew in the morning with a horse to move you up to the Castle. Rest assured I'll get your news to Whitley as soon as possible. He'll be relieved to know we've got them all."

"Thanks, Jack." Anthony lay quiet on his pillows and watched Jack walk to the door. "But why the hurry to leave?"

Jack paused. "A little matter of propriety I have to discuss with my wife. Not something a rake like you would understand."

Closing the door on his friend's "Oh-ho!", Jack strode to the stable. He hadn't actually caught her in her breeches, but it was close enough, surely?

Anticipation was riding high by the time he reached the house. He entered through the side door, picking up the single candle to light his way. He went straight to his wife's room.

And stopped short when the light from his candle revealed an undisturbed expanse of green satin, with no deliciously curved form snuggling beneath.

For a moment, he simply stared, unable to think. Then, his heart thumping oddly, he went through to his own room. She was not in his bed, either. The sight of the simple white square propped against his pillow caused his hand to shake, spilling wax to the floor.

Drawing a deep breath, Jack put the candle down on the table by the bed and, sinking onto the mattress, picked up the letter. Kit's delicate script declared it was for Jonathon, Lord Hendon. The sight of his proper given name was warning enough.

His lips set in a grim line, Jack tore open the missive.

Her formality had apparently been reserved for the title. Inside, her message was direct and succinct.

Dear Jack

I've had enough. I'm leaving. If you wish to explain anything, I'm sure you'll know where to find me.
Your devoted, loving, and dutiful wife,

Kit

His first thought was that she'd omitted the obedient, obviously realizing his imagination wouldn't stretch that far. Then he read it again, and decided he couldn't, in all honesty, take exception to the adjectives she had claimed.

He sat on his bed as the clock in the hall ticked on and struggled to make sense of what the letter actually meant. He couldn't believe Lovis had given him George's message but forgotten to tell him his wife had left him. Trying to ignore the empty void that was expanding inside his chest, threatening to crush his heart, he read the letter again. Then he lay back on his bed, hands locked behind his head, and started to think.

She was annoyed he hadn't told her the details of his mission. He tried to imagine George telling Amy and felt a glow of justification warm him. Abruptly, it dissipated, as Kit's image overlaid Amy's. All right – so she wasn't the same sort of wife, theirs wasn't the same sort of marriage.

He and his mission were deeply in her debt – he knew that well enough. That she yearned for excitement and would follow wherever it led was a characteristic he recognized. He could understand her pique that he wouldn't involve her in his schemes. But to leave him like this – to walk out on him – was the sort of emotional blackmail to which he'd never succumb. Christ, if he didn't know she was safe at Cranmer Hall, he'd be frantic! No doubt she expected him to come running, eager to win her back, willing to promise anything.

He wouldn't do it.

At least, not yet. He had to go back to London tomorrow, to convey Anthony's news to Lord Whitley. He'd leave Kit to stew, caught in a trap of her own devising. Then, when he came back, he'd go and see her and they could discuss their relationship calmly and rationally.

Jack tried to imagine having a calm and rational discussion with his wife. He fell asleep before he succeeded.

Chapter 29

Heaving a sigh of relief and anxiety combined, Kit plied the knocker on her cousin Geoffrey's door. The narrow house in Jermyn Street was home to her Uncle Frederick's three sons whenever they were in London. She hoped at least one of them was there now.

The door was opened by Hemmings, Geoffrey's gentleman's gentleman. He'd been with the family for years and knew her well. Even so, given her costume, a long moment passed before she saw his eyes widen in recognition.

"Good evening, Hemmings. Are my cousins in?" Kit pressed past the stunned man. Brought to a sense of his place, Hemmings rapidly shut the door. Then he turned to stare at her again.

Kit sighed. "I know. But it was safer this way. Is Geoffrey here?"

Hemmings swallowed. "Master Geoffrey's out to dinner, miss, along with Master Julian."

"Julian's home?"

When Hemmings nodded, Kit's spirits lurched upward for the first time that day. Julian must be home on furlough;

seeing him would be an unlooked-for bonus in this thus-far-sorry affair.

She'd left Castle Hendon on Sunday afternoon, more than twenty-four hours ago, dressed as Lady Hendon with no incriminating luggage beyond a small black bag. She'd told Lovis she'd been called to visit a sick friend whose brother would meet her in Lynn. The note she'd left for her husband would, she'd assured him, explain all. She'd had Josh drive her into Lynn and leave her at the King's Arms. When the night stage had left for London at eight that evening, a slim, elegant youth muffled to the ears had been on it.

The stage had been impossibly slow, reaching the capital well after midday. From the coaching inn, she'd had to walk some distance before she'd been able to hail a sufficiently clean hackney. And the hackney had dawdled, caught in the London traffic. Now it was past six and she was exhausted.

"Master Bertrand's away in the country for the week, miss. Should I make up his bed for you?"

Kit smiled wearily. "That would be wonderful, Hemmings. And if you could put together the most simple meal, I would be doubly grateful."

"Naturally, miss. If you'll just seat yourself in the parlor?"

Shown into the parlor and left blissfully alone, Kit tidied the magazines littering every piece of furniture before selecting an armchair to collapse in. She'd no idea how long she lay there, one hand over her eyes, fighting down the uncharacteristic queasines that had overcome her the instant she'd woken that morning, brought on, no doubt, by the ponderous rocking of the stage. She hadn't eaten all day, but could barely summon sufficient appetite to do justice to the meal Hemmings eventually placed before her.

As soon as she'd finished, she went upstairs. She washed

her face and stripped off her clothes, wryly wondering what it was Jack had intended to do if he found her in such attire. The thought brought a soft smile to her lips. It slowly faded.

Had she done the right thing in leaving him? Heaven only knew. Her uncomfortable trip had succeeded in dampening her temper but her determination was undimmed. Jack had to be made to take notice – her disappearance would accomplish that. And he would follow, of that she was sure. But what she wasn't at all sure of, what she couldn't even guess, was what he'd do then.

Somehow, in the heat of the moment, she'd not considered that vital point.

With a toss of her curls, Kit flung her clothes aside and climbed between the clean sheets. At least tonight she'd be able to sleep undisturbed by the snorts and snores of other passengers. Then, tomorrow, when she could think straight again, she'd worry about Jack and his reactions.

If the worst came to the worst, *she* could always explain.

She was at the breakfast table the next morning, neatly attired in Young Kit's best, when Geoffrey pushed open the door and idly wandered in. He cut a rakish figure in a multicolored silk robe, a cravat neatly folded about his neck. One look at his stunned face told Kit that Hemmings had left her to break her own news.

"Good morning, Geoffrey." Kit took a sip of her coffee and watched her cousin over the rim of the cup.

Geoffrey wasn't slow. As his gaze took in her attire, his expression settled into dazed incredulity. "What the bloody hell are you doing here?"

"I decided a week or so away from Castle Hendon was in order." Kit smiled. "Aren't you pleased to see me?"

"Dash it, Kit, you know I am. But . . ." Geoffrey ran a harassed hand through his dark locks. "Where the hell's your husband?"

Abruptly, Kit dropped her pose. "Coming after me, I hope."

Geoffrey stared. Abruptly, he reached for the coffeepot. "Cut line, my girl. Start from the beginning. What kind of dangerous game are you playing?"

"It's no game." Kit sighed and leaned both elbows on the table. Geoffrey drew up a chair. When he waved at her to continue, Kit related her story. In the cold light of morning, it didn't sound particularly sane. And trying to explain to Geoffrey why she felt as she did was even more futile. She wasn't surprised when he showed every indication of taking Jack's part.

"You've run mad," was Geoffrey's verdict. "What the hell do you suppose he's going to do when he finds you?"

Kit shrugged, dreaming of the moment.

Geoffrey stiffened. "Did you tell him you'd be here?"

Kit's shaking head let him breathe again. "But he'll figure it out."

Geoffrey stared at her. That wasn't the assurance he'd wanted. He studied Kit, then asked: "You're not breeding, are you?"

It was Kit's turn to stare. "Of course not!"

"All right, all right." Geoffrey held up both hands placatingly. "I just thought it might be a good excuse to have handy when Hendon makes his entrance. Everyone knows women do strange things at such times."

Incensed, Kit glared at him. "That's not the point! I want him to realize I won't be put aside, tucked safely away in some niche, every time he decides what he's doing is not . . . not suitable for me to be involved in."

401

Geoffrey clapped a hand to his forehead. "Oh, my God!"

The door opened to admit Julian, the youngest of the three brothers, the only one younger than Kit. Geoffrey sat, staring into his coffee while Julian and Kit exchanged joyful greetings over his head, and Kit filled Julian in on the reasons for her present excursion. When they finally turned their attention to their breakfasts, Geoffrey spoke. "Kit, you can't stay here."

Her face fell. "Oh."

"It's not that I mind, personally," Geoffrey assured her, ignoring the dark look his brother was throwing him. "But can you please try to understand how your husband is going to feel if he arrives here to find you cavorting about Jermyn Street in breeches?" Geoffrey paused, then added: "On second thought, rescind that 'personally.' I *do* mind, because it's my hide he'll be after."

"I've got a dress with me."

Geoffrey cast his eyes to the ceiling. "With all due respect, Kit, trotting about Jermyn Street in a dress is likely to prove even more dangerous to your reputation than the other."

Kit grimaced, knowing he was right. She'd lived in London long enough to know the rules. Jermyn Street was the haunt of the well-to-do bachelors of the *ton*. Women of her standing definitely did not live in Jermyn Street. "But where can I go? And for God's sake, don't suggest your parents."

"I'm a coward, not daft," returned Geoffrey.

The three cousins sat considering their acquaintance. None of it was suitable. Then Julian bounced to life. "Jenny – Jenny MacKillop!"

Miss Jennifer MacKillop had been governess to Frederick Cranmer's sons and had filled in a few years more as governess-companion to Kit until the time of Kit's first Season.

Subsequently, she'd retired to look after her aging brother in Southampton.

"I had a letter from her a few months back," said Kit. "Her brother died and left her the house. She thought she'd stay there for the rest of the year, before making up her mind what to do."

"Then that's where you'll go." Geoffrey sat up. He studied Kit sternly. "How far behind you do you suppose Hendon is?"

Kit looked uneasy. "I don't know."

Geoffrey sighed. "Very well. I'd better wait here in case he arrives, breathing fire. No!" he said, as Julian opened his lips. "From everything I've heard about Jonathon Hendon, he'd eat you alive before he paused to ask questions. At least I'll have my wits to help me. You may escort our lovely cousin to Southampton."

Julian beamed. "May I use your curricle?"

Geoffrey's sigh was heartfelt. "If I find a scratch on it, you'll be painting it with your eyelashes."

Julian whooped.

Geoffrey raised his brows. "You wouldn't think he shaves yet, would you?"

Kit giggled.

Geoffrey smiled. "That's better. I'd started to wonder if you'd forgotten how."

"Oh, Geoffrey." Kit put out a hand to clasp his.

Geoffrey gripped her fingers. "Yes, well, I suggest you leave as soon as possible. You should be able to make it by nightfall if Julian keeps a proper eye on the cattle. It sounds as if Jenny will be able to put you both up."

Her immediate future decided, Kit poured herself another cup of coffee. She didn't want to go to Southampton. It was too far away from Castle Hendon. But she had to agree with Geoffrey's reasoning. Jack wouldn't be pleased to find her frequenting a bachelors' residence. And she would enjoy seeing Jenny again. Perhaps catching up with her old mentor would distract her from the problems of her new role.

Jack woke on Friday morning feeling thoroughly disgruntled. He lay on his back and stared at the ceiling, his eyes devoid of expression. Life, full to brimming but short days before, had taken on a greyish hue.

He missed his wife.

Not only did he miss her, he couldn't seem to function, knowing she wasn't here, where she belonged. He couldn't sleep, he couldn't recall what he'd eaten for the last three days. His faculties were enmeshed in a constant retreading of their last encounters, of the opportunities he'd missed to read her mind and head off her startling, but characteristic action.

It had been a mistake to leave her at Cramner Hall. He saw that now. But he hadn't known then how much the thought of her would prey on his mind.

With a half groan, he pushed back the covers and hauled himself upright. Without more ado, he'd rectify his error. He'd ridden in from London late the previous night, his hope that Kit might have reassessed her objectives and returned home dashed by the sight of her empty bed. His empty bed had proved even less inspiring.

He dressed with unusual care, choosing a morning coat of simple elegance, determined to impress his wife with every facet of his personality. He knew exactly what he'd do. After greeting her coolly, he'd insist on seeing her alone. Then, he'd *explain* to her why her action in leaving him was unacceptable behavior in Lady Hendon, why no

404

circumstance on earth could excuse her absence from the saftey of his hearth. Then he'd kiss the damned woman witless and bring her home. Simple.

He grabbed a cup of coffee and ordered Champion brought around.

"If she's not here, where the devil is she?" Jack ran an agitated hand through his hair, dragging golden strands loose to fly in wisps about his haggard face. He paced the Gresham's morning room like a caged and wounded tiger.

Amy watched him, sheer amazement in her face.

"Perhaps, my dear, you should get us some refreshment." George smiled reassuringly into Amy's eyes. Drawing her to her feet, he steered her to the door and held it for her.

Once Amy had escaped, George shut the door and fixed Jack with a stern eye. "I told you not to leave Kit alone." His voice held a note of decided censure. "And if you left without explaining what was going on, I'm not surprised she's left you."

Jack paused to stare at him.

George grimaced and rummaged in his coat pocket. "Here," he said, holding out the note Kit had sent him. "I'd hoped I wouldn't need to show you this, but obviously your wife knows your stubbornness even better than I."

Puzzled, Jack took the note and smoothed it out.

"Read the last sentence." said George helpfully.

Jack did. *I feel sure that you, being so much more in Jack's confidence, will know better than I how to proceed.* Crushing the note in his hand, Jack swore. "How the hell was I supposed to know she felt that strongly over it?" He glared at George.

George was unimpressed. "You knew damn well she wanted to know. Dash it – she *deserved to* know, after what she

405

did that night on the beach. And as for her recent efforts in the cause – all I can say is she's been damned understanding."

Jack was taken aback. "You don't even approve of her!"

"I know. She's wild beyond excuse. But that doesn't excuse you."

Hands on his hips, his eyes narrowed and smoky grey, Jack glared at George. "You're not going to tell me you've told Amy of our mission?"

Unaffected by Jack's belligerence, George sat on the *chaise*. "No, of course not. But the point is, Kit's not Amy."

Jack's lips twisted in a pained grimace. He fell to pacing once more, his brow furrowed. "If I'd told her, God knows what she'd have got up to. Our dealings were too dangerous – I couldn't expose her to such risks."

George sighed. "Hell, Jack – you knew what she was like from the start. Why the devil did you marry her, if you weren't prepared to accept those risks?"

"I married her because I love her, dammit!"

"Well, if that's the case, then the rest should come easily."

Jack shot him a suspicious glance. "What exactly does that mean?"

"It means," said George, "that you wanted her for what she was – what she is. You can't start changing bits and pieces, expecting her to change in some ways but not in others. Would you be pleased if she turned into another Amy?"

Jack bit back his retort, his lips compressed with the effort to hold back the unflattering reply.

George grinned. "Precisely. Not your cup of tea. Thankfully, she is mine." The door opened at that moment; George looked up, smiling warmly as Amy entered, preceding her butler, who bore a tray burdened with a variety of strong liquors in addition to the teapot. Dismissing the butler, Amy poured tea for George and herself while George poured Jack a hefty glass of brandy. "Now that we've resolved your differences of opinion, what exactly has happened?"

With a warning frown, Jack took the glass. "I came back from London on Monday evening and got your message – as you'd instructed, as soon as I'd crossed the threshold. I went to see our friend, then returned to the Castle. Kit wasn't there." He took a swallow of his drink, then pulled a letter from his pocket. "As we seem to be passing my wife's epistles about, you may as well read that."

George took the letter. A quick perusal of its few lines had him pressing his lips firmly together to keep from grinning. "Well," he said, "you can't claim she's not clear-headed."

Jack humphed and took the letter back. "I assumed she'd gone to Cranmer Hall and reasoned she'd be safe enough there until I got back from reporting Anthony's news to Whitley."

George's gaze was exasperated. "Hardly a wise move."

"I wasn't exactly in a wise mood at the time," Jack growled, resuming his frustrated prowl. "I've just endured the most harrowing morning of my life. First, I went to Cranmer. I didn't even make it to the Hall. I met Spencer out riding. Before I could say a word, he asked how Kit was."

George raised his brows. "Could he have been protecting her – throwing you off the track?"

Jack shook his head. "No, he was as open as the sky. Besides, I can't see Spencer supporting Kit in this little game."

"True," George conceded. "What did you tell him?"

"What could I tell him? That I'd lost his granddaughter,

407

whom I vowed not a month ago to protect till death us do part?"

George's lips twitched but he didn't dare smile.

"After enduring the most uncomfortable conversation of my entire life, I raced back to the Castle. I hadn't thought to ask my people about *how* she'd left, as she'd obviously made all seem normal, and I didn't see any point in raising a dust. As it transpired, she'd told Lovis she'd been called to a sick friend's side. She had my coachman drive her to the King's Arms in Lynn on Sunday afternoon, from where according to her, this friend's brother would fetch her. I checked. She took a room for the night and paid in advance. She had dinner in her room. That's the last anyone's seen of her."

George frowned. "Could someone have recognized her as Young Kit?"

Jack threw him an anguished glance. "I don't know. I came here, hoping against hope she'd simply laid a trail and then gone to ground with Amy." He stopped and sighed, worry etched in his face. "Where the devil can she have gone?"

"Why the King's Arms?" mused Amy. Sipping her tea, she'd been calmly following the discussion. George turned to look at her, searching her face as she frowned, her gaze distant.

Then Amy raised her brows. "The London coaches leave from there."

"London?" Jack stood, stunned into stillness. "Who would she go to in London? Her aunts?"

"Heavens, no!" Amy smiled condescendingly. "She'd never go near them. She'd go to Geoffrey, I suppose."

George saw Jack's face and leapt in with, "Who's Geoffrey?"

Amy blinked. "Her cousin, of course. Geoffrey Cranmer."

The sudden easing of Jack's shoulders was dramatic enough to be visible. "Thank God for small mercies. Where does Geoffrey Cranmer live?"

Frowning, Amy took another sip of tea "I think," she began, then stopped, her frown deepening. "Does Jermyn Street sound right?"

George dropped his head back and closed his eyes. "Oh, God."

"It sounds all *too* right." His jaw ominously set, Jack picked up his gloves. "My thanks, Amy."

George swung about as Jack made for the door. "For God's sake, Jack, don't do anything you'll regret."

Jack paused at the door, a look of long suffering on his face. "Never fear. Aside from giving her a good shaking, and one or two other physical treatments, I intend to spend a long, long time *explaining* things – a whole *host* of things – to my wife."

At five o'clock, Geoffrey studied the elegant timepiece on his mantel and wondered what he could do to fill the time until dinner. He'd yet to come to a conclusion when the knocker on his door was plied with the ruthless determination he'd been expecting for the last three days.

"Lord Hendon, sir."

Hemmings had barely got the words out before Jonathon Hendon was in the room. His sharp and distinctly irritated grey gaze swept the furniture before settling with unnerving calm on Geoffrey's face.

Geoffrey remained outwardly unmoved, rising to greet his wholly expected guest. Inwardly, he conceded several of the points Kit had attempted to explain to him. The man standing in the middle of his parlor, stripping riding gloves off a pair of large hands and returning his welcoming nod with brusque civility, didn't look the sort to be easily brought to the negotiating table. Now he could understand why Kit had felt it necessary to flee her home purely to gain her husband's attention.

His knowledge of Jonathon Hendon was primarily based on rumor – not, he was the first to admit, a thoroughly reliable source. Hendon was a number of years his senior; socially, their paths had crossed infrequently. But Jack Hendon's reputation as a soldier and a rake was close to legendary. Undoubtedly, had the country not been at war, he and Kit would have met much sooner. But how his slip of a cousin coped with the powerful male force currently making itself felt in all sorts of subtle ways in his parlor was beyond Geoffrey's ability to guess.

"I believe, Cranmer, you have something of mine."

The steel encased in the deep velvety tones brought Geoffrey's well-honed defense mechanisms into play. Angry husbands had never been his cup of tea. "She's not here." Best to get that out as soon as possible.

Arrested, the grey gaze trapped him. Some of the tension left the large frame. "Where is she?"

Despite Kit's instruction to tell her husband precisely where she was as soon as he appeared, Geoffrey found himself too intrigued to let the information go quite so easily. He waved his guest to a seat, an invitation that was reluctantly accepted. Smoothly, Geoffrey grasped a decanter and poured two glasses of wine, handing one to his guest before taking the other back to his armchair. "I've been expecting you for the past three days."

To his surprise, a slight flush rose under his guest's tanned skin.

"I thought the damned woman was at Cranmer. I went to fetch her this morning, only to find Spencer hadn't seen her.

410

It took some hours to uncover her trail. If it hadn't been for Amy Gresham remembering you, I'd still be chasing my arse in Norfolk."

Hearing exasperation ring behind the clipped accents, Geoffrey kept his expression serious. "You know," he said, "I don't think Kit intended that."

"I know she didn't." Jack fastened his gaze on Geoffrey's face. "So where is she?"

The commanding tones were difficult to resist but still Geoffrey hesitated. "Er . . . I don't suppose you'd consider allaying my cousinly fears with an assurance or two?"

For a moment, Jack stared, incredulous, until the sincerity in Geoffrey's eyes struck him. Here was another who, while recognizing Kit's wildness, had learned to overlook the fact. With a grimace, Jack conceded: "I've no intention of harming a single red hair. However," he added, his voice regaining its sternness, "beyond that, I make no promises. I intend taking my wife back to Castle Hendon as soon as possible."

The strength in that reply should have reassured Geoffrey. Instead, the implication revealed a glaring gap in Kit's plan. "I'm sure she has no other intention than to return with you." Geoffrey frowned. Had Kit explained to her intimidating spouse why she'd taken to her heels as she had? "In fact, I was under the distinct impression she was waiting for you to arrive to take her home momentarily."

Jack frowned, not a little confused. If she didn't want to bargain with him, her return against his promises, what was this all about? Admitting she wished to return with him would leave her no leverage to wring promises from him.

His bewilderment must have shown, for Geoffrey was also frowning. "I don't know that I've got this entirely straight – with women one never knows. But Kit led me to

411

understand that her . . . er, trip was solely designed to make you sit up and take notice."

Jack stared at Geoffrey, his gaze abstracted. Was she wild enough to do such a thing – simply to make him acknowledge her feelings? To force him to do nothing more than admit he understood? The answer was obvious. As the memory of the sheer worry he'd endured for the past four days washed through him, Jack groaned. He leaned his brow on one palm, then glanced up in time to catch the grin on Geoffrey's face. "Has anyone warned you, Cranmer, against marriage?"

Jack stretched his long legs to the comfort of the fire blazing in Geoffrey Cranmer's parlor. Kit's cousin had invited him to dine and then, when Jack had confessed he'd yet to seek lodgings, Hendon House being let for the Season, had offered him a bed. By now at ease with both Geoffrey and the younger Julian, who'd joined them over dinner, he'd accepted. Both he and Geoffrey had been entertained by the conversion of Julian from guarded civility to hero worship. Aside from the ease of an evening spent with kindred spirits, Jack doubted Kit would find support from these two the next time she made a dash for town.

Not, of course, that there'd be a next time.

Before leaving with Julian for a night about town, Geoffrey had filled Jack in on Jenny MacKillop and her relationship to the Cranmer family. Julian had painted a reassuring picture of a genteel household in one of the better streets of Southampton. Kit was safe. Jack knew where he could lay his hand on her red head whenever he wished. He wished right now. But experience was at last taking root. This time, he would take the time to think before he tangled with his loving, devoted, and dutiful wife.

412

His record in paying sufficient attention to her words was not particularly good. He'd ignored her requests to be told about the spies because it had suited him to do so. He'd not listened as carefully as he should have to her warning about Belville, oblique though it had been, too engrossed in delighting in her body to pay due interest to the fruits of her brain. And he'd put off fetching her from Cranmer, knowing it would involve him in a discussion of topics he had not wished to discuss.

Uneasily, Jack shifted in the chair. Admitting to such failures and vowing to do better was not going to come naturally.

It would have to come, of course. He knew he loved the damned woman. And that she loved him. She'd never said so, but she proclaimed it to his senses every time she took him into her body. Even when she'd offered herself to him that night in the cottage, he hadn't imagined she'd done so lightly; that was what had made the moment so special. For her, and now for him, although it hadn't been so in the past, love and desire were two halves of the same whole – fused, never to be split asunder.

So he would have to apologize. For not telling her what she'd had a right to know, for treating her as if she was outside his circle of trust, when in reality she stood at its center. He'd never imagined a wife would be close to him in that way – but Kit was. She was his friend and, if he would permit it, his helpmate, more attuned to his needs than any man had a right to expect.

Jack grinned at the flames and sipped his brandy. He was a lucky man, and he knew it. Doubtless she'd want some assurance that he'd improve in the future. No doubt she'd assist, prodding whenever necessary, reminding him of this time.

413

With a confident snort, Jack drained his glass and considered his next meeting with his wife. His part was now clear. What of hers?

There was one point he was determined to make plain, preferably in sufficiently dramatic fashion so that his red-headed houri would not forget it. Under no circumstances would he again endure the paralyzing uncertainty of not knowing where she was, of not knowing she was safe. She must promise not to engage willy-nilly in exploits that would turn his golden brown hair as grey as his eyes. She'd have to agree to tell him of any exploit beyond the mundane before she did her usual headlong dash into danger – doubtless he'd arrange to block quite a few; others he might join her in. Who knew? In some respects, they were all too alike.

Jack stared long and hard at the flames. Then, satisfied he'd established all the important points in their upcoming discussion, he settled down to plan how best to take his wife by storm.

Despite her interest in some of his affairs, she'd neglected to ask about the family business. Perhaps, as the Cranmers relied totally on the land, she hadn't realized there was a business to ask about? Whatever, one of his brigs was currently in the Pool of London, due, most conveniently, to set sail for its home port of Southampton on the morning tide. The *Albeca* was due to load at Southampton for a round trip to Lisbon and Bruges before returning to London. Like all his major vessels, the *Albeca* had a large cabin reserved for the use of its owner.

He'd commandeer the *Albeca*. It could still do its run, but, after Bruges, could lie in at one of the Norfolk ports to let them ashore. As a means of transporting his wife from Southampton to Norfolk, a boat had a number of pertinent advantages over land travel. Aside from anything else, it would give them countless hours alone.

It was definitely time to reel Kit back.

Back where she belonged.

Chapter 30

Kit stared at the forget-me-nots bobbing their blue heads in Jenny's small walled garden and wondered if Jack had forgotten her. It was Monday, more than a week since she'd left Castle Hendon. She'd been absolutely confident he'd be after her the instant he returned from London, which should have been on Tuesday at the latest. A minute should have sufficed to tell him where she'd gone. Cranmer was out of the question; likewise, her aunts could not be considered candidates. Her cousins should have stood out as the only possibility, and she'd mentioned Geoffrey was her favorite. Of course, her move to Southampton would have delayed him for a day, maybe two. But he'd yet to show his arrogant face in Jenny's neat little parlor.

Worry creased Kit's brow; she chewed her lower lip in something close to consternation. It had never occurred to her that he might not behave as she'd expected. Had she misread the situation? Men often had peculiar views and certainly, her flight was not the sort of action any husband would view with equanimity. But she hadn't expected Jack to be overly concerned with the proprieties,

416

or with how her actions reflected on him. Had she miscalculated?

She knew he loved her; where that certainty sprang from she couldn't have said, but the fact was enshrined in her heart, along with her love for him. The whens and wheres and hows were beyond her. All she knew was those truths, immutable as stone.

But none of that answered her question – *where was he?*

Kit heaved a heavy sigh.

So deep in contemplation was she that she failed to hear the footsteps approaching over the grass. Nevertheless, despite her distraction, her senses prickled as Jack drew close. She whirled with a gasp to find him beside her.

Her eyes locked with his. Her heart lurched to a standstill, then started to race. Anticipation welled. Then she saw his expression – stern, distant; not a flicker of a muscle betrayed any softer emotion.

"Good morning, my dear." Jack managed to keep his tone devoid of all expression. The effort nearly killed him. He kept his arms rigid at his sides, to stop himself from hauling Kit into them. That, he promised himself, would come later. First, he was determined to demonstrate to his errant wife how seriously he viewed her actions. "I've come to take you home. Jenny's packing your things. I'll expect to leave directly she's finished."

Stunned, Kit stared at him and marveled that the words she'd so longed to hear could be delivered in such a way that all she felt was – nothing. No joy, no relief – not even any guilt. Jack's words had been totally emotionless. Searching his face, she waited, more than half-expecting his austere expression to melt into teasing lines. But his frozen mask did not ease.

For the first time in her life, Kit did not know what she

felt. All the emotions she'd expected to experience upon seeing Jack again were there, but so tangled with a host of newborn feelings, disbelief and resurgent anger chief amongst them, that the result was total confusion.

Her mind literally reeled.

Her face was blank; her mind had yet to sort out what her expression should be. Her lips were parted, ready to speak words she could not yet formulate. It was as if she was in a play, and someone had switched the scripts.

Wordlessly, Jack offered her his arm. Speech was still beyond her; her mind was in turmoil. Kit felt her fingers shake as she placed them on his sleeve.

Jenny was waiting, smiling, in the hall, Kit's small bag at her feet. Still struggling to grasp what tack Jack was taking, and how she should react, Kit absentmindedly kissed her erstwhile governess, promising to write, all the while conscious of Jack's commanding figure, an impregnable rock beside her.

Surely he hadn't missed her point entirely?

Kit sank onto the cushions of the hired carriage, puzzled that it wasn't one of the Hendon coaches. She blinked when Jack shut the door on her. Then it dawned that he'd elected to ride rather than share the coach with her.

Suddenly, Kit was in no doubt of what she felt. Her temper soared. *What* was going on here?

Ten minutes later, the carriage jolted to a halt. Sitting bolt upright on the carriage seat, Kit waited. Jack called an order. The keening of gulls came clearly on a freshening breeze. She narrowed her eyes. Where were they? Before she could slide to the window and peer out, Jack opened the door. He held out his hand, but his eyes did not meet hers.

Her temper on the tightest of reins, Kit coolly placed her fingers in his. He handed her down from the carriage. One glance was enough to tell her that she would have to delay giving him her reaction to his stoic performance. They stood on a wharf beside a large ship, amid bales and crates, ropes and hooks. Sailors rushed about; bustle and noise surrounded them. At Jack's urging, she stepped over a coil of rope. His hand at her elbow, he guided her along the busy wharf to where a plank with a rope handrail led up to the ship's deck.

Kit eyed the gangplank, rising and falling as the ship rode the waves of the harbor. She drew a deep breath.

Her chillingly civil request to be carried aboard never made it past her lips.

As she turned, Jack ducked. The next instant, Kit found herself staring down at the choppy green waves as Jack swiftly climbed the gangplank. Fury cindered the reins of her temper. She closed her eyes and saw a red haze; her fingers curled into claws. She'd wanted to be carried, but carried in his *arms*, not over his shoulder like a sack of potatoes!

Luckily, the gangplank was short. The instant Jack gained the deck, he set her on her feet. Kit immediately swung his way, her eyes going to his. But Jack had already turned and was speaking.

"This is Captain Willard, my dear."

With an almighty effort, Kit shackled her fury – aside from not wanting to scare anyone else, she wanted to save it all for Jack. Her face set, expressionless, her lips a thin line, she turned and beheld a large man, potbellied and jovial, dressed in a braided uniform.

He bowed deeply. "Might I say what a pleasure it is to welcome you aboard, Lady Hendon?"

"Thank you." Stiffly, Kit inclined her head, her mind racing. The man's manner was too deferential for a captain greeting a passenger.

419

"I'll show Lady Hendon to our quarters, Willard. You may proceed on your own discretion."

"Thank you, m'lord."

The truth struck Kit. Jack owned the ship. Yet another not-so-minor detail her spouse had failed to mention.

Jack steered Kit aft, to where a stairway led down to the corridor to the stern apartments. With every step, he reminded himself to hold firm to his resolution. He had endured a full week of the most wretched worry – surely an hour of guilty misery was not unreasonable retribution? That Kit was shaken by his retreat, his withholding of the responses she would have expected from him, was obvious. The stunned, searching expression that had filled her eyes in Jenny's garden had wrenched his heart; the quiver in her fingers when she'd laid them on his sleeve had nearly overset his careful plans. He hadn't been game to meet her eyes after that.

Carrying her up the gangplank had nearly done him in. Even with her tossed over his shoulder, he hadn't been sure he'd be able to let her go, which would have shocked Willard out of his braid.

He couldn't take much more of his self-imposed reticence. He'd leave her in his cabin until her hour was up, then surrender as gracefully as possible.

As he followed Kit down the narrow stairs, Jack closed his eyes and gritted his teeth. His resolution was fraying with every step. The sight of her hips, swaying to and fro before him, was more than he could stand.

His quarters lay at the end of the short corridor, spread across the vessel's square stern. The door he held open for Kit led into the room he used as his study and dining room. A single door led into the bedroom, the two rooms spanning the stern. Both rooms had windows instead of portholes, set in under the overhanging poop deck.

420

The bright light reflected from the water hit Kit instantly as she entered the room. She blinked rapidly; it took a moment for her eyes to adjust. Then, drawing a very deep breath, she swung to face her husband.

Only to see him disappear through another door.

"The bedroom's through here." Jack reappeared immediately. Kit realized he'd left her bag in the room. His demeanor hadn't altered in the slightest. It was still politely blank, almost vacant, as if they were mere acquaintances embarking on a cruise. He still hadn't met her eyes.

"I'll leave you to refresh yourself. We'll be departing with the tide." With that, he turned to leave.

The rage that gripped Kit was so powerful that she swayed. She grabbed a chair back for support. *Just like that?* She was being deposited in the cabin like some piece of baggage, and he thought he could walk away?

She was beyond fury, even beyond rage. Kit's temper was now in orbit. "Will you be back?"

The words, uttered in precise and icy tones, halted Jack.

Slowly, he turned. He was nearly at the door; Kit stood with her back to the windows. The light streaming in left her face in shadow; he couldn't make out her expression.

Jack stared at his wife and felt a familar ache in his arms, in his loins. She was so damned beautiful. Despite her less-than-placatory tone, his righteous anger melted away, leaving a hollow ache. "Strange," he said. "That's a question I've been asking of you."

The sincere doubt, the vulnerability revealed, pierced Kit's rage; nothing else could have hauled her back to earth. She blinked – and suddenly felt cold. "You *couldn't* have thought I intended to leave you permanently?"

When Jack's face remained shuttered, Kit frowned. "I didn't intend . . . that is, I . . ." Abruptly, she shook her wits into order. This was ridiculous! What misguided notion had he taken into his head? Drawing in an exasperated breath, she laced her fingers together, fixed her gaze on her husband's grey eyes and clearly enunciated: "I only meant my absence to focus your attention on my wish to be informed as to what was going on. I never intended to be away from Castle Hendon for longer than a few days."

Slowly, Jack raised his brows. "I see." He paused, then, strolling forward, said: "I don't suppose it occurred to you that I might be . . . concerned for your safety?" Kit turned as he neared; he could now see her face. "That, given your propensity for landing yourself in dangerous situations, I might, with justification, feel worried over your wellbeing?" The arrested look in Kit's large eyes stated quite clearly that the idea had never occurred to her. Abruptly, Jack's mock anger crystallized into the real thing. "Damn it, woman! I was *worried sick!*"

His bellow shook Kit. She grasped the chair back with both hands and blinked. "I'm sorry. I didn't realize . . ." Her words trailed into fascinated silence as, wide-eyed, she watched her husband fight to shackle his temper, a temper she'd never seen unleashed. He vibrated with angry tension, muscles clenched as if to hold the violence in. His grey eyes burned with a dark flame.

Jack heard her words through a haze of conflicting emotions, the suppressed fears of the past week unexpectedly erupting. Anger overrode all else – the damned woman really *didn't* understand. "In that case," he said, his voice a steely growl, "I suggest you listen very carefully, my love. Because the next time you endanger yourself recklessly, without me by your side, I swear I'll tan your pretty hide."

Trapped in the grey fury of his gaze, Kit felt her eyes grow rounder, a species of delicious fright tickling her spine.

He'd called her *his love* – that would do for a start. His confession sounded promising.

With an effort, Jack forced himself to remain where he was, a bare three feet from his wife. If he touched her now, they'd go up in flames. He fixed his eyes on hers and enunciated clearly: "I love you, as you damned well know. Every time you head into danger, *I worry!*" Her eyes searched his; he saw her lips soften. Abruptly, he swung away and started to pace. "*Not* a passive emotion, this worry of mine. When in its throes, I can't think straight! I know you've never run in anyone's harness before. But you married me – you vowed to obey. Henceforth, you'll do precisely that." Jack came to a halt and fixed Kit with an intimidating stare. "Henceforth, you'll tell me *before* you embark on any escapade beyond what your dear friend Amy would countenance. And if I forbid it, so help me, you'll forget it. If not, I swear by all that's holy, I'll lock you in your room!"

His voice had risen. His final threat struck Kit while she was still engrossed with his first revelation. He loved her. He'd said so, in words, out loud. In silence, she stared at him, her gaze softening, caressing the angry lines of his cheek and jaw. Her mind belatedly scrambled to catch up. Did worry over her truly affect him so? Is this what love did to him?

With a frustrated groan, Jack turned and strode from the room, slamming the door behind him. He swung up the short stairway and headed for the foredeck, his only aim to cool his heated brain before he returned to his cabin and made passionate love to his wife. He was so wracked with violent emotions he didn't trust himself to lay hands on her delicate limbs. She bruised easily enough as it was.

Kit stared at the cabin door. Her face drained of emotion, then she stiffened. Her eyes flared, purple flames erupting from the violet depths.

How dare he? One moment, vowing love and demanding obedience, the next, walking out on her, as if he'd said the final word.

"*Hah!*" Kit drew a deep breath and drew herself up, her hands on her hips. Her eyes narrowed. If he thought he was going to so easily escape the rest of their discussion, the clear statement of what *she* wanted henceforth from *him*, he was wrong! She'd wanted his attention – she'd got it. But he hadn't left it with her long enough!

With a determined stride, Kit made for the door.

His arms on the foredeck railing, Jack watched the waves slide under the bow. They'd slipped their moorings and were heading for the mouth of the harbor. Soon, the heavy swell of the ocean would tilt the decks. He drew a deep breath and felt sanity return.

Looking back, he couldn't recall a single instance throughout their association when Kit had allowed his plans to proceed without remodeling. He'd had their recent discussion carefully organized. He'd intended explaining to her what he felt when she went into danger, that she'd have to learn to cope with the ramifications of his love. He'd managed that but her patent surprise that he should feel so strongly for her had slipped under his guard and distracted him. His statements of intent had been far more aggressive than he'd planned.

He grimaced. That wasn't the worst of it. He'd forgotten the rest of his orchestrated performance, arguably the most important part. He'd omitted to tell her that he understood her need to know what he was about and that, henceforth, he was prepared to share even that aspect of his life with her.

Jack was drawing a last deep breath of calming sea air

when he sensed a disruption behind him. He swung about to see Kit making for the foredeck, oblivious of the sailors she swept from her path. One glance at the set of her chin told him she was about to upset the plans he'd just made.

For one instant, Jack paused to admire the magnificent figure she cut, her lithe body outlined by her elegant carriage dress, her halo of curls gleaming in the sunshine. But he couldn't afford more time to stand transfixed by admiration. His Kit was no angel. In another minute, when she reached the foredeck, she was going to irretrievably damage his reputation – if not worse.

Kit had to concentrate to manage the ladder to the foredeck with her skirts held before her. She'd seen Jack's tall figure at the rail and made straight for him. The foredeck looked a perfectly wonderful spot to tell him what she thought of his henceforths, limited, as they were, to her.

Gaining the foredeck, she dropped her skirts and smoothed them down, then glanced up to find her husband. To her surprise, he was directly in front of her.

Angry violet eyes locked with laughing grey ones.

Laughing? Kit opened her mouth to wither him.

She'd forgotten how fast he could move. Before the first syllable of her tirade tripped from her tongue, his lips had closed over hers, stifling her angry words. Kit struggled and felt his arms lock about her, a tender trap. Her heart was already accelerating, leaping with anticipation. It was too late to close her mouth. He'd taken immediate advantage of her parted lips to lay claim to the softness within.

Damn him! She wanted to *talk*! This was precisely why she'd left Castle Hendon in the first place.

Disgruntled, Kit tried to hold firm against the tide of need rising within her. It was impossible. Little flames of desire greedily flickered and grew, swelling into the familiar warmth in her belly. With a stifled groan, Kit rearranged her plans and surrendered to the urge to press herself against the hard body that surrounded her, savoring the pressure that would bring her relief.

When Kit melted into his embrace, Jack knew he'd won the round. Despite the catcalls and whistles that rose about them he kept kissing her, too hungry after the starvation of a week to call an early end to their exhibition. The need to repair to a place of greater privacy to embark on the next stage of their discussion finally brought his head up. He stared down into her wide eyes, already purpling with passion.

Jack smiled, his slow, wicked smile. Kit's heart lurched crazily.

"I'm going to carry you down to our cabin. Don't, for the love of God, say a word."

One arrogant brow rose, but Kit could only stare. Talk? That required being able to think. She was witless – how could she say anything?

Then, as Jack stooped and tossed her over his shoulder, reality returned to her with a thump. Heavens – everyone on the ship was staring at them! Kit felt her cheeks burn crimson as Jack went down the ladder. She could just imagine the grin on his face.

Her fears were confirmed when he shrugged her from his shoulder into his arms. He strode the length of the deck smiling down into her anguished eyes. Cradled in his strong arms, Kit knew it was useless to struggle but she'd have given a great deal, at that moment, to wipe the triumph from his lips. Still, it was only a battle – she had set her sights on winning the war. He juggled her back to his shoulder to manage the narrow companionway and corridor, then strode through the door to their stateroom and kicked it shut on the world.

Her hands on his shoulders, Kit waited to be put down. Now was the time to make her stand, before he kissed her again. But Jack didn't stop in the stateroom. Kit blinked as she was carried into the bedroom beyond, ducking her head at his command to avoid the lintel.

She looked around wildly. Her stomach contracted as her gaze fell on the bed. Jack stopped at its foot, his intent clear. Any doubts she might have had on the point were banished as he let her slide down until her toes brushed the carpeted floor. Clasped against him, Kit could feel the evidence of his need pressed hard against her soft belly. Her eyes met his; her breath suspended as she saw desire etched in silver flame against the smoky grey.

With an effort, Kit pulled her mind free. She drew a deep breath. "Jack?"

"Mmm?"

He wasn't interested in talking. His large hands spread across her waist, moving down to mold her hips against his. One hand remained at the top of her thighs, trapping her in that intimate embrace, gently fondling her bottom. The other hand went to the laces of her gown. His lips grazed her ear, then lazily drifted to where the pulse beat strongly at the base of her throat.

Kit clenched her fingers on his shoulders, trying to hold on to her mind, but the heat trapped between their hips rose and cindered her resolution. She felt Jack tug at her neckline and the material ripped. As his lips moved down to taste the fruit revealed, Kit decided against protest.

He had stated that he loved her. Now he would show her, his loving a vibrant reiteration of what he'd found so hard to say. She'd be a fool indeed to interrupt him. Instead, she would enjoy him, enjoy his love and claim it as hers – then return to her point later, once their love had tamed him.

With a satisfied murmur, she dropped her arms to free them of her sleeves, then whimpered as Jack's tongue teased her sensitive nipples, aroused and covered only by the thin film of her chemise. She heard his knowing chuckle, then he moved closer to the bed, letting her down so she stood on unsteady feet, trapped between him and the end of the bed.

Her petticoats drifted to the carpet, freed by expert fingers. Gentle hands divested her of her stockings and shoes. Clad only in her fine silk chemise, she stood before her husband, half-expecting him to rip the garment from her. His eyes burned brighter than she'd ever seen them.

Jack feasted his eyes on her bounty, the ripe globes of her breasts tipped by ruched pink, duskier now that he'd claimed her. Below the swell of her hips, her sleek flanks beckoned, the heat between pulsing with her heartbeat. Every sweet inch of her was his – his to adore, his to devour.

Kit's heart was pounding, a slow steady beat, a march to take her to paradise. Her breathing was shallow. It dissolved into short little gasps as Jack's hands closed about her breasts. Long fingers slid beneath the lace edge of her chemise to draw her fruit to his lips. He suckled hard. Kit dropped her head back, her eyes closing, her senses burdened with sensation too exquisite to bear. Her fingers tangled in Jack's hair, frantically pulling the long locks from the riband that confined them. One strong arm slipped about her waist to support her as she arched her body, exposing her breasts fully to his mouth and tongue.

She was on fire. Kit drew a ragged breath as she felt one large hand drop to her silk-clad thigh.

"Oh, yes," she whispered, as she felt Jack shift her in his arms, so that her hips were now angled against his. Slowly, his fingers drifted beneath the silk chemise, tracing a long curve all the way up to her hip. She felt him tuck the end of her shift, which had risen with his hand, into the fingers at her back. The edge of the garment was now draped from hip to knee across her body, revealing the satin expanse of one thigh to her husband's ardent gaze, but hiding the red-gold curls of her mound from his view. Kit lifted her heavy lids. The silver eyes were indeed examining what they could see. Then she felt his fingers drift down and closed her eyes the better to savor the pleasure to come.

As his fingers reached her knee, Jack's head dipped to take one rosy nipple into his mouth, torturing it with his tongue. The effort to breathe became that much harder as he reversed the direction of his caress, languidly trailing his fingers up the back of her thigh. Delicate caresses, tantalizingly explicit, trailed fire over the fevered skin of her bottom. Kit moaned, delighted he'd chosen the long way to paradise.

Slowly, the tracery of flame laid down by his fingertips moved over the curve of her hip to encroach on the silken skin of her stomach. His mouth on her breasts played havoc with her senses. When he finally raised his head, his fingers hovered just above her curls, already damp from the fever surging through her. Kit kept her eyes shut, knowing he was watching her, watching the way her senses flickered in heated anticipation of his next move.

"Open your eyes, Kitten." The growled command was one she wished she could disobey. Her lids fluttered and she opened her eyes just enough to see the devilish smile that twisted her husband's lips.

"Wide."

Kit glared weakly, but obeyed, her breathing tortured and waiting.

His smile grew.

One long finger slid into her.

429

Her body arched slightly, invitingly, her thighs parting to give him greater access. He reached deep. Kit shuddered and closed her eyes.

His lips found hers in a long slow kiss as his fingers found her heat, stroking and teasing until she clung to him, fever raging in her veins, her body straining for release.

Then he laid her on the bed. He shed his clothes and joined her, his hands, his mouth, quickly, expertly, restoking the flames before, in a fire of need, he possessed her, riding her hard, her urgency driving him on. Kit raised her legs and wrapped them about his waist, tilting her hips to take all of him, drawing him in, reveling in the slickness that allowed him to drive so deeply into her.

The end was shattering, leaving them both gasping. As the fires about them died, they slipped into sleep, limbs entangled, sated and content.

Kit woke to the sensation of Jack kissing her, soft, nibbling kisses that stirred her body to life. Before she was fully awake, he possessed her, quickly, expertly, taking the edge from her need before she even realized it was there.

Lying wrapped in his arms in the warm afterglow, Kit smugly considered the benefits accrued through having a rake for a husband. Then she remembered their discussion, and the fact that she'd yet to have her say. She tried to sit up, but Jack's arms held her firmly.

"Jack!"

At her protest, he shifted onto his elbow and kissed the frown from her brow. "I know, I know. Just keep quiet for a moment, you redheaded houri, and let me explain."

Redheaded houri? *Explain?* Kit dutifully stayed silent.

"I apologize, all right?" He nuzzled one ear, then placed a trail of kisses along her jaw to the other ear.

Kit frowned. "Exactly what are you apologizing for?"

Now she'd finally got him to the point, she wanted to be sure she got her due.

Jack drew back and considered her through narrowed silver eyes. "For not telling you about the damned spies."

Kit smiled beatifically.

Jack humphed and kissed her long and hard. "Furthermore," he said, when he was finished, "I promise on my honor as a Hendon to *try* to remember to tell you the details of any of my endeavors which might conceivably cause you concern."

Kit narrowed her eyes as she considered his wording.

Jack raised his brows, at first arrogantly, awaiting her acceptance, then more thoughtfully. "In fact," he mused, considering the delightful picture she made, lying naked in his arms, her skin aglow in the aftermath of their loving, "I'll make a bargain with you."

"A bargain?" Kit wondered at the wisdom of making a deal with such a reprobate.

Jack nodded, inspecting her nipples, shifting over her so he could weigh her breasts in his hands. Then he raised his head and smiled, directly into her large purple-shaded eyes. "We share – I'll tell you what I'm doing before you have to ask, and you'll tell me what you're doing before you do it."

Kit bit her lip on her acceptance. "That's not quite fair," she said, weighing his words every bit as carefully as he was weighing her breasts.

"It's the best you'll do, so I'd advise you to accept." The raspy reply jerked Kit's mind to attention. Too late. He was already lying between her thighs, her long limbs wide-spread. Even as her mind dealt with that discovery he lifted her hips. The sensation of warm steel pressing into her over-rode all other interests.

431

Kit arched her back, pressing her head deep into the pillows behind her, her lids drooping over her darkened eyes.

"Oh, yes!" she breathed.

Above her, Jack smiled and wondered just what she was agreeing to. As he flexed his hips and thrust deep into her welcoming heat, he decided he'd assume she wanted to share her life in the same abandoned way she shared her body. Then he stopped thinking.

"Lisbon?" Kit turned to look at Jack in surprise. "Why Lisbon?"

Jack chuckled and turned on his side to look at her. The ocean swell had finally registered and she'd got up, draping the counterpane over her nakedness, and gone to the window. "Because it's where the cargo is bound. This isn't a pleasure craft."

Kit's frown took in the sumptuous cabin. "I did think it was a bit big for a yacht." At Jack's laugh, she climbed back on the bed. "So where do we go after that?"

Tucking her curled warmth into one arm, Jack told her of their projected trip, six days in Lisbon followed by the long haul to Bruges, keeping well away from the French coast. After four days in Bruges, they'd head home to Norfolk.

She lay quiet in his arms, and Jack marveled at the peace that held them. They were both wide-awake, but content in their closeness.

Gradually, the perfume of her warm body reached out to flick his senses. He felt his body react and smiled at the ceiling. She'd been well loved, and it was a long way to Lisbon. He closed his eyes. He'd give her another hour or two.

He was woken by Kit scrambling over the bed. "My dress," she said, catching hold of the garment and kneeling on the bed to inspect it. "You've ripped it." She turned to

432

throw an accusing stare his way. Then she glanced at the large armoire against one wall. "I don't suppose that contains any dresses?"

Jack grinned and shook his head. Then he frowned. "Haven't you got another in that bag of yours?" Her black bag had been left near the door.

Kit shook her head. "I didn't expect to be away from home for long, remember?"

"What's in there?"

Warily, Kit eyed the long muscled length stretched, relaxed, on the bed. "My breeches. Both pairs."

Jack's head came up; his eyes found hers. Then, to her relief, he chuckled and dropped his head back on the pillow. "Actually, I'd hoped you'd be reduced to wearing them when I found you at Jenny's. I spent the entire trip down from London fantasizing about your punishment."

Kit stared at him. Fantasizing? She licked her lips. "You never did say what my punishment would be."

"Didn't I?" Jack raised his head. One brow rose; his eyes glinted wickedly. "But that's half the delight. Your imagination running riot in anticipation."

"Jack!" Kit frowned and shifted on the bed, drawing the counterpane about her. Her imagination was stimulated enough already.

He dropped his head back again, then she felt the bed rock with his deep laughter. "I just had a thought."

She could see the smile on his face. It grew. He came up on one elbow, the look on his face growing more wicked with every passing second.

"If your breeches are all you've got to wear, then perhaps you'd better put them on now. Then we can get your punishment over and done with and you can wear them in Lisbon, until we can buy you some new clothes."

Kit stared as one arrogant brow rose, sending delicious shivers skittering through her. His gaze held hers steadily, as if what he was suggesting was the most straightforward proposition in the world. Dazed, Kit reflected that if she had a single proper bone in her body, she would tell him that married women did not indulge in realizing fantasies. Particularly not his fantasies. She concluded she didn't have a proper bone to her name.

She ran the tip of her tongue over her dry lips. "What sort of punishment did you have in mind?"

Jack smiled. "Nothing too drastic. Nothing that would hurt. I'd intended it as a purely educational exercise." He sat up in bed and leaned back to study her, his arms crossed behind his head. "I thought I should widen your experience by showing you what could happen should you be caught by a man while wearing breeches. But you'd have to promise not to squeal."

Squeal? Kit blinked. This was madness. But she'd never be able to sleep without knowing what he'd planned. Now he'd told her that much, and no more, sometime, somewhere, she'd wear her breeches again just to learn the rest. Why not now?

Jack knew she'd never be able to refuse, to walk away without knowing. Curiosity was something his kitten possessed in abundance. He sat back, entirely confident, and waited for her agreement.

"Perhaps –"

A knock on the stateroom door interrupted Kit's tentative acceptance.

"Lord Hendon?"

Jack got up and reached for his breeches, a smile still on his lips. "I'll take care of whatever it is. Why don't you get dressed?"

Buttoning his breeches, he went out.

Kit stared at the door through which he'd disappeared. She could hear talk in the next room, the voices muffled by the panels. Her gaze dropped to her small black bag, resting where Jack had dropped it, just inside the door.

She was buttoning up the flap of her riding breeches, her back to the door, when she heard Jack enter.

He saw her and, with a half-suppressed whoop, swooped down on her, one arm slipping around her waist to drag her up hard against him, her back to his chest. Without effort, he lifted her feet clear of the floor.

"Jack!" Kit struggled, keeping her voice down, remembering that she mustn't squeal. She assumed his surprise attack was what he'd meant. He'd certainly startled her. Her hands fastened on the muscled arm about her waist. "Put me down."

A rumbling chuckle ruffled her curls. Then his lips nuzzled her ear. "Remember, this is your punishment, love. Not something you have any say in. Just something you *feel*."

Kit closed her eyes. She wished she hadn't heard that. Her nerves were in turmoil. What fiendishly arousing act had he planned? She hadn't a single doubt as to its nature. His shaft was already hard and throbbing, pressed between the firm hemispheres of her bottom.

She didn't have to wait long to learn her punishment.

"I really don't think," her husband continued conversationally, his fingers rapidly undoing the buttons she'd just done up, "that you appreciate just how fast a man can have at you when you're dressed in breeches."

With that, he pulled the offending garment down, letting it slip from her thighs to hang from the closures above her calves.

"And given that you're so easily aroused," he went on,

moving closer to a chair which was facing away from them. He let Kit slide down until her toes touched the ground. With a gasp, she grabbed the back of the chair with both hands as she felt Jack's fingers slide effortlessly into her. They withdrew and returned, delving deep, then left her.

"It takes but a second before you've . . ."

She felt him, hard and hot, behind her.

"Been . . ."

He lifted her hips slightly, the head of his swollen shaft nudging into her.

"Had." Then he drove home.

The young cabin boy was leaving the Master's cabin when he heard a very feminine "*Oo-oh!*" emanate from behind the oak door at the end of the corridor. His eyes widened. He cast a glance at the stairs but there was no one about. Quickly, he put down his tray and hurried to press his ear against the door to the bedroom.

At first, he heard nothing. Then his sharp ears caught a low moan, followed by another. One particularly long-drawn moan made his toes curl. Then he heard, quite distinctly, a definitely feminine voice sigh, "*Oh, Jack!*"

The boy's brows flew to astronomical heights. He'd heard tales of Lord Hendon. Obviously, they really were true. With wide eyes, he hurried to pick up his tray.

Epilogue

November 1811
The Old Barn near Brancaster

The wind whistled in the eaves of the Old Barn. It sent cold fingers sneaking through the crevices between the boards to set the lamp hung from the rafters wobbling. Shadows dipped and swayed eerily, ignored by the men gathered under the derelict roof. They were waiting. Waiting for their leader to return.

Captain Jack had led them to success afer success. Under him, they'd enjoyed stability and strong leadership; he'd welded them into an efficient force, one they all felt proud to be a part of. They'd steered clear of the Revenue and of any more heinous crimes. They'd suffered no losses, other than poor Joe. And, thanks to Captain Jack, his family had been well taken care of.

All in all, Captain Jack's reign had been one of prosperity. The news that he'd been forced to retire had hit them hard. George, Jack's friend, had brought the news, more than a month ago. Since then, they'd done little, too demoralized to reorganize.

Then, last week, the message had gone around. Captain Jack was back. They'd gathered this foggy Monday night in the expectation of seeing their leader return.

George and Matthew had arrived. As ever, they'd taken up positions on either side of the door. The men chatted quietly, anticipation riding high.

A sudden gust howled about the roof; fingers of fog wreathed about the rickety door. Then the doors opened and a man strode in, fog clinging like a cloak to his broad shoulders. He walked in as Jack had always walked, to stand directly under the lamp, swinging high above.

The smugglers stared.

It was Jack, yet a Jack they'd never seen. His clothes marked him clearly as one born to rule. From the high gloss of his Hessians, to the faultless crease of his cravat, he was Quality. The grey eyes they all remembered scanned their faces, impressing power just as they recalled, only this time the personal strength was backed by social standing.

"Jack?" The puzzled question was asked by Shep, his grizzled brows knitted in consternation.

The slow smile they all remembered twisted the man's lips. "Lord Hendon."

The name should have sent shivers down every spine, but they all knew this man, knew he'd smuggled alongside them, that he'd saved their hides a good few times. So they sat and waited to have the mystery explained.

Jack's grin grew. He took up his usual stance, feet apart, under the light. "It's like this."

He told them the story, simply, without detail or embellishment. The essential points were enough for them to grasp. He made no mention of Young Kit, a fact some noted but none made comment upon. When they grasped the fact they'd been helping His Majesty's government to

438

apprehend spies, the atmosphere lightened considerably. When Jack showed them the pardon he'd brought for them all, and read the official decree, they simply stared.

"This will be posted in all the Revenue Offices in Norfolk. It means that as of today, you're absolved of any crime under the Customs Act committed up until last night." Jack rolled the parchment up and tucked it into his pocket. "What you do with your lives from now on is up to you. But you'll be starting with a clean slate, so I'd urge you all to think carefully before you re-form the Hunstanton Gang." He smiled, wryly, convinced that no matter what he said, after a spell, the Hunstanton Gang would live again "You'll doubtless be pleased to know that I'm retiring as High Commissioner. In fact, it's doubtful there will be another appointment made to the post."

His glance took them all in, every last unlovely face. Jack smiled. "And now, my friends, I'll bid you farewell."

Without looking back, Jack walked to the door. Matthew opened it for him, then he and George followed him outside. There was a murmur of farewell from the men in the barn, but none made any attempt to follow.

Outside, Jack stood under the open skies, his hair glinting in the moonlight. He dropped his head back, his hands on his hips and stared at the pale orb, glowing amid the clouds.

George drew near. "And so ends the career of Captain Jack?"

Jack swiveled about. In the moonlight, George saw his devilish smile. "For the moment."

"For the moment?" Incredulous horror filled George's voice.

Jack threw back his head and laughed, then strode toward the trees.

Puzzled, George watched him go. Then he gasped and

grabbed Matthew's arm as a rider burst from the band of firs directly in front of Jack. Jack's stride didn't falter; if anything, he moved faster. Then George recognized the horse, and noticed Champion behind.

"Dangerous fools!" he said, but he was grinning.

"Aye," said Matthew. "Imagine what their young'll be like."

"God preserve us." George watched as Jack swung up to Champion's saddle. Kit tossed some remark over her shoulder and set Delia for the road. Jack followed, bringing Champion up to ride by his wife's side.

George watched until their shadows mingled with the trees and disappeared. Smiling, he turned to fetch his horse, his ride home made light by anticipation of Amy, now his wife, waiting safe at home in their bed.

"Incidentally," Jack said to Kit, as Champion led the way up the narrow path onto Hendon lands. "You'll have to give up riding Delia."

Kit frowned and leaned forward to pat the glossy neck as Delia followed the stallion at a slow walk. "Why?"

Jack grinned, knowing his wife couldn't see it. "Let's just say you and she have more in common than you might at first suppose."

It took Kit a moment to work that one out. On the ship, her bouts of queasiness had become more pronounced day by day, until, when they'd left Bruges, she'd had to admit to Jack that she suspected she was carrying his child. To her abiding irritation, he'd admitted he'd known she was since he'd first made love to her in the big bed in their stateroom. Ever since, he'd gone around positively glowing with a smug pride that never failed to get her goat. His protectiveness, of course, had reached new heights. She'd been surprised he hadn't yet taken exception to her riding;

doubtless that would come. But what could Delia and she have in common?

The answer made her rein in with a gasp. "You mean . . .? How . . .?" Jack drew up and turned to look at her. The truth was easy to read in his smile. Kit's eyes narrowed. "Jack Hendon! Do you mean to tell me you've let that brute of a stallion get at Delia?"

Her husband's eyes widened with unlikely innocence. "But, my love, surely you wouldn't deny Delia a pleasure you take so much delight in?"

Kit opened her mouth, then abruptly shut it. She glared at her aggravating husband. Would he always have the last word?

With an irritated humph, she clicked her reins.

Jack laughed and fell in beside her. "Well, are you satisfied you've shared in Captain Jack's end?"

Wide eyes turned his way. "Has Captain Jack died?" Her voice was sultry. "Or has he simply changed his clothes for a while?"

Jack's eyes widened as he read her look. But before he could say anything, Kit urged Delia ahead. She led the way homeward, but pulled up in the clearing before the cottage.

Jack drew rein beside her. "Tired?"

Kit eyed the cottage. "Not exactly." She slanted a look at her husband.

Jack saw it. He groaned, mock resignation not entirely concealing his anticipation, and dismounted. "I'll take care of the horses, you take care of the fire."

Kit laughed as he lifted her down. She reached up to draw his lips to hers, pressing her body against his in flagrant promise. Then, smugly satisfied with his immediate reaction, she released him and ran for the door.

Jack watched her go, a slow smile curving his lips. Despite

all her adventures, Captain Jack's damned woman was every bit as wild as she'd ever been – outwardly conservative, in reality as untamed as he. She was headstrong but his, in his blood as he was in hers; there could be no tighter bond. Caring for her would fill the empty center of his life; she'd already filled his heart. He could count on her to exasperate, frustrate and infuriate – and love him with all her soul.

She would keep him on his toes. Jack glanced at the cottage. He hoped she was getting impatient.

With a conspiratorial wink for Champion, and a last smiling glance at the moon, he took the horses to the stable before swiftly returning to the cottage – and the warm, loving arms of his wife.

If you enjoyed *Captain Jack's Woman*,
don't miss the following books now
available in Stephanie Laurens'
Bastion Club series . . .

MASTERED BY LOVE

As the mysterious leader of the Bastion Club, Royce Varisey,
10th Duke of Wolverstone, served his country for decades,
facing dangers untold. But as the holder of one of England's
most august noble titles, he must now take on
that gravest duty of all: marriage.

Yet the young ladies the grand dames would have him consider
are predictably boring. Far more tempting is his castle's wilful
and determinedly aloof chatelaine, Minerva Chesterton.
Beneath her serene façade lies a woman of smouldering
sensuality, one who will fill his days with comfort –
and his nights with unadulterated pleasure . . .

978-0-7499-4013-3

THE LADY CHOSEN

Tristan Wemyss, Earl of Trentham, never expected he'd need to wed within a year or forfeit his inheritance. But he is not one to bow to the matchmaking mamas of the ton. No, he will marry a lady of his own choosing – the enchanting neighbour next door. Miss Leonora Carling has beauty, spirit and passion; unfortunately, matrimony is the last thing on her mind . . .

Once bitten, forever shy – never again will Leonora allow any man to capture her heart and break it. But Tristan is a seasoned campaigner who will not accept defeat, especially when a mysterious blackguard with dark designs on Leonora's home gives him the excuse to come to the lady's aid – as her protector, confidant, seducer . . . and husband.

978-0-7499-4023-2